BOOK 1

ZENITH ACADEMY

CASSIUS LANGE

Thank You!

I cannot overstate how much it means that you took the time to read Zenith Academy. Your support means the world to me. Please consider logging on to Amazon or the retailer's website where you purchased this copy *and leaving a review*. For indie authors like us there is no better way to show that you appreciate our work. It also helps convince others to give it a read, as well. If you would like to take it another step forward consider:

JOINING MY PATREON. Here I provide early access to chapters for books still in the works, offer early looks at cover art, and so much more. Sign up at: **https://rebrand.ly/acarspb**

FOLLOWING ME ON MY FACEBOOK PAGE. I provide updates. and can communicate directly from here. I will publish release date information, chat about existing books and characters, and share other fun stuff from the community. Check it out at: **https://rebrand.ly/ygc7oal**

FOLLOW ME DIRECTLY ON AMAZON. This is the best way to get updates directly from Amazon when books are either scheduled for pre-order or they are released ninja-style in the middle of the night. Sign up at: **https://rebrand.ly/7dk8kqv**

Again, thank you for your support. While you tell your friends about Zenith Academy, I'll work on getting you more exciting adventures to read!

Strange Customer

"YOU WANT ME TO LEAVE?" the beautiful woman asked.

She squirmed in the booth as if making to leave. I studied her for a moment, calling her bluff. And wouldn't you know it, she settled back down.

"I'll take that as a no," she said. She had a peculiar accent that I couldn't quite place. Possibly Eastern European? Maybe Russian? Regardless, it was a delight to hear.

She watched me dry a glass, set it down, and pick up another. Her eyes were hazel-brown, her nose slender, and her cherry-red lips pulled up into a disarming smile. She had long, black hair, pulled up into a bun and held in place with golden sticks. They looked like the kind of things only cosplay girls used. My gaze caught on her cheeks; specifically, how incredibly pale her complexion was. It was only thrown into contrast by her unusual outfit. It was a kimono, but it wasn't buttoned at the top, so there was more than a little of her ample cleavage on display. I didn't see bra strap lines, so my curiosity immediately deepened.

"I just manage this joint. I only kick people out if they are drunk, or rowdy, or harassing my staff," I said.

"Are you saying I haven't been trying hard enough? I have been trying to harass you since I sat down."

She bit her lip and shifted, drawing my attention down to where a freaking sword lay across her thighs. It didn't look like it was made out of cardboard, but real metal. A replica, maybe? Either way, the flirting aside, she'd proven to be the weirdest customer I'd had in a *very* long time. If she was hungry, she was about an hour too late.

"I like the company," I admitted, "But I gotta say. We closed an hour ago, so I hope you aren't hungry."

She and I were the only people in Judson's Bar and Grill. Maybe she was looking for a hookup, which was okay with me... any other time or day, but tonight was one of the rare occasions where I had somewhere to be.

My staff had gone home thirty minutes before. Being the manager, I was normally the last one to leave... after all, I was responsible for final checks and lock up before heading out for the night. I had been well on my way to that phase when I happened upon this woman, sitting straight as an arrow in the booth, her hands clasped in front of her.

"You like the company, but..." she whispered.

"The grill's closed, lady. We've been closed for half an hour. I'm not sure how you got in here, but you've got to go."

"I'm not leaving until," she said, pushing a crumb across the table with her fingernail, "I get what I came for. And what I came for is you, JD. You're coming with me tonight."

I laughed. "Is that so?"

It always felt weird hearing someone else say my name the way she just did.

She nodded once, then folded her arms in her lap and looked up at me expectantly. Almost as if begging me to say no for the second time. I hesitated, more than a little confused by her behavior. She was drop-dead gorgeous and dressed to kill, but there was something off about her, too. It wasn't necessarily something I could put into words, but I had a suspicion she wasn't exactly what she appeared to be. Was she lonely, seeking help? Was there a Con in town I didn't know about? Was she into recreational drugs and just looking for someone to mess with?

I looked at the door, then back her way. I considered kicking her out for the umpteenth time. Then maybe I could go home, but maybe that wasn't the best idea. Perhaps I could entertain her for a while. Besides, she looked like she was alone, and walking back to wherever it was she'd come from might put her in danger. After all, the way she was dressed, she was bound to catch all the wrong kinds of attention.

Judson's was perched between a few seedy clubs and dive bars, which meant there'd be no shortage of drunk dudes on the prowl. And if I tossed her out and later realized that something had happened to her, well that would be on me.

Then I remembered her sword. I'd suggest a Mossberg eighty-eight for most women's self-defense needs. But I guess a sword would work just as well in the "deter the leering creeps" department. And yet, this woman had a dangerous air about her, as if she wasn't as innocent or helpless as one might think.

I finished drying the rack of glasses and stowed them on the shelf, struggling with the feeling that the woman wasn't just some confused or lost cosplay damsel. And I had to wonder if she was the real deal. What? As though she might *actually* have been some femme fatale who had stepped through a portal and come to Earth for... me?

Damned sakes, I watched entirely too many movies. Or, it could have been the three fingers of whiskey I'd had since closing. I explained away my runaway daydreams to a long day and pulled off my apron. I was wishing for things that...weren't quite normal.

I flashed her a warm smile, but it was hard to look gracious when I was tired and just wanted to go home. Only after I dropped off my payment at the phone company. Yes, that was my "big" thing I had to do. Sue me. I was behind and didn't want them to shut off my internet.

I didn't know how she'd gotten into the place, and she was clearly acting coy, so maybe one of my buddies told her to find me. Hell, maybe they had snuck her into the bathroom before I locked up. They were always trying to set me up with women.

Yes, I had excuses for being single. I worked long, late hours. Plus, I spent all my free time on my art, leaving me almost no time for dates or women. Aside from the ones I managed to draw on paper. But I was really close to a breakthrough with someone at Marvel Comics, so I couldn't give up now.

Taking my keys off the hook behind the bar, I walked out and slid onto the seat across from the mystery woman.

"So," I said. "You're not going to leave unless I go with you, huh? And where is it we're going? If it's someplace worth visiting, I just might join you. But I have to warn you, I've been up since five this morning, so I don't know how much fun I'll be."

"I suppose that might have been a little forward of me," the woman replied.

I struggled to read her tone and expression, but she sounded somewhere between pissed off and amused. Maybe amused. Both?

"We haven't even been properly introduced. Which isn't fair, because I already know *your* name, JD. You are the general manager at Judson's Bar & Grill, an aspiring artist, and the man I just happened to be looking for."

"Sounds like you know me. Are you a fan of my hamburgers? Or did one of my buddies set me up?"

"No. See, this is the second time you've asked the wrong question. Third time's the charm, right? Unless you're not the man I think you are. I hope I wasn't wrong about you, JD."

I frowned and stared into her eyes, only then realizing how remarkable they really were. They weren't just gray but shone almost silver in the bar's soft light. And what question? Had something interesting happened outside? Like a world-ending event that only I wasn't aware of? I sure as hell hoped not.

"How about you tell me your name," I said.

She smirked, looking from my face, down to her napkin. She was…drawing my eyes. And she was very good.

"Hmm, slightly better. Although that wasn't a question." Her smirk widened, and she went so far as to wink. "Fine, it was close enough. My name is Mistress Salina."

I raised my eyebrow. "Mistress? As in a domina? With a whip and all?"

She chuckled, then stuck out her tongue and dragged it across those supple, ruby-colored lips. "Mistress of Finances, actually," she said, immediately dropping her attention to her doodle. Had I offended her? I immediately started to panic.

"I suppose the next question would be, why me? You said you're going to take me somewhere. Where, a faraway land like Wakanda? Because that would be awesome."

She leaned her elbows against the table, and as she did, her breasts squeezed together. My eyes wandered. It was hard not to look, like they had gravity and were pulling my gaze down to them. And let's be honest, she knew exactly what she had on display.

"I was sent to find you," she said, "And to deliver something into your hands."

"Well, you found me. What is it you are delivering? An old inheritance from a long-lost relative? Wait, I have no relatives. You aren't serving subpoenas, are you? Or is this one of those scams where I find out that some prince somewhere died and left me the keys to a kingdom?"

Her cool smile wavered just a bit, and I caught a glimpse of annoyance. It seemed that, while we had been flirting up to this point, her patience was running thin.

"No," Mistress Salina said with all the finality of a bullet to the cranium. "I'm here to give you something much better than an inheritance. Something better than anything this world could possibly offer. You've been yearning for more, haven't you? Even your drawings say as much."

"Oh?" I frowned as something she said caught my attention. "Wait, did you just say, 'this world'? And are you being serious right now? You aren't trying to seduce me, only to have my friends pop up from around the corner and laugh their asses off, are you?"

I silently wondered if a bathtub full of ice was in my immediate future.

Salina shook her head as her smile returned, this time much broader than before. That was a good start as I rather liked her smile.

"Take this orb and hold it in your hands. We'll talk more after."

She held out her left hand, while still doodling with her right, but it was empty. I blinked, only to find a square box resting in her open palm.

"You are a magician," I said under my breath. "Someone has hired me a magician."

"Where I am from, to call someone a magician is a great offense," Salina said, her voice dropping. She pressed the pen down, the tip biting clear through the napkin and tearing it in half. She quietly placed the box on the table between us.

"I am sorry. I mean no offense," I said not quite getting what she was talking about. Where she was from? An offense?

I leaned over the table and looked at the box. It was lacquered wood with a symbol of a large tower etched into its surface. The craftsmanship looked outstanding. It was almost like a puzzle, the one Pinhead liked to use in the Hellraiser movies. *Shit.*

"Wait, are you trying to send me to hell?"

Salina raised her right eyebrow and considered me for a moment, evidently not catching the reference. Story of my life. Wrong joke, wrong crowd. That was my motto.

"Hell?"

"Never mind. Tell me about this orb?" I asked. "This is a box, and it looks quite expensive."

"The orb is inside," she explained, pressing a finger into the side of the box. It popped open, just like a puzzle box would. I repelled and let out a silent scream, but nothing happened.

She sighed and tilted the box toward me so I could see the insides. A shimmering, bright orb sat there. It looked similar to a fortune teller's scrying orb, translucent but foggy and mysterious at the same time.

"So, you are a…" I started to ask, looking up at the beautiful woman, "psychic?"

"My affinity is with the element of metal, young JD. I'm not a psychic. Or like any of those other false practitioners. Please consider your words wisely. I enjoy a bit of idle banter, but if you insult me any further, I will get…physical."

"Noted," I replied but caught on to what she had said. *False.* What did that mean? And physical? Was she offended, angry? Or was she talking about the other physical activities? Honestly, I'd never struggled reading someone so much before. She was an enigma.

"Take the orb in your hands," Salina said, interrupting my thoughts. It definitely sounded like she was growing impatient now. But why? If she wasn't just a girl my friends sent to play a joke on me, then who was she?

Rather than keep her waiting and delay whatever trick was coming next, I reached for the orb and picked it up. It was cold and smooth, almost too smooth. A tingle bit into my palm, and then my fingers spasmed.

A loud, buzzing noise filled my ears, but it went quiet almost as fast as it started. The orb vibrated then, just as a floating screen appeared in the air above my hand, translucent with bright blue letters.

NAME: JD **AGE:** 24
WORLD: Earth **CITY:** Los Angeles
WEAPON AFFINITY: Unknown
POWER LEVEL: Unknown

"Wait, what?" I asked. "This is all correct information, and not that hard to find on the internet. Except for the 'Weapon Affinity and Power Level' things. What's that supposed to mean? And 'World: Earth?' Come on, you can do better than that, right?"

"You'll understand everything in time, JD. Now, are you ready?"

"Oh, shit. Wait," I said. "Are you trying to induct me into a cult? No-No-No! My buddy Ryan is into that kind of crazy stuff. He went to a meeting just last week and said a freaky hot woman was all over him. Then she 'inducted' him into their little group? He said she wanted him to drink goat's blood and do this weird chant."

"I don't know this Ryan, nor do I know of the cult you speak! I do not have any beast blood with me." Salina's expression hardened, taking her beauty along with it. I realized then that she was utterly, absolutely, without a sliver of a doubt, serious.

I swallowed my tongue and realized that I knew next to nothing about the armed woman sitting across from me. Nervously, I glanced at the sword lying in her lap. Right then, I could have bet that the blade hidden inside the scabbard was razor-sharp. It didn't help that Salina was stroking it like a pet cat, and I subconsciously waited for it to purr.

Salina sighed. "It seems that, just like with most earthlings, you require far more evidence than is necessary. In this case, as I have neither the time nor the patience, I will provide you with it! So, we might move along before old age claims you."

She slid off the bench and stood before me. With her scabbarded sword held parallel to the ground, she broke the blade free. A sound like wind chimes filled the air as the weapon slid free. The blade glowed a dull blue, waves of what looked like energy rippling into the air.

If it was a trick, it was a damned good one. But I saw no projectors, speakers, or other hardware. Was she using a hologram?

"Here," Salina said and flipped the sword around, holding the handle towards me. I stared at it for a long moment, taking in its beauty—the gleaming, dangerously sharp blade, and intricate carvings on the hand guard.

How in the hell did she know I liked swords? I mean "like" is an insignificant descriptor, really. I was a major fan of movies like *Crouching Tiger, Hidden Dragon*, and *Hero*, but that was a secret I kept close to my chest. I'd never even told my friends.

I reached out and let my hand drape over the weapon's handle, but as soon as my skin touched, the blade stopped glowing and the rippling energy disappeared. *Weird*. Stranger yet, a glowing square appeared in the air above it, much like the one I saw over the orb.

NAME: Moonlight Chain Sword
TYPE: Weapon, Elemental
DESCRIPTION: Sword crafted using the moonlight by imbuing the power into every sheet of steel. Has two forms: the basic sword form, and the chain sword whip.

FORM 1: Moonlight Sword
POWER LEVEL: 750, **RANGE:** 3

FORM 2: Moonlight Chain Sword
POWER LEVEL: 600, **RANGE:** 12

"Moonlight Chain Sword?" I asked, studying the blade and the glowing square. I'd done some HEMA and studied medieval weaponry, so I knew a little bit about how to handle a blade, but not much beyond—don't cut off your own hand or leg.

Besides, the sword felt like the real deal. It had a solid heft in my hands, and damn, the edge looked sharp enough to shave with.

"It looks like a regular sword to me. Sure, when you were holding it, the blade glowed, but—"

"Give it to me," Salina interrupted, and only then did the moment truly register in my brain.

Hot girl in weird clothes made me hold a glowing orb—okay, strange. Then she pulled out a glowing, freaking sword and made me hold it—weirder still. And that wasn't accounting for the odd, glowing boxes filled with words and stats.

What in the ever-living hell had I stepped into?

"So, is it LED's? Are there some tiny lights hidden in the hilt, maybe a special glow-in-the-dark coating on the blade?" I asked, fighting to hold back my sarcasm. I was quickly running out of patience and answers for the weird stuff.

"I don't know what those are," Salina said. "But no."

I shrugged and handed her the weapon, making sure I didn't cut myself in the process.

"This is most certainly *not* a regular sword." Mistress Salina flicked her sword arm, the blade snapping out and splitting into multiple segmented sections. They swung through the air, connected by a long, incredibly thin, and glowing wire. Then it struck me. The weapon was eerily similar to the Snake Sword Ivy used in *Soulcalibur*. Damn. I loved that game.

"That is," I said, pausing as the blade hung, shimmering in the air, "definitely not a regular sword."

Salina smiled and then leapt away, twirling the bladed whip around her like a lasso. She flicked the end past my head to the left, and then to the right, the wind rustling my hair. I watched in awe, holding my breath and afraid to move. A little pee might have come out. Don't judge.

"Alright," I said, holding my hands up. "I get it. It is not a regular sword. Would you mind putting it away before someone—uh, me, gets cut?"

"Oh, I'm only getting started," Mistress Salina said. She spun and brought the chain sword down hard, and with a loud crack, the counter next to me exploded in a shower of wood splinters. I turned away, raising my arm to protect my face.

The strange woman then proceeded to launch herself back, moving in an impressively destructive dance, her chain sword striking and tearing apart every piece of furniture in the room.

"I'm definitely losing my job," I said, slumping against my knees. Of course, that would happen after I tried to clean everything up. "Or prison. Yeah, I'm getting arrested, too. Shit!"

"You won't end up anywhere except where I take you," Mistress Salina said as the segments of the sword pulled back together. A heartbeat later it was just a gleaming short sword again. She sheathed it in her scabbard and fixed it to her belt. "I'd say you no longer have a reason to stay here. In this…bar. In this…world."

"This world? Lady, you are all sorts of weird," I replied, struggling to process what she said and just did. I watched too much anime and read too many manga and comic books to be taken completely off guard. I expected the worst but hoped for the best. No, that wasn't right. I hope for the sensational. But damn. This was weird, even for me.

"I just want to close up. Pay my internet bill and maybe eat a shitty, frozen pizza when I get home. Then I can go to bed only to wake up tomorrow and do all of this crap over again. It sucks, but it is predictable."

"You have a task ahead of you, JD. A destiny, if you will. Your legendary weapon awaits you, as does the tower. I am the Mistress of Finance at the Zenith Magical Academy, and you are coming with me, like it or not. The headmistress spent too much time searching for you only to have you to choose frozen pizzas and internet over destiny."

"Destiny? Headmistress?" I scoffed. "Wait, and why a Mistress of Finance? Don't you guys have recruiters?"

Her silvery eyes narrowed, and she tapped a finger against her scabbard. The hint was clear enough—stop wasting my time or I'll use this on you.

"Because they are currently out recruiting someone else. And our window to acquire you was relatively small. You see, the barrier surrounding Earth doesn't open very often, so I had to come. Anything else I can explain? Anything else I need to cut apart or destroy? This blade works just as well on flesh and bone."

14

"Well, if you're offering, I have a bowl of apples behind the counter. Tell me, have you ever played *Fruit Ninja?* It is a strangely addictive—"

She snapped her fingers, cutting me off. A bright, shimmering portal popped into existence in the middle of my now ruined bar. The surface rippled and surged, like liquid metal.

"Wow, is that a Stargate?" I asked, mesmerized.

The portal flickered and danced, before finally calming. Then I could see the other side. Clearly.

Young men and women walked past, almost as if I was staring through a round window. But they were dressed...differently. The men, even the women, seemed to be wearing robes, all made from colorful and well-trimmed fabric. The young women I spotted were dressed similarly to Salina, with a few showcasing long slits on one side, revealing plenty of legs.

"It is real?" I asked, staring through the portal. "You didn't just slip something into my drink? A roofie, maybe? Are you telling me magic is real? That you are from a magical academy? And there are magical girls? They're real, too?"

"Indeed," Mistress Salina said, watching me with obvious amusement. "How much time do you need? The last earthling needed almost ten minutes before she was ready to enter the portal. Chloe. Yes, that was her name. You don't know her, do you?"

I laughed, the sound far giddier than I was comfortable with. "I don't know how much you know about Earth, but it's a *really* big place. There are probably thousands, if not tens of thousands of women named Chloe in my state alone. Anyway, I don't think I know her."

Salina shrugged. "I'm sure you'll get the chance. The headmistress tends to pair earthlings together and since there are only two of you in this recruitment cycle, you two are destined to meet very soon."

I decided then and there that I wouldn't be like the other people from Earth Salina had likely encountered. Besides, I liked proving people wrong, so instead of sitting around, waffling over

15

my choices, and drooling on myself in disbelief, I pulled myself together. Figuratively. But I did drool, a little.

What would my dear old dad say now? After ridiculing me for the time spent with anime and manga, all the comics I had read. They prepared me for this moment. Besides, who would be stupid enough to say no to such a gorgeous lady? Even if she was a little scary and weird. *Eat your heart out, Harry Potter,* I thought. *On second thought, no eating hearts,* I added, realizing I was about to step fully into the unknown. That very well could be a thing.

"Please don't wake up tomorrow in a bathtub of ice," I muttered.

"What is that?" Salina asked.

"Oh, nothing," I said, "I've been waiting whole my life for this, Mistress of Finance. Keeper of coins and notes. Why have you kept me waiting for so long?"

Salina chuckled, her hauntingly gray eyes reflecting the portal's light. Then she held out a hand for me to take.

I gave the restaurant one final look. The authorities could sort out the mystery on their own time—the destroyed furniture and missing manager. No doubt the security cameras caught everything. Or did they? I wasn't planning on coming back, so it wasn't something I planned on losing any sleep over. But it did make me wonder what people would say. I felt my grin widen, and my heart pounded in my chest. Shit, I was nervous. Like my first day of school. At least I didn't have an uncontrollable, teenage boner to hide. Or...I subtly grabbed my crotch and confirmed. Only mildly aroused.

It took every ounce of self-control not to fist-pump, or worse, offer Salina a fist-bump. I composed myself as best I could and took her hand.

"About that chain sword," I said, as she started forward. "Do you think I could have one?"

"Not unless you have an affinity for it."

"Oh." That immediately filled my mind with a jumbled pile of additional questions. But realizing there was only one way to answer any of them, I stepped forward and into the portal.

The Test

Bright light burned my eyes, even after I closed them tight. It lasted only for a moment, but it was intense—like staring directly up at the sun. I felt the ground change beneath my feet, the air growing slightly cooler around me.

When I opened my eyes again, I found myself standing in a large, circular room. The tall, marbled walls rose easily a hundred feet high, gracefully curving into a glass dome. Sunlight shone through, the ceiling scattering the bright light into a dozen, intense beams. A single exit sat directly ahead, maybe a hundred paces away.

Tiered bleachers rose all around me, the furthest reaches of the stone seats disappearing into heavy shadows. The space looked like an arena or stadium, perhaps something out of Ridley Scott's *Gladiator.*

"What is this place?" I asked.

Salina shifted next to me, brushing a few stray pieces of broken furniture off her clothes. She finally looked up, glanced around, and smiled…mischievously.

"Your new home," she replied.

"I'm going to live in an...arena? Or do I have to prove myself first? Maybe strip off my shirt and fight one of those girls I saw through the portal earlier?"

"Don't be foolish. You don't want to fight them. They would pull you apart, piece by piece. And to answer your question, no. You'll be living elsewhere. For now, though, you should prepare yourself. If you don't pass the affinity test, you'll die. You can take off your shirt if you want. After all, you will face a bare-chested beast. But that is entirely your call."

"I change my mind," I said. "Can I skip fighting the beast and stay here?"

Salina turned from me and started walking deliberately toward the door.

"Good luck," she whispered, and yet her voice carried as easily as if she had shouted.

"Uh, thank you. But did you hear me? About the not fighting part?"

She half-turned my way and peered at me from over her shoulder, then smiled. "You need to stay here to test your affinity. Just be a good boy and stand in the middle of the room. Someone will come by to help you real soon."

"Wait, no! This is the time when that monster appears and eats me, right? And I'll have nothing but my bare fists and a nearly bottomless pool of insults and foul language to throw at it?"

Maybe I went a little over the top, but when someone takes you to another world, leaves you in an arena, and then tells you that you must fight some kind of beast, it has a tendency to induce panic. Activate—drama mode.

I kicked forward and ran after Salina, but she spun and drew her sword in one fluid motion.

"Stay!" she snapped, thrusting the point of her blade at me.

A bright glow washed over her sword, just before a pulse of light erupted from the weapon. It narrowly missed me and hit the far wall. I cursed effectively, nearly soiling my Superman undies. Yes. I said Superman. Don't judge me.

19

A second beam blasted forth and hit the stone by my feet, forming a translucent wall of yellow light. I pressed my hand against it and found that it was as tough as stone and immovable as a wall.

"I guess I won't be coming with you then?" I asked. "Too bad, I was looking forward to seeing what you had for snacks before the tour."

I wasn't sure whether she'd be able to hear me through the wall, but the question was more for me. I tend to get chatty when I get nervous or threatened with bodily injury.

"No, you won't. Now, be a good boy and fetch a weapon. Trust me, you'll need it."

Well, shit, that didn't sound good. I had to find a weapon and face something monstrous if the various Isekai stories I read were anything to go by were accurate. No, they wouldn't, would they? In those, the MC would face a goblin or small monster. They wouldn't dare pit me against something strong right away. Would they? If the freaking Balrog stepped out of the shadow I was leaving.

I swung around, my gaze scouring the walls for weapons, but turned to find that Mistress Salina had vanished. With my exit cut off and left with no other choice, I turned around and resumed my search.

Another portal sprang to life not six feet to my right. It barely rose to my height, but that wasn't what startled me. An equally beautiful, but much younger woman walked through. Long, blonde hair flowed down her shoulders and over her rose-colored robe. Her icy-blue eyes took me in as I stared. The garment was long, silken, and tight, leaving absolutely nothing to the imagination. Like with Salina I found my gaze drifting towards the neckline, where her perfect breasts pressed against the silky fabric.

"Are you the other prospective student?" she asked, her voice catching me off guard. I lifted my eyes but could tell she knew I had been ogling her. She smirked, then chuckled, throwing me a startlingly white and disarming smile. She reached up and flicked the hair off her neck, the action drawing my attention to her ears. Yes, they rose into points.

"Are you an elf?" The ears were a dead giveaway, but for some reason, I couldn't keep the words from tumbling out of my mouth. As I said, I get nervous, and things happen. Awkward things.

She nodded and curtsied. "The name is Mabel, human."

"I'm JD, elf. My mom thought I was an ogre when I was born, but it just turned out I was a fat baby and had jaundice. Who knew?" Ah. *Stop trying to be funny!*

Mabel laughed, lifting her hand to cover her mouth.

"The pleasure is mine, JD. And yes, I am an elf. A moon elf, to be precise."

"Oh, a moon elf! So, exotic! No wonder your skin is so pale."

She chuckled and shook her head. "Don't, you'll make me blush. You seem surprised to see me, do you not have elves where you come from?"

"No, we don't. And I will tell you, now that I have seen you, I believe it is a grave crime against all that is holy that we do not. Your beauty is truly unparalleled. But...apparently, there is a test that is going to begin at any moment," I said.

I stopped and tore my eyes away from her. There was something about the girl—about her looks, or maybe it was in her eyes, or the way she smelled, that made me want to drop to my knees and pledge myself body and soul to her safekeeping. Was I just overwhelmed? Or did she have some power over men? Or...was this just a byproduct of the cranial trauma and the coma I'd obviously slipped into?

"Mistress Salina said something about needing weapons. She also didn't say we couldn't work together. Care to join forces?" Man, there it was again. Why did I sound so funny when talking to her?

"An excellent idea, JD. This test is extremely hard. Unfortunately, many young men and women die in the attempt."

"Die?"

21

Mabel nodded. "It is a test to enter a Tower Academy. Not just *anyone* can be allowed entry. Young contestants must prove themselves worthy of their placement, thus the danger must be real."

The magical portal notwithstanding, I had started to believe this was all a joke. An elaborate prank. Maybe I had angered some obscure deity, or more realistically, my friends had slipped me some fantastically strong hallucinogens and I was tripping balls in a dirty stall in the restaurant's bathroom right now. A lot of them died? Pick up weapons? Monsters?

Shit. Hell no! That wasn't what I signed up for!

As if mocking my thoughts, a rack of weapons appeared in front of us. A sword, a bow, a spear, what looked like a battle staff, a wand, and a...zither? Wait, why would anyone place a zither in a weapon rack? Last I checked, it was a musical instrument.

I closed my eyes, took in a deep breath, and let it out slowly as I tried to push away my panic. I opened them again and let them roam over the last few items. Shield, crossbow, some kind of dual-bladed staves, and other things I had never seen before. And what was that last one? It looked like a damn quill... or a bladed pen?

"Are you people serious? You want me to fight with a zither or a pen?"

Before Mabel could even reply, a loud, screeching noise came from my left. And then my right. I swung around and froze. A truly horrific creature stood not twenty feet away. It was almost as tall as me, with long, slender arms. The head looked small for the rest of its body, with sharp, pointy ears. White, pupil-less eyes burned in its sockets, radiating enough malevolence to dislodge a small drop of pee.

The beast wore a piece of ragged cloth tied around its waist, the loincloth not quite sufficient to cover its beastly bits. Damnit, why did I have to look? I'd never be able to burn that image out of my mind. Drink, you fool! Drink the trauma away!

"Pick a weapon," Mabel hissed. "Or are you planning on fighting that thing off with your bare hands?"

22

"I'm uh…" I stammered, eyes still stuck on the…what was it? It looked like a mixture between a goblin and a very malnourished orc. A goblin? An orclin?

"I'm just not sure what would work best with me," I laughed, nervously, trying to hold the rest of my bladder's contents in.

"Hold out your hand and trust…the right weapon will speak to you! Trust me, you will feel it."

Mabel's hand shot out toward the zither, and she took up a position to my left. I closed my eyes. You can do this, JD. If she said I would feel it, then dammit, I had to try.

My hand moved across the rack, but I felt nothing. Nada. Zilch. Whatever. Damnit. I'm going to end up a snack for Captain McStinky Balls and he would spend the rest of his life retelling the story about how I cried and peed myself when he slow-roasted me over a campfire. His children would laugh, thus making his drunk uncle fall over and break his hip, and then they would sue my estate for damages. Fuck!

A freaking sword then, I decided. My hand wrapped around the sword's handle, and I pulled it free just as the first monster came at me. I swung the weapon in a wide arc, but it glanced off the monster's thick skin. Shit, I felt like a toddler trying to swing a freaking wiffle bat. Probably looked like one, too. I found my balance and stabbed the creature's chest, only to have the tip hit the skin, catch, and then glance off.

"Okay, what in the-serious-fuck!"

I dodged a swipe of the creature's clawed hands, retaliated, and hit only air, then about fell on my ass. This wasn't off to a great start.

"Dear lord! No one said anything about being in a Lord of the Rings movie! What, does this thing have iron skin or something? Am I fighting a damned Uruk Hai!"

The monster lunged at me, swiping those sharp-looking claws at my face. I ducked but lost my balance and rolled sideways. I came up again just as its claws came in at eye level. Shit. Here I go. Dead already and I just got to the party.

The creature froze, its hand twitching in the air, and then with a loud *snap*, it folded backward. Mabel appeared next to me, her hand strumming the zither. A thread appeared as if the notes were given form. It wrapped around the creature, tightening around its arms and legs.

"Try another weapon. You've obviously got no affinity for the sword," she yelled.

She didn't sound angry, just frightened, like me. Okay, maybe there was some impatience there, too. After all, if I were her, and some bumbling idiot was falling all over the place instead of fighting, I might get a little pissed. Point taken.

I dropped the sword and took the bow, but there were no arrows. Where was the damn quiver? Why wasn't it there? Damn it! Why were there no arrows?

"Where are they?"

"What? The arrows? They should appear in your hand if you have an affinity for it! Try something else! Choose something that comes naturally! Something you're familiar with! As I said, feel the right weapon!"

Mabel cried out then, as she strummed a bad chord and her hold on the beast broke. It snarled, cried out, and with crusty balls swinging, dove for her.

"Why would I be familiar with any type of weapon? I'm a friggin' artist!" But then my eyes veered off to the end of the rack and lingered on the pen-blade. Yes, I was an artist, after all, right? The pen-blade could be what came naturally? I've held one for thousands of hours. If anything, it should be that.

I grabbed the pen-blade, shamefully screamed like a girl, and almost let go as a jolt of energy ran up my arm and into my body. I could feel it, the energy that came from the strange-looking weapon. It made me feel alive, my body running hot as if my blood was about to boil. But then the sensation faded away. A familiar, infuriating window appeared in the air above the pen-blade.

You have completed the affinity check!

AFFINITY: Pen-blade
NOTE 1: You are the wielder of the legendary pen-blade!
SIDE NOTE: We're deeply sorry and wish you well in your next life. It is bound to come soon, after having bonded with what we believe to be the most useless weapon of all the legendaries!

NAME: Pen-Blade (R1)
TYPE: Weapon, Upgradeable
POWER LEVEL: 1, **RANGE:** 5
DESCRIPTION: Blade crafted from the feather of a ??? and steel mined deep within ???
Can be used to cast magic and as an ordinary sword. Maybe. We don't know, as we've never really wanted to use one.
STORED SKILL: Air Slash (B)

I frowned at the side note. What in the hell was that note about? Was it sending me its condolences over my shitty weapon's affinity? Did they just tell me I was screwed and about to die? Crap. Crap. Crap.

"No!" I growled. I'd just gotten there. I wasn't going to die already. Beautiful, exotic women were everywhere, and I was going to learn magic. *Don't say it, you idiot.* "Or die trying."

And what was that about usable skills? Air Slash?

Mabel ducked a slash, tried to snare the creature again, and failed.

"Are you going to help, or what?"

I turned, jumped forward, and kicked stinky balls in the midsection, sending it sprawling onto his butt. And his loincloth flapped up, putting his swollen monster bits on full display. Again. Burned right...into...my...brain.

It snarled and sprang at me, swinging its long claws, jagged, green teeth snapping. Air Slash. Air Slash. Right. It should have to

25

do with slashing the pen across the air, right? Crap, I don't want to die.

I raised the blade and slashed it in a downward, diagonal cut, aiming from the right shoulder to the left hip. A brushstroke appeared in the air, glowing bright, freaking-angry red. Nothing happened. I pulled the sword back up and traced the same line on my second try as I narrowly evaded a disemboweling swipe of the Uruk Hai porn star's claws.

I screamed and cut straight across with the pen-blade, the resulting brush stroke pulsing with my anger's intensity. The creature lurched right through the stroke, squealed, thrashed, and promptly fell into two, sloppy pieces. Blood and stinky intestines spilled out onto the ground. As if to mock me, the right leg flopped over, the monster's giblets waving at me in response.

I watched in horror and awe, a considerable weariness hitting my legs. I barely held on to my weapon. Shit. This isn't what I had in mind when I activated the skill. Or was it? I turned to Mabel for confirmation, maybe a thank you or high five, and found three more of the glowing-eyed, dangly ball creatures moving in from the shadows.

"Hah! I knew it! I knew you'd survive! Thank you for not dying," Mabel said as she gave me an honest smile.

"Your—welcome?"

So there really was a chance I could have died? Damned sakes.

"Come on. We can do this," she said, strumming her zither. Three snares appeared, lashing around the three monsters.

"You want me to do it again?"

"Yes. I will hold them, and you attack," she yelled, excitedly bouncing on the balls of her feet. My eyes dropped, immediately drawn to her bouncing breasts. I froze. Damn, why did she have to bounce?

"What are you staring at? Attack!" she cried, as the monsters started breaking free.

"I'm drained! You didn't even ask if I *could* do that thing again! I don't know if I can."

I sucked in a breath and straightened my back. An idea blossomed. If I was using air to hit them, then I might use air to do other things? I thought about spinning them around and focused my pen-blade. I drew a downward trajectory, followed by a stroke to the left and back up diagonally.

I finished the drawing in the air and felt the magic bite into my heart again. A gust of wind rolled in and hit the three creatures, spinning them up and off the ground like spinning-top toys. They screeched and howled as the wind held them in place.

Yes. Their loin cloths didn't stay in place. Argh.

I couldn't leave them hanging out all day, so I changed my approach and drew a sickle in the air, and imagined the wind slicing into them. Three new trajectories appeared, mimicking the sickles I drew in the air. I swung them forward, catching the three dingle berries right in the chest.

The creatures exploded into a fine, smoggy mist and disappeared, leaving behind three crystals that floated in the air. I looked to Mabel, who released a pent breath, and together we approached.

"What are core crystals?" I asked, reading the window that popped up above the glowing and shimmering pieces of... stuff? I had no idea.

Mabel ran over and plucked them out of the air.

"Here, take them," she said, holding the glowing cores out. "I can't use them anyway, as you dealt the killing blow. Besides, they're nothing to me, but to someone just starting out, they're worth a fortune."

"Are you sure?" I asked, gladly shifting my focus to the glowing cores.

"Most certainly. You look like you need them, anyway. Here, I will help you open your rift."

"My what?"

"Your rift. Some races call them clefts. Here, I will show you."

She reached out with her right hand, just as a small, shimmering portal appeared in the air before her. Her fingers, then her whole hand disappeared inside. She pulled it back out a moment later, her fingers now wrapped around a much larger, red core.

ITEM RECEIVED:
Core Crystal Rank 5: 1

"So, I'm guessing that thing is worth a lot, especially if a rank one is worth a fortune?"

"It is," she said, and extended it towards me.

"Wow, heh. I can't accept something that valuable."

"It's okay. The academy gave it to me. As for a **rank one,** yes, they are incredibly valuable. To certain people, especially those just starting out. Now, hold out your hands, palms up, and I'll do the rest."

I did as she instructed, though I wasn't necessarily sure what she was going to do. Nor was I extremely excited about placing absolute trust in someone I didn't know. Mabel approached with the red core, its haunting light reflecting in her eyes.

"So," I said, as butterflies fluttered their wings in my stomach. "What, uh, did you mean by *just starting out?* At the academy? Or, in online gaming? Or maybe competitive shoe polishing? Poker? Go fish?"

The core glowed more intensely as it drew closer to my hands, releasing what looked like sparks of something... energy, maybe. My fingers jerked and twitched, the same jolting sensation pushing up my hand that I felt when I grabbed the pen-blade. The power burned bright and strong, even pushing the core to catch flame. One of the sparks jumped over to my left palm, and another to the right, burning right through my skin to the bone. An intense pain shot up my arms, forcing me to my knees. Pain erupted inside me... no, pain was stubbing a toe. This was anguish beyond compare. Soul blackening, crushed to dust and then swept away by gale-force winds, anguish.

The energy had burned holes right through my skin and muscle. Gaping holes, blackened and smoking. I gagged as my stomach threatened to revolt. Just as I was about to puke, the wounds healed, and the pain evaporated.

I pulled my hands back and stared at my palms, but I only saw soft, unblemished skin. How? I'd seen the holes, smelled the charred flesh. There wasn't even a scar. Magic was cool but burning holes through people with it wasn't. Damn, maybe next time she could provide a warning, a courtesy grope. Or, shit, I don't know, buy a guy a drink first.

"Why the pain?" I grunted, staring at my hands. Mabel winked at me and even went so far as to stick out her tongue playfully.

"It was all in your mind. Now, do this," she said, after stashing the core away. Then she grabbed my hands. Yes, I flinched. But it was out of surprise. And damn, her hands were soft, and she smelled really good. Like fresh flowers or Pez candies. I loved those things!

Mabel rubbed my hands, somehow knowing the exact spot the energy had touched me. Then she bent my fingers and moved beside me.

"Imagine that an invisible chest sits next to you. It can be a box, or a bag, too. Then reach out towards it. But use your mind, not your hands. Try to open it."

I did as she instructed, focusing my thoughts on a box. A large treasure chest adorned with gold and diamonds. Just like the ones you would find in mangas when the main character would stumble upon the treasure vault.

It took roughly ten seconds, but holy shit, one appeared. The beautifully gilded box opened, a hundred spaces ready to hold my loot. I placed the cores inside, neatly stacking them into a single slot. A small white number 'three' hovered above the image of a crystal core.

ITEM STORED:
Core Crystal Rank 1: 3

"You can do the same with your pen-blade. Just store it inside and pull it back out when you need it. It is as simple as that."

I did as Mabel instructed, and to my great satisfaction, it worked.

"A rift, huh? I'm going to call it Smaug's Vault. Because I'm going to lord over that loot like a greedy dragon," I said, letting my inner dork speak freely.

Mabel chuckled, just as a slow clapping sound came from the direction of the massive room's solitary exit. I turned and spotted Salina slowly approaching, a wide grin plastered to her face. And not just any smile, but that mischievous one I'd seen before. It was infectious and enticing like she could ask me out or pull a fuming, angry troll out of her pocket at any moment. I liked one option more than the other.

"Impressive, JD," she said, her voice echoing in the large space. "You did even better than I hoped."

"Yes, I was quite surprised as well, Mistress Salina," Mabel added.

My gaze moved between the two women, studying them, watching, and waiting. Were they *actually* impressed? Or were they mocking me?

"Thank you, I think."

"You are the first to successfully wield the Pen-blade in ages. What's more, you survived. It didn't blow you up or tear poor Mabel in half. I'll have to keep an eye on you, JD, or the other mistresses might snatch you right out from under me."

Her wording struck me-*under her.* I wanted that very much.

"Oh, Mistress!" Mabel laughed. "They wouldn't dare."

Salina shrugged.

"And you. Why did you reach for the Zither?" she asked, turning to Mabel. "Didn't your mother use the same weapon

30

when she died on the tower's 13th level? Now she was a formidable woman, your mother."

"Yes, she was, Mistress. She really was."

"A pity. I mourned her for many seasons. But did you know she was the last woman to wield one and come so far? She was destined to become a master, that is until pride got the better of her."

Mabel's expression changed, her features hardening. She stared at the mistress for a long moment, neither speaking. I reached up and awkwardly scratched my neck, feeling very much the third wheel on a rickety tricycle, quickly approaching a sheer cliff. There was obviously bad blood between them, but it definitely wasn't my place to pry.

"We mourn her death every day, Mistress," Mabel finally said, her jaw muscles visibly tight.

"Good," Salina said, studying her nails. "Anger is good, Mabel. But you must learn to channel it. We will teach you how, and so much more... if you prove to be a worthy successor."

Mabel looked away, meeting my eyes for a brief moment, and then looked away again, as if suddenly remembering that they weren't actually alone. The story of my life.

I didn't hold it against Mabel, even if she went at the older woman. Insulting someone's parents was bad manners, especially their memory.

"What now, Mistress?" I asked, trying to change the subject. Her expression didn't betray any of her feelings, at least not to me, but then she was all smiles again.

"Oh, right. How silly of me." She let out a throaty laugh, one that sounded surprisingly phony, especially after all I had witnessed. "Follow me, both of you."

Salina set off quickly towards the distant door. We waited a moment before following.

"She seems like kind of a bitch," I whispered, leaning in close to Mabel.

31

"You can say that again. No matter how nice I am, or how good a student I become, she never fails to insult my mother. I want to shove this zither so far up her tight ass, that her tonsils start plucking the strings!"

I couldn't help but laugh. This elf was beautiful, skilled, and had a way with words. Just my type.

"Probably not the way you envisioned your first day at... wait, what was this place called again? Zenith?"

Mabel nodded. "Zenith Magical Academy. It is one of many magical schools located inside the Elemental Tower. You and I have just become their newest students."

"Wait, I thought you were a new teacher or something?"

Mabel chuckled and shook her head. "No, I am new. But thanks to my family lineage, I have been surrounded by this knowledge my whole life. Us appearing in this chamber at the same time was not a coincidence, you know. They usually put students in pairs to see if they can work together."

"So, we've just become students then?"

She nodded. "Welcome to the academy, JD."

I wasn't terribly interested in becoming a student, especially not in going back to school, but if it meant that I could keep this awesome weapon and draw things in the air, command magic with my actions and thoughts, and hang around incredibly attractive, magical women, then I was definitely the man for the job. I'd always wanted to become a Jedi, anyway. Or a fucking samurai.

A pen-blade might have sounded like a ridiculous weapon, but I'd read enough anime and manga to know that silly, underestimated things could possess the greatest potential. Especially in the hands of someone with a lot of knowledge. Mostly useless knowledge, yes, but knowledge, nonetheless.

"Mind if I ask a question or two?"

"You may," she replied, flashing me a warm smile. I watched her as we slowly made our way toward the far exit, and it was only when she coughed that I realized I was staring.

"Sorry, it's just that I'm not used to seeing real-life elves. And you're so pretty and strong. This whole thing just caught me completely off guard," I said. She shrugged and looked away, but I caught her little smirk. "What about my air slash? Is it normal for magic to be used as one sees fit?"

"No, it's not. I think that it's one of your special powers. Every magic skill has a design. If it is a gust of wind, then that is what it is. Maybe it is a slash of air that turns physical mid-air. But with you...I don't know. You used a single skill in two different ways, and it was fantastic."

"That's interesting," I said as we stopped right in front of the exit. "What's with the Power Level stats?"

"Mana is the energy infused into magical items. Each one has a power level. That's basically a power output value. It depends on the type of item, but when it comes to consuMabels, like cores, it's how much energy you can absorb or transfer."

"Wait, what? How much energy—err mana, right? How much mana I can absorb? And do what? Cast spells?"

"Well, yes and no. Look, they'll talk about it later, so let's leave it at that for now. Salina is waiting, and I'm already on her bad side."

I could get behind that. People that talked trash were a bad breed, one I disliked, even if they had a great rack and long legs. And a beautiful face.

"Can we talk later? After... whatever comes next?"

She nodded and graced me with a wink as she pushed through the door.

"I'd like that!"

Meeting The Mistresses

WE FOLLOWED SALINA INTO A LARGE HALL. It was roughly rectangular, with large, exposed beams that arched high overhead. Stained glass filled the space between beams, the shining light beyond depicting a massive battle. A tower sat in the middle of the scene, while fantasy beasts charged in from one side, and an army of magic-using heroes on the other.

Matching fireplaces sat at either end, roaring, crackling fires glowing in their hearths. Long tables filled the middle of the space, each covered in trays, as students clustered on long, dark wood benches. Besides the castle stone, beams, and magnificent stained glass, I was immediately struck by how much the rest of the room reminded me of a High School cafeteria. My heart immediately jumped in my chest and my palms started to sweat. *Not again.* My first go-around in school hadn't been that great. Back then, it was a dirty word to be a "nerd". Now it was a fashion choice.

Students noticed us and turned, their eyes lingering on Mabel, and then on me. Yes, I felt like the new kid who was last to arrive on his first day of school. Well, I was in a way. But I subtly checked to make sure I wasn't naked. *Clothes,* check. Good. At least I wasn't living that nightmare.

Everyone turned as Salina stopped, her heels tapping angrily against the hard floor. The chatter and whispers went quiet and most of those present straightened in their seats.

"How commanding," I whispered to Mabel. My lips were only inches away from her ear, and I'd spoken so softly that only she could have heard, yet Salina turned and considered me, her scowl deepening. Could she have heard ten steps out?

"Later," Mabel whispered under her breath and shied away a step.

"Why are you two lollygagging?" Salina asked, her gaze potent enough to melt the skin right off my body. "You are expected, so pick up your feet. It is time to introduce yourself."

Salina turned around and walked off, moving with the slink and confidence of a hunting predator. She abruptly turned right and moved towards a rectangular table, practically sagging under a pile of food. We approached, and to my surprise, most of the food looked foreign, almost alien. Some of it didn't look appetizing and I immediately wondered if I'd be able to eat any of it. What would it taste like? Could I even digest it? Would I want to?

My stomach growled just then, as if saying "eat first and ask questions later", but I wasn't sure I agreed. Mabel's hand brushed against mine, and she leaned in to whisper.

"Can you go first?" she asked. "I'm... shy."

I barely stifled a snort, and not because I doubted her shyness. But more because I *was* the poster child for shy people. Hell, I think my face is in the dictionary next to the word. Then my eyes dropped to her... gravitational cleavage, because darn it, they kept trying to pull my eyes in. It felt strange that someone shy would wear something so... revealing.

"Yeah, no problem. Sure," I replied, not wanting to put her on the spot. I'd be willing to suffer through a bit of discomfort for the unusually attractive... elf. Damn, that thought felt weird.

I followed Salina and stopped before the table, standing quietly while she sat down. I struggled to hold my smile back. I was simply too excited, nervous, and everything in between. Although, I wanted to pinch myself because part of me still wondered if I was stuck in a drug-induced wet dream. Sure, I hadn't fought well, but Mabel helped me in the affinity test. Yes, I could have died, but it was behind me now. And in front of me spanned the promise of adventure... a whole new life, the kind I had only read about in books and comics.

"Greetings, everyone. The name is JD, and I'm incredibly happy to be here," I said, my voice radiating my feelings. "I am human and promise I will do everything I can to show you just how much I appreciate this opportunity."

Five gorgeous women sat across from me, six if you counted Salina, and I struggled to not stare at each one in turn. It didn't even matter that several hundred pairs of eyes were staring at my back now, as the mistresses demanded my undivided attention.

The Mistress of Finances sat to the right, while a woman I could only describe as a witch, sat to her left. She wore a dark robe, trimmed in red silk. A tan sash was tied around her waist, the elaborate fabric accented by gold and copper thread. She had pulled up her voluminous sleeves, revealing long, sheer gloves, the fingers cut off to reveal glossy, painted nails. I focused on her hat, as to not stare at her slender, bare neck. It was an almost comically oversized cone-shaped witch's hat, complete with a long, blood-red feather.

"JD," the witch said, repeating my name. Damn, I loved the way it sounded when she said it. "That is a lovely name. I am Scarlet, the Mistress of Magical Cultivation. I also serve as the headmistress."

"Magical Cultivation? Is that like what I did with my pen-blade? The air manipulation, writing thingy?"

"Oh, he catches on quickly," the woman next to Scarlet laughed. "My name is Freya, and I am the Mistress of Martial Arts Cultivation. I am the assistant headmistress. So, try to keep that in mind, young man."

I looked back at Scarlet, and she nodded playfully.

36

"Yes, ma'am," I said, "Martial arts. Using your body as a weapon, right?"

She winked, but it was Scarlet that spoke first.

"My school teaches magic that commands the elements, be it explosive, offensive, defensive, and anything in between. Truly awe-inspiring, universe-changing power. Freya's muscles should tell you what she is adept at—punching, kicking, and breaking things."

"I could make one of those *things* you, Scarlet. After all, we haven't had a sparring match in ages. Care to partake?" Freya asked, turning in her seat.

"Oh, that sounds exhausting," Scarlet breathed, then adjusted her hat. "Raincheck."

"I will teach you how to guard against foes four times your height and weight, harden your muscles and punch clean through full-sized trees. You will see," Freya said, leaning into the table. The pressure just exaggerated her already prominent gifts. She was brunette, with short hair, piercing, sky-blue eyes, and a wide, genuine smile. She *was* muscular, too. And strangely, I found it both alluring and intimidating.

Was every woman in this place built like a goddess?

"That sounds magnificent," I said, appreciating the view. I knew what she was doing—flaunting her gifts next to the older woman. While Scarlet had the air of importance, wisdom, and patience, Freya gave me the impression she was far less "books and study".

Mabel shifted next to me, catching my attention.

I smiled at the collection of beautiful women in front of me and waited.

"My name is Leona," the third woman said proudly. "I teach Weapon Cultivation, be it the sword, spear, bow, or even that pen-blade of yours. Every weapon, every style... that is my motto. If you are curious about a certain style, just bring the weapon, and I'll teach you how to use it."

Mistress Leona had long, red hair. It flowed down her shoulders, gleaming in the light like a silky sheet of soft fabric. Her pale skin stood out in contrast to her hair, making her perhaps the most recognizable of the women arrayed before me. She was just as beautiful as the others yet dressed far more conservatively than Scarlet or Freya. Her kimono was made of pearlescent blue silk, adorned with blooming, white cherry blossoms.

"I'll keep that in mind, Mistress Leona. Thank you."

"Another thing to keep in mind is that your weapon is everything here. Take good care of your blade and it will save your life. If you don't, it will certainly fail you in battle, and that means death in this world, JD."

I nodded appreciatively and returned her smile. The fourth woman pushed her glasses back to the bridge of her nose as she studied me.

"If Leona is done making eyes at the boy," the next woman said, again pushing the glasses up her nose. "Good. I am Eliana and I head the department of Cultivation Crafting. The most important field of study at this academy."

"Most important? They are all important," Freya snorted.

Leona cleared her throat and adjusted her glasses. She mumbled something under her breath and Freya visibly stiffened. Scarlet abruptly shifted in her seat, and then her hand was on the other woman's shoulder, yet I hadn't seen her move it.

"Ladies, enough! We are all far too old to be sniping at one another like this."

Freya relaxed and whispered something quietly in response.

I watched in uncomfortable silence, wondering exactly what I had stepped into.

Eliana looked the part of a sexy librarian. Donning a short-sleeved tight-fitting dress, she had her blonde hair tied up in an economic ponytail. And I was delighted to see she was an elf. I already had a thing for the ears.

Someone coughed to the left, and I turned to track the noise. I hadn't noticed it earlier when I first walked in, but the crowd was far from human. Sure, human-looking students accounted for about a third, but a good chunk appeared to be elves, which again were divided into several groups differentiated by their hair and skin color. The rest was a mix of... what I could only describe as human-like beasts. Some had animal traits like proud lion's manes around their necks and sharp-looking claws, leathery, or hairy skin. I swear one girl had ears like a fox.

And once again, I wondered if I was on drugs. *Don't wake up, JD. Don't wake up.*

I quickly looked back as the last woman at the mistresses' table waved. She looked human-ish, but with the ears of a wolf, a collarbone and neck covered in white fur, and with elongated fingers and toes. White fur covered her wrists up to the elbows. And the same went for ankles and calves.

"Hi, JD. Last but not least. I am Lamora, the beastmaster or mistress, I guess. I teach others everything they need to know about the world of beasts, both magical and mundane. And those who belong to my kin, well, I teach them how to change into beasts. It is a pleasure to meet you, young pen-blader."

Lamora didn't just stand out because of her fur, ears, and totally cute nose. But also because of her outfit. She was wearing a tank-top, a rather short skirt, and what looked like flip-flops. How did I know all this? Well, I had a perfect view under the table. And she didn't seem shy.

I nodded and bowed, my eyes meeting Salina's as she tapped her long fingernails against the table. She remained quiet but otherwise seemed amused.

"And who is the young lady behind you?" Scarlet asked. "Is that Mabel from the moon elves?"

Mabel stepped forward and took her position next to me. She tried to give them an honest smile, one that equaled mine, but I saw right through it. And so did the ladies. There was no way this young elf was comfortable being here, stared at from all sides. I put my hand over hers to lend her some strength and offered a

39

reassuring smile. Shit, I almost felt like a pimp about to sell her to these wolves. Bad thoughts. Shoo.

"Yes, Mistress Scarlet. I have finally decided to join. Lady Salina gathered me today."

Scarlet looked at Mabel, her expression comforting and warm. "Good, good. I see you share your mother's affinity. And what a tragedy. She was a good cultivator and a good woman. Bless her soul."

"Thank you, Mistress," Mabel replied, her voice wavering. I squeezed her hand gently and moved a touch closer. Some might think it stupid, or that I was trying to play the "protective" part, and maybe I was, but I liked the girl. She had her demons like everyone else, but she seemed genuine. Plus, she helped me when she didn't have to.

"Right," Mistress Scarlet said, adjusting her hat so it didn't droop. "We don't normally introduce new students to all the mistresses right away, but since everyone was already here, it only seemed appropriate. Now, why don't you two get some food, find a seat, and start meeting some of your classmates? We were just about to finish, but I don't think a little longer meal will harm anyone."

"Thank you, Mistress," I said and bowed.

I pulled Mabel after me and picked up an empty tray and several plates. She watched me, her expression somewhere between horrified and curious, but I didn't care. I was hungry before Salina showed up, and the battle just made the hunger worse.

"What are you doing?" she whispered, casting a glance at the mistresses behind us. "You shouldn't take so much food."

"I'm making sure I can function properly," I replied. "You should, too. The one thing I've learned in life so far is that you don't always know where your next meal is going to come from. And yes, it was probably stupid that I didn't eat anything all day. But still..."

She let out a sigh and nodded, adding several other things to her tray. I looked around, struggling to identify empty seats. Mabel stared down at her tray, her cheeks flushing red.

"We should skip food. It's embarrassing."

I nudged her with an elbow, and she looked up. I gave her a grin and said, "Watch this."

The tables were full, yes, but the table holding the empty trays was currently available. So, I swapped my tray to my left hand and started shoving the empty trays towards one side, clearing enough space for Mabel and me. I pushed the table closer to the other students but stayed far enough so we could chat without being overheard. Then I dropped my tray down, ran over to the wall, grabbed several empty chairs, and pulled them over, first motioning Mabel to sit, and then joining her.

I had done the same in High School... forging new territory when the bullies tried to block out all the places to sit. The bullies hated it, naturally.

"You're crazy," she chuckled. "And thanks. I'm famished. I just hate eating in front of other people," she added with a whisper. Her pink cheeks only added to the whole, adorable elf package. I found myself at a loss for words. Yes, I was sitting across from an elf.

"Everyone," Scarlet said, loudly. "Give the newcomers some privacy. You can pester them with questions later."

The crowd returned to their trays and conversations, or at least most of them. I still caught some glares, especially from the elves.

"What's with the other elves?" I whispered, tearing off a chunk of warm bread and stuffing it into my mouth. At least, I thought it was bread. That's what it tasted like, along with what I was sure was butter and herbs. It was damned good!

Mabel started nibbling on what looked like a mix between a donut and a hamburger patty. I'd taken two of the small, round pastry-like things as well aside from two loaves, several pieces of meat, something that looked like a roast potato, and lastly something I recognized. Cake. Someone made cake! With chocolate chips, no less!

"Now that everyone has food, go on and eat as you listen," Scarlet said. "I will go over some of the basics. Everyone here has had ample time to consider their options, so make sure to have your mind made up before lunchtime is over. Everyone but JD, that is. He is still new to this all, a special case, so the mistresses will work with him after."

"What Scarlet means is that JD has been given the pen-blade," Leona added. "He doesn't necessarily have to work under me, maybe Scarlet's class will be of more use, or even Eliana's. The pen-blade is a strange weapon and can be used in many ways, across many different disciplines."

"That's right," Scarlet said, taking over once again. "It is important that you are solid on your decision, as once your direction is selected, you will not be able to change. Most of you have been groomed all your lives, prepared for a specific discipline or weapon, so don't lose confidence now. Trust me, you will regret it."

"Is that true?" I whispered to Mabel. She barely lifted her eyes from the plate and then slowly nodded.

"It is. You are so lucky, you know?"

I chuckled. I'd never been lucky, just a dude doing things to get by until the next paycheck. Mabel glanced over to the large group of elves and then back down to her plate. Several students from the far side of the room were staring back and whispering. The signs were all there and easy to read. She was a black sheep. But how and why?

"Luck is something I don't have a lot of experience with," I said, trying to help her understand that she wasn't alone. Her eyebrows rose along with the corners of her mouth, but just a bit.

"There are some missing students," she said, changing the topic. I dug into the meat next and found it strangely chewy but flavorful.

"What do you mean, missing?"

42

"Well, there is supposed to be another human in our class. Chloe, I think? The mistress warned me about her. And you as well. They tell us that humans are troublemakers, that you lack any true sense of morals, belonging, nobility, or authority. Most blame all of their problems on your kind. Tell me, though. Is that true? Do your people not have morals or values?"

I thought about it for a moment, chewing through a bite of... steak? It was green, so who knew. If I was being honest, her words rang true, but only to an extent. No people were that black or white.

"Our history, of the human race, that is, is one of war and slavery. We've enslaved each other since early times. There are always those who rose to power, but even more like me, just ordinary people trying to get by. It also depends on your definition of bad behavior. For example, I would very much like to go back in time and punch some of humanity's worst d-bags right in the face. If you consider that kind of random, unsolicited violence bad, then yeah, we're trouble."

"What is a 'd-bag'?" she asked.

"It is someone that does bad things to innocent people when you don't have to. And if you're a man like me, you are opposed to stuck-up assholes like that. Most think they're better than the rest just because they were born into a wealthy or influential family. So, it's not like they've actually made lasting contributions to... anything."

Mabel stopped eating and looked up at me. Her icy-blue eyes flashed for a moment and her pale-golden hair moved on its own as if she'd just been caught in a gust of wind, or... magic. I was definitely going with magic.

Then I felt it. The power radiating off her. It wasn't that strong, but it was there.

"I think we can become good...friends," she whispered. "If what you just said is true. I like that you are honest. Most would keep those feelings to themselves."

43

"Thank you," I smiled. "You just keep on smiling that beautiful smile of yours and I will continue to be the nerdy guy that says anything that crosses his mind."

Mabel's mouth fell open as she gaped at me. Her ears gained some of that rose color from earlier. Elves really were beautiful. And Mabel was no exception, although she had haunted eyes.

"So, umm, where were we?" she asked.

"That other human girl. You were saying something about her."

"I was?" Mabel asked, staring off and seemingly getting lost in thought. Then she shrugged and started whispering. "She's a problematic young woman, I hear."

"Hear when? I thought you arrived right after me."

"I did, but this isn't my first time here. See, because of my mother, I was... purposefully..." she faltered, her eyes dropping to the tray. Several long moments later she looked up and said, "I was groomed to come here for a long time. But only when I was truly ready."

"Oh. I'm sorry about your mother. That has to make being here even more difficult. If you need someone to talk to, just let me know. From what I hear, I'm not a horrible listener."

"So, you're one of those men, huh?"

"The listening, type?" I asked, struggling to interpret her change in tone.

"The kind that likes to search for trouble."

"Sometimes. I mean, not really. I don't like drama. But I was serious when I said that I'm not a bad listener. And I don't want anything in return. This isn't some creepy attempt to win your trust and then demand something from you."

"Okay. That's good," she whispered.

"Can I ask you a not-necessarily related question? What are you going to choose?" I asked after chugging down some sickly-sweet drink.

"Weapon Cultivation. The zither is a support weapon and is very important, but is useless without the proper cultivation skills. And team members."

"Oh, I see. Just like the time when you bound those monsters together? You could hold them, but not kill them?"

She nodded. "Exactly. The zither's sound can provide special buffs to allies, yet devastating debuffs to enemies. But only at a high level. Early on we can't do much, so we can only provide support. If you weren't taking the test with me, I would have only been able to tie up the monsters with the zither's ethereal threads. Eventually, I would have run out of mana, and they would have killed me."

"Surely, Mistress Salina would have intervened before then?"

Mabel didn't reply, and after a long moment of silence, she shook her head. "The test is meant to, well, test you. It's not for the mistresses or anyone else to intervene. I'm just lucky I was paired with you. On a wrong day or with the wrong mistress, I could have been forced to take it by myself."

"Then we are both lucky," I said, trying to not dwell on the dark implications of her words. And that was tough. Because, damn. That sounded like straight murdering someone.

"If it weren't for you, Mabel, I probably would have run through every single weapon before even giving the pen-blade a second look. Those stinky-ball bastards would have torn me apart."

"We helped each other," Mabel said with a nod and a smile.

"That's right," I agreed. "The way magic works here, it all feels like a video game."

"Video game?" Mabel asked.

"Oh, right. I guess you guys don't have them here. Let's just say that I'm kind of familiar with the system that guides the magic. Or at least similar versions. It seems overpowered though. Being able to use magic and skills is something everyone can do if they have an affinity for a weapon. And then being able to manipulate it by drawing different strokes. I'll have to spend some time practicing, that's for sure."

"Indeed," Mabel said. "It beats practicing with a weapon you have no affinity with for years. A lot of our younger generation isn't happy with what their weapon turns out to be, but they learn proficiency, at least. Most of the time."

"It sure does but having some knowledge about your weapon can only help."

Mistress Scarlet's voice rose above the din, and everyone promptly went silent. She had a domineering presence, one of a king or queens, but not an ordinary one, but perhaps more warrior nobility. Power radiated from her very presence and voice.

"Freshmen, students of the first year, now that the time for pleasantries is over, please stand behind the mistresses that represent your choice. They will lead you to your dorms and show you where you'll be staying for the coming years. As for you, JD, please stay behind."

Scarlet turned with a flourish, the other mistresses scattering from the table. I nodded and got up, but then hurriedly gulped the rest of my drink. Mabel got up as well, and she leaned in to hug me. I froze, startled by the sudden show of affection. She was warm and smelled like vanilla. Strange, as I was sure she smelled like flowers before.

"Say, where are the other students?" I asked after she had pulled away.

"Oh, this is only a portion of the first-year students. The rest have yet to arrive. For students in their second year or above, their dorms and classrooms are elsewhere. It's only the…five hundred or so of us that are here."

I scratched what little stubble I had and nodded. Five hundred new students. The academy was quite large if it could afford such numbers.

"Thanks, Mabel, for uh, putting up with all of my questions."

"No, JD, thank you for everything. Especially earlier when we stood in front of the mistresses," she whispered, leaned in, and kissed me on the cheek. "You did well today. I'm sure we'll get the chance to spend time together, whichever discipline you end up choosing. You seem like a good guy, and I'd like to talk again."

"Of course," I chuckled, inwardly glowing that a cute elf thought I was a good guy. "With such a strong and beautiful young elf by my side, we could take on anything they throw our way!"

She leaned in again, but further this time.

"Don't trust everything they say, JD. We know who's the boss around here, but that doesn't mean they're the good guys. Pay attention, be a good student, and trust your heart. Alright?"

I nodded. It was good advice. "I'll make sure to find you, even if we don't have the same classes."

Her smile was weak but genuine, full of affection. Yet, those eyes. So full of sadness and remorse.

"Take care," she said and made to leave, but I grabbed her hand as feet started shuffling in the cafeteria. Hundreds of students made their choices as we stood there, holding hands. I knew how it looked, but I didn't care.

"I know that you've got... problems, but know that you're not alone. Find me. Ask me for help, and I'll be there for whatever you need. Alright?"

A tear welled up in the corner of her right eye, but she wiped it with the back of her hand and pulled free.

"Thank you, JD." Mabel walked past me and took her place in line behind Leona, the Weapon Cultivation Mistress. She stood there, surrounded by a mass of other students, and yet somehow alone.

I understood the feeling better than she probably realized. Avoided, sometimes despised for who or what you were. Maybe even just because of an interest or the way you talked. Hell, sometimes it wasn't for anything more than a birthmark or the way you wore your hair. I tried to push away my past resentment, and instead moved towards the nearest fireplace. Thick, white bark-covered logs sat neatly stacked in the rack. Peculiar, magical flames bit and leapt, crackling joyfully, and throwing off drifting spark.

The mistresses filed out of the cafeteria then, the students following like lines of little ducklings. But not before one of the red-haired elves stopped and stared at me. It was a guy, probably somewhere in his mid-twenties if looks were any indication.

He bared his teeth. I immediately knew that I had made a mistake, just not *what* mistake. Hell, I used to joke at the bar that "Mistake" was my second middle name.

The man-elf didn't speak, just snarled silently before finally turning his back and moving away. He fell into line behind Eliana and strode out through the door. Shit, he gave me the creeps. The "stand quietly in the corner and drag your finger across your throat" kind. And that was saying something, considering I spotted the two-head-taller human-looking students. Giants. Shit. We even had giants.

I turned to find the red-headed man-elf standing in the doorway, staring at me. Confirmed. Creeper. He waited for the last few students to leave, then chuckled and said, "Watch what you wish for, JD. You just might get it." Then he turned and swept out into the hall, the door closing behind him.

"Great," I whispered. "We are already off to a good start."

THE WAY AROUND

"EVERYONE IN MY CLASS," Scarlet said, clapping her hands. "Please wait outside in the hallway until I'm done with JD here."

The Magical Cultivation students made their way to the exit and soon the last one closed the door behind him. Not a single one had sent me a glare or even a glance for making them wait. Scarlet motioned me forward with an index finger, so I did as instructed. It wouldn't do to disrespect someone who could tear me apart with a mere glance, or at least that's the vibe I got from her.

"Do you know why I mentioned you to the other students, why I explained your circumstances?" she asked, her lips turning up in a coy smile.

"I figured it was to provide me with a challenge," I guessed. "Whenever someone is singled out, they become a target. Or *the* target, in my case. I'm the only human here, that I could see, at least. I also the one who just happens to wield a strange weapon. Am I close?"

She chuckled and nodded. An orb appeared in her right hand, and she started stroking it like a pet. I half expected it to start purring. Thankfully, it didn't. Scarlet got to her feet and straightened her robe. The smooth fabric, having looked loose while sitting, stretched around her rather gifted figure.

Don't stare. Don't stare!

She had a perfect hourglass figure, one most of the women I knew from the bar would kill for. And it appeared that she knew it. And she also appeared to know that I appreciated it, as well.

"You're special, JD. Not so much that you could change the world, but you're not average, either. And that's good. That is why I had you fathered," Scarlet said, chuckling quietly. "We need special students, individuals with potential. But not those that will bring us the wrong kind of attention."

"Is that another way of telling me to keep a low profile?" I asked. Honestly, I had no idea what she considered the wrong kind of attention. Or how I was special, for that matter. I was just a nerd with a penchant for comic books and video games.

"By the gods, no. Not at all. You progress as you see fit. And in a school like Zenith, it is win or lose, do or die. So, I would advise you to avoid making more enemies than you already have. Blood elves are rather sensitive when it comes to their servants, the moon elves."

Oh, shit! I groaned inwardly, cursing myself for not figuring it out earlier. The way that elf had looked at us earlier, it wasn't disdain for me... well, maybe it was. But, no, it was jealousy and fear. Fear that I might get into Mabel's good graces.

"Thank you, Headmistress. I appreciate you taking the time to explain that. I'm a rather simple person. I see someone I find interesting, and I want to be their friend and get to know them. They just have to treat me right in exchange."

"Stick to that philosophy and you should have a marvelous time here. There are many royals in attendance at Zenith, from many different worlds and races. Just mind your toes and your gaze and remember that they are used to everyone bowing and scraping around them. Don't bump too many heads or ruffle too many feathers your first day, alright?"

I nodded and offered her my most earnest smile.

50

"I'll do my best, Mistress Scarlet."

"Oh, I know you will," she chuckled and motioned for me to join her in the hallway. I waited as she walked past me.

I swallowed, set my feet, and took a breath. Scarlet was an intimidating woman, but I mentally patted myself on the back for how I was managing myself, so far. Truth be told, I'd never been good at talking to the opposite sex. But...I got better at it thanks to tending bar. Most of my regulars were older women, and I played the part of the drink filler and part-time therapist. I listened while they lamented about their cheating husbands or their snotty kids that didn't appreciate all the money they spent on college.

My least favorite? Freshly divorced middle-aged men. They were like predators, and everyone could sense it. I chased them out regularly, like a benevolent lion god, protecting the animals as they clustered around my watering hole. But now, I was the outsider looking into someone else's water hole. I had to learn a whole new rulebook, perhaps customs, too.

"Coming?" Scarlet asked, turning to find me still standing in place.

"Oh, no, sorry. I was just lost in thought," I said, chuckling. Busted. "How good is the pen-blade anyway?" I asked, trying to change the subject.

"It can be a powerful tool in the right hands, and utterly wasted in the wrong ones."

"It only has a fraction of Salina's power level. The chain sword had six hundred or so? And I take it you saw her put that to the task?" She chuckled, telling me she already knew that I saw it used. Yes, to destroy my bar. Still not over that.

"Just remember, your weapon's power grows alongside you. The stronger you become, the stronger your weapon will become, as well. Salina's blade would have nowhere near the same bite in a lesser being's hands. Someday, with the right training, your pen-blade will demand the same respect."

I nodded again, content to listen, respectfully. And truthfully, I didn't have anything to add. Everything was new, strange, and getting stranger. It would take time to digest it all.

We exited the cafeteria and I took in the hall beyond. The sweeping wall to my left was gray stone, pocked with iron brackets, holding burning torches. Colorful tapestries filled the spaces in between. But where the right wall should be was just... nothing. We were in a tower, it seemed, and the center was open space, extending up and beyond the seemingly endless floors above.

Dozens of floors lay below ours, so I leaned over the ledge to have a look down. We weren't that far off from the ground, not in comparison to the vast open space above. Still, I held no delusions about what would happen if I decided to fling my body into the open air.

Splat.

I gulped, yes, I know, and it was as comical as you would think. A trickle of cold sweat ran down my neck but was comforted by the wide eyes and whispers from the other students. They clustered around me, staring out into the impressive space. So, I wasn't the only person that felt incredibly small and out of place.

"What is this place?" I whispered. The craftsmanship was truly beyond anything I believed possible—the size, the grandeur, the fucking majesty of it all. Magical? Yes.

I moved off to the side and studied one of the intricately carved pillars, the stout, stone structure effectively holding the floors above us... up. Then I looked at the beautiful murals and tapestries. I felt like I was in a castle, and it was freaking awesome!

"That is usually one of the first things people ask when they come here?" Scarlet chuckled. "This is a tower that can grant you almost anything you wish, but it can also take everything away. Countless academies fight every year, vying for the right to climb to a higher floor, and thus earn favor from those at the top."

52

"Wait. There's not just this one academy, but instead, there are—?"

"As many as there are floors," she answered. "Every floor you see is an academy, but we are all governed by laws. Most academies can only pick students from certain worlds. That's why you don't see any dwarves, lizardfolk, or even dragon kin amongst you. They are far above us on higher floors."

"That... is... crazy," I gasped. "This place is so much... cooler and weirder than I ever imagined."

"Oh, it is. Once we have reached a certain level, we were given access to dungeons twenty-four hours a day. Before that, we were limited to a measly six hours. And before you ask, dungeons exist on another plane but are bound to our floor. If we ever manage to climb to say…the thirtieth floor, we'll be given access to the world dungeons where you can battle other students while hunting monsters and beasts of all sizes. You can go there to earn points, cores, their body parts to sell to the crafters, to gain random loot generated within the tower, or simply to gain strength. It is a place where the strong thrive, and the weak die. It's as simple as that."

"Simple?" I laughed, doubting that anything in my new world was simple. "I was in a bar, pouring drinks to my regulars earlier, now I'm carrying a pen-blade." I paused. "Mabel was surprised that I had the affinity for it. And I saw a strange notification. It said, 'good luck, you'll die soon'. What did that mean?"

Scarlet let out a hearty laugh as she tapped me on the back and then pushed me on, moving slowly. She seemed rather amused, and her demeanor had changed to that of an older sister, or an aunt.

"An inside joke, never mind that. But yes, you're quite sharp, I have to give you that. Not everything is simple, especially not this year. Let's put it like this. There are three brackets of academies: the top, middle, and low-rankers. We don't have special names for them because there is no need. But there are differences even inside a bracket. We've hit rock-bottom in the mid-grade bracket, and if we don't have a remarkable student step forward soon, we'll be degraded to the lower bracket once more and will struggle accordingly. That will mean fewer resources and favors from the tower."

"Oh, so it's a power struggle? I'm not sure how much I can help right away, but you can bet your silk-covered behind that I will learn as fast as possible," I laughed. She stopped for a moment and watched me. I immediately stopped. *Where in the hell did that come from? Silk-covered behind?*

"You can devote your heart and life to *our* Academy?"

Her emphasis on the word "our" immediately registered.

"Yes," I said, then corrected. "I can, Mistress Scarlet. See, where I come from, the world is filled with... the ordinary? And this place is magical. It has everything I ever wished for, so why not dedicate myself?"

And there are so many gorgeous women... I mean girls. I would be a fool to throw my chance away, I added silently.

Her right eyebrow rose slightly, and I immediately wondered if she had read my mind. Was that possible? Damn, if so, I needed to get my thoughts under control.

We moved further along the sweeping walkway and stopped near a large door.

"This is the Weapons Cultivation entrance. Within lies its dorms and training areas. Everything is in there and is accessed by entering one of the portals. Every portal leads to a rift, with doorways affording access to the other facilities."

I nodded and followed as she started moving again, only to stop several more times to show me the other entrances. Each had a plaque above the door.

The first plaque featured a sword crossed with a spear, the second two fists, the third depicted what looked like tools, the fourth a mage hat and staff, just like the one Scarlet wore, and the fifth the image of beast claws. A sixth entrance was further ahead but it was different. A large lounge sat in front of a fifteen-foot-tall shimmering portal.

"That leads to the dungeon entrance," Scarlet said as I eyed it curiously.

"And where will I be staying?" I asked.

"Over there," she said and pointed toward an ornately decorated doorway. The sweeping, chiseled stonework was gilded with veins of gold, the highly polished door inset with sparkling gems. "That's the staff entrance, but also a dormitory for those students selected to wield legendary weapons. No matter how strong the users, or what grade they are in, we need to keep them close. We cannot allow that much destructive potential to walk about unsupervised. Space is limited, however, so you will need to share a room with another first-year student. I hope that won't be a problem."

It wasn't as much a question as it was a statement, but even if it hadn't been, I nodded, suddenly thinking about Chloe. Mabel had mentioned she was missing and that she was a troublemaker. I immediately wondered if other students were saying similar things about me behind my back.

I nodded, my heart beating faster in anticipation. I was beyond excited to sink my teeth into... whatever studies they deemed to throw my way. And I wanted to meet my roommate.

"When do we start? The classes, I mean," I asked.

"Tomorrow. So, spend today acclimating yourself to the grounds. But count yourself lucky, Salina caught you at the last moment. A day later and you never would have come here. That aside, let me show you to your dorm."

If the floor was painted into a clock, the cafeteria would be roughly at 7 o'clock, the classrooms and dorms for the five main branches would be 8, 9, 10, 11, and 12. The dungeon was at 2 o'clock, and the staff and VIP dorms at 4 o'clock. That left several empty spaces, namely 1 and 3, with translucent and shimmering portals, but I had no idea where they led or how to use them. I filed that information away for future research.

Scarlet led me into the VIP area and down a long corridor, stopping at the last door, and nodding her head towards the door with the number 13 on it.

"Is this—?" I started to say.

"Go in and rest. You'll need it for what's to come."

I bowed. "Thank you, Mistress Scarlet. Truly."

She offered me what looked like an honest smile and nodded.

"JD, I feel the need to be honest with you. We don't expect much from humans here at Zenith. For starters, your people have no innate traits or magical prowess. But you have been selected by a legendary weapon, and your partner has, too. Put in some effort and you will likely be rewarded. And if you fulfill your promise to fight hard, I'll make sure to reward you handsomely. And not just with items or laurels."

"Oh? Money? I could sure use some. See, I'm a man of culture and hobbies. I like to fill my time with…"

"No, not money or tools. Don't be a fool. I noticed how you looked at me earlier, and Mabel. All the women here. Human men are…special, in that regard. I trust you will find that the almost toxic timidity your people possess regarding sex does not exist here."

She snapped her fingers and disappeared, leaving me confused but strangely aroused. Human men are special in that regard, meaning? We're awesome? We smell better than some? We are more passionate lovers? "Toxic timidity towards sex does not exist here…"

Damn, I hoped it was the last one. I absently traced my tongue across my lips and laughed, fantasizing about Scarlet and what waited beneath that tight, black robe. I'd never been a horn ball or a perv. Hell, I'd never really had much luck with women. But if she was right, things really could be different in this world. Damn, that felt weird to think.

I exhaled excitedly and walked through the door, only to find myself stepping through a portal that transported me into what I

56

thought Salina had called a rift. Interesting. I hadn't felt anything... magical.

I gave the place a good look and I had to say that I was impressed. If you liked lavish furniture made from wood, then this was the place for you. The room was rectangular, and at the far left, stood two large closets, the doors open and waiting. Two beds sat to my immediate left, with a little more than four feet of space between them. A chest of drawers sat at the head of each bed, a small, crystal-shaped lamp glowing happily.

A wooden wall separated what I would call the bedroom from the rest of the space. A living room and kitchen filled the rest of our new home, containing a small dining table and four chairs near the entrance. Several kitchen cabinets lined the wall in the furthest corner, but I spotted no appliances.

"What, no microwaves or dishwashers in the magical tower?" I asked, attempting to break the silence.

Two wood-frame sofas sat next to the kitchenette, their leather, overstuffed cushions beckoning to me. The walls were bare, but that was okay. The gold veins running through the stone and inset jewels made up for it.

"Hello?" I said, walking into the bedroom. I moved to the living room, testing how soft the sofa cushions were, just as I heard a voice. It was female and seemed to be coming from behind a sliding door. Did it lead to a bathroom?

I inched forward and pulled it open, only to be hit in the face by a billowing cloud of hot steam. It dissipated around me but practically filled the other space.

The voice filled the air, singing a sweet melody of honey and vinegar. I inched into the steam, my heart racing. Then I spotted someone. It was a young woman with wavy, blonde hair and tan skin. She stood in the middle of what looked like a Roman-style bath, her naked back towards me. It wasn't a huge space, maybe some fifteen feet across, but the luxurious marble floors, columns, and bronze fixtures gave it a broader feel.

The young woman stood in the middle of the recessed bath, a waterfall of steaming water falling down her body. She was quite tall, almost as tall as me If my eyes were to be trusted in the steam. I knew I should have turned and given her privacy, but my brain locked into stare mode, especially as I considered the graceful curves of her backside.

She turned suddenly and her song abruptly died away, replaced only by the beating of my heart and the dripping of water. Her eyes widened and her mouth fell open, likely considering that I was in fact a guy. Maybe she was admiring my jeans and Iron Maiden t-shirt. Or, that I was just watching her bathe like a freaking stalker. My stomach dropped.

"Oh, shit," I muttered. "I'm sorry. I didn't think anyone was in here."

I'd come to this world less than a few hours before, and I had already had the headmistress lowkey hit on me and now, I was the academy's Peeping Tom. Another few moments ticked by. Except the woman didn't scream, cover up, or throw anything at me. Shit, where I came from, she would have been hollering for the police or brandishing a knife from…somewhere.

She flashed me a smile and waved.

What in the hell?

She promptly wrung out her hair and moved towards me.

CHLOE THE EARTHLING

"UH. . . SORRY. I thought this was the... balcony," I said, cringing at how utterly ridiculous it sounded. "I didn't realize you were in here until I had opened the door and heard you singing. Marvelously so, by the way."

The woman's feet shuffled against the marble floor as she walked past me. I turned around and stared at her retreating form. She hadn't said a word strange. Nor had she screamed or run away—worse. Had she enjoyed the attention? I knew I had.

"Are you going to just stand there, trying to catch flies with your mouth?" the woman called, without turning around. "Why don't you come in here and make an introduction. After I've put on some clothes."

Like a dog pulled on a leash, I followed the blonde back into the room only to find she had moved to the bedroom and was digging through clothes. To my relief, she came back with a bath towel wrapped around her waist and a robe in her hands. She dropped the robe on the kitchen table and turned toward me as she unwrapped the towel and started drying off.

"Do you want me to—?" I started to ask but she cut me off.

"I've been a stripper for three years, so it's not like this is new to me. And you'll see me walking around naked or in my underwear more often than not," she replied and straightened, then started drying her hair.

"I see," I replied, trying to keep my cool, but this is not how I had envisioned this moment going down in my mind.

"Yeah, it paid for school. Graduated with zero student loans."

"Oh? What did you study?"

"Psychology," she replied, letting the word hang in the air.

Again, not what I had expected, especially not from a rather attractive blonde parading around naked.

"I managed a restaurant. Los Angeles. You?"

"Miami," she said. "I love the beach. If you can tell by my tan."

I nodded and then found myself sitting on the sofa across from her. I remained quiet, however, as she started whipping her hair around. Was she drying it? Or headbanging to some late nineties garage band music?

When she stopped, I looked away, not wanting to get caught staring. Sure, it wasn't the first time I had been in the same room with a beautiful, naked woman. But her nonchalant demeanor left something to be desired in the modesty department.

She dropped her towel and picked up the robe. Her movements were precise and in mere seconds she had slipped into the garment. They looked similar to what Salina had worn. A kimono-like robe that was A: generously cut at the neckline and B: was made of shiny, rather tight material.

"Hey there," she chuckled, turning to face me when she was finally done. "I'm your roommate, Chloe."

"Yeah, hi. It is nice to officially meet you. I'm JD," I replied slightly lost in all of what just happened. "Didn't see you earlier in the cafeteria."

She shrugged and dropped in one of the chairs.

"Yeah, JD. Salina told me. She said we were going to be roommates for a while. I mean, sharing a room with a guy I'm not involved with... at a school is... odd, but since we're from the same place, I guess that is like the best-case scenario. They wanted us to feel comfortable, or something."

"It makes sense, but yeah, a little weird."

She snorted, which turned into a chuckle. Her hair was still wet, that water dripping down onto her cleavage only made her look hotter and wilder. Shit. I would need to thank the mistresses for this...gift.

"Us humans aren't popular in this place," Chloe said. "We're troublemakers or something like that. We don't respect the hierarchy and nobility. That's what a few students told me, at least. That is okay with me. I tend to stick to myself, anyways. Besides, I already know what area of study I want to pick, and don't need their approval."

"That's good. Me, too," I said, quickly, even though I had no idea. But the lie felt weird, and I quickly turned it around. "You know, I have no idea where they'll put me. But to see someone else, another person... like me, so far from home. Now, that's something I didn't expect. But do find incredibly comforting. It is nice not being the only earthling."

"Oh, come on, don't be like that. I might just think you don't like me."

"Now what would give you that impression?" I grinned. "I just walked in on you naked in the bath... and didn't run away screaming. You're very pretty."

"At least you're honest. I can appreciate that, mister professional burger-flipper with a bit of tortured artist on the side."

I snorted. "Seems like Salina told you everything. That puts me at a disadvantage. I don't know anything about you."

"Maybe it's because I'm not as interesting as you? Other than being a trouble magnet and a wildcard."

"Interesting? How so?"

"Well, for starters, you are an artist, right? That is super cool. As for me? I was a student with zero hobbies or aspirations, spent most of my time playing video games and reading comic books.

Aside from studying, that is. Oh, yeah, and I stripped to pay my tuition and put food on the table. You might have been flipping burgers while I was crunching words, but you still had something beyond your day job. I'd practically given up before that weird lady... what is her name, Salina? When she came to my home and brought me here."

"She's a little different," I said.

"She's not so bad. From what I hear, she is one of the better masters."

"They're a rowdy bunch. Not what I pictured teachers of a magical academy to be, honestly. Salina pulled her sword and destroyed everything in my bar. That was how she convinced me to come here."

"Seriously? Shit," Chloe breathed. "They're pretty weird, right? But super-hot. Did you catch Mistress Lamora? I'd give anything for those wolf ears. Or the muscles on Freya? I never thought buff women were all that attractive... but she proved me wrong."

I chuckled. "They're all ridiculously good-looking. Maybe it is magic? From my perspective, every woman I've seen in this place is a solid ten."

"That so?" Chloe said with a smirk.

"Uh-huh," I said, not breaking her gaze. I had a nagging suspicion she wanted me to comment on her performance from the bath earlier, but I wasn't going to jump the gun. There was no need to complicate the room and board situation on my first day.

"Well," Chloe said, "then it seems like you came to the right place."

"I'd say so."

"What are you thinking about for a focus? Probably too early for you to tell what you want to do, right? Especially with your strange affinity."

"Yeah," I said. "I think I need time to chew on my options. But I like the sound of crafting. I have always been good with my hands, and this world seems to be full of possibilities."

"Crafting is good. That's what I'm looking at, although I'm thinking about narrowing my focus to weapon classes only. Along with general training and meditation, my schedule is pretty full anyway."

"So, you've already started?"

"Not really. I was one of the first to be brought here... uh, collected? Recruited? Anyways. A few masters spent time talking with me, giving me some pointers, so I wasn't bored." She paused and ran her fingers through her hair. The silence stretched between us before she finally continued.

"So, I hear you ended up with a legendary weapon. That's a pretty big deal," Chloe grinned, almost seductively. And I immediately wondered how long she had been waiting to bring it up. "I'll show you mine if you show me yours."

"Are you sure? It is pretty big," I said with a laugh.

She chuckled, her eyes rolling. "You're handsome, but we only just met. Maybe another time?"

"Oh, shit. No, I didn't mean that," I said, wanting to facepalm. "It's just I still find it funny how small it is."

She chuckled again.

"I'm just going to stop now."

"You want to see mine?"

"Sure," I said.

Chloe pulled a sword from her rift. It was shaped vaguely like a hunting knife but on a much larger scale. One side appeared razor-thin and sharp, while the other was serrated. In total, the weapon looked to be around three feet long.

The sword shimmered as Chloe turned and tilted it, showing off the runes carved in the flat of the blade. They glowed with a subtle and haunting bluish light. The hilt was inlaid with gold and studded with small, multi-colored gems. It was a pretty, lethal-looking blade.

"That's a nice-looking blade," I said. "What do the runes do?"

63

"I guess they give some kind of boost to my powers, but they haven't activated yet. Salina told me I would need to become stronger first."

"And do you know what kind of bonus you'll get?"

She nodded and walked over to me, sat on the coffee table, and laid the sword across her lap.

"There are five major types of runes. The red runes boost the general power level or attack, as we might think of it. The blue ones boost mana circulation and the skills that use it. Green makes you faster, both while moving and fighting. Yellow affects your defenses, be it against physical or magical damage. Lastly, the purple ones are the rarest of all. They boost skill power."

"And you know they work?" I asked curiously. "It all sounds like something taken straight out of a video game. Chloe was only inches away, her smell accumulating around me in an invisible but hard to ignore cloud. I couldn't identify *what* it smelled like...sweet vanilla with a touch of something spicy?

She looked at me and it was only then that I realized I was leaning into her, my nostrils flared.

"I was going to push you away or hit you, but then I remembered. It is probably the first time you're smelling this, isn't it?" she pointed to her body, then wafted the robes. The smell around us doubled. "We would call it body wash. To them, it is a cleansing elixir. What you're smelling are blood roses. Their flowers are potent but have many benefits—detoxifies and cleanses the skin, blood, and even deeper, the organs. Salina didn't explain further, but I have come to suspect that it has certain aphrodisiac properties, as well. I can see it in your eyes. Your pupils are blown wide, man!"

"Shit. I was going to say. It is strong. My heart started to race and everything. But that reminds me. I could use a shower, but...I don't have any clothes."

"There are some robes in your closet. It is the one on the right. They don't use underwear here so keep that in mind. It gets a little breezy at times," she said, pointing. "You mentioned video games. Are you a gamer yourself?"

"RPG's all the way, baby!" I nodded and raised my eyebrows, my inner nerd getting excited.

"Slap hands," she said, lifting her hand for a high-five. I happily obliged.

"What flavor? Final Fantasy and Monster Hunter were my jams. Damn, I spent so many hours hunting monsters and making gear out of loot. It's how this world functions, so I guess that makes me uber qualified."

"Really? You're not fucking with me?"

"I never joke about that, lover boy," she teased and winked. "But no, it is the truth."

"Okay! Color me excited," I said. "Here, check this out." I opened my rift and fished around for the pen-blade.

"What is it? A dagger? A bow? Some kind of staff? Or maybe a chain whip?"

I didn't want to piss on my own parade, and the excitement on her face was contagious, so I pulled out the pen-blade and held it up in the air.

Chloe's mouth froze open. "The pen-blade? Really?"

"You know what it is?"

"Uh-huh."

"Did you try it during your test?"

Chloe shook her head. "Nah, but I've heard about it."

"Before you got here? How's that possible?"

"I did a bit of reading in the library. It is inaccessible to new students, but apparently, the mistresses thought giving me access would help keep me out of trouble."

"And did it?" I asked with a smirk.

"You bet. It is the most incredible library I've ever seen. Just wait. It's next door to the left. I go there every chance I get. You should see all the scrolls, and tomes, and other things in there. Crazy stuff. But anyway, the pen-blade has crazy potential. If you can get the hang of it, that is. If you can learn how to create brush strokes, and imagine what you want your magic to be, you could go on to become a legendary... whatever. The pen-blades are so overpowered, but very hard and dangerous to use. That is why they aren't as common, because they are just as likely to backfire and kill the user as they are to effectively kill the enemy. Especially in the early stages where most wielders die before getting the hang of it."

"And you got all that from scrolls and tomes in the library?" I asked.

It wasn't necessarily that I didn't believe what she said, but more that it supported my growing doubt. Had I really ended up with a weapon just as capable of killing me just for wielding it?

"I did. And from chatting with the mistresses."

I looked down at my relatively humble-looking weapon. It suddenly didn't look so legendary or safe anymore. It felt more like holding onto a live grenade.

"I'll figure it out," I said. "I have to. I want to make the most of this chance. It's not every day that you get transported to a fantasy world and granted access to a magical academy."

"That's for sure."

"This library. . . what else can we learn there?"

"Everything, JD. They have books about our world—and even a few back issues of Silver Age comics. Don't ask me where they got them from, but they're in there. And not only books from this world and Earth. There's stuff there from *other* worlds. Hundreds of them. We are smack dab in the middle of a real multiverse there, and we've only visited two worlds."

"This whole experience has been a little... mind-blowing," I whispered. It sounded too crazy to be the truth, but there we were. Like two peas in an alien pod.

"You bet your ass it is." She agreed. "I was starting to go a little crazy though. Everyone and everything is so different here. To be honest, I'm really glad you're here. I think we can help keep each other stay grounded. What do you think?"

"I like the sound of that. I don't think everything has soaked in yet, but it is going to at some point. Having a familiar face around will help for when it does. The books in the library might help. I figure if they have some stuff from back home, especially comics, I can read them now and then. Although, at this point, I'm a little more interested in learning about the new... worlds."

"If you want access to the library, you'll have to ask Salina or Scarlet. Like I said, they have to grant entry. They are the only ones with authorization."

I nodded, only then realizing how close we'd been sitting. She was practically in my lap. It didn't bother me, on the contrary, her warmth and smell were welcome comforts.

"I'll ask them about it next time I see them."

"What now? Do you want to hang out? Maybe I can give you a rundown on everything I've learned."

"Sure. I'd like to know more about the academy, the tower, and the other universes. Maybe weapons, the beasts, and magical creatures. Oh, if there are deities and gods."

"So, basically everything, then?" she laughed. "I'm not sure where to start. Why don't you start with some questions, and I'll do my best to answer them?"

"Alright," I said, taking a moment to think through those things most pressing on my mind. "So, what is this tower? Scarlet didn't give me any details other than it is incredibly competitive."

"Hmm. Imagine this place is a one-tower country. The academies are the political parties, and everyone is fighting to get in on the pie. It's that simple. Or rather that complicated."

"But there's much more to it, right? The fighting and climbing levels?"

"Well, yeah, naturally. I've heard rumors that whoever reaches the top is granted immortality. Or my favorite—that there's an immensely powerful being waiting up there that can grant any wish."

"Immortality and wishes?" You could say my interest was suddenly piqued. Living forever in such a world didn't seem so bad. Especially if I had Mabel and Chloe as company.

"That's what I've heard."

It made me think about all the people here and the various reasons why they all attended this academy. Could something that powerful exist? One capable of granting any wish?

"If someone told me yesterday, that I would be sleeping in a fantastic new world, I would have recommended they seek treatment," I said, then my thoughts stuck on her second rumor. A being that powerful had to rival death itself. And rewards were always tied to risks, so the greater the risk, the bigger the reward. And vice versa.

"I guess we'll just have to make our way to the very top," I whispered.

Chloe furrowed her brow, but her smile didn't waver. I think she found me entertaining.

"You have a long way to go, mister artist. First, you need to learn how to cultivate, then you can start thinking about what comes next."

"Cultivation? Like farming? Do we do that here?" I didn't mind getting my hands dirty, but planting, tending, and reaping crops wasn't what I had planned for my time in a magical academy.

Chloe laughed. "It's not farming. It's way cooler than that."

"Something like special training?"

"More or less. See, you'd have to wait and learn about cultivation in classes, but seeing as we're both earthlings and classes won't start for a while, I guess I might help you if you return the favor."

"Oh, I'll pay you back. Just let me know... anything!" I joked.

"Pfft! How about you focus on cultivation for now, lover boy?" she said and looked down. I followed her gaze and found my hand on her leg. *Shit!* When did I put that there?

I flashed her a sheepish grin and pulled it back. She winked and put her hand on mine, squeezing gently.

"So, how about you tell me what cultivation is?"

"It is... the easiest way to explain what cultivation would be to compare it with leveling up in games. It's different in the way that it directly affects your body. The different realms all do something different to your body. The first realm is cleansing your body and establishing a mana container. Or mana pool. Or whatever you want to call it. Every breakthrough helps you temper your body, skin, blood vessels, your outer appearance, power in your arms and legs, and even your control over mana itself."

"And mana is the thing used when I do the things with my pen-blade?"

"Exactly. And so eloquently stated, might I add. The second realm is the bone forging realm. Your bones are reinforced and strengthened to a degree they won't shatter or break unless someone from a higher rank hits you, and even then, you will withstand more damage than before."

"But it's still possible. Then we'll have to get stronger, huh?"

"If you give it your all, I'll do my best not to fall behind. Now, the third realm is all about your skin. Hardening the skin to the degree that you can deflect blows from a sword, or arrows, or any kind of weapon."

"You're kidding?" I exclaimed. "Really?"

"Really. I've seen Lamora do it."

"Shit. Now that's intense."

"Hah, you sure got a way with words," she chuckled and went on. "The fourth realm is supposed to strengthen our inner organs to the point they can never die. Grow sick. Whatever you want to call it. They will keep regenerating, as will your body. The fifth realm allows you to expand your mana circulation, your mana pool, the attack power of your skills, and anything that has to do with power and skills."

"What's beyond that?" I asked curiously. "And how hard is it to get there?"

"Well, I'm still a rank one first realmer. From what I've read, it's possible to get to the second realm within a few years, or even in a year if you get lucky with core drops from the dungeon, but for every upgrade, you need to let it all settle or you can end up with broken cultivation. Compare it to a level-five game character without gear and with gear. They're both level five, but their stats are different."

"So hard, huh?" I asked, all excitement suddenly leaving my body. I had expected it to be hard, but years...did we have that much? How long could we live here anyway? A hundred years just like back on Earth?

She nodded slowly.

"So hard, but it's tangible. See, there's a basic system in place in this world. It's like games. We have several stats the 'system' uses to show our state during battle. That way we can see how close we are to defeating our opponents. It also works for cultivation, so you can see and manage how far you are from... well, as cheesy as it sounds, leveling up. That's not what they call it, but it's the best I have."

"Interesting," I whispered. "But I first need to become a rank one, right? Before I can see my stats?"

"Exactly. Did they let you keep the cores from the monsters?"

I nodded. "Yes, three of them."

"Great. We circulate all the mana this tower and world give off, then condense it into power and absorb it. Cores help us skip a step. Their mana is already highly concentrated, so think of it like power on demand. Crystals work in the same way, only with less capacity."

"And they differentiate with rank, right?"

"Yeah, they do. The higher the rank, the more power they can contain... and the more expensive they are. We just have to be careful to not waste what mana we collect. It is highly frowned upon."

"Absorb something you can't see or feel? Sure, why not?" I said, more than a little nervous about the prospect.

70

"Trust me, it's much easier than you think. How about you give it a shot? I can help you activate your first rank and stats."

"Time to earn my keep and find my place in this world, right? Let's do this!"

Cultivation Unlocked!

"ALRIGHT. IT'S VITAL YOU SIT STILL and do as I say, exactly as I say it. Clear?" Chloe said.

"Uh-huh," I said, nodding excitedly.

"This will open your first rank and nothing else. To go further we'll need to gather ingredients or spend time meditating to draw in mana."

"Sure," I said as Chloe took my hands. I met her gaze. It was only then that I realized she had one blue and one light brown eye. How wonderfully unique.

"Thanks for this. Any head start is a good one. I really appreciate this."

"Hah, now that is precisely the kind of attitude that will get us to where we need to be," she said and leaned in closer. I tried not to breathe too deep, to ignore the intoxicating smell swirling around us. Damn, it was distracting.

Forcing my eyes down to focus on anything but her smell, my gaze caught on her dress. The leg slit went high up her hip, showcasing more than a little of her thigh. Maybe a little of what sat above that, if I was being honest. I blinked and looked up, right at her breasts. *Damnit!*

Chloe chuckled, somehow aware of my struggles.

She let go of my hands, pulled her hair up into a ponytail, and tied it off with a hairband. I don't even know where the band came from. It wasn't there one moment, and in the next, it was. Weird. And now she was only a pair of thick, black glasses away from pulling off sexy librarian.

"Okay. Close your eyes and focus on your breathing," she said, leaning in again. I immediately wondered if she wanted me to close my eyes so I *could* focus, period.

"Got it," I said.

"Now put your hands on your knees, palms up. Relax and make sure your body isn't tense. If it is, mana won't flow through you properly, it will just bounce off and be wasted."

I nodded and did as she said, breathing in and out slowly, taking my time to feel the air enter and leave my lungs. I immediately became aware of something around me. Not the air, but something swirling around it—a tangible mass of streaks and strands that somehow did and did not have form at the same time. It touched my skin, prickled me, and tried to enter.

"Do I—?"

"Shh, I'll tell you what to do. Don't speak." I remained quiet and relaxed my body as much as possible. "I'll place two crystals in your palms next, but don't move your hands. You need to remain loose and relaxed. Understand?"

"Yes."

"Understand, this will hurt, but there can be no progress without pain. And if I survived the process, so can you."

The last comment hurt my pride, but just a little. Truth be told, I was no macho man, that was impervious to pain, but I had a decent pain threshold. When the two crystals touched down on my palms, a sudden jolt of pain cut into my skin, digging through my muscles, and worming their way up my arms and into my chest. My skin lit up as if on fire, literally, but I clenched my teeth and grunted through it.

The fire bled deeper, through muscle, and into bone. My grunt turned to a wheeze, then a groan. I wanted to cry out, to push the pain out of my body, but I couldn't be the one screaming.

The crystals were like burning coals in my hands, my skin crying out like bacon sizzling in a hot skillet. Then I felt them burn through, forming small holes in my flesh. They widened quickly and the crystals sank through, burning inside me until they hit my veins, my lifeblood.

I was sweating, clenching my teeth so hard my jaw ached, and ready to fall over. I felt the beads of perspiration run down my brow and neck as a cool wave washed over me, bringing my temperature down. But a wave of heat rolled in right after, only to be replaced again by that cooling wave. I was about to immolate and then freeze to death.

"You're doing great, JD. Keep your cool, maintain focus. It hurts, but only this first time. We're almost done."

Her voice was soothing and calm, melodic, and just what I needed to stay grounded. I made it my anchor, focusing on her presence to keep me from screaming and flailing.

"Now, I want you to pull on the mana inside the crystals. You have established a link to them. Can you feel the power course through you?"

"I—can!" I growled. "I can feel the—strands wanting to enter!"

"Alright. Good. Now focus on them, pull the mana in, easy and steady. Keep it flowing. Just picture a fishing line in your mind. One end is connected to the crystals in your palms, and you control the other end. Pull at it, steadily. Just like that," she said calmly. "You're doing great."

I followed her instructions and focused on the mana trickling out of the crystals. It was indeed a thin strand, barely the size of a spaghetti noodle. Whenever new mana flowed into my hands, there was an excess of the matter and it blocked out the path up my arms. Every time there was an excess of mana, the hole became deeper, and it burrowed itself further up my limbs.

74

The pain disappeared gradually as her hands pressed down on my back. I could feel her energy intermingle with my own, pulling at the two strands and forcing my mana veins to open and widen. We broke through to the shoulders and I silently wished that the mana would kill me. The coursing, surging energy cut down into my chest and moved straight toward the heart.

I gasped, clenched, and cursed as the new pain threatened to break my concentration and cut me off from the flow. But Chloe was there again, her presence and voice just enough to anchor me and keep my concentration from scattering completely.

"Keep. . . speaking, please," I gasped as the pressure built in my shoulders. More and more mana gathered but it had nowhere to go. It was pooling, expanding, and searching for a path of least resistance. My skin ruptured right next to my collarbone, distended bones pushing through the surface.

"Shit! JD! Keep it in! Close the gaps or you'll burn up!"

"H... how? Tell... me!"

Chloe's hands jerked free from my back and all the calm I felt radiating from her disappeared, but then they were there again. Not just the hands, but something cold, and smooth. She pressed it with both hands against my back and then a new pain pierced me from behind. Drilling... yes, it could almost be compared to someone drilling holes into me, one directly into my spine that stopped at the center of my chest, and then branched out toward the shoulders.

The pain stopped momentarily, as the excess mana had a new direction. I pushed, focusing on my heart, which was only inches from the new center of activity. Again, the burning pain gathered in my chest, right where she stopped drilling.

"I can't do anything else for you!" she hissed, her mouth right next to my ear. "If you can't... bring it under control, it will cripple you!"

My heart skipped a beat, and then another. What did she mean by, cripple me? Did that mean I'd have to stay mundane? An ordinary human? Fuck no! Drill, you son of a bitch! Drill!

75

I redoubled my efforts, smashing my eyes shut and directing every bit of focus inward. I felt the mana moving, pooling, and waiting. The inner wall of my mana canal exploded straight toward my heart, tearing a hole inside me. I didn't know if it was what was *supposed* to happen. I could only hope that it was.

I forced out a pent-up breath, and Chloe laughed nervously. I opened my eyes and looked up at her, but was startled to find Scarlet standing over me, not Chloe. Her expression was pinched. She was annoyed and I immediately knew we had fucked up.

I turned to Chloe, the blonde watching the mistress with obvious apprehension. Then Scarlet started to laugh.

"Why are you laughing?" I asked, my jaw aching from clenching it so hard. The pain was still present but fading quickly. Chloe looked to me, then back to the mistress, shaking her head in confusion.

"I need another bath. Just look at what you did!"

I looked down and noticed the black, tar-like substance covering her legs and part of her chest. The same strange substance covered me as well, head to freaking toe.

"What *in* the hell is that?" I growled, trying to wipe it off my arms, but it stuck in place like glue. Hot, sticky glue.

"You need to rinse it off. There is no way you'll ever get it off like that. I'll help?"

"Now? In the bath? You and me?"

She nodded.

"Don't tell me you're embarrassed," Scarlet said, finally speaking.

Chloe stopped and looked up as if noticing Scarlet for the first time.

"You almost destroyed his heart, young woman. You almost killed my prized possession, but I guided the mana and your hands. No thanks needed, although a touch more caution would serve you well in the future."

"Thank you, Headmistress," I added, quickly. "I am alive, thanks to you."

"This whole scene would have been amusing, if not so troubling. Please, try to avoid tearing any holes through one another, or through the fabric of the universe, if it's not too much trouble. Now go get cleaned up, both of you. You smell like sour pitch. I will use mana to clean the floor."

I got to my feet and bowed, my arms and legs shaking. Then muttered "thank you" another hundred times as I made for the bath."

"You're so cute!" Scarlet chuckled, "But think of this as an investment. Prove to me it was a wise one!"

She swiped a hand across the floor, the black, sticky substance just... disappearing, and then with a sly grin, the headmistress vanished. I hated it when she did that. Had she really gone, or was she just invisible?

"So, does this mean we can start working on that... o-o-other stuff you m-m-mentioned?" I asked, unable to keep my teeth from chattering."

"Come on, I'll tell you as we rinse off. The hot water will feel good." She started towards the bath but stopped when she noticed I hadn't moved. "Don't worry, I don't bite."

"Hard, I hope," I whispered.

"I heard that," she said and slapped my back, propelling me forward.

Chloe made me feel...appreciated, accepted, and part of a whole. I couldn't call it love after only knowing her for such a short time, but there was definitely affection there. Yes, she intimidated me, with her unabashed, straightforward way, but that was something I quickly grew to like. I didn't have to wonder where I stood with her.

She backtracked, plucked two fresh robes from our closets, and joined me inside the bathroom.

"Come on. Take those dirty clothes off. It will only get harder to clean if it dries," she said and pulled her previously clean clothes off. After folding the garment several times, she threw the robes into a bin near the door.

77

I slowly started to take off my burger-flipping clothes—her words, not mine.

Shit. The act of stripping off the t-shirt and jeans did something, it made this whole thing real. I followed Chloe's lead, and as much as I hated the notion, pulled the shirt over my head, then pulled off my pants, shoes, and boxers. I was by no means a shy man, but this was something new to me. Especially to strip for a stripper when it was usually the other way around.

"You coming?" she called, having already waded into the water.

"Yeah, I'm coming," I replied and struggled with a moment of confusion. Shit, what *in* the hell was I doing? It wasn't rocket surgery. Just lift a freaking left and get in the water. Show her that your bite is better than hers!

I followed Chloe with all the confidence of a praetorian—my chest out, shoulders straight and head held high. She spotted me, chuckled, but then dropped beneath the water to wet her hair. I dropped in, immediately savoring the hot, steaming water.

"So, do we use the special soap?" I joked after Chloe resurfaced.

"Yes, we do. From what I understand, they condense down the blood roses, mix it with a host of other extracts, then mix it with pure mana and tiny shards of crystal cores. It is the only thing that will remove this black muck."

"Oh," I replied. "Can I help you get clean first? After all, you're here because of me."

She nodded, letting the soap slip from her hand and fall into mine, and then she turned her back to me. I dipped the soap into the water, wetted my hands, then rubbed them together to create foam. Gently, I rubbed it against her pale, soft skin. She was as smooth as silk, the contact between us making the hair on my neck stand on end. And to my horror, the hair wasn't the only thing that perked up.

Chloe started to hum quietly as I washed her back, and then without warning, turned to face me. Her eyes met mine and a mischievous smile formed on her lips.

"I want to share something with you, and I would like you to be man enough to listen, and then give me an honest answer."

I frowned, at first thinking that she was just going to crack a joke about our compromising situation. But the smile faded. A few, wet strands of hair clung to her neck, and on impulse, I reached to move them, but I caught myself and pulled back.

"I will. I promise."

"There aren't many stories of humans excelling in this world. In fact, we are expected to fail. That has grown into more than just an expectation, but a prejudice. But I found a book in the library, a truly ancient tome. Within those pages, I found a story passed down from a scribe with no name. It tells the story of two human warriors, collected from warring tribes somewhere in the ancient world. Their names were Lydos and Chloe."

I felt my eyebrow rise at the names. I didn't understand their significance to the story, but I could feel it, somehow, distantly.

"They were brought to a tower, not unlike this one. But not for the same reasons as you and me. Back then, the other races viewed humans as inferior, barely more civilized than beasts. They used them as slaves or disposable sparring partners for promising students. But Lydos possessed an undeniable thirst for life, as well as an uncanny skill with a spear. Chloe, on the other hand, was smart. Their cultures were different, their beliefs at odds, but somehow, they found more than just a common ground. They came together in secret and formed a pact of flesh, a bond so strong that none could break it. Together, with Lydos' strength, and Chloe's wit, the pair didn't just survive, but they conquered every champion that came against them. They were lovers and fighters, bonded of spirit. The two escaped the tower and were never seen again. There are no other stories of human warriors rising to prominence in the academies. Not one."

"And you want...?"

"I want a chance," Chloe said, cutting in and moving closer. Her breasts were practically touching me, her nipples perked. Goosebumps covered her skin, indicating she was either cold or affected by what she was telling me. "We're here because the academies recruit from all the civilized races, from all worlds. But that is where favor ends. If we fail in a dungeon, get torn apart by some beast, or catch a jealous elf's blade through the ribs, we are just... done. Another girl like me is collected from some city somewhere. And she'll never know about either of us."

"They made a pact of flesh," I said, turning the story over in my head. I had a suspicion that I knew what that meant but wanted to hear her say it, to understand her justification.

"They became lovers, JD, when everything they knew told them not to. Their tribes were killing one another. Their cultures clashed. Hell, they didn't even worship the same gods. And yet, they accepted one another, intimately, and did what none had done before them, or since. I'm telling you this, JD. I want what my namesake had."

And before I knew what was happening, Chloe came forward and kissed me. I felt her body press into mine, her hands sliding around my back and pulling us close, her soft, sweet lips on my mouth. We sank into the hot, steaming water, and I gave in to her embrace.

I returned her kiss, brushing my tongue across her lips before it met hers. We kissed passionately, the perfumed soap and Chloe's smell filling my nose and every thought. I didn't necessarily understand everything she'd told me, but it had fed on an already existing fear growing in the back of my mind—that there were dozens of every creature imaginable everywhere I looked. But Chloe and I were the only humans. Judging from what Mabel said, those other races raised and groomed their young for opportunities like ours at Zenith. But why was it like that for them, and not us?

Chloe was right. If we were to survive and succeed, we needed not only to capitalize on those opportunities that presented themselves, but we needed to make our own. I let my hands drift down her back, my fingers sliding under the curve of her shapely and muscular rear and pulled her into me.

She kissed me, then my neck, and whispered into my ear.

"I have been weighing this decision for weeks. So, don't think this makes me easy. Yes, I've done things most would frown upon, but my life hasn't always been easy. You are here, and I like you... so far. But make me this promise. Don't take advantage of me. Please."

Her breath was hot on my neck, her lips tickling my ear. It just added to my already growing excitement, my heart racing and pooling even more blood into my throbbing member. I managed to push the fog of lust aside long enough to understand what she was asking for and didn't think it unreasonable. After all, she had already gone out of her way to help me begin my journey, why shouldn't I give a little... maybe a lot, back?

"I promise," I said."

Chloe pushed me then, her lips brushing against my ear before I felt her teeth bite. She bit playfully at first, the pressure increasing until it almost hurt. I felt my back hit the edge of the bath just as she released her hold.

I scrambled up the stone stairs but couldn't even get out of the water before Chloe pulled herself atop me.

"Okay. First thing," she said, leaning down to kiss me. Then I felt her hand slide between us and wrap around my cock.

I had a level view of her as she ran her hand down my length, gently tickled my balls, and ran her hand back up. My hands crawled up her thighs, the muscles tight, then to her hips, and up her sides. She stroked me several times, then eased her hips forward and rubbed my swollen head between her warm and incredibly wet lips.

"Oh, damn..." she breathed, easing me back and forth, teasing it just around the entrance of her hot sex. "First... thing. Yang is not the same as mana. It is *your* energy, *your* life force. You have to focus inward... and... force it towards where we conjoin."

"Conjoin?" I grunted, loving the sound of it. "How do you know...?" I started to ask, just as Chloe eased down, my throbbing head slipping inside her. I watched it disappear, inch by veiny inch, the sight of her beautiful body accepting me throwing my brain into a sex-drunk stupor.

She eased up and moved down slowly several times, before finally, with a shuddering moan, met my lap.

"... know all of this?" I finally managed to finish.

Chloe caught her bottom lip between her teeth and eased upwards, guiding her tight body up until I nearly pulled free, and then pushed down again. Her perky breasts jiggled happily with the movement, and I reached up to squeeze them.

"Do you feel it yet? Come on... this isn't just for the... pleasure. This is for... survival," Chloe said, grunting.

I almost laughed—having sex with a beautiful woman the day we met... for survival.

My eyes ran down her body, her abdominal muscles flexing impressively. I struggled to focus, to not fall completely into my passion and look past the pleasure. But, how? I had never had much luck with women, and now, in a single day, I had been whisked away to a magical world, met an insanely attractive girl, basically been propositioned into some strange flesh pact, and boom, we were having sex on the stairs of our personal, Roman bath. It was every daydream fantasy I had ever had in High School... made real.

Chloe abruptly stopped and lifted, threatening to pull free. I looked up at her face.

"Are you even trying? How long has it been for you?" she asked.

"I am, yes. It has been..." I paused, ashamed to admit that, although I had been propositioned for sex many times, all by fairly drunk and desperate women at the bar, I hadn't consummated a successful relationship with a woman my age for over two years. "A while."

82

"I can tell. You look sex drunk. You need to focus. Feel the energy building inside you. There is a reason why your energy peaks during intimacy and we need to forge the bond now, before..." Chloe abruptly went quiet. There was a look in her eyes then that I couldn't quite read. Was it fear? Uncertainty? Doubt?

She slowly slid down into my lap and leaned forward, letting her hands come to rest on my chest. Then she slid her hips forward and back.

"Feel me," she said, gently digging her fingernails into my pecs.

"Did you learn all of this from books in... the library?" Damn, she was tight and warm, and that smell... those whatever kind of roses... affected me like Viagra. Not that I know how it affects me, but I'm just guessing.

She nodded, moaned, and let her head droop forward.

At least I'm not the only one enjoying it.

"Some call it dual cultivation. But the mistresses intentionally have... oh my god," she whispered and suddenly ground us together with more force, "the mistresses have removed most of the literature referencing it from the library. But I got... oh... lucky. The Hindi discovered it, too. I found a book on the Kama Sutra in the back, covered in... dust and apparently forgotten."

I watched, listened, and savored. But moreover, I focused, searching for the surge or swirl of energy she was talking about. What a weird thing to do... looking for energy inside their body. A day ago, I probably never would have known what I was looking for, but my experience with the crystals in the other room changed all that.

Whether it was the near immolation-death experience with Chloe and the mana now simmering peacefully inside my body or just the magical aspect of the tower around me, the result was clear. Every time Chloe slid against me, I felt a decided uptick of something hot and energetic inside me. I closed my eyes and pushed everything else away.

83

I bottomed out inside her—the strangeness of the moment, the new magic to my body, and the surreal aspect of all of it having swollen me beyond anything I'd ever known. And then I felt it. Shit, I saw it. Moving against the dark backdrop of my mind's eye was a swirling, red mass. It looked like a swarm of birds, or a school of fish, curving and sweeping together. It was my yang, the energy of my lifeforce.

"I feel it. I found it," I gasped, and I felt Chloe abruptly pull away. I opened my eyes, both shocked by the sudden lack of her body around me and the cold air that rushed in after. I took a breath to speak, to find out what I had done wrong, but she was faster.

"I felt it, too. Okay. It is time. Sit up and cross your legs," she said.

I accepted her hand and sat up on the set tile, then with more difficulty than I was comfortable showing, I crossed my legs. Then, without warning, Chloe put her hands on my shoulders and carefully lowered herself into my lap. She wiggled her hips for a moment, but I slid back inside without any unnecessary manipulation. It just felt right.

"Okay, now put your arms around me and I will do the same. The closer we are, the better. This position is called Om. I don't know what will happen when our Yin and Yang mingle, but I'm guessing we'll both feel it."

She pulled me closer and hooked her legs behind me. I pulled her in tight, her soft breasts pressing in against my chest. Chloe leaned in and pressed her face against mine, her mouth right by my ear.

The position felt strange... close and incredibly intimate. I wondered how much movement it would allow and immediately started to doubt until she moved her hips. Chloe ground against me, the movement pulling me back and thrusting me in, rubbing sideways, and every other direction all at once.

And it didn't stop there. It was her soft breasts against me, her arms hooked around my back, and her legs pulling us closer. Every bit of skin-on-skin contact felt amplified, that small amount of motion more than I could ever hope for.

"Focus. Feel it. Push it towards me," she whispered, her lips brushing against my ear. The contact flared like a spark, the energy inside me immediately swirling faster and brighter. My member swole inside her again, responding to the Yin energy.

"Feel me. Bring us together."

I pulled her in tighter and Chloe immediately kissed my cheek and ran her tongue against my ear lobe. The tickle almost pushed me too far, but I just managed to keep my orgasm from hitting. I closed my eyes and buried my face in the crook of her neck. My Yang filled my mind again, and I focused on moving it, pushing it towards the warm, pulsing spot where my body slid feverishly against hers.

It moved willingly, no, eagerly, as if it had been waiting for that very prod. A profound sense of warmth slid down from my chest and into my stomach, then settled into my pelvis. I felt Chloe warm against me, too. And I knew she felt it. Her breath caught in her throat, a desperate, almost strangled growl vibrating out of her chest.

She slid back and ground us together hard, and then our energies met. Red, swirling energy met a no less impressive, swirling mass of greenish light and I ceased to be. I didn't fall away or feel Chloe leave me, but somehow, we melted into one another.

We were together, floating in the black canvas of my mind, two glowing forms, conjoined, radiating enough heat and life to light up a city. Then she tipped sideways and pulled me over on top of her. Spreading her legs, Chloe pulled on my hips. I thrust hard, pulling back, and driving forward until our bodies slapped together.

The light and heat grew, swirling in and between us like a cloud of fire.

"Harder. Faster," she moaned, her voice echoing right into my mind.

I responded, thrusting harder and faster. The swirling green and red energy compressed suddenly, blooming in a blinding flash of light and heat. I saw it but felt it inside as we climaxed together. Chloe grabbed my arms and wrenched me down, my hips still driving me into her with fevered need.

It lasted moments, that thrum of light and heat, or orgasms pulsing as one. And then as quickly as it happened, it was gone.

FIRST RANK AFTERMATH

"HOLY SHIT," I gasped and slumped forward.

"That might not be far off," Chloe grunted in response.

We laid there for a while, fighting to reclaim our breath and digest what had just happened. But what *had* happened?

"I thought you were putting me on at first," I said, pushing up onto my knees. "But that. You were right. I saw it, felt it... my energy. Then when it met yours, it was like..." I mimed an explosion with my hands because I still couldn't put the sensation into words.

She grasped my hand and pulled me back down, so I snuggled in close, then studied her large, and strangely, lust-filled eyes. The way she moved against me, breathed, and watched me... I could tell, she wanted more.

Unfortunately, I was spent. Both from the ordeal of opening my first rank and then our unexpected romp. It had been a day of firsts. Exhausting firsts, yes, but highly enjoyable, nonetheless.

"So, what next?" I asked, "I mean, do we need to do anything? Light incense, meditate, eat? Because I can't lie, I am hungry again."

"I don't know," she whispered. "All it said was—if two bodies are mutually attracted and aligned, and they successfully pair their energies, then they can form a basis for dual cultivation and share each other's absorption and mana circulation."

"Pair?" I asked and watched her. There was something there. I had a feeling. It was what she hadn't said when in the bath, the urgency and perhaps the motivation for matching with me so quickly. I mean, as a guy, I wasn't going to complain about it, but it wasn't an altogether normal thing to get pulled into a magical world, meet someone, share introductions, and then jump right to copulating. Unless it was normal in this world. Hell, how was I to know?

"I'm guessing it is important to form a connection quickly, right? You said not to take it as you being 'easy'," I said, looking for a little clarity.

She nodded and a strand of hair fell over her face. I plucked it away and tucked it behind her ear. She really was very pretty. No, she was beautiful. And beyond that, she was honest and direct. I felt like the luckiest guy in the world, at that moment.

"This place is different. You will see it in time. Keep your eyes open and watch the other members of the academy. And I don't just mean the students. The mistresses have their own ambitions, too. Did you notice how they dress?"

I nodded. Of course, I had.

"Scarlet is the strongest here, but not by much. They have their little power struggle going on between them. Ever wonder how they got so powerful, came to live so long, and yet still look young?"

"Wait, are you saying the mistresses use dual cultivation, as in, having sex with the students to get more powerful?" I asked.

Chloe shrugged, the movement temporarily dislodging my head. It made sense, in a way I had considered before.

"When you asked me not to take advantage of you, what did you mean?" I asked.

"It isn't anything I can substantiate," she whispered, and that darkness flashed in her eyes again. "Everything I read about dual cultivation supported that it had to be a mutual pairing... from the start."

"And if it isn't, 'mutual'?"

"It's quite simple if you think about it. Whatever progress you manage to make, whatever strength you gain is added to mine, and vice versa. But it isn't based on your use of mana, at least I don't think it is. It is the strength of a person's Yin and Yang energies. So, a powerful cultivator like Scarlet or Freya could draw strength from a man, despite the disparity in cultivation ability."

"Is that why there aren't any male teachers? The mistresses are essentially using young men to slowly but surely become immortal? Does it not work with the other races? Are they warned about these things ahead of time?"

"I don't know. It is all just guesswork on my part. But think about it. If a man and woman pair successfully, and her use of mana is stronger, then she might be able to slowly and steadily use him as a... battery of sorts. If he weakened or his cultivation abilities failed him, then they would simply kick him out of the academy and bring in a younger, stronger man to take his place."

"Shit, that is downright diabolical," I breathed.

"Listen," she said and turned on her side to face me directly. "It is all just conspiracy theory on my part. It could all be true, or none of it. I just don't know. But Lydos and Chloe's story struck me, and the relative lack of human cultivators here just added to it. If I was right, then you were in...danger. And as weird as it sounds, the only way I could protect you from them was to—"

"Yeah, no, I get it," I said, as some of my new home's magical luster chipped away. "Thank you."

"Don't get me wrong. It wasn't all for you," she said with a smirk. "I wasn't joking about the first part. About *me* not wanting to fail in this world. And if we can succeed together, even better. We got lucky. Our Yin and Yang energies were complementary to each other, and now that they have mingled, we're..."

"Paired?" I asked.

"In a way, yes. Don't take it like we're married or anything. According to the stories, Lydos and Chloe took other lovers, but none that came between them."

"Married?" I snorted, "We just met today."

"But for this to work, we will have to do this again. Repeatedly."

I shrugged. "If it is for survival, I am game. But what about the mistresses?"

"Keep your head on a swivel, I guess. Pairing requires several elements to be present. Intimacy is key. That's why you can't simply lock a bunch of people up and turn them into cultivation sex slaves. There needs to be mutual attraction, trust. and willingness to give and receive. You can't force someone to dual cultivate."

"So, beyond the whole—protect me from potentially predatory mistresses, thing—does this at least mean you find me attractive?" I asked.

She frowned. "What in the hell kind of question is that? I literally just fucked you on the bathroom floor. I'm not sure there is a more damning sign of attraction than that. But, yes, beyond the other stuff, I think you're... good looking."

"Why, thank you. I think you are... 'good looking', too."

She playfully punched me. In truth, I thought she was beautiful—a dynamite body, silky smooth skin, eyes as deep and blue as the ocean, a rack to die for, and beyond that, she seemed like a genuinely good person and loved video games. Um, point-set-match.

"Hey, do you want to get dressed and go visit the store?" she asked. "We won't have classes for a while, so I might as well show you around the place and finish some chores while we're at it."

"I'm feeling... reinvigorated. Are you sure you don't want to stay here for a bit longer?" I whispered, tracing my index down her neck and between her breasts, ending at her navel. She shivered, pulled back, and giggled.

"Don't push your luck, buster. We'll be here for a long time. Don't worry, you'll get your fair share of this. Trust me," she said, slapping her butt and rolling away.

I stood and helped her up, all the while trying to hide that I was once again growing... excited. It had a mind of its own, especially when around beautiful, naked women.

Chloe grabbed two towels and I dried off and got dressed. Or tried to. I honestly didn't understand how my garment was supposed to work, save for the sleeves. Those I got right. I leaned around the corner to ask Chloe for help just as she fished a lace thong out of her closet and slowly pulled it on.

"I thought you said they don't wear underwear here?" I asked.

She turned her head, threw me a wink, and blew me a kiss, and pulled on a clean robe.

She finished getting dressed and then turned to help me. If I didn't know any better, I'd think she'd been living in this place far longer than she led on, but I wasn't going to start our relationship with mistrust.

"You're quite handy," I said as she finished tying my peculiar garment into place. "And attentive."

"Oh? I'm usually very shy around men."

I snorted. "Shy? I find that hard to believe."

"Believe what you want. But just because I took my clothes off for money, that doesn't mean I loved or even liked it," she said and leaned in, pressing her weight into me. But before I could plant a kiss on her lips, she pushed away.

"We need to get to the store, lover boy."

Hearing her call me 'lover boy' gave me a special tingle inside.

Some ten minutes later, we exited the dorms and walked down the circular path, the expansive, open-air of the tower looming beyond. I wasn't sure that I would ever get used to the sight. Nor did I want to.

The portal leading to the market was located at the one o'clock position. We stopped before it and I gave it an appraising glance. It wasn't glowing.

"Can you open it?" I asked, "The portal?"

"Oh, I can do much more than just that," she whispered.

Chloe held her right hand out, palm towards the portal, and moved it in a circular, clockwise motion. Then she tapped three indentations in the stone and the portal glowed to life. It gave off a green aura, unlike the other portals, which all seemed to be blue.

"What... did you just do?" I asked, glancing around the massive space. Blue-blue-blue—green. "Why is this one...?"

"Easy, killer. You just got here. Remember, if you try to question everything at once, your head will explode," Chloe said, laughing. "I just opened the portal that leads to the market, and yes, I'll teach you later. And yes-yes, I will tell you why it is green. But first, come on, it only stays open for a short time."

She hooked me by the arm and promptly pulled me into the glowing ring. I felt nothing when we exited on the other side. There was no discomfort or pain, just nothing. Like walking through a normal doorway. Part of me was disappointed, as I'd loved every dorky science fiction or fantasy show, and those had always depicted people throwing themselves through portals, screaming, faces frozen mid-snarl, while their bodies were pulled apart and immediately thrown back together. Yes. Part of me felt gypped.

"What are we searching for?" I asked as a bazaar opened up before us.

"Food."

"Food? Now you are speaking my language," I said, just as my stomach gurgled ferociously. "But isn't that why we have the cafeteria?"

She chuckled and shook her head. I watched her damp hair move, how it clung to her neck. Shit, she was hot.

Focus, dude. You two are already pretty much magically welded together now. Chill.

"Formal dinners are hosted once a week. I've only eaten there twice since coming here. The rest of the time, we buy food and necessities right here."

"With cores?"

"No, with money you get from dungeon dives. There you can find cores, beast corpses, and ingredients, or random drops that you can sell for money in the bazaar. The best part is, no matter what you get in there, someone will want it. And if you do happen to find something no one wants, the academy will normally take it off your hands at a slightly smaller price. They don't want anyone to starve."

"I see. Well, my stomach appreciates that." I turned and took in the bazaar. The place looked like the Grand Bazaar in Istanbul. I walked through it with my grandfather when I was ten. I remembered how the myriad smells, sounds, and colors overloaded my senses. It was incense, patchouli, tea, roasted coffee, fresh bread, and so much more, all swirling together. It was the only trip my grandparents ever took me on. They both died just a few years later.

"The people here will look different," Chloe said, quietly. "They use a glamor that makes them look…" she paused as if searching for the right word. "Let's just say, to make them look like people you're most familiar with. It is a comfort thing. Evidently, glamor works both ways. So, they see us differently, as well."

"Interesting. I can live with that. Better to stare at something familiar than alien, right? Imagine the queen from the Alien movies selling you meat or bread."

"Hah!" she laughed. "But she had those little arms on her chest. She would make a great vendor… could pass out twice as many samples!"

God damn, I literally just fell in love with her, just a little more.

"So, do we have to work for our food?" I asked after our laughter died down.

I remembered saying something to Mabel about eating. What was it? *Eat up, because there was no telling when we'd eat next.* I suddenly worried about the elf and hoped that she was doing okay.

93

"Yep. You'll work for it, alright," Chloe snickered and pulled me forward. "Come on, let's go to my regular spot."

We waded through the crowd, ducking and weaving through men and women in colorful, embroidered robes. Merchants pushed out into the crowd, chanting and yelling, singing about their products, swinging massive platters, and foisting treats onto any that would look their way.

I saw fruit and vegetables, nuts, sausages, barrels of spices, dried flowers, clothing, boots, and weapons, and we'd only managed to go a dozen stalls into the place. We moved around a crowd and Chloe pulled me into an open tent. An elderly woman stood on the other side of an ancient-looking wood counter, a heavily wrinkled and permanent-looking grin on her face.

"Chloe, dear! How nice to see you again. What can I get you? And who's this young man? He's so handsome for an earthling!"

"He's the pen-blader that joined earlier today," Chloe replied, her voice filled with pride and joy. Her demeanor shifted the moment she stepped into the tent. I respectfully waited for the old woman to turn my way.

"Oh, a pen-blader? It's my honor, young man. The name is Reline."

"JD, the earthling," I said and offered her my hand. Reline grasped it gently, her hand radiating warmth and genuinely good vibes. It was peculiar. As in, I felt a degree of *goodness* encompassing her.

"They don't shake hands," Chloe interrupted, and I promptly pulled away. Probably looking the part of an idiot.

"I'm sorry. I'm pretty new here."

"Oh, there is no harm. No harm at all," Reline said, that unusual vibe fluctuating as she laughed.

"What can I do for you?"

"Can I have double my usual order? JD is my new roommate and we both need to eat. We can wait."

"Oh, certainly! I'll whip it up right away. Give me a few moments."

94

Reline disappeared behind a curtain and the telltale sound of pots and pans banging together broke the silence.

"A few moments?" I asked, but Chloe winked and pressed her index finger to my lips, shushing me.

Reline pushed back through the curtain a moment later, carrying a tray filled with food containers. Chloe bowed, accepted the containers, stored half in her rift, and pushed the rest into my arms. I stored mine away.

"How much do I owe you?"

"Because he's new and you're my *favorite* customer, let's make it 200 Fres."

"That's... barely half what it should be," Chloe noted.

"See it as an investment, young Chloe. I have a feeling he is going to be a good customer."

Chloe snorted and shook her head, but then offered Relina some strange-looking coins. They had holes in the center, along with an etching that looked eerily similar to our tower. I noticed a number etched on the opposite side. It was the same number on every coin, although the numbers themselves varied slightly.

"What's with the coins?" I asked as Reline busied herself searching for change. Chloe fished one out of her purse and held it up. It looked ordinary enough.

"Every level of the tower has its own coins, so if we change floors, the coins magically change. You can't use money from this floor on another, or the other way around."

"Relina, thank you for your kindness. I look forward to eating your food. It smells delicious."

She chuckled and seemed to blush, although that heavily wrinkled smile didn't waver. Odd.

"Oh, you two make such a nice couple! How cute! Do grace me with some cute babies, someday. Maybe you could even let me take care of Chloe once she becomes with child!"

"Relina!" Chloe hissed. "Come on!"

"Oh, you young ones are so shy!" the older woman laughed. Chloe lifted an arm to hide her face.

"Bye, Relina! See you again sometime, maybe in a decade, or so!" Chloe said loudly and stormed out.

"You can take care of her, don't you worry," I said to Relina as I followed her out. "We'll make loads of babies. Dozens maybe!"

Chloe grabbed my shoulder and pulled me along once I stepped outside.

"Enough of that talk," she snorted, and shook her head, then turned to me and said, "You'll have to pay me back when you get money. I'm pretty tight myself right now, but I don't want you going hungry."

"Oh, don't you worry," I said, lowering my voice. "A JD always pays his debts."

"A JD?" she snorted, "Did you really just drop a Game of Thrones reference?"

"That was a test. And you totally passed!"

She groaned. "Don't think I'll accept anything other than cold-hard-cash, Casanova."

"What? I have to pay it back with interest?"

Her scowl immediately turned into a smile. She leaned in and kissed my cheek before running off.

"Now you get it!"

INTERLUDE

I followed Chloe out of the bazaar and stopped to appreciate the place's sheer enormity and boisterousness. Such a large area hidden within a portal was something...yeah, I got it by now. Unheard of. But this was a fantastic, awe-inspiring place and I couldn't wait to come back and explore it more fully.

Chloe hooked her arm around mine and tapped the portal. It flashed to life with a miniature explosion of green light and pushed us out into the circular walkway. Several larger groups of students stood just off the side and gave us room, evidently waiting to go to the bazaar.

I heard someone grumble from the crowd, and they moved to push past us and get to the portal.

"You will not cut in line!" a giant of a young man bellowed as an elf with blood-red hair moved towards us. The elf froze, looked at us, then back at the... big kid.

"I'm royalty too, long-ear!"

Bristling, the elves turned with fight shining in their eyes, but red-hair put his hand up. They looked like peacocks, all dressed in bright colors, their chests held out and backs straight. I moved

97

forward to say something, to speak up and tell them that they were being ridiculous, but Chloe pulled me back and out of the crowd.

"Don't," she hissed under her breath, "We don't want any part of these spoiled shits."

Chloe pulled me off to the side and we made for our dorm room.

"And where do you think you're going?" a voice rang out from behind me as a hand landed on my left shoulder. It squeezed hard, my momentum halting as my arm went numb. "I don't think we've been introduced yet, newbie."

I suppressed an eye roll, took in a deep breath, and turned. Then I came face to face with the elf that sent me mental death threats in the cafeteria. He looked almost identical to the one arguing with the giant. Almost. Save for the dangerous and almost violent air about him.

"Hold on," I said, just as he opened his mouth to speak. "Is this about Mabel?" I asked, trying to sound calm, though I was anything but calm. "I haven't spoken with her or seen her since the cafeteria."

"Oh, I know. Because if you had, then you wouldn't be standing here, you would be on the ground, cradling your broken, fragile little legs."

I slapped his hand away from my shoulder and he frowned.

"I prefer to think of them as petite," I said, barely stifling a laugh. They were anything but, as when I was given the chance to exercise, I didn't skip leg day. But the look on the elf's face was priceless.

Red-hair tried to reach for my shoulder again, but I swatted his hand down, the slap echoing loudly in the hall. He recoiled and rubbed the spot.

"You've already opened your—," he started to say, then stopped, cursed silently, and shoved the elf next to him. He turned back to me and said, "Mabel and her kin belong to my family, so keep your hands off... if you know what's good for you."

Most of the crowd had already dispersed by the time the Giant and the other elf stopped arguing.

"Watch where you're going, midget!" the Giant laughed as he pushed the elf aside.

"That's kind of been my thing... my, uh, what's the word?" I asked, turning to Chloe.

"Issue?" she asked.

"Yeah!" I said, lifting a finger. "My issue is, I don't usually know what is good for me."

Red hair sneered, shoved his buddy again, and they moved through the portal. I turned and walked away with Chloe.

"Seriously? Did I come all this way just to land in another place where all people can think about is how to be the first one to walk through a door, move through a portal, or threaten each other?" I muttered. "This place feels like High School all over again."

"Except the bullies are royal and from other dimensions," Chloe added.

"Fuck him and his holier-than-thou attitude. And what in the crap is this all about them owning people? Are we from the only world that has come to understand that shit is bad?"

"Yeah, well that could have gone better," Chloe whispered. "And worse as well, I guess."

We hurried along and soon we were standing in front of the VIP portal. She was whistling some tune I faintly recognized but couldn't place. Shit, music. It just hit me that this place was as quiet as death. There was no music. No elevator muzak, bad shopping store radio, odd Bard in the corner playing the lute, or even an old drunken Chinese man playing the zither. There was just nothing.

We passed through the portal, down the hall, and into our room. And it was then that I realized how tired I was. It was only my first day and I already had royal snobs targeting me. And for no other reason than I'd eaten lunch with a pretty elf named

Mabel. I sighed dramatically... okay, perhaps a little too dramatically. But as I said—tired.

I followed Chloe into the kitchen.

We sat down around the table and pulled out a portioned container of food each and opened them. Both packs contained a fork, a knife, and a spoon. Disposable of course. The containers were thin as paper but felt as cold as stone from the outside, but on the inside, they were piping hot. Magical to-go containers. Why not?

"What is this stuff?" I leaned over the steaming food and drew in a breath through my nose. It looked like... well, I couldn't immediately rationalize what it looked like. But it was hot and smelled good.

"It's called Eldaran Breel. It is comparable to rice, with chunks of cooked beef, and some kind of sauce. It's spicy, so be warned. I never liked spicy stuff before, but strangely, I really enjoy this."

"Interesting. Eldaran Breel, huh? I'll have to remember the name and recipe just in case we ever get back to Earth."

"Oh? And what kind of meat would you use?"

"Umm...cow? Duh."

"Then it wouldn't be Eldaran Breel, now, would it? Duh," she laughed. "Go ahead, eat. I'm curious to see if you like it."

"Here goes," I whispered and pulled up my sleeves. I leaned in and gave it another sniff. The pungent aroma was somehow stronger this time. I could actually smell the heat! Still, I didn't give up and picked up my fork, grabbed some of the rice-like stuff, and then a piece of meat. I tentatively placed it in my mouth and chewed.

"So? How is it?" she asked.

"Surprisingly good," I heard myself say before I could even register the complex explosion of flavors. Sure, intense... that was the only word I could think of for it. Spices overlapped with savory, and an interesting cool undercurrent kept it all from becoming too much. It was almost like the best parts of Mexican food, mixed with Chinese, held together with the creamy saltiness of macaroni and cheese. So... strange. "It does remind me of rice and beef. And in a good way."

"Told you! There are others you'll like, too. Give it some time. Just be cautious, some can be rather expensive. We'll have to earn some money first, but you have to try Levran Cobblecake. Oh... my... god!"

I snorted and almost spat the food from my mouth.

"Levran Cobblecake?"

"Imagine a lava cake on drugs."

"Honestly, you had me at lava cake. I love sweets. And meat. And a good drink. Cake, though, is one of my truest loves. I like sour candies, too. Oh, and brownies. I so..."

"Okay," she interrupted, "you went off a little there."

"Yeah. Sorry. I get excited about food." That was no joke. I once talked to a group of Jehovah's Witnesses for four and half hours at the bar. What did we talk about? Hamburgers. They had come in to save my soul, and instead, I sold them all double cheeseburgers, hold the pickles, with extra bacon, and side orders of fries. They all hugged me before they left.

"Hello?" Chloe said, waving her hand in front of my face. "Did you just check out?"

I chuckled. "Sorry I am tired. And I got thinking about the time I sold cheeseburgers to a bunch of Jehovah's Witnesses."

"That sounds truly epic."

"It was. Truly. And cheesy. So much cheesy paper." I groaned and stuffed another bite of food in my mouth. It wasn't a burger, but it wasn't bad.

"I'm glad you're a gourmand, nevertheless. I like to eat as well, so it's good to have a companion to share it with. Even more, someone to make the food with. And best yet... someone with riveting food adventures."

"Hah! So, the cat's out of the bag!" I laughed.

Chloe leaned back into her chair and laughed, then accidentally snorted, and laughed some more. Damn, she was beautiful, even when darn near choking on her food and blowing a snot bubble. I was in love.

"You're funny, JD. I like that. But don't... make... me... snort, you hear? Or blush. It is not becoming of a lady."

"Which cheeks are we talking about? I just want to make sure we're straight."

"I feel the need to reiterate that I am not accepting physical satisfaction for food, or the information I just gave you about the cake. You still owe me 135 Fres, buster."

"Cheapskate. I already said I'll pay you back," I said, "The satisfaction... that is for free."

"Free, eh?" she asked, suddenly sitting forward. "What makes you think you're so good?"

I leaned forward to match her, then slowly lifted my fork and inserted a bite of food into my mouth. While chewing, I said, "Lady, I'm dead sexy."

Chloe snorted and almost toppled backward out of her chair. We ate and talked for a long time after that. And she snorted many, many times.

"When do classes start, exactly?" I asked after we came to a natural lull.

"The real classes start in three days? Or four? Don't know exactly. We need to go through basic classes and cultivation first anyway. I've already learned most of it from Scarlet in private, but I'll have to learn it alongside everyone else... officially. Otherwise, the other students will bitch about it."

"She told me we had a day."

"Yeah, until the basics start. But we can skip those as you've already unlocked your first stage. That is all they really do there. Talk for hours about what your first stage means, then talk some more about what comes after. Then take breaks. Then look at books about the first stage. And then after reflecting on everything they had talked about, they will help you open it."

"I get to miss all that? I feel cheated."

"You can go if you want to," she said.

"You know, I wouldn't want to distract any of the other students. Learning is so important."

"You really have the smartass thing down, don't you?" Chloe asked.

"Please," I snorted. "That was what drew you to me. That and my undeniable animal magnetism."

"And here I was thinking it was because you are the only human male within a thousand miles," Chloe said, absently scratching her chin.

"You take that back. Hurtful," I said, with mock outrage.

She snorted and we fell into laughter again. Crap. Our first day together and we were already fast friends. But I had to wonder if that was because we were kindred spirits, or was it some new and lingering effects of our cultivation pairing?

"They teach basic mana manipulation?" I asked.

Chloe nodded. "You can use it for things like covering your body for protection or infusing it into your weapons or tools. I guess, in the more advanced classes they show you how to use it in cooking, crafting, and fighting. Anything really."

"Outstanding. And you already know a part of it?"

She nodded. "I do." Then she polished her nails on her top and inspected them. "I know enough to be your senior despite only being here for a week, but you've got one on me with the whole pen-blade thing. It could even open up opportunities at several schools. If," she said, pausing and holding up a finger, "you can perform well enough with it. You will need to complete some special missions to prove yourself."

"Oh? What kind?" This was getting more and more interesting. It was almost like a game of go do this, get a reward, and then accept another quest. A real-life quest-based life. Bring it on.

"Dungeon dives for special beast ingredients? Or to perform school-related tasks. It is hard to predict. What's more, since you're special like me, you'll have a much easier time when it comes to the cultivation part. But be prepared, plenty of students will hate you for it. We receive special treatment from the mistresses, and you know how the masses look upon that. Even more so when you're human."

I sighed and shook my head. It was annoying to consider how horrible we humans were to one another. And as icing on the cake, everyone dogpiled on.

"Isn't it like that everywhere? School was bad enough. If I was good at something, the other kids would bully me about it. And if I sucked at something else, they would bully me about that, too. I stuck to the middle after that."

"Well, it's not just about being bullied here, JD. Like I told you before. You know? Before we…" she pointed back towards the bath, and for the first time, showed a hint of shyness.

"Played Patty Cake by the bath?" I asked.

"Seriously. You can die here, and no one will bat an eyelash. So, keep that in mind. Always. Do you want to take it easy for the next few days and rest up?"

"Hell no! I want to get a head start! I want to go dive in a dungeon and kick some beast ass. Like D&D style."

"Bah! You're no match for the stuff out there. The beginner test was rigged. Those imps were bound, magically weakened to be easy kills."

"Rain on my parade, why don't you. Although, I did wonder why they just kind of stood around and waited forever to attack."

"The monsters and beasts you'll find in the dungeons are much worse."

"I don't care. I've got a few days, right? Why not use them to cultivate, practice, and make some headway? Don't you want to get out as well? What else can we do in here but…" I turned and looked back at the bath, then the other direction at the beds. "Wait a minute. Yes. Let's stay here for the next couple of days."

"Oh, boy. What have I done? Do you think I'm that easy?" She tried to sound stern, but I stared her down, and she laughed.

"Well, it is an option," I said, nodding towards the bed. "Staying here and helping you cultivate... it is a sacrifice I am willing to make."

"Well, if you prove to be a good student and can cultivate, then I'll think about letting you touch me again," she said with a wink.

"Sorry, are you talking about the sex or the dungeon?"

"You are horrible." She laughed. It was an infectious sound. One I wanted to hear every day for the rest of my life. "And both, by the way."

"Hit me!"

And she did. Hard.

With the food gone, we settled down. We didn't have any spare crystals, so we couldn't break through to another stage. So, we did something that Chloe said most people neglected. Widening our pathways.

The first several minutes were the worst. Stabilizing the flow of mana that made its way into my system was a task all in itself. It burned its way through my veins, singing its way through my system. Chloe had me sit on the bed. And good thing, too. Because I blacked out the first time.

Inch by painful inch, I pushed that mana, letting it burn its way through my body. But my pathways opened, allowing a greater flow, and by the time I got to my elbows, the amount I could push against the walls doubled from what I started with, allowing for faster burning.

Pain. It was an almost ignorable factor once I reached my shoulders. Then it came back, so intense that tears welled up in my eyes and ran down my face. I blacked again and woke up with my head on Chloe's lap. Evidently, it was later in the day. Evening?

It burned, it hurt so bad that I wanted to curl up and cry. She fetched a bag out of her closet and deposited a pile of small cores onto the bed. They were rank 1, from what I could see. I kind of wanted to curl up in a ball but knew I couldn't give up. Chloe was investing her time and energy in me, and I owed it to her to return the effort. Seeing my endurance and will, she held my hand and encouraged me the whole way. I clenched my jaw and maintained the pressure for several more hours, before I managed to burn through to the heart, reaching rank two. My meridian veins opened fully from my palms to my heart.

"Hah! Good job! You fucking did it!" she cheered. "I knew all the reading would serve a purpose."

"Shit, how much do I owe you?" I asked, wobbling drunkenly on the bed. A wave of energy shot out from me and hit a chair, almost knocking it over. Chloe launched herself at me, tackling me to the ground. I slammed my head against the stone floor, but strangely, it didn't even hurt.

"On your tab, buddy. Seven cores. Oh, and the 135 Fres. Don't forget!"

"Yes, my lady. Whatever you say."

To my delight, I recovered and found that I wasn't covered in black muck this time. Chloe watched me expectantly as I sat up.

"You can open your cultivation progress now. You can check your status by holding your hand palm-up in front of you and saying the word 'status'."

"Wait? Just like in a game?"

She nodded.

"Go on, give it a try."

I did as she said and held my hand up.

"Status."

NAME: JD, AGE: 24
WEAPON: Pen–Blade
CULTIVATION: Realm 1, Rank 2
POWER LEVEL: 112 (1)
HEALTH: 320, MANA: 110
ATTACK: 25, DEFENSE: 15
MANA SHIELD: 170

"Shit, that's quite overpowered," Chloe muttered. "You shouldn't even be in the high teens, even less in the early tweens."

"Teens? Tweens? And is that 1 power level stat from the pen-blade?"

"Most likely it's from your weapon. And sorry, let me explain. When you rank up, the stats go up depending on what kind of...luck you had? It isn't the same for everyone, but there's a general modifier that you can usually count on."

"Usually? Modifier? As in how many stats I get every level, like in video games?"

"The norm is anywhere between one and five points from the first to the third stage or rank. How much did you go up? Five points? See my meaning? And health. The norm is between ten and twenty points, yours went up twenty. Everyone is different, so you'll have to keep an eye on your stats as you progress."

"So, you're saying I'm... special? Right? I'll be able to kill everyone with a single stroke of my pen!"

She slapped my shoulder playfully, but her eyes didn't leave the small screen.

"You sure are. But... actually. Let me check something!"

Chloe held up her palm and pulled up her stats.

"Mine have all gone up, too? Could it be? Is this from the dual cultivation, already?" she whispered, and then looked at me. I could only shrug and collapse onto the pillow.

First Dungeon Dive Part I

I WOKE UP THE NEXT MORNING EXHAUSTED. Hell, I didn't even remember laying down to fall asleep. We had cultivated all night, and I had a suspicion that our bath experience was more than a little responsible for my exhaustion, too. But did I regret it? Not even a little bit.

I stood and stretched, surprised at the fact that I had continued to absorb mana throughout the night and morning, albeit at a much slower pace. I didn't know if that was normal, or a side-effect of our successful pairing. I didn't need to be special. But I sure as hell didn't want to be the guy that stood out for all the wrong reasons. Life was hard enough as an underdog, and I held no delusions that it would make life impossible here. Especially after our run-in with the elf brigade outside the portal.

Chloe and I managed to break through to the third rank, which she kept saying was practically unheard of. But dammit, we did it. But it took a toll on my body. And judging from the way she was moving, Chloe wasn't doing any better.

"Are you okay?" I asked.

She grunted and rolled over, smashing her pillow over her face.

"Okay. Good talk," I replied and padded painfully to the bath. I poured some water into the basin and splashed it into my face. The cold helped. I snagged a towel and dried off, then turned just as Chloe appeared around the wall.

"Ugh!" she groaned. "Do you feel as shitty as you look? What happened to your face?"

Startled, I flinched and turned back to the mirror. I looked like me, albeit a little healthier version. The dark circles that had developed beneath my eyes were gone, and the little, gray hairs that had infiltrated my stubble over the past few years, were gone as well. Yes, I had gray hair coming in at twenty-four.

Chloe laughed and leaned against the corner. "How do I look?" she asked, pursing her lips and holding her messy hair up.

"I plead the fifth," I muttered. I rubbed my eyes and yawned, stretched, and leaned against the sink.

"Oh? Are you afraid of how I'll take the truth?" she chuckled. "You're supposed to lie to me and tell me how beautiful I am... even if I wake up looking like a scaly, twelve-eyed she-beast."

"Hey, this is survival!" I joked and leaned in, planting a kiss on her nose. "How do you feel about hitting the third rank so easily?"

"Easily?" she snorted, "What about last night would you consider easy? I'm sore, spent, worn out, caput, snockered... done in."

"All those things at once, heh?"

She nodded wearily.

Yes, we had burned the candle at both ends, but I imagined what we could accomplish after several more similar sessions? If I managed to live through it, that is.

We had breakfast and got cleaned up. Chloe was worn out, but incredibly upbeat. I fed off her attitude as I dragged my feet around. It felt strangely like my midterm all-nighters in college, except I didn't have the benefit of caffeine pills and Mountain Dew.

"It's weird. This," Chloe said, sticking her head out of her closet and pointing between us.

"What is weird?" I asked. She had a nasty habit of just randomly throwing something out there between us with no context or warning.

"Us. I'm usually not so open with people. Or rather, men. I've been burned before... just when I let my guard down."

"That won't happen this time. The worst that can happen is... we die," I said, trying to make her feel better. "Oh, shit, that didn't come out right."

She chuckled and shook her head. A strand of hair fell free and she tucked it back behind her ear. "No, it didn't. You are absolutely right."

"I don't know, Chloe. We both have our own baggage, but if this," I said, gesturing to the tower around us, "is what we've got to look forward to, then I am more than happy to give it, and us, my all."

We left our dorms a little while later, only to find a large crowd milling around in front of the dungeon. It appeared that no one was able to get inside. No one but the VIP students, it turned out. Which meant us.

We caught more than a few glares as we picked our way through the crowd, then entered through the portal. Strange, milky tendrils flickered and danced around us as the portal activated. And unlike the other gateways I'd been through so far, I felt this one. It was like walking through one of those rubber curtains at the car wash, the ones that shimmy from side to side and are always covered in road grime and soap. I felt the portal's magic on my skin, like something cold and wet. But when I moved to flick it away, nothing was there.

We stepped out into a considerably darker space. It looked and smelled exactly as I thought it would. A ring of stone formed the portal, strange markings having been etched on the front face. I thought it looked like a Stargate but kept that outburst to myself. Chloe might have admitted to being a gamer, but I didn't want to risk scaring her off with my sometimes-overwhelming nerd powers.

The portal room ended in a wall ahead of us, the floor made up of smooth, natural stone, while the walls curved up and rounded overhead. Large iron brackets extended from the walls to our right and left, the hanging braziers burning brightly.

"And we're in a dungeon," I said, matter-a-factly.

"First thing you need to know," Chloe said, turning to me. "We are weak as shit, so we can only go into the first dungeon."

"Mean," I said, "I am feeling particularly brawny today."

"We just hit rank three last night, He-Man, so slow your roll. And this isn't the dungeon... yet. The place we're headed for, well I'll call it the plant-type dungeon. It sounds corny, but that is the best I have, right now. Most of the enemies we'll encounter there are insects."

"Bugs?" I asked, blowing a raspberry.

"Not your garden variety... ha, pun intended... plants and bugs. They're big. And vicious. And always hungry. So, underestimate these things at your own peril. Just so you know, I am not signing up to get eaten alongside you."

"Fair point," I nodded, and Chloe led me forward.

We exited the portal room and entered what looked surprisingly like a tavern from a fantasy game. The walls were covered in rich dark wood, paintings, and candelabras holding glowing candles. A large counter sat off to our left. Two young women stood behind it. I squinted, my eyes struggling in the dim light, but I could have almost sworn that they were twins... down to their outfits.

A sitting area opened up to our right, featuring wooden tables and benches, along with a few booths. Wooden separators, like the one in our room, were set up to divide the space, but they did little to control the noise or provide privacy.

Another portal sat on the far wall, the cool, gray stone standing out in immediate contrast to the wood... everything. But unlike

111

the one we'd entered to come here, it was already active. And it was purple. Violently purple.

An open, rectangular fireplace sat just past the counter. And yet, there was no hood or chimney above it. And as I watched the logs burn, I noticed that the burning embers and smoke just sort of disappeared. Magic. Freaking magic! Yeehaw. The sight made me want to break out in the Snoopy dance.

Several small groups of people sat around, drinking from large mugs—some lacquered wood, others glazed clay, but one student drank out a cup that resembled a skull. He caught my eye, and not just because of his totally awesome taste in drinkware, but also his fine robes and fantastic armor.

"A lot to take in, huh?" Chloe asked, elbowing me in the side. "I had the same expression my first time, too. It makes movies and television shows pale in comparison, doesn't it?"

I nodded taking it all in with another generous visual sweep and then nodded some more. "Sure do. Just look at this place! I want to live here! Right here. In this room."

"Is that so?" she asked. "First glimpse of a dungeon tavern and you're already to cast me aside for a beer wench and a crackling fire?"

"Who said anything about leaving you?" I asked, turning to meet her gaze. "We'll stay here together. Fuck, fight, and drink all day... every day!"

Chloe rolled her eyes and playfully slapped my chest. "We need to pay the fee first," she said and pulled me up to the counter. "Hello, ladies."

I raised my hand and flashed them an honest and warm smile. They stared at me strangely, but only for a moment. Darn skippy. They were identical, the only difference being their outfits. Otherwise, their long, blonde hair flowed the same way and their emerald-green eyes shone like gems. Elven clerks. Interesting.

"Hi, Chloe. Going in again?" the lady on the left asked.

"Yeah, I'm going there with my... boyfriend."

"I knew you'd come around, you bad girl!" the one on the right laughed. Her voice was different, huskier. Was she the rowdy one? As if privy to my thoughts, she eyed me from head to midsection. Her expression made my blood run cold and I immediately felt like prey being sized up as a meal.

"JD, this is Belma," Chloe said, gesturing to the woman on the right and then gesturing to her counterpart, "and this is Selma. They're sisters and work the counter most of the day. Ladies, this is JD, he is a pen-blader."

Their eyebrows rose, and Belma, who had been eyeing me like a steak, suddenly looked a little friendlier.

"Now isn't that interesting? We haven't seen one of your kind for... well, decades. Good to see one of your breed again, even if you're just human."

"Just human? Is our species a dirty word around here?" I asked, unable to swallow down my immediate and snarky response. She hadn't sounded condescending or unfriendly, but I didn't like how she said: *just human.*

"No, but you have no racial bonuses. Us elves are proficient in magic, while other races possess proficiencies with weapons, spirit summoning, conjuration, or their body. You humans? Nothing special."

"No bonus isn't the same as nothing special," Chloe interjected, brightly. "We just happen to be good at everything." Then she slammed the coins down on the counter. "Thanks for the chat, ladies, but we've got dungeon crawling to do."

"Very well," Selma laughed. "Talk to you after!"

Chloe pulled me along to a notice board next to the portal.

"Stuffy, pretentious bitches," she hissed. "They act so high and mighty! Everyone does! Shit, JD, we need to get stronger and show all of them that humans aren't weak!"

"Wow there, sparkplug. I can't say I dislike that fire in your eyes, but shouldn't we be focusing on getting up to rank six first, and then we can talk about conquering the world."

She huffed and turned to me.

"Remember what I told you? About there being *no* recorded history of humans achieving anything of note here? Are you starting to see it yet? The other races expect us to fail. Hell, if they aren't taking bets on how soon we will die, they are probably actively trying to curse us or put poisonous leeches in our beds."

"I get it," I said, squeezing her shoulder. "And we've already taken the first step towards showing them up. But we need to keep our heads down and our noses to the grindstone." I reached out and *bopped* her nose, and thankfully, her scowl lifted.

I turned to have a look at the notice board. It was broken up into different sections, with a single piece of parchment dominating the space. But as I leaned in to read, the writing disappeared, and new words started to appear on the blank surface.

DUNGEON: Plant, 1ˢᵗ floor
RESTRICTION: Realm 1, Stage 12
BEAST TYPES: Plant, Wood, Insect, Bird
LOOT DROP: Rank 1—5
BEAST WEAKNESS: Fire Mana, Weapon
CLEARANCE RATE: 95%
BEAST KING: ???

"Okay... the basics," Chloe said as she noticed me staring at the board, "No one over Realm 1 can enter. These are the beasts that spawn," she said, pointing at the line about plants, wood, insects, and birds. "So, anything from plants that can eat us, trees that can crush us, insects that can cut us in giblets, and birds that can swoop in from above and carry us off."

"Carry us off?"

She nodded. "Haven't had it happen to me, but I heard a story about a dark elf that was picked up, carried all the way across the dungeon, and dropped into a nest. They found his clothes and bones wrapped up in the... what do they call those things? Oh, pellets."

114

"Super gross," I said, suddenly feeling much less confident about our task.

"Right?" she asked, agreeing. "It's really dangerous, so you might think about getting serious once we're inside."

"Trust me, lovely, I'm not throwing away this chance. I'm going to become the strongest, and best pen-blader there ever was! Besides, getting turned into a poo ball sounds uncomfortable."

"Careful. Your enthusiasm might just rub off on me. I just peed myself a little," she deadpanned, turning back to the board.

"Really?" I asked, leaning in as if to check her pants.

She chuckled and punched my shoulder playfully.

"Don't overdo it, lover boy. Now, loot drops can be anything from Rank 1 to Rank 5. His loot includes small mana crystals, beast cores, random gear, coin, beast ingredients, even skills and spells, crafting techniques, and blueprints. I have no idea what metrics manage the drops, so don't ask."

"Feisty."

"Don't you forget it," she said, sticking out her tongue. "And since you brought up resistances and weaknesses, they're pretty simple."

"I didn't bring them up."

"But you were going to. Any who... magic is identified by its elemental bias, for both attack and defense. Weapons, as in swords," she said, holding her hands out to indicate a long weapon.

"Okay, that's just mean. It is small but mighty."

"I know," she said, with a wink. "And the unknown Beast King? Well, that is pretty self-explanatory."

"When do we fight that?" I asked.

"Dunno," Chloe said, absently turning to watch the adventurers drinking. "You see, the Beast King can manifest wherever it chooses. Some might make it all the way through and never see them. But the only way to get a 100% clearance is to make it all the way through and defeat the Beast King. That is the only way to get a super reward from the dungeon, the academy, and the tower. Three rewards."

"Does it happen often?"

"In other academies, yeah. In ours? No. Most ramble around, picking fights and looking for chests. Some go in just looking for the king. But most leave before the end. I have no idea how it works beyond that. As for the Beast King, he respawns once every twenty-four hours. Someone killed him for loot, so once the twenty-four hours are up, he'll respawn somewhere in the dungeon."

I listened, taking in the freaking awesome ambiance around us.

"Just like a freaking game," I breathed.

"Yeah, except in a game, if you die, you just restart from the last checkpoint. Here, if you die, they paint warnings on the walls with your guts.

"Okay, that is bad," I agreed. "But at least we're used to playing games and have certain knowledge other races don't. I'm guessing the elves don't play Final Fantasy or Warhammer in their free time."

"Or Skyrim. That was my jam," Chloe said, agreeing. "But those two you mentioned. Awesome sauce. I love Final Fantasy and the Warhammer universe. They rock!"

"Sure do!" She put up a fist, I bumped it, and hers blew up.

"It's almost like I made you in a lab."

"Is that a weird science reference?"

"I love you," I said.

"I know."

"Say, is that a leaderboard?" I asked, pointing at another board nailed to the wall.

"It is. Rankings for the fastest dungeon run from beginning to end, with the end being the entrance to the second level. Fastest boss kill, most boss kills, most types of beasts killed, and completion rate. They're self-explanatory."

"And if we beat them, we get a reward?"

116

"Exactly. Anyway, are you ready to go?" Chloe asked as she pulled me toward the large purple gate.

"JD! Hey, JD!" someone called out from the portal chamber behind us.

I froze and turned around, both excited to see Mabel, but also nervous as to who might see us together. My feelings on the pretty young elf were... complicated. Her zither was beneficial in battle. Darn handy. But being around us would possibly get her into more trouble. And that wasn't cool.

"Mabel. What are you doing here?" I asked as she ran up to us.

Now if only Chloe hadn't been there, this conversation would have been a lot easier. Mabel's eyes dropped between us, and it was only then that I realized Chloe and I were holding hands.

She recovered quickly. "I was thinking of going into the dungeon."

"By yourself? With only a zither?"

She glanced at the wood floor and nodded, but then her gaze lifted to our hands again.

"Yeah, I've got no one to go with, and... you know, I sort of followed you here."

"Hey, aren't you going to introduce us?" Chloe protested, squeezing my hand.

"Oh, right, sorry. Chloe, this is Mabel, an elf I met during my first test. She came in and totally helped me survive."

"And I am Chloe. His girlfriend and a VIP student."

Mabel's face screwed up when Chloe mentioned the world *girlfriend*, but it was nothing compared to her mouthing her name.

"Okay," I whispered, more than a little uncomfortable between the two women.

Chloe muttered something about "getting going" but she said it while turning away, so I couldn't hear it properly.

"Chloe, the troublemaker?" Mabel asked.

"In name only," I chuckled. "And only because she is human. They don't like our kind very much here."

117

Mabel looked at me and then Chloe's back, before moving closer to us both.

"I don't feel that way about you or your kind," she said, tapping on Chloe's shoulder." I just want to be friends. I've never really had any before and for the first time in my life, I would like to find people who see *me* for me. I'm good in battle, and I know dungeon lore and structures. Please, feel free to tell me if my offer isn't on the level. But do you think you would let me tag along for a bit?"

It was an understatement to say that I was surprised. But, damn, I was pulling for Mabel in every way possible.

"I... I see," Chloe muttered. "Sorry, I just assumed... since you're so pretty and you two knew each other. I just thought that...well, I guess I don't know what I was thinking. I just got jealous and bitchy. Sorry."

"You don't need to apologize. Really. I know that I don't know what it is like to be human. But most of my race are slaves, so I know what it is like to be looked down on."

"It is okay with me," I said, looking at Chloe. "I'll never forget that you saved my life in that test."

"She did?" Chloe asked. I nodded.

"Then that makes you good in my book."

"Really?"

Chloe and I nodded together.

Mabel beamed and moved towards us, stopping just short of throwing her arms around both of us in a hug. She clapped her hands quietly and danced in place.

"Is it true that you can project a mana extension to her blade? I mean, that is what I heard. That you are a sword-wielder but also counted as a mid-range damage dealer?"

Chloe nodded excitedly.

"That's me, baby!"

"Ahh! I've heard so much about you! Even though you're just a freshman, you're pretty good with a blade! It's an honor! I can't wait to see you in action."

Chloe looked over her shoulder and mouthed something I didn't catch.

"Shit, I like you already, Mabel!"

"Are you still using the zither?" I asked, trying to cut back into the conversation. "Your support back then was marvelous!"

Chloe's eyebrows rose.

"You're a supporter!"

"I am. Why?"

"Why? Because no raiding party is complete without a bloody great supporter!"

I was forced aside as the two young women started chatting and laughing. It was awesome to see them immediately bond, but annoying, too, as they immediately ignored me and moved off. I followed, now the third wheel in our troop.

I knew Mabel would be able to pull her weight, now I only needed to see Chloe in action. But Mabel's response gave me pause. My new "roommate" was already a famous freshman?

"Are you girls ready?" I asked, cutting in and wedging between them.

"Born ready!" Chloe laughed. "Wait, did you say you knew dungeon lore and structure?"

"Just a little bit," Mabel said, and immediately started rattling off the beast types, weaknesses, drops, regions best frequented, the possible boss spawns, and so much more.

"Firstly, how do you know all of that? And second, where the hell have you been all my life?" Chloe whispered.

"My father was a cartographer, in service to our Matron family. And I have been far away from here, Chloe. A very dark and faraway place," Mabel replied. She tried to sound funny, but her humor couldn't fully mask the darker undertone. She had said her father was in service to their "matron" family, and red-hair said something about his family "owning hers". I wasn't going to push on the issue, yet, but it seemed Mabel needed our help more than we needed hers.

119

"You can't even understand how happy I am that you are here right now!" Chloe practically squealed.

"What about our formation?" Mabel asked as we stepped toward the gate.

"Formation?" I asked.

"We can use a formation and fill in battle slots to get a bonus boost to stats and skills. We can... yeah, we can only use one. Solidary of Heart. It gives us an attack boost of **+15%** and a defense boost of **+10%**. You will have to act as a tank, JD, while Chloe will fill the mid to long-range damage role, and I will be your support."

"Outstanding. How do we adjust the formation, though?" Chloe asked. "I have read about them, but never used one before. "

"Simple. At the gate, you just input each person and their role. As to what a formation is, well, it's quite simple. A single party can consist of up to five members, six including a pen-blade, as they can technically fill several different roles. If we successfully fill each slot with another class, we can get a bonus. But seeing as there are just the three of us, we are limited to this formation for now."

"So, if we add a fighter, or a mage, or beastmaster then we'd get higher stats?" I asked.

"Most likely, yeah," Mabel chuckled. "I'm not a hundred percent sure myself, but once we've formed a real party, we're allowed to share and manipulate some group stats. Only from different classes, though. It gives groups an incentive to fill up all the classes."

"Well, Mabel, I think I speak for Chloe *and* myself when I say, we are blessed to have you."

"It's a pleasure to be here, JD. Chloe. Are you ready to squash some bugs?"

First Dungeon Dive Part II

WE STEPPED THROUGH THE PORTAL, a flash of green light fading into... swaying branches and leaves. The world that greeted us was—anticlimactic in a sense. It looked like a jungle, but what I found odd was, it looked like every jungle I had ever seen. I know it was irrational, but I expected something more... spectacular... fantastical. Outrageous?

The trees had wide trunks, and grew straight up, reaching for the sky. But they seemed to have no end. The brush and foliage were so thick I couldn't see an end to the forest above or around us.

The soil was rocky and hard, the space between trees broken by large fan-like ferns. Limited sunlight filtered down from above, but the wind shifted the trees, making the light dance and move.

"Well, at least it isn't wet. I wasn't crazy about the idea of fighting in the mud," I said, tapping the ground with the toe of my boot.

"Don't like mud?" Chloe asked, watching me with a smile. "Just wait five minutes. The weather here is so horribly random."

I looked up at the clear sky wearily, half expecting a crack of thunder to echo at any moment. That's all I needed on my first *actual* dungeon crawl—get caught in a magical thunderstorm and struck by lightning. Boom... dead. End of story.

But there was no story. Just a strange sky... at least, that portion of it I could see between the trees. Yes, it was a dungeon inside a tower, with trees, and a clear sky above us, and then a bright sun floating somewhere overhead. Now that's what I call fantasy!

"So, where are the monsters?" I asked, trying to sound as excited as possible. I struggled to suppress a very real pang of fear. Who knew what would come at us?

"They'll spawn as we move around, don't worry," Chloe replied, her voice barely a whisper. "We shouldn't speak much here."

"She's right. And since you're the tank, take the lead," Mabel added, pulling the zither from her rift. The movement was so swift and elegant that it looked heavily practiced.

I nodded, swallowed hard, and moved forward. We passed between two mammoth trees, and an obvious roadway appeared. I made sure to look around and stared at the lush greenery and the trees above with equal fervor. Despite being on guard, I physically jumped as two plants suddenly started moving toward us from the shadows between trees. Or, rather, they tried to.

"Are those plants coming for... us?" I asked, pulling my pen-blade out of my rift. Yes, I should have already had it out and ready, but the idea of carrying a real weapon was still a novelty.

The plants moved towards us with all the speed and dexterity of a toddler on all fours. It made me think of horror movies, especially where 'entities' would walk backward while leaning on their hands and feet. Now that shit was creepy!

The monsters looked like a mixture between a rafflesia and a Venus flytrap. Their 'feet' were short and stubby, like the stalks of mushrooms, but there were many of them and the plants seemed to float. Truth be told, it was their heads that unnerved me. Their diameter was easily three feet across and once fully opened, I guessed they could eat any one of us whole. Gross. What a horrible way to go.

122

Green tendrils flailed from their pale bodies, but they were fairly short from what I could see.

Information about the monsters appeared above the closest creature, but I could see it clearly, thanks to the massive shade trees.

NAME: Venus Lorana
POWER LEVEL: 35
HEALTH: 60, **MANA:** 40
ATTACK: 15, **DEFENSE:** 10
WEAKNESS: Fire, Sword

"Watch out for their poisonous gas!" Mabel yelled just as green spores appeared from their bulbous heads. They drifted towards us, along with several sharp needles. They all missed, but the poison spores struck me. To my surprise, I didn't receive any damage, instead, my Mana shield started dropping, one point every second.

The sound of Mabel's zither broke the silence, as she started to strum the instrument. Magical snares appeared, wrapping around the plants and snapping their mouths shut. I felt a sudden spike of annoyance when she stopped. I half expected Chloe to start singing to her music.

"Don't focus too intently on my music, JD. It can put you in a trance," Mabel warned.

"Now you tell me!" I yelled and pulled my blade back. *"Think about that later!"* I imagined the ordinary Air Slash and a brushstroke appeared in front of me. Just an ordinary diagonal line, thick and inky, just as if someone had painted it with a calligraphy brush. I slashed the blade along the brush stroke and a blade of wind appeared in response, hitting the plant and dealing damage.

SKILL USED: Air Slash
MANA USED: 7
DAMAGE DEALT: 25

123

I swiped both messages aside as Chloe moved around to the left, carefully staying out of the thrashing tendrils. Her sword cut in a downward arc but came nowhere close to landing a blow. And yet, the plant monster shuddered, slumped over, and died. An afterglow remained fiery, red in the dim light.

"That's fucking cheating!" I protested. "You can use fire magic and hit from so far away!"

"Hey, I'm not special for nothing, baby. I'm fire incarnate!"

"Fire incarnate?" I echoed, "Does that mean you are going to go live in a mansion with a bunch of other mutants when you finish at Zenith?"

I immediately turned towards the second Venus Lorana. I slashed my blade across the head and followed up with an upward slice, then a sideways cut. The strokes all flared to life, cutting into the plant and killing it effectively. I intentionally avoided using another skill, therefore conserving my mana. We would be here for a while, and I needed to conserve my power.

The plants didn't disappear, but their bodies turned translucent.

"Go on, pick it up," Chloe said, motioning towards my kill. I moved in, a prompt immediately appearing.

Would you like to loot the corpses?

Naturally, I accepted.

ITEMS RECEIVED:
Venus Lorana: 2
Core crystal Rank 1: 3
Fres: 72

"What's with the corpses? I remember monsters dropping body parts in games," I asked, turning to Chloe. "Do we have to cut them up?"

Both girls shook their heads and opened their mouths to reply at the same time, but then chuckled as they stopped short. Mabel nodded to Chloe, giving her the chance to answer. I sensed that she was struggling with how to fit into our little group. Perhaps she felt like a third wheel? Or maybe she was jealous of how quickly I had formed a relationship with Chloe?

"No, you don't have to cut them up. Every corpse that drops is considered good enough by the dungeon. By good enough, I mean that it's usable and therefore can be sold. Whoever buys it, which usually is the tower, will cut it."

"I see. What if we meet a wild boar or something? Can we eat them?"

She chuckled and shook her head. "No, silly, not like that. We can sell them but ask for the meat in return, and then they charge you for processing it. Food made using beast ingredients adds temporary stats, perks, or boosts, so it's useful. But it does require special skills."

"I see. There are so many things I have to learn," I said, scratching the stubble on my chin. I'd have to shave when I got the time. No. I'd grow a beard and show those beardless elves what a real man looks like!

"Yet," Mabel said, finally joining in on the conversation. "I would like to offer my services to teach you, Lady Chloe seems very knowledgeable, but there are some areas where I believe I can be of service."

"Oh, why thank you," Chloe said and curtsied. "You're too kind, Mabel."

"Anyways," I said, interrupting their back-patting session. "We should move on. We are here to fight monsters, right?"

Neither argued and they quickly readied themselves, so I took up the center of the road and prepared to move forward. I paused. The forest's silence struck me. It was nerve-wracking—the absence of sound. Not a single bird chirped, snake hissed, or bush rustled. It felt like someone forgot to hit play on the "forest noises" tape player.

We moved up the road and walked for five minutes before the next group of Venus plants charged us. If you could call their adorable, bobbing, and incredibly slow saunter a charge. I started humming *Flight of the Valkyrie* as they approached, Chloe chiming in for good effect.

They proved to be even less of a problem than the first two, and so half an hour passed with us killing eight more, coming in at a total of twelve Venuses, but only seven corpses.

"Is this it?" I asked.

"Dungeons are separated into zones," Mabel said, beating Chloe to the punch.

The two girls were competing now, and for some reason it made me feel... good? Sure, I promised Chloe something, and I would keep my word no matter what, but seeing another incredibly attractive female competing for my attention felt great.

"See that over there?" Chloe asked, pointing ahead, "That shimmering wall?"

I spotted a barrier at least one hundred paces ahead.

"That's the entrance to the next zone," she said, continuing. "Every zone holds different monsters and beasts, and some have mini-bosses. Others contain full-on zone bosses. There's even a floor boss you need to kill if you want to move to the next dungeon floor. Most of the bosses can also appear as mini-bosses."

Something caught in the corner of my eye. A hint of movement. I turned around and raised my blade as a floating tendril came into view, one much larger than those before. The sound of dozens of planty knob-like feet reverberated around us as first one Venus Lorana appeared, and then another, but the second creature was several times larger. It was gigantic, with a bobbing, red head, several flowers growing out of the top, each filled with long, sharp teeth. Bones and torn cloth were stuck between them, telling me these plants had eaten more than dirt and plant fertilizer lately. Had it been a student? Someone we might have known?

I immediately felt guilty, as I'd hope it was our redheaded elf friend.

126

"Are you guys seeing this?" I asked as the plant monster inched closer, flailing its tentacles around and hitting the ground, the bushes on both sides, and the empty air.

"I think so," Chloe muttered. I both heard and felt their feet shuffle behind me, and before I knew it, they stood on either side and just behind me.

"It's one bad-looking plant," Mabel whispered. "It looks so angry."

Both Chloe and I frowned at her.

"Bad-looking and angry? You can curse if you want, Mabel. We won't judge you," I said.

"Yeah. Just say that it's a fucking asshole!"

"Fucking—asshole? That doesn't make sense."

I groaned, both from Mabel's inability to swear properly and the approaching murder plant. The tentacles were almost in reach, and we still hadn't talked tactics. And before I had the chance, the status window popped up above its head. The plant monster even stopped for several seconds, giving me ample time. How considerate.

NAME: Venus Lorana Queen
TYPE: Mini-Boss
POWER LEVEL: 238
HEALTH: 900, **MANA:** 240
ATTACK: 55, **DEFENSE:** 45
WEAKNESS: Fire, Sword

"Here goes, girls!" I focused on using my skill, not wanting to hold back in case it had some strange power not listed in the pop-up. Wouldn't it just be our luck if this particular murder plant was capable of spitting digestive juices over great distances, and we ended up melting into puddles right there in the middle of the first... freaking... dungeon? That would suck.

The now-familiar brush stroke appeared before me and I sliced through the line, sending a wave of mana-charged wind at the Queen.

SKILL USED: Air Slash
MANA USED: 7
DAMAGE DEALT: 31

I followed up with three more attacks and slashed through the strokes that appeared. Each blade of wind cut into the Queen, slashing through tentacles and digging deeper into her skin, but she wasn't slowing down, if anything, her small knobby feet churned even faster.

Bindings suddenly appeared around its head and legs. They were followed by the familiar and soothing sound of Mabel's zither. The bindings, however, weren't doing a good job. Several snapped and she had to recast them over and over.

Chloe ran off to the side and used one of her skills. I didn't know what it was, but her sword glowed bright red, just like the previous times, no, not the same. It glowed brighter and then even started burning. A searing flame appeared along the edge of her blade and flashed out at the plant boss. The monster's weakness was apparent as it caught fire.

She let out a deafening screech and threw herself to the ground and rolled. The flames disappeared and the queen, showcasing more agility than seemed reasonable, sprang to her many feet.

"Any other bright ideas, Chloe? She knows stop-drop-and-roll!"

I drew a curved brush stroke—a "U" and pushed mana into it. The attack hit the bulbous plant, creature, thing, severing a leg and flailing tendril, but she kept moving. The mouths were bending low now, snapping and biting.

I dodged aside but felt strange. I could feel sweat forming on my brow as nausea twisted my guts. One of the creeping horror's snapping mouths suddenly twitched and started to swell like a balloon.

I didn't even have time to shout a warning before the head exploded in a fine mist, pluming into the air like a detonated vacuum cleaner. It was too much to escape, so I did the best I could counter.

"Whirlwind!" Four brush strokes appeared in front of me, glowing to life one by one. I followed the pattern and let the wind fly. A small tornado appeared in front of me, tearing through the deadly spores and blowing them up and away from us. The magical wind attack hit the Queen and knocked her back, but she was far too heavy for more than that. A few errant spores landed on my bare arms, the skin instantly burning.

"Good, now move!" Chloe yelled as she swung her sword upwards, casting another wave of fire at the Queen. It struck a growth on the creature's side, tearing through a branch-like appendage, scorching leaves, and bulbous flesh.

A buzzing noise echoed in from the trees overhead. "Heads up!" I yelled. Dark, flying shapes appeared through the columns of shifting sunlight. They were too fast to see properly, but I knew by the sound of their wings—

"Take them down!" Chloe snapped. "Mabel! Snare them!"

Mabel's fingers stopped strumming the zither, and she immediately started playing a different tune, the notes higher and faster. The snares binding the mushroom queen disappeared, and new lines of magical energy appeared above us. They grew and linked, connecting between the trees like a glowing spider's web. The flies dropped...the swarming beasts hitting the web and sticking fast. Several of the creatures tore free and fell to the ground, their adhered body parts still stuck to Mabel's web.

"We need some more flames!" I stressed as I drew several hard cuts in the air before me. The pen-blade made them real, the resulting slices splitting two of the dark bugs in half.

The queen screeched and moved right at Mabel, her lashing tentacles regrowing in a messy explosion of green ichor. She

129

lowered her mouth and snapped at our zither player, just as I hacked into a one-winged fly, the creature's sticky blood spattering my pants.

The boss Lorana spewed something green, the ground immediately sizzling and smoking on contact. I dove to the side, narrowly escaping the spitting attack. It hit the third fly, however, and the beast immediately dissolved into goo.

"Ahh! That's so nasty!" Chloe squealed. "Die, you bitch!"

Mabel spun and dodged a fly, as it pulled free from her web overhead, then added another chord to her tune. A new series of snares appeared on the queen's left side, latching onto and pulling at her body.

Mabel was maxed out. I watched and listened, my mind struggling with how she would be able to add additional notes or magic to her tune. We had to act, and fast.

I ran right at the trapped mushroom queen and threw my weight into her side. It toppled over and landed on its back, the tentacles flailing and lashing to pull her upright once again.

I checked its health.

NAME: Venus Lorana Queen
TYPE: Mini-Boss
POWER LEVEL: 238
HEALTH: 192, **MANA:** 75
ATTACK: 55, **DEFENSE:** 45
WEAKNESS: Fire, Sword

Almost there!
I gathered myself and started cutting into it, but the ordinary slashes barely broke her thick skin.

DAMAGE DEALT: 6
DAMAGE DEALT: 4
Shit!

I stopped hacking as it did very little good and was just sapping my strength. I prepared a new attack, planning out my mana usage just as the mini boss rolled over, her remaining heads snapping out and eating the fly carcasses right off the ground. I glared at it.

"Chloe! Some fire!"

"I'm out of mana!" she yelled back.

I cursed under my breath and lunged in, swiping at the stalks holding the queen's heads aloft, but I managed a single attack before something slammed into me, knocking me off my feet.

I struggled to my feet immediately, rubbing my sore ribs and raising my blade, only to come face to face with a fly the size of a damned minibus. Its wings buzzed as it fluttered just off the ground.

"Fire or not, Chloe, keep that walking bag of fungal spores busy," I yelled, imagining several slashes between myself and the fly.

Numerous brush strokes started appearing, flashed several times, and disappeared again. I hit them all dead on and the fly buzzed as the attacks connected. A single snare appeared around its wings, and the bloated creature tumbled out of the sky, one wing ripped free.

Chloe's sword finally started glowing red and burned with a blazing fire. Then it struck me. Wind and fire. Could it work? It was a fantasy world, after all. Right? I hoped my hunch was correct, as I only had enough mana remaining for a single skill.

A complex sequence of patterns appeared as my thought was turned into reality.

"Mabel, I yelled. Drop your web above and snare the fly to the Venus Queen! Chloe, target her with the strongest fire skill you can manage!"

I darted toward the still flailing plant as its tongue flew out and wrapped around the fly's mid-section. Two more tendrils flew out and started pulling it in. I dove out of the way at the last moment as the wounded fly fought to break free, its hooked legs almost skewering my midsection. The Venus Queen rolled and thrashed, finally pulling the fly within range of its mouths. She immediately started trying to ingest it whole.

Mabel's zither rang loudly as new snares appeared around the two, cinching down like glowing lassos and pulling the two monsters together.

"Now!"

Chloe wound up and swung, almost baseball-style, sending a wave of mana-infused flames from her legendary blade. It split the air and flew right at the two mini-bosses. My mind immediately spun a complex pattern of brush strokes ahead of me, and I slashed quickly and precisely, just in time as the wave of flames moved past me. Right upper corner straight down and up to the left upper corner, then down again and in a circle to the starting point.

"Down, down, up, high kick," I growled, as my mana spun forth.

Her wave of mana fire combined with my tornado, the two attacks morphing into something truly terrifying. I stepped back as the heat increased, captured by the wind and magnified into a blistering firestorm. It engulfed the queen and the fly, scorching them and everything around them in a torrent of swirling death.

The fly tried to push through the barrier of fire, but I used my last **5** points of mana on a relatively weak Air Slash. Mabel's snares did the rest, as the winged beast fell back and started to burn. I checked my stats and cursed under my breath as I watched my mana slowly tick up to **1** and then a moment later **2**. I would be relatively helpless for some time. The firestorm suddenly weakened and then disappeared, leaving our forest battleground almost insufferably dark and cold.

Chloe grunted and brought her blade up. I did the same, a little embarrassed how paltry my pen-blade looked as I brandished it before me. But the Venus Queen and the lord of the flies didn't move. Their bodies sagged and became translucent.

"Hah! We did it!" Chloe laughed, whooping with relief.

"Yes," Mabel gasped, sagging against her knees.

"You girls rocked," I said, dropping to my rear. "Shit. That was a bit harder and more dangerous than I imagined."

"And these were only mini-bosses," Chloe whispered. "Just imagine how much stronger the real bosses are. But..."

"But what?" I asked, gulping down some air.

"Did you just say, 'down, down, up, high kick' when you summoned that whirlwind?"

"It just felt like the right thing to do."

"I am confused," Mabel said, "What does that mean, down, down...?"

"He thinks he is a ninja, murdered and damned to the underworld, now returned to the land of the living to get his revenge," Chloe laughed.

Mabel turned to me, her eyes widening. "Is this true? Were you murdered? Are you a... wraith?"

I wiped some perspiration off my forehead. "It is from a video game. One about a tournament of fighters."

"Video game?" she asked, her confusion deepening.

"I'll tell you about it later," I laughed, still out of breath. I was exhausted, my heart was beating an angry tapenade against my ribs. But it was worth it—the fight, the win, the danger, and the praise for my girls. But also, the power I had acquired since arriving here. I could fight. I could cast magical skills! How fucking cool was that?

"Did you loot it?" Chloe asked as she sat next to me. I shook my head and then held my hand out toward the two boss monsters. "Shit!" Chloe cursed. "Is that a boss core?"

"The green glowing thing?" I asked.

"Yeah, go on, take it."

"Wait, but the two of you did as much as me. Hell. Or more. Without Mabel's snares or your fire, we would have been plant food."

Mabel walked up to me, the zither hanging at her side. "Go on," she said, prodding my leg with a foot, "Take it. The lady is being pretty nice to offer. That is a valuable prize."

133

"I like this elf," Chloe snorted.

I pushed myself off the ground and walked over to the glowing core. Then, with more difficulty than I care to admit, I bent over and scooped it off the ground. It looked like a hexagonal crystal, unlike the cylindrical ones I saw earlier. It was larger, too. Almost the size of my fist.

ITEMS RECEIVED:
Venus Lorana: 2
Venus Lorana Queen: 1
Mutated Swapper Fly: 1
Core crystal Rank 1: 28
Core crystal Rank 2: 3
Fres: 912

SPECIAL ITEMS RECEIVED:
Venus Lorana Queen Core: 1

"So, how about you ladies tell me about this special core," I said and held it out for them to see. Chloe's eyes widened and she grabbed it from my hand.

"A named core!"

"Wait, what?" Mabel hissed. "Really?"

"Yeah, just look at it!" Chloe said. She scooped it out of my open palm.

I had no idea what the fuss was about, but considering the trouble we'd gone through to acquire it, I gave it a second look. I almost asked Mabel what it was worth? But paused. Maybe it was worth approaching someone like Salina on my own—she was the mistress of finances, after all. Perhaps being a guy, I could negotiate prices, especially if the biases of this world towards humans went deeper. Did the all-female gang of mistresses underpay for items when the seller was a girl?

"It gives off such a strong power signature," Chloe whispered, interrupting my train of thought. "It feels so much different than ordinary cores."

"Because it *is* different," Mabel whispered in equal awe. "See, ordinary rank one core crystals hold a day's worth of mana, rank two holds three days, and a rank three does seven days. Rank four through six could be anywhere from two weeks to months. Boss cores are different. They're much more of a gamble, but sometimes even weaker cores like this queen could hold up to a year's worth of mana cultivation once absorbed. Two years, hell, even five years."

"Here, take it," Chloe muttered and gave the core back. "I don't want it."

I reached out and wrapped my hand around the core but didn't lift it free yet.

"Are you sure you don't want it?"

Chloe shrugged. "You're the tank, aren't you? It's an investment as I see it."

"As she said," Mabel added, cutting in. There was a hint of sadness in her eyes, one I saw mirrored on Chloe's face as well. We all felt it, the core's power, the promise of its boost to any one person's cultivation ability. It would make Chloe's fiery sword more potent, perhaps unlock new skills and abilities. At the same time, it would make Mabel's snares stronger and more plentiful. Perhaps it would level her up to new and fantastical skills, too. But I was the tank, the one intended to absorb the damage and keep them safe. Safe so they could manipulate the battlefield and deal the damage. If I couldn't stand my ground and died, they wouldn't stand a chance either.

"If it is the price to dungeon dive with you two, I will pay whatever it takes," Mabel said, interrupting my thoughts. "I will claim no loot or coins. I just want..."

"Absolutely not," I said, cutting her off. "We don't work that way, Mabel. Sure, I might show favor to Chloe, but you are one of us. You fought, you risked, and you *will* share in the reward. I

135

don't know what is up with this world, but long as you are part of our little group, you will be equal. Always."

She nodded and searched my face for a moment, then her mouth pulled up into a smile. She looked from me to Chloe. Their eyes locked for a second too long and Mabel looked away, a bit of color having blossomed on her cheeks. The blush might not have been noticeable on Chloe or me, but with Mabel's moonlight-colored skin, she practically glowed.

The silence stretched on for several moments before Mabel cleared her throat.

"Chloe didn't mention one important thing," she said, her voice soft at first. "Named cores are special but have to be handled in specific ways. They need to be set up in a formation, and not just any formation. It has to be constructed using monster core crystals of the same rank. If that is a rank 2 named core, it will require rank 2 core crystals to bridge together. That will form a barrier that will prevent the power from bleeding away over time."

"Oh, I didn't know that," Chloe replied. "Guess I haven't been here long enough to find out about those things."

"And how long *have* you been here?" I asked curiously. "For real this time. There's no way you've only been here for a week."

She smiled sheepishly. "Three weeks?"

"Are you asking or telling?"

I had to take into consideration that she had already lied about her tenure once. That was before we became 'an item' so I decided to let it slide.

"It has been a busy three weeks, then. You hit the first rank, amassed crystals, explored the academy, pillaged the library, and amassed a healthy pile of knowledge."

She shrugged. "I told you I'm special, didn't I?"

"You sure are," I laughed, but then cursed inwardly. Mabel was here. "You both are. The way you two worked together during that battle just proved it."

Mabel blushed even more deeply. A fact Chloe noticed right away.

"Did something happen between you two? Something you didn't tell me about?"

"No," I said honestly. "She was the first person I met when Salina delivered me here. Besides, you know how it was for you during the first few days, right? The loneliness, the strangeness of it all. We hit it off, battled some dangly-ball imp creatures, and then sat together at dinner."

"Oh," Chloe said, simply. But I gathered there was far more to it than that.

I glanced over at Mabel who looked more than a little uncomfortable. Somehow, we stumbled right back into the third-wheel territory.

"I can help... set up a formation for you. As a thank you. And I'd be willing to join your party. As an official member."

"Thank you, Mabel," I said.

"You have to know. It is an honor beyond imagining just for me to acquire two... friends," Mabel whispered.

Her sudden change of character, her meek, almost afraid side came out so quickly. Was she *that* lonely? I'd have to add that to my list of things to learn. But first, the red-haired elf kids' comment about owning her family. That shit bothered me to no end.

"Is it possible to make a formation large enough that would allow all three of us to siphon the core's power?" I asked, wanting to dispel any tension and bring our group back onto equal footing.

"It is," Mabel replied. "With the right number of materials, that is. With five ranked core crystals per person, we could make it work." Judging from the look on Mabel and Chloe's face, I guessed that was well beyond our budget. But heh, it was possible.

"Rome wasn't built in a day. And it gives us something to work toward. Now, how about we kill some more mushroom monsters and other freaky beasts? I want to eat well this week."

BULLY

CHLOE, MABEL, AND I spent most of the afternoon hunting. But most of that time went into searching, unfortunately. We walked, looked around, and found a creature or two every once in a while. But those fights were short and relatively easy.

Then we came across a valley and were picking our way down the slope, the only passable terrain taking us right through a sizable bramble. I was pulling my leg free from a thorn when we heard something massive approach.

Chloe leaned out and immediately cursed. Mabel crawled through the underbrush next to her, leaned out, and echoed the same curse word. The creature's shadow extended, covering the underbrush as it moved to stand almost directly over us.

It looked like a massive, reddish-brown cockroach, and it was as big as a school bus. To our luck, it hadn't spotted us beneath the tangled brush. I watched it walk slowly by, its hooked legs tearing small trees and shrubs out of the ground and gouging the soft earth.

It looked like a monster, complete with large, black segmented eyes and an armored, glistening carapace. I immediately longed for an RPG. Maybe a missile? A nuke would be overkill, although I loved overkill. It was so satisfying, the heat, flash, and the mushroom cloud rising in the sky—yeah, I got off track a bit.

"Same tactic?" I whispered. "Bind it with snares, hit it with a firestorm, and run if things go south?" I looked at both Mabel and Chloe. They nodded but kept looking up at the lumbering beast, more than a little uncertainty flashing in their eyes.

"Are you sure it's worth it?" Chloe asked. "That thing is a tank. I mean, is it worth the risk?"

I knew what she meant. We had been lucky, up to that point. But this beast was well beyond anything we'd tangled with. Yes, we were running out of opportunities to get our hands on resources. But picking a fight with the wrong kind of creature here didn't just mean game over, it meant lights out—the forever kind.

"Don't you want to be taken seriously?" I asked, mock nudging her with my shoulder.

"I'd like to, you know, live a while longer, JD," Chloe muttered and pushed me away. "I'm sure that I'll make for a hot corpse, but let's not find out."

"I am confident I can subdue it for... maybe three seconds. Would that be enough?" Mabel asked.

I nodded, my excitement barely outpacing my apprehension. A beast that size would undoubtedly drop fantastic loot. And not to mention its core. The possibilities almost made me giggle. I had already decided that it was worth the risk, but I needed to make sure the girls were okay with it, too.

"This is a kill that could set us up for major breakthroughs. But the decision isn't just mine. We attack, but if things go sideways, we can run. Deal?"

Mabel nodded first, her zither already in hand. Chloe looked at her, then me, and said, "Just don't get us killed, okay?"

"I got you," I said and pulled the pen-blade out of my rift.

We moved together through the brush, Mabel flanking left, and Chloe right. I double-checked my mana, confirmed the girls were ready, and jumped out of the bramble to get the monster's attention.

I wanted to yell something witty and funny to get the beast's attention, to add to the story when we told it later. Hey, I threw a one-liner at a bus-sized cockroach and then we roasted it with a magical firestorm. Nope. I stopped, took a breath, and my mind went completely and utterly blank. Damn. So, I screamed borderline unintelligible sounds and waved my arms.

The monstrous bug stopped, its hooked feet catching and tipping over a tree, then it slowly turned toward me, two massive pincers gleaming in the light. They opened and snapped shut, sliding together like dangerously sharp blades. Okay, that wasn't something I had expected from a fucking cockroach, but it was already too late to do anything about it.

"Now!" I yelled, gesturing to where Mabel hid.

The zither came alive, numerous snares erupting from the ground and binding the roach's legs. Another appeared in the air and cinched the pincers shut. Chloe jumped up to my right, immediately activating her flaming sword skill. The fire flew right past me as I activated my air slash. The two combined as before, the mana and elemental heat blossoming into a spinning, raging firestorm. It hit the insect-like mini-boss head-on.

Chloe abruptly swung her sword, launching another wave of fire in. I drew out another air slash, this one with an extra stroke or two, and launched the larger windstorm in to meet it. The second, larger firestorm hit the cockroach. The two conflagration spells merged, exploding with so much heat that I was pretty sure it singed my eyelashes.

The carapace held for several seconds, but under the onslaught of hellish flames, it started to burn and flake to ash. Antenna burned away as the creature's pinchers glowed red-hot. Greenish blood and flesh spurted forth, catching fire as soon as it met air. I pulled back further, shying away from the scorching heat. Mabel and Chloe closed in on either side, their arms raised to shield their eyes.

"Do we—?"

A borderline manic laugh echoed from somewhere nearby, interrupting Chloe as she was about to speak. Mabel jumped and cursed. So did I, although I tried to hide the fact.

I spun, searching for the source of the sound as something twisted deep inside my guts. It was one thing to interrupt someone, but to do so while hunting? I'd seen enough of that in games to know it was usually for one of two reasons—to steal bosses, loot, or kill someone while they were compromised.

"Weaklings! You dare to try and take what is mine!" The voice echoed from all around us, that dread in my guts twisting a little tighter.

Then I spotted a figure ahead and to the right, merging almost flawlessly with the shadows. They stepped forward, revealing an elven man, the light from the firestorms revealing shimmering gold robes. Shining red embroidery scrolled over the garment, creating a tapestry of geometric shapes and patterns.

The elf snapped his fingers and the monster exploded into a fine mist and instantly dispelled our firestorm. He approached, exuding power beyond anything I had felt since arriving at Zenith. I tried to rationalize his cultivation ability, his power level, and his intentions, but it all felt beyond me. *He* was beyond us, many times over.

"That was our *kill!*" Chloe snapped, stepping forward. She clutched her sword tightly at her side, and I immediately wondered if she was picking the wrong fight.

My gaze finally broke free from the elf's robes, allowing it to slowly slide up over his face, and—blood-red hair and pointy ears. He was... pretty in a way that made me uncomfortable, as he was clearly a man. He was tall, lean, but well-muscled, with smooth, attractive facial features. If he lived on earth, I was sure he'd be able to steal pageants from equally pretty ladies.

"No, stop! He is a blood elf!" Mabel whispered, tugging at Chloe's sleeves and trying to pull her back. "He is the heir to the house my family has served for centuries!"

I froze, my blood immediately boiling in my veins. Who in the hell did this ass think he was to take what was ours? No... I was getting ahead of myself. He probably thought he was a *particularly important* someone—with his fancy clothes, his snobbish attitude, and his freaking slaves.

Elven slaves. Mabel. Shit!

"Hey, I'm sorry, my guy," I said, stepping up to Chloe and pulling her back. "I think we got off on the wrong foot here. You see, we attacked that giant, skittering critter first! The lady is right. That monster belonged to us!"

"Oh?" he asked, elevating his nose to a characteristically snobbish angle. "It didn't belong to you *three*, it belonged to *one* of you. In particular, the *one* who did the most damage. In this case, it was you, pen-blader. But since you never formed a party, the overall damage rule applies, which means that it's *my* kill."

I sucked air in through my teeth, fighting to control my temper. But it was so... damned... hard, especially the way he emphasized words and drew them out.

"Never heard of *that* rule," I spat, dropping an H-bomb of emphasis on the word 'that'. "And I suppose *that* means you can just come and take whatever you want? Aren't you a little strong for this place?"

"Oh, the questions," he snickered. "Yes, I am stronger than you. So, that *does* mean I can take whatever I want, from whomever I please. As for this paltry dungeon, well, you can always go to lower floors, even if it is miles beneath you... ability-wise."

The loathing, condescension, and malice practically dripped off his voice. He hated us, he hated the beast we had just been fighting, and the dungeon in which we stood. But his pleasure seemed to stem directly from lording his power over us... like every other bully. No matter how much things changed, they always seemed to stay the same.

"Please, Master Emron," Mabel pleaded. "We aren't hurting anyone, and we didn't mean disrespect."

He narrowed his eyes on her and took a step forward. I put up my pen-blade, stopping him in his tracks. His smirk just pissed me off even more. It said—I'm amused, not threatened.

Sure, maybe he was stronger than me, but that didn't mean I had to back down. It was one thing having to bow and scrape back on earth, subjugating myself to the all-mighty dollar and those that had more than two of them to rub together, but this? I was going to make a future for myself here. I was going to do more than just survive.

"It appears that your little *human* friend wants me to back down, Mabel. It's clear he doesn't understand how things work around here. That he doesn't know how insignificant you three truly are."

"Insignificant." I spat, but he continued, talking over me.

"I thought when your mother died that you had learned your place. Maybe you had learned from *her* example. But no. You've started rebelling again. How... sad."

"I am not rebelling, Emron. This is the academy! I don't serve you here! At least not until I have finished my studies!"

I grabbed Mabel's hand and gave it a reassuring squeeze, showing her she wasn't alone. The poor girl trembled in fear, her hand shaking and mana practically bleeding off her skin.

"Studies," the elf sneered, "The idea of teaching a moon elf anything is laughable. Your mother didn't understand her place and look where it got her. If you are... how about that? I almost said 'smart'." Emron said his horrible sneer like a mask I longed to peel off.

"If you are *smart* you will learn your place. But if you wish to be mistreated even worse once the academy is over, then simply continue along this path. Here, let me give you a glimpse of what awaits you when your time here is done."

Mabel flinched, her hand reaching out to him, almost as if he had somehow silently compelled her. I bared my teeth, jumped in front of her, and blocked him.

143

"Who in the flaming Cheeto farts do you think you are?" I spat, my hand holding the pen-blade shaking at my side. "For someone that carries himself with an air of ridiculous importance and sophistication, you sure are an unsophisticated bag of rotten dicks. Learn some manners, fucker! Mabel is smart and talented, and from everything I've seen around here, a far better elf than you."

I lifted my pen-blade, arm shaking, teeth bared. But Emron didn't attack. Nor did he shout back at me. He just frowned, his arrogant sneer turning to confusion.

"A bag of rotten dicks?" he whispered as if silently working out what that was.

"Yes, sir. Diseased, stinking, and rotten. In a word... putrid. And your hair is stupid. Your father is a zombie, and your mother is a banshee!" I honestly didn't know what else to say, as I was so driven by anger. But his hair pissed me off. It looked like a wig from a Strawberry Shortcake Halloween costume. And not a good one either, but one of the super cheap ones you bought at a gas station.

"Stupid? My family... is holy!" he snarled.

It appeared that I finally touched a nerve. Why is it always the hair?

"Do you know who I am?"

"Leonard Landy? The red-headed kid from Little Rascals?"

"I am Emron of house Harken and that elf," he growled, pointing right at Mabel, "is my property! You petty earthling! You should be grateful we even allowed your kind to mingle with ours, allowed you to come here at all!"

My mind whirled as he raised his hand, mana gathering around his open palm. I started visualizing my defenses, planning my first frantic brush strokes. But before I could raise the pen-blade two searing bolts of lightning struck the ground between us. The intense light and heat pushed us both back, the hair on my arms and neck standing on end.

144

Mistresses Scarlet and Salina were standing between us when I put down my arms. Scarlet held her staff up toward Emron, while Salina held one out towards us.

"Stop bickering at this instant!" the headmistress snapped. "I have already warned you once, Emron. Your aggression towards other students stops today!"

"Step back, you three," Salina whispered, gesturing for us to move. "This isn't a fight you can win. Not by a long shot."

I lowered my pen-blade and stepped back, taking care to keep the girls behind me. I felt them both bristling, but whereas Chloe seethed with rage, Mabel was practically catatonic with fear.

What a monster! What a creep! What a... horrible person. I vowed silently to protect the two girls behind me. No matter the stakes. No matter the personal harm. I had never managed to stand up to bullies before, but here? I would do whatever it took to gain the strength needed.

"Mistress," Emron hissed. "This pale grubworm made a slight against my family, my name, my hair. You know our ways. Our code. You wouldn't want to displease my father, would you?"

"I think it's you who should be thinking about your father. I already contacted him, you see. He knows that I will kill you if you harm any more of my students. Now run along, little prince. Your family is pressing on my last nerve."

Scarlet didn't sound angry, but she didn't sound amused, either. Honestly, I think that made her sound more frightening. I knew I was dense and lacked situational awareness, but watching Scarlet and Emron stare each down scared me even more. He'd killed the boss cockroach with a snap of his fingers—after we'd softened it up for him. You're welcome, d-bag. And Scarlet didn't look intimidated. Part of me wanted to push the girls back before the two titans started picking up mountains to throw at one another.

Emron moved first, his eyes sliding towards the cockroach corpse. He took a step and reached for it, just as Scarlet tsked and shook her head.

"Nope. Not today, Emron. Move along."

"What?" he asked. "You expect me to leave my loot to these plebs?"

"They tagged the boss and did first damage. And a considerable chunk, at that. Get lost before I lose my cool."

Emron's eyes flicked from Scarlet to me, and then back again. We had made an enemy for life, I just knew it. It was something I couldn't afford to take lightly. If he had ties to Mabel, and his family was as horrible as they sounded, our time at Zenith was going to get very interesting.

As if I needed more incentive to get stronger.

"I won't forget this, trust me. And I'll be seeing you around, human. Mabel."

Emron snapped his fingers and disappeared without so much as a sound. I let out a breath I didn't realize I'd been holding. Then I cursed as Scarlet burst out in laughter. Theoretically, it wasn't our fault, but I might have poured some fuel on the fire... especially with the comment about his hair.

"I hope you know what you just did," Scarlet said after putting away her staff. "You just made a blood enemy, JD. And a strong one at that. Emron's family is one of the oldest and strongest of his race. The blood elves are not kind people, nor do they have short memories. But you stood your ground. I can admire a man who shows bravery against overwhelming odds. And one who fights for what is his... possession or acquaintance. How romantic."

I grumbled something about liking a challenge but was too busy trying to piece together a strategy for... not dying via murder.

Scarlet chuckled and nodded, sizing me up. "You're so cute, all three of you."

"Headmistress," I said, finally able to break away from the daunting task of staying alive. But Salina cut in.

"Emron not only insulted our academy, but I'm fairly sure he just admitted to wanting at least one of these three dead. When are you going to deal with him properly? He is going to bring shame or disaster down on us all."

146

"Enough, Salina!" Scarlet hissed. "I will handle it!"

Stunned by her outburst, I didn't even see Salina disappear. She was just there one moment and gone in the next. A faint cloud of mana hung where she had been standing.

"Thank you, Headmistress. I think you would have had at least one more corpse to deal with if you hadn't arrived when you did." I flashed her as honest a smile as I could summon, but damn, that woman scared me. I wasn't sure if it was her unpredictable mood or that red glint in her eyes. Or both.

She shrugged and favored me with a wink.

"He should not have been here. It is as simple as that. Perhaps he was on his way back from a higher dungeon and happened upon you, or he was *slumming* it in the lower dungeons. I don't know. Either way, Emron has been prowling lately, slinking about like a cat, looking to poo in a place he's not supposed to. And from the looks of that core drop, I'm guessing this beast might have been carrying what he was looking for."

I turned to the monster's corpse, only to see an even larger core waiting for us. It was as long as my arm and dark brown. A haunting, gray light pulsed from within.

"Can we take it?" I asked, silently craving its promised strength. Sure, we might not have killed it, but it was just as she said: we tagged it. Who was to say that our firestorm wouldn't have finished off the beast, had Emron-what's-his-nuts not stepped in?

"Go ahead," Scarlet said, gesturing dismissively at the core. "I feel the need to tell you something. We have been running through this dungeon for a while now, but none could get above ninety-five percent completion. It appears you three found that missing five percent. Consider that core special. I'm sure of it. Don't waste it on cultivation, keep it for now."

"We will, Mistress," Chloe said, bowing. "And thank you."

"Don't mention it. Truly. I hate excessive gratitude. I dealt with Emron because that is my job as headmistress. But tell me, why are you three hunting together? I can understand JD and

147

Chloe, as they have been roomed together. But you, Mabel? You know pairing with humans will only bring you more animosity from your people."

"I... there were..." Mabel stammered.

"It is okay, no need to explain. I'm only glad you took the initiative and found these two. That is half the reason why I intervened. I very much would like to see the three of you grow stronger, and perhaps, form a real party."

"Wouldn't that bind us to the same dorm? And to each other?" Mabel asked.

I had no idea what that meant, but for some reason, the idea of "binding" people felt oddly permanent. If that was the case, was I ready for that kind of commitment? I looked over to Chloe and Mabel and felt my curiosity deepen. First, I needed to know more and then I'd decide.

Scarlet nodded and I immediately feared that I was in the dark on something my two female counterparts understood. Why? Well, for starters, Chloe looked quite flustered. She was shy about important or decisive matters, and she was holding back now. My curiosity turned into anxiety.

"It does. You will have to move into Chloe and JD's dorm. Then the three of you can formalize the party. Here, take this," Scarlet said, a glowing sheet of parchment appearing above her outstretched hand. "Read this contract. Every line. Then follow the instructions at the bottom. I will know when it is signed."

I accepted the parchment from the headmistress and stashed it safely into my rift. Right next to my pen-blade.

ITEMS RECEIVED:
Party Contract: 1

SPECIAL ITEMS RECEIVED:
Hulker Gargantua Core: 1

I read the two messages. Another named core. Well, how about that? If I didn't know any better, I'd say that they were pretty common. Or... we might have been in the middle of a rather lucky streak. Who knew?

"So, Mabel can move in with us?" I asked, typically slow on the uptake. "If we agree on it and she wants to, I mean."

"Yes," Scarlet said, her voice breathy and almost bored. "Emron will make trouble for her wherever she goes...that is, whether she is with you or not. But she will be protected in the VIP dorms, thanks to the limited access. I very much want to see you stay safe, Mabel, as Emron's violent appetites have already proven difficult to manage."

Then Scarlet turned to me, and I jumped, startled by the amber glow in her eyes.

"I am entrusting her safety to you, JD. Mabel's mother was my good friend. Do not make me have to mourn her daughter, too. She deserves a real chance. All of you do."

"I will do my best," I said, taken aback by her intensity. My stomach twisted on itself as I made the promise. How would I do it? That was the question. Because I had to keep the three of us safe and... this was a big "and" do my best to help her get stronger *and* shed her fear of Emron and the other blood elves. If I could empower her, then we would all be better for it.

"*We* will do *our* best," Chloe said, echoing my sentiment and making her support for me known to the public. Then, in a move that surprised the hell out of me, she put her arm around Mabel and pulled her close.

"I am warmed," Scarlet said, but her smile faded, "But there is just one problem."

"Which one, headmistress?" I asked, trying to guess what came next. "A favor for a favor?"

Scarlet's eyebrows rose along with the corners of her mouth. Damn. She looked even more dangerous than she did when she was mad.

"You won't have enough room... for now, but once you have gathered the necessary ingredients you can upgrade your dorm. Then you can add the space to accommodate a third person."

"Does that mean she'll have to sleep in one of our beds?" Chloe asked. "I don't mind, though. I can bunk with JD, and she can take my bed."

"It is your... sleeping arrangement to manage," Scarlet sniggered. "But don't tell anyone about your room level. It's against the rules. Just so you know, I like underdogs. They make for the best stories. I'll be keeping my eyes on you three." Scarlet winked and snapped her fingers, disappearing in a small cloud of red mana.

I immediately walked to where she had just stood and searched the ground as if there might be some magical trapdoor in the ground.

I looked up to Chloe, and together we said, "Freaking magic."

"I can't lie," I said and scratched my beard, "I don't like this new development, but I won't back down either. We'll make it work, Mabel."

"Go get the rest of the loot before it disappears," Chloe said, not giving the moon elf the time to respond. "I think it would be best if we headed back to our dorm and talked this through. The party contract, the rooming situation, the cores we've gained today, and the murderous blood elf."

She sounded tense, which at least matched how I felt. Hell, if my guts wound any together, knots would start to appear beneath the skin. Mabel hovered between us, evidently unsure about whether to move or speak. So, she danced from foot to foot.

I walked over to our dead cockroach friend, giggled excitedly, and read the prompt as it appeared in the air.

ITEMS RECEIVED:
Hulker Gargantua: 1
Core crystal Rank 1: 14
Core crystal Rank 2: 5

Fres: 673

"Shit, we just got another 5 rank 2 crystals and 14 rank 1's. I think we need to consider this a highly successful start to our little party's dungeon diving career."

"We have more than enough for that formation now," Mabel said, her voice a tense whisper. "When do you guys want to absorb the core?"

"Let's not get ahead of ourselves," Chloe interjected. "We'll talk about it when we get back, but we should first wait until after we've completed our basic cultivation classes. There's no need to hurry anyway."

Chloe sounded different when she spoke. I wouldn't go as far as to say she sounded pissy, but there was definitely something there. Fear? Apprehension? Jealousy? Then I realized we were potentially adding another female to our dorm room. And although we'd become pretty close very quickly, I had to consider that Chloe was wondering if I was already looking to replace her.

Well, shit. I'd have to talk to her about it as soon as we got back. Openly and honestly.

CASH OR CARD?

WE MADE OUR WAY back up through the bramble and onto the main road. We half expected to find more monsters, until a small display appeared.

ALL BOSSES ARE CURRENTLY DEAD.
TIME UNTIL NEXT SPAWN - 01:13:58

"I take it that our walk back will be much quieter!" I said as Chloe and Mabel looked in to read.

"I think we should talk about the monster drops now before we get back," I said, as the tower exit came into view. Money was a topic no one liked, but it needed to be discussed. Especially when we all had an equal stake. Better to tear that bandage off fast and hard.

"Sell it," Chloe said. "We can live off the proceeds for a month. Maybe use some of it to furnish our dorm, get new clothes, more food, necessities, and so on."

"I agree," Mabel added. "If we are going to be together moving forward... uh, as a party, that is, it seems like the most practical course to spend it on our dwelling."

Dwelling? I watched Mabel talk. She had a way with words, an innocence, that, mixed with her honey-sweet voice and dimples, made her oh so adorable.

I nodded.

"Then we all agree. We're selling some stuff and buying some different stuff! Let's do this!"

I started making a mental shopping list, but there were simply too many unknown variables. For example, what if I decided to take up crafting as my specialty? What would I need to buy to get me started there? Would we have to buy our own toiletries, armor, repair, and upkeep on our weapons? Could I buy a magical pet? Because, yes, I really wanted a magical pet. Something small. No, larger... and maybe have it breathe fire. Oh, or walk-in shadows to help me sneak into places I wasn't supposed to be. My god, the freaking possibilities!

"JD!" Chloe said, jabbing me in the ribs.

"Wha...?" I stammered.

"You just went completely blank. I think you kind of started drooling."

"Oh," I laughed, swiping at my mouth. Thank god, no drool. "I just started thinking about all the steps that we need to take next and kind of... well, I got lost in my thoughts."

"Let's put it all on the table when we get back," she suggested, and together we passed through the portal and appeared in the tavern. The place looked just as it had before... literally. I think there was even the same number of people sitting around drinking and talking. Part of me wanted to walk up to them and see if they were NPC's.

Is that a thing here?

The sisters greeted us cheerfully as we walked up to the counter.

"Greetings and salutations, JD," Belma chuckled. "We are glad to see you survived."

"Hi, Belma, right?"

"Certainly! See, this butterfly here is Selma. She doesn't like to wear tight clothing, like me. That alone should help you tell us apart."

"We're wearing the same outfit!" Selma said, slapping her sister's shoulder and pushing her aside.

"Right," I replied, stepping away from the counter. Nothing like stepping into the midst of a real, sister-on-sister spat. "I like both of your outfits, ladies."

"Nevermind her, young JD," Belma said, squeezing back in. "What can I do for you and the ladies? Do you have some loot to sell?"

"As a matter of fact, we do!" I said and moved to pull the corpses free. Well, I tried to, but it wouldn't let me. Instead, small squares appeared in front of the two women, the corpses stored neatly inside.

"Oh, you found all the spoils," Belma laughed. But it was strange... her humor, her demeanor. It felt as if the sisters weren't used to conversing with people. Or, humans, for that matter.

"Is that normal?" I asked, pointing at the nearest translucent square. "That the corpses are in those?"

"Why, yes. Perfectly normal," Selma answered. "Wait, did you think that you would have to cart around the bodies of dead, five-ton-creatures?"

"Umm, no?" I replied honestly. I had no idea what to think of other than that they would appear...somehow. Burnt and quartered. And shredded. I sighed. "So, what now?"

I pulled the glowing cubes from my rift and placed them on the counter. The pile looked relatively small now, but I did catch a glint in the two sisters' eyes. They looked quite happy with the catch.

"Can we get the meat from the Gargantua?" I asked.

"Just the Gargantua?" Belma asked. "Why not the others?"

"Well, I'm no vegan," I replied stoically but immediately noticed their confusion. "It means I love meat, not plants."

"Silly," Belma chuckled. "The Venus Queen's meat is highly sought after. Trust me, after one bite you'll be itching to come back and hunt her again!"

"You said her meat," I said, "I thought she was a plant?"

"You earthlings are adorable. It's always one thing or another with you. Creatures are different here. You'll see," Belma said and winked once. "How about this? I will butcher it all for you, at no cost, but divide it into two portions. Selma and I will take half, as payment for the labor. The rest goes to you. If you like it, which I know that you will, we can negotiate a rate for the next time. Deal?"

I looked at both Chloe and Mabel, but they didn't seem to have any objections.

"Yes, please. What about the rest? How much can we get for the usable components?"

"Give me a few grains of sand and I will tell you," Selma said as she pulled an hourglass out from beneath the counter, turned it over, and then slapped on some strange-looking goggles. The items moved from hand to hand while Belma started scratching a quill against a long piece of parchment.

"Alright. You have a total of **31** Venus Loranas, **12** Swapper Flies, and **3** Hulkers. Also, there is a Venus Lorana Queen, a Mutated Swapper Fly, and finally a Hulker Gargantua."

Numbers appeared in the air around the sisters as they spoke, glowing brightly to match the spoken words. I found my eyes flicking up as they appeared, only to glance back at their faces. It was strange and horribly distracting.

"That sounds about right," Chloe replied, as I counted the squares quickly.

"What are they worth?" Mabel asked.

"Venus Lorana bring anywhere between **10** and **100** Fres, per corpse. You have more bad than good corpses, so we'll give you a batch price of **1,500** Fres for those. The Swappers are worth the same money. They were pretty beat up, so I can only offer you

500. As for the Hulkers, they were in pristine condition, and I can give you top Fres for them. **1,200**."

More numbers appeared in the air between us, popping like fireworks.

I did some quick, mental ninja math. "So, that comes out at **3,200**, right?"

"Exactly. As for the mini-boss corpses, the Queen goes for anywhere between **1,000** to **10,000**. The Mutated Swapper— **1,500** to **6,000** as it isn't as rare, and the Gargantua, well, that beauty is worth anywhere from **15,000** to **50,000**. Yours was severely burnt and partially disintegrated, so you'll only get the low end of that."

I felt my eyebrows rise, my surprise and excitement building at the numbers she was throwing around.

"Is that a good offer?" I whispered, leaning into Chloe and Mabel.

"I think so," Chloe hissed back. "This place will almost always pay out on the lower end. But they buy everything. And if we sell enough stuff, we can rise in levels and get better prices. Later, we can always shop around in the bazaar. Some might offer better prices, but there are no guarantees."

"Oh?" I asked and turned to Mabel. She nodded in silent agreement. The girls and I turned back to find the sisters leaning on the counter, listening in.

"That's right," Selma said.

"Once you've sold a total of **500,000** Fres in goods we extend a **10%** discount on future purchases and **+10%** on the price you get from us," Belma added, "That is why you want to do all your buying and selling through us, right?!" she said, raising and lowering her eyebrows in almost comical fashion. I couldn't tell if she was hitting on me or an animatronic person struggling through a bad software update.

"Enough, sis," Selma hissed and slapped her sister right on the ass. The *slap* echoed loudly around the whole tavern. "JD, we can have your meat ready in ten minutes if you agree with the prices."

I nodded. "I'll take the deal. So, I'm getting **23,200** Fres and the meat?"

"Exactly," Selma replied. "Would you like it on a card or in coin?"

"Card?" I asked, confused.

"They're a bit different than credit cards," Chloe explained. "You carry the money inside these cards instead of keeping it in a bank. This is way more convenient."

"And where can I pay with the card? Everywhere inside the tower?"

"No, only in here," Belma explained. "But keep in mind, the more money that goes onto your card, the quicker you'll move towards the next level. Only the money inside the card is counted towards the VIP services we provide."

I stared at her, troubling over exactly how to break it up. Was there interest? Small print? I'd had some bad experiences with credit cards in my old life and I sure as hell wasn't going to bring those same troubles here. Mabel shifted between her feet and Chloe started tapping her toe against the ground. I understood the message—decide.

"Put **10,000** on the card," I said, the number glowing to life between us. "And give me the rest in coin. Is that doable?"

Selma nodded and immediately started molding and shaping a small slab of stone. Her mana flowed in and around the slab, thinning and straightening it until it was roughly the height and length of my ID. The main difference was, this was made out of stone and was about as thick as my finger.

"I am happy to have received your patronage, JD," she said and offered me the card. I plucked it from her outstretched hand, a screen appearing above it.

CARD BALANCE
*F*10,000

"Okay. That is pretty cool," I said, stowing it securely into my rift.

Then Selma dropped a sack onto the counter. "And here is the rest."

Chloe picked it up and gave it a hearty shake, the merry sound of jingling coins filling the air.

"Hah I like the sound of this," I said, accepting the bag and pulling it open. 13,200 Fres. There were several different kinds of coins in the sack, and as my eyes fell on each in turn, their name and value appeared in the air. I saw **5** coins worth **1,000** Fres each, then **10** of **500** Fres, **10** of **250** Fres, and the last **7** appeared to be of the **100** Fres variety.

I stashed the pouch away just as Belma hefted a small wooden box onto the counter. It was roughly the size of a shoebox, with brass hinges, and a highly polished finish. I moved to lift it and found it much heavier than the pouch. My hand slid across the lacquered wood and the top popped open.

SPECIAL ITEMS RECEIVED:
Venus Lorana Queen Steak: 5
Gargantua Steak: 7

"Thanks, ladies." I stored the box in my rift and turned to Chloe and Mabel. "Shall we?"

The girls grabbed an arm each, and while Chloe did give Mabel a bit of side-eye, we made our way back out of the tavern.

"First things first. I have a debt to repay," I said and pulled out **3,200** Fres. I dropped them into Chloe's outstretched hand. She excitedly stashed them away.

"I'm not gonna say no to money, lover boy. We can't live on an empty stomach."

"No, we can't," I said and turned to Mabel. I pulled out **2,000** Fres, and gently pushed it into her hands. She fought me for a moment, and the coins almost fell free.

158

"No, JD, please. I don't need the money and I'm... very humble. I don't really have needs."

Chloe swooped in and grabbed her hand, closing it around the money.

"You are a fucking keeper, Mabel," Chloe cooed, "A girl that doesn't need money for make-up and that superficial crap because she's already so beautiful. As if the ears weren't enough."

Chloe turned to me, looking for my confirmation, but I didn't give it. I couldn't tell if she was trying to flatter the elf or put her on the spot. Part of me was still trying to figure her out.

"I'm not fucking around," Chloe whispered when I didn't respond. "We need to make sure the others regret losing her, right?"

"Yeah, right. They'll come running but it will be too late," Mabel said, but I gathered that she didn't fully understand what we were talking about. I was more concerned with keeping her safe from that flame-haired psychopath and his power trip.

"Exactly. And for that, we need a little help. You're fine with that, aren't you, JD? Having two fine ladies by your side? I mean, a guy is willing to pay for quality, right?"

I chuckled, but my heart wasn't in it. I wondered if Chloe was building Mabel up as a way to keep her mind off the encounter earlier. The idea that we... okay, I had maybe started a potentially violent feud with a blood elf family.

"I want to get Mabel out of her old dorm and moved in with us. And I would like to do it as soon as possible. Then we can go shopping."

"I vote to get cleaned up first!" Chloe said, "I'm not feeling the blood and guts I'm wearing right now.".

"Mabel?"

"I can get cleaned back in the dorm. When I'm done, I'll wait for you inside my room. Just knock..." Mabel paused and thought for a second, "twice, then pause, then knock twice again."

"The weapon dorms?" I asked.

"Yes. Room one hundred and thirteen."

159

I nodded and flashed her my warmest smile. She returned it, but the smile didn't meet her eyes. Why? Did she think we weren't serious about taking her in? Had she been abandoned before? The questions immediately started to pile up.

"Don't worry, Mabel. We'll be there..." I started to say, but Chloe spoke up.

"Why doesn't she stay in our room while we get cleaned up? Then we can all go to her dorm together. Emron has had time to get a head start. He's likely already planning to cause trouble, especially if she were to go alone."

"I don't think that is a good idea," Mabel whispered. "Not yet at least. Not until we have had a chance to look at the party contract."

"Then what about the benches in front of the VIP dorms?" I asked. "You can wait there. I doubt he'd do anything in front of that place."

"I don't love it, but it will work," Chloe replied. "And when we get there, you don't fucking move no matter what. And if someone tries to mess with you, you get us. Got it?"

Mabel nodded silently. That hollow, dark look continued to haunt her eyes, and it only served to make me angry again.

We exited the tavern and immediately made our way toward the VIP dorms. Several groups of students milled around, but no one seemed all that interested in us—even after seeing that an elf was walking openly together with the only two humans.

Mabel melted onto the bench as we arrived, her arms wrapping around the armrest as if she was afraid a sudden wind might kick up and carry her away.

"I'll...be here."

"Mabel, you've got us now, alright?" I said, kneeling beside her. Although with the inherent bias against humans in the academy, I didn't know if that truly made her feel better. "Don't worry about that asshole. Just block out what he said. We are going to watch each other's backs, get stronger, and show them that we are not to be trifled with. I promise."

160

Her tight frown softened a bit, but there was no smile, no brightening of the hollowness in her eyes. It was going to have to be enough for now.

"Go, I'm fine. I'll be waiting."

Chloe grabbed my hand and pulled me towards our dorm. She wrenched our door open, pulled me through, and slammed it shut behind us. We were already halfway to the bath when a thought struck me.

"Chloe, where does that bastard live? He is somewhere in the tower, correct?"

"Yes," she said, already starting to strip off her clothes. "Somewhere above, on one of the other floors. The upperclassmen live up there. Why?"

"Does he have access to this floor?"

"Not unless Scarlet permits him. And judging from their encounter, I don't think she is likely to do that any time soon."

"Do you think he has family in this academy? Perhaps a little brother?" I asked, my thoughts immediately spinning back to the night I arrived. There had been another red-haired elf... shit maybe more than one.

"Maybe. I don't know everyone's familial connections. Let's not risk it. Hurry up," she said, sliding the rest of the way out of her clothes.

I followed suit, tossing my dirties onto the same pile, then we jumped into the water. It was less a bath, and more a cannonball contest. We scrubbed frantically, getting as much mud and caked blood as we could, then rinsed and were done.

We got out of the bathroom and Chloe tiptoed over to the closet, snagging clothes for us both. Someone must have restocked our closets while we were out. Handy.

Chloe helped me get dressed and then I helped her, but we both slipped and slid on the wet ground. I caught my balance, but she sprawled, and I just managed to catch her. She playfully slapped my chest, kissed my cheek, and pushed free.

"Come on, she's still waiting."

161

I stopped Chloe and pulled her back for a moment.

"Do you like her?"

"Why wouldn't I?" she asked, obviously confused.

"It has only been a few days, but it has just been you and me in here. If she stays with us, everything will get a bit more crowded. Plus, you know, she's an elf. I also think she... likes me," I said, not intending to say the last part. But shit, it just toppled out of my mouth.

"Pfft!" Chloe spat, blowing an exaggerated raspberry. "Don't flatter yourself," she chuckled, which grew into a full-on laugh. I felt my insides twist up and my cheeks grow hot.

"Got you there," she said, coming forward and poking me in the belly. "It is fine. We'll make it work. And yes, I'm sure she does like you. You're cute and usually smell nice. Which is more than I can say about a lot of the guys I've known."

I pushed out a breath, letting the anger release. Holy crap, it flared quickly! It was yet another reminder of how little I knew about my new... roommate... battle buddy... girlfriend? Hell, I didn't even know how to define what we had.

"Got nothing better to do than to pick on the newbie?"

"Aww, come on! You clearly showed you ain't no noob. And in case you forgot, I already..." Chloe nodded back to the bath, and the spot where we had formed our dual cultivation connection.

"That's right," I joked, "I almost forgot. You'll have to refresh my memory."

"As if..." she scoffed and pulled on a fresh pair of slippers. "But fine. You want my take? Here it is. Elves are usually so stuck up that they can't play nice with others. That is what I've heard, at least. I doubt she'll fit in with us, but I am willing to make an exception for two... no, three reasons."

"Oh? And those are?" I asked, coming up behind her, spinning her around, and pushing her against the wall. Then I leaned in close, pressing our bodies together.

162

"I like where this is going, but should we be doing it now?" Chloe purred.

"No, we shouldn't, but you *should* tell me your reasons."

"Simple. One, she's a support, which is exceedingly rare. People don't like playing support, so she is a natural fit with us. Two, you already know her, and I think I like her. She's easy to please, which is important. And thirdly, she's subservient, so I won't have to worry about her stealing you away. If anyone's going to do something, it will be *you* doing *things* to her."

"Oh, come on!" I protested. "We're not even married and you're already making a priest out of me!"

"Priest? JD, haven't you noticed? Maybe take a moment to ask yourself why I made such an effort to bond with you so quickly? There are at least five women here to every man, and that is just this academy. Some are worse. This is the truth. Men are scarce here... talented men more so... and cute, fuckable guys, well, you're kind of a unicorn."

"You have a point there," I muttered. "But damn, where did I put my horn?"

Just then she reached down between my legs and firmly grabbed my dick.

"Careful, lady, they say a unicorn's power comes from its horn. If you handle it wrong, it just might go off. Lucky for you I have the self-control of a deity!"

"Pffft! Really? A deity?" Chloe flashed me a grin and shook her head, showing me all her pearly-white teeth. They were perfect, every single one of them.

"How about you put this away," she said, teasing me back and forth, "and we go get our elf damsel in distress? I'm worried she might be getting cold feet."

We walked out of our dorm and into the circular corridor. Mabel was still sitting on the bench, alone, with her face buried in her hands. I felt sorry for the elf. Slavery was something I knew of, but nothing I had ever experience personally. What must it feel

163

like to be owned? Hell, what would it feel like to have your entire family owned by someone else?

"We're done, Mabel," Chloe said, kneeling next to the girl. "You alright? Do you need more time?"

The elf shook her head weakly and got up, pulling Chloe up with her.

"No, I need to get the hell out of there. That's all I care about now. Getting away from them."

"We're right here at your side, alright? We'll be with you the whole way—two promising first-years, both wielding legendary weapons, escorting their elf friend, Mabel. We won't be taking shit from anyone!"

"You're silly," Mabel chuckled as she looked up at Chloe. "But we just got here and are years behind almost everyone else. What can the three of us do?"

"Much more than any of us can alone," I said.

Tears appeared in the corners of Mabel's eyes, as she nodded, stoically. I turned her towards me, reached up, and wiped the tears away. Chloe stared at us intently, but she didn't say anything. I kissed her forehead, pulled her in for an embrace, and whispered into her ear. "You're one of us now. Don't forget that."

"Friends?" Mabel whispered back.

I nodded. "Friends." I held my right arm up and Chloe pushed in, throwing her arms around me and sandwiching Mabel between us.

We broke apart and Mabel wiped her face dry.

Chloe pulled something from her rift. It looked suspiciously like a mascara pen. She helped the elf correct her make-up and then promptly stashed it away again. A brush came out next, and then...yeah, they primped one another. I stood off to one side and tried to not look... bored.

"Friends forever, alright?" Chloe asked, as they finally finished.

Mabel nodded, then leaned in and whispered something in Chloe's ear. I couldn't hear, so instead, I watched their faces. My

164

blonde counterpart scowled, then smirked, and finally fell into that infectious and strangely sexy chuckle.

"You two, no whispering when other people are around! It is so rude!" I scolded and made to leave. The girls stuck their tongues out and ran off.

"Catch us if you can!"

"Damn it," I muttered and set off after them.

I caught up several minutes later. But not because I was faster. No. While they were running, screaming, and chasing one another around the massive, circular space, I walked patiently. Eventually, they came around again. Work smarter, not harder. Another of my mottos.

We approached the dorm together, only to find a small group of elves clustered outside. Several had pale skin and silvery hair, while the others had the telltale scarlet red locks. More blood elves? Shit. Not now!

"... and I'm not the only one who thinks that way," one of the reds said as I stopped behind them.

I was a head taller, so it was hard to miss me. Someone in their group hissed at the speaker, while others "pretended" not to see me. Although I had no idea what they were talking about, I felt Mabel bristle. Apparently, she knew.

"That's a fucking lie, and you know it!" my downtrodden elf friend cursed, but her voice was weak.

"What's wrong?" I asked, pushing past them and getting up into the face of the red-haired elf. "Do you have something to say to my girls?"

"What? Your girls? Pfft! Serves a moon elf right to end up a human's girl!" he laughed and looked around at his supporters. Some sniggered and laughed, although it sounded forced. I was bolstered to see that not everyone seemed to agree.

Bullies were bullies, no matter the color of their skin or the shape of their ears. Unfortunately, it appeared that the blood elves were an entire race of stuffy pricks. The bad behavior and manners,

165

notwithstanding, were not an exclusive trait to that anal worm Emron.

I sniffed, taking in a pungent odor. It wafted from the elf's hair and his clothes. It wasn't pleasant... kind of like burning tires and Indian food. And that shouldn't be taken as a slight against Indian food. I love me a good Butter Chicken or Curry. But this... not good.

I stepped even closer to the offensive prick, quickly growing numb to the stench. I puffed out my chest and bumped into him, getting right into his face. He didn't seem to like me being so close and stepped back, scowling and narrowing his eyes. I wasn't a fighter, but I had learned quickly in High School that bullies were often running off bluster if little else. Yeah, I did get beat up a lot, though. Can't win them all.

"Listen up, you cocky piece of shit!" I hissed. "Mabel is a sweet, kind, and wonderful person. I don't know why you Cherry Kool-Aid-haired snob-jobs are so desperate to drag her down to your level, but it isn't going to work. She's too good to stoop to your games. But you know what? I'm not. If you want to get your hands dirty, feel free to have a go at me." I bumped the blood elf bully back, the heat growing on my neck and face. My knuckles popped, and I realized then that they were balled up into fists. I had never been more ready for a fight.

The blood elf sneered and lifted his nose, baring his teeth.

"Is that a yes? Otherwise, get the fuck out of our way! You're wasting our time."

"Wasting your time? You're just a filthy human... barely better than a dirty ape..."

My hands snapped out and I pushed him back. He stumbled and tripped, his friends catching him before he could fall. He gathered himself and straightened his robe, all the while licking his lips. His eyes darted from me to Mabel, and then back at me again.

"You're a dead man, human. A very dead man." But he turned and disappeared down the dorm's hallway. I stood and watched him go, my body trembling from the rage. I gambled and called the bully on his bluff. This time I won, but fortune wouldn't favor me forever. Especially when I had to consider someone like Emron and his power.

I wasn't liked, and to be honest, I could live with that. People hated what they didn't understand, and I didn't have the time or the patience to bring the other races up to speed on what it meant to be human. And quite frankly, I didn't think they cared to know, anyway. We were going to have to learn to march to the beat of our own drum.

"Just imagine if we hadn't come with you," Chloe whispered. "Come on. Where's your room? Let's get packed and get out of here."

"Seven doors down," Mabel whispered.

Where had all of my self-confidence come from? I mean, I wasn't a cowering wreck before, but I wasn't someone who was going to stare down a bunch of renegade elves. Was this just the new me? The academy me? Or was I experiencing perks from my pairing with Chloe? Ahh, too many freaking questions.

"You go first," Chloe whispered. "We'll be a step behind you."

"Let's hurry. Let's not give them a chance to find some more courage and come back. Just grab your stuff and come with us. You can take a bath back at our place."

There were at least forty-to-fifty students milling around, staring at us. Some did so in admiration for standing up against the bullies, but others wanted to get on the blood elves' good side and stared daggers at us. I heard them mutter threats and call us names. I kept it all in and would do so for a while longer. If we fucked up here, it would mostly hurt Mabel.

I could stand their looks... their petty names. Hell, they could scold or yell at me. I'd even take a torturing if someone felt so inclined. But I would absorb it all, so Mabel didn't have to.

The seventh door was wide open when we got there. The closet was emptied, and everything was on the floor, clothes cut

167

to ribbons and furniture knocked over. On the other side of the room, everything was in order.

"Mabel, did you bring anything important with you to the academy?" I asked.

"No. I don't own anything of real value. They don't allow it... the masters."

"Great, let's go then. There's nothing for you to pack. It's all... ruined."

I pushed them back towards the exit, just as I spotted him—that red-haired bastard from the dungeon. He stood with his back to us, leaning against the wall. A sizable crowd of elves stood around him. And there were elves everywhere. They were the most numerous race. I spotted a healthy population of giants, beasts, and other races, some I couldn't immediately identify. But they appeared to be in the minority, and eager to stay out of the way.

Mabel noticed me staring and leaned in.

"The others should be arriving today or tomorrow. It's a general rule that they arrive last. It is an honor thing."

"What others?" I asked. But she shrunk away, either too afraid to answer or too cowed by the oppressive air of her kind. Damn, I could feel it, too. The combined weight of judgment and scorn.

"Alright. I won't make a scene, for your sake. But I'm going to find a way to show those red-headed snobs a thing or two."

She graced me with a weak smile. It wasn't much, but it was more than I had seen since we met before the affinity test. I hoped that meant she trusted me.

"Let's just go," she whispered and pulled on my sleeve. "It feels good to leave everything behind. It is a new start, a blank slate."

"Some things are better wiped clean, heh?" Chloe asked, speaking overly loud on purpose. And if everyone wasn't looking at us before, they were now. "Where is a biblical flood, when you need one?" I heard her mutter the last part as she grabbed Mabel's hand and pulled her towards the exit.

I slowly turned and made my way out, following close behind the girls. No one stopped us, but they called us names, whispering just loud enough for us to hear.

I felt as if a colossal weight had been lifted from my shoulders when we finally stepped out into the free air of the central chamber. The door slammed behind us, shutting us off from the pretentious stares, bigotry, and overt hatred. My hands shook at my side, my body practically toxic with adrenaline and stress. Standing up to bullies was one thing but facing down entire magical races was another. I was going to need to watch my back.

"So, it appears we need to go shopping. Where can we buy Mabel some nice clothes around here?"

"To the bazaar!" Chloe said, forcing a smile. I could see it on her face, too. The strain and discomfort as she fought to push off the ugliness of our encounter.

"I know a couple of cherry spots, Mabel. I have been meaning to get myself some new stuff as well. Now we can shop together. Money shouldn't be an issue... as long as we don't go too crazy."

"Can you teach me how to open the portals?" I asked as we approached. "There might come a time when I want to sneak out on my own to get someone a gift."

"It is simpler than you probably realize," Chloe said. "Feel the mana around you, then trace the pattern for the portal. Done."

"Geez. That is simple."

"You could have just told me you wanted to buy me something. I'll leave you a list of ideas if you like," Chloe said and threw me a wink.

"A list? But then it wouldn't be a surprise."

"So, at what rank do I need to be to open the portal to the Bazaar?"

"Rank one is already fine. You just need to focus, JD. That's how most things work around here. The mana is the medium that connects you to the world. Think it, will it, and the mana will make it so."

We stopped in front of the portal to the bazaar. I immediately studied the gate, focusing on the mana coursing through the air around me. It came from everywhere—every surface and molecule. And if I really focused, I could almost see the currents swirling through the air. And they weren't all the same. The mana from the inanimate objects produced quieter, lazier threads, providing a contrast to its more vibrant and active counterpart.

I stared at the portal for a moment, the center dark and inactive. The girls waited behind me, content to allow me to figure this out on my own. They knew that the only way to figure something like this out, was simply to do it.

I held out my hand and allowed a bit of my mana to trickle forth. I felt it immediately react to the magical potential floating in the air. It formed a bridge, in essence, allowing me to span the open air between myself and the portal. I studied the glyph carved into the stone and copied it in the air. The portal responded, the glyphs glowing with blue light. A spark formed in the dark center, and a heartbeat later, the magical gateway opened.

"Freaking magic," I whispered, staring at the portal and then my hand. I was everything I had ever wished for, everything I had ever dreamed and fantasized about. Now it was real.

I turned triumphantly to the girls. Mabel clapped her hands, beaming happily. While Chloe's expression was far more complicated. She lifted her hands and golf clapped, a mischievous smirk forming on her lips. Then she blew me a kiss. I had a feeling I was in for a treat when we got back to our room.

Not Alone, After All

WE PASSED THROUGH THE PORTAL TOGETHER, stepping out into the bazaar almost immediately. An electric tingle shot down my body, Chloe visibly twitching next to me. I was confident that portal transportation wouldn't get old anytime soon.

The bazaar's sights, sounds, and smells washed over us. Somehow, the sprawling maze of tents, shacks, and awnings looked more colorful, more vibrant, and boisterous. It was an entirely different world, equally wondrous and no less busy than our previous visit.

"Do we get food first?" I asked, meeting Chloe's eyes.

"Sure. Necessities first. Then see how much money we've got left. Perhaps buy enough for a week? The drops might not be as lucrative on our next dive, so it wouldn't hurt to be prepared."

"Sure thing," I agreed, and Mabel nodded her silent approval.

I hooked arms with both Chloe and then Mabel and we made our way into the bazaar. We took up a good quarter of the road, but I didn't care. People watched us pass—students, shopkeepers, and marketgoers. Mabel pushed into me, but it felt more defensive than affection. Part of me couldn't blame her, especially after the scene we just left in her dorm. This many eyes couldn't be easy to take.

Chloe pushed into me from the other side, and I looked down just in time to catch her looking at Mabel. I followed her gaze over when the elf was tucked under my arm, specifically her breasts pressed against me. Mabel looked up and noticed Chloe's attention, the two women immediately looking away.

"Heh, why don't you two go ahead without me? I need to find some personal effects," Mabel said, separating.

"Yeah. No. I'm going with you," Chloe said, snagged the elf by the elbow, and then stormed off with her in tow.

"What have I gotten myself into?" I whispered as the two disappeared into the crowd.

Chloe hinted at jealousy but actively advocated to bring Mabel into our dorm. Did she have a thing for the elf? Was there some attraction there? Or did she see something in Mabel, perhaps the helplessness, that compelled her to protect?

I couldn't lie to myself. Chloe was confusing, but the spark initiated during our intimate time together was compelling and I longed to explore it more deeply. And I'd be lying if I said I wasn't attracted to Mabel as well. I loved her honesty and her emotional purity. It was all there, worn openly on her sleeve. But the signs were all there, the markers of abuse. If Emron and the other cretinous blood elves in his family had abused her, then the last thing she needed was some horny human pushing her for a physical relationship.

I looked around, taking in the bazaar. Everything I saw and smelled told me I was in the food quarter. And I saw every kind of food imaginable—cooks tossing food in wok-like skillets, meat roasting on spits, ovens puffing aromatic smoke into the air, and that didn't include the carts, dividers, barrels, and stands crammed full of produce, stringers of sausages hanging from the tent frames, or other goods propped on the display. It all made my stomach rumble and mouth water.

172

I followed the girls to Relina's stand. The older woman, or at least that's what she looked like, greeted me with that warm, albeit strange smile.

"JD. Chloe's…friend," she said, greeting me and showing off her solid memory.

"Yes. Her…friend. Hell, Relina. I'm in charge of food, so I would like to place an order. We need meals for three people," I said, for some reason holding up three fingers. "We need food for seven days. Breakfast, lunch, dinner, and two snacks a day. And maybe, if you have it, throw in something sweet for the girls."

Relina watched me but didn't write anything down. "Yes, yes. Meals are needed. Humans get hungry. Tell me, young JD. What kind of food do you crave? Relina can make it all—sweet, savory, spicy, light, heavy, rich, or delicate. Don't you worry, I am quite familiar with human food. Yes, quite familiar. I have been studying it for so long now."

"Oh?" I asked, more distracted by her strange manner than the noise around us. "What would you suggest?"

"For two humans and a moon elf?" Relina asked, gesturing to our group. I nodded.

"Hmm, let me ponder," she mumbled and pressed an index finger to her lips. Her eyes narrowed and she fell quiet, evidently deep in thought. We stood and watched, waiting for the peculiar woman to finish.

"I have it!" she gasped, suddenly, startling all three of us. "Human delicacies, every one of them. No doubt, to satisfy elf and human. We will start you off with a strong breakfast of meat, eggs, and bread. Some garnishes? Yes. Salsa for flavor. Then for lunch, we'll have soup. Hearty and thick. Then spaghetti and hamburgers. Yes! A pizza even? I think so. And for dinner, we go lighter. Perhaps a day of salads and steak, perhaps a roasted chicken or pheasant. Yes. All splendid."

I took several breaths, planning to respond every time she asked a question. Chloe chirped several times, trying to speak as well, but Relina continued, answering her own questions. It was

173

perhaps the strangest conversation I ever had. But highly entertaining.

"Sounds fantastic. All of it," I replied, comforted by the idea of steady, familiar meals.

"Splendid." She pulled out a piece of parchment and waved her hand around above it. Writing appeared. Words and numbers rearranged themselves, duplicating until evidently, everything was written down and summed up. "Feasts for one will cost **1,600** Fres," she said, the glowing number appearing in the air between us. **4,800** for the three of you. I can add some delectable sweets, which will round it all off at **5,500**. Agreeable?"

I nodded thoughtfully, watching the last number glow in the air and then fade away. That wasn't going to get old any time soon. Part of me silently hoped that dialogue boxes would follow. Maybe with some dialogue options.

"Relina, what about this?" I asked, pulling our prepared meat from my rift. Somehow, it was still cold to the touch. "Could you use it in our meals or accept it as barter?"

She immediately motioned for me to join her behind the counter and only spoke when we were safely behind the curtain. "Be cautious, young one. Steaks of that quality are hard to come by, therefore highly sought after. I *can* prepare it for my higher-end customers anywhere, but the cost is high. **4,500** to **8,000** Fres. The Queen meat. And the Gargantua meat, those can go for even more!"

"That is expensive," I said, watching the numbers dissolve from the air. Then an idea hit. "Relina. What if you prepared three steaks for us, and took the rest as payment towards our week of food?"

The cook's eyes bulged, and she immediately started whispering, silently counting figures. "With the value, you would receive **30** days' worth of food. That is the best I can offer."

"Fair deal," I said, trusting that it was. I didn't really have a grasp on commerce here yet, nor did I want to offend her with excessive haggling. Besides, trading one day's worth of hunting meat in exchange for a month of prepared food felt like a phenomenal deal.

"I'll even add additional salads and sauces to this week's order."

"Thank you. That is very much appreciated."

A silence fell between us next, and I started to gather that there was something *more* she wanted to tell me. I cleared my throat and scratched my chin, but it was another long moment before she spoke.

"You make sure to care for those girls, yes? They both seem like good, honest students, so you do your best."

I had an idea of where this was going, but with Relina, I couldn't be sure. She was odd, probably only looked human, and far older than she looked. I figured it was best to let her say her piece.

"I will," I promised.

"I have seen more students come through here than I can remember. More than I can count. And I have a mind for numbers, mind you. But Chloe, she is different. I have taken a liking to her. She is special, young JD. Mark *those* words. Keep her close. Keep her safe."

I nodded, withering a bit under the odd woman's intense gaze. What was she? And was she really just a cook?

"Come back in a few hours and I will have your order ready," she said, waving me away.

I left, gratefully, and immediately started searching the chaotic bazaar for the girls. I found them ten booths away, picking through clothing. Chloe saw me first and waved excitedly. I hurried over and put an arm around her waist.

"You done?" she asked and then leaned in, planting a kiss right on my lips. She drew it out a little longer than was necessary. I had a feeling it was to remind Mabel of her place. But also didn't think it was entirely necessary. I detached, firmly but gently.

"We're set. We need to go back in a few hours and pick up our order."

"What did you order?"

"It is going to be a surprise. But I think there will be something in there that'll make each of us happy. Earth food, baby!"

"What!" Chloe hissed. "She never told me I could get food from home!"

"Guess she likes me, huh?" I chuckled and then pulled her in for a tight hug.

"How much did it cost?"

"Nothing. I bartered our meat, too. We're paid up for **30** days for all three of us. Breakfast, lunch, dinner, snacks, and sweets for you two."

Chloe watched the number flash to life, then fade, and held up her hand. I moved to give her a high five, but she wrapped her arms around me instead.

"Hah! I knew it! I picked a good one!" Chloe laughed.

"Are you sure?" Mabel asked, cutting in. "I was given…allowance, so I'm not without any money. I really should contribute towards our food."

"Nope," I said, brushing the idea away. "You did a third of the work fighting those monsters, so it only stands to reason that you get to eat a third of the profits. Besides, that means we can use the money we would have otherwise spent on food and buy Mabel new stuff. Maybe a few new outfits for Chloe." *And a magical pet for me,* I added silently.

Neither protested, which was a good thing. I mean, what rational person argues against the idea of free stuff? But still, Mabel was an unknown. Until I learned more about elven culture, I would have no idea what to expect.

I looked up and down the bazaar's main thoroughfare as Chloe and Mabel returned to their shopping. It was a marvel, the colors, and fabrics, but also the myriad of races present. I recognized a few, or at least, I thought I did—one man navigated his way through the crowd, yet his shoulders were twice as wide as the next largest man. His face was piggish and squat, his skin dark gray

176

and heavily cracked. Was he an ogre? An orc of some kind? I spotted a woman placing peppers into her basket. She wore a long dress, and although a silken hood covered her head, a reddish, bushy tail stuck out the back and swished the air.

I watched them all shop, captivated by each and every one. I wanted to know their names, their stories, where they came from. Every detail. But I knew this wasn't the time or place. This was their world, and it would be rude to ask. So, I filed it away for later research.

I turned and looked behind us, to where the food stalls stood, a mental image finally growing in my mind, although it was far from complete. Chloe and Mabel moved on to another shop, and then another. Larger tents appeared ahead, items like dressers and beds on display. A man with scaly skin and large eyes stood before a tent directly across, shouting and holding something aloft. I squinted. It looked oddly like a clothing iron. *Fantastic,* I thought.

We meandered into another tent. An elven woman stood on the opposite side of the counter, reading from what looked suspiciously like a tablet. It was translucent and glowed, appearing eerily similar to the messages that kept popping up in the air. A shiny, silver bell sat on the counter, a small sign hanging before it. It read:

Ring bell for service. I might be "out of body". Thank you and have a good day.

I tapped the bell, a ringing, magical note filling the tent.

"Greetings and welcome. What can I do for you?" the elvish woman asked, not bothering to look up from her screen. She didn't seem overly friendly, but neither did she seem unfriendly, at the same time. I could work with that.

"The girls here are looking for some clothing," I replied and nodded towards them. "We're in the market for a whole wardrobe, so it can't be *too* expensive, though we'd like quality and comfort, too."

"I'm sure the girls will be fine without your input, human. Please, come in." She stepped aside and motioned for us to join her.

Chloe and Mabel slid past the clerk and walked into a room filled with dresses, robes, underwear, and shoes. I spotted accessories like belts, pouches, and even suspenders, but most of it looked like stuff you'd find back home. I hung back, fighting the urge to say something snarky.

"All of my wares are of good quality, but nothing is enchanted, so if you want stat bonuses or perks, you'll have to scrounge your own crystal cores and do it yourself. That's why it's cheap."

"Enchanted? Crystal cores?"

"Yes, that is what I said." The elf turned, casting a rather annoyed look my way.

"Sorry. We're pretty new here."

"Then I would recommend you seek out a formation master. They will be able to teach you how to enchant articles of clothing and armor. It is an amazing process. Once *properly* enchanted, clothes can stay clean forever, become harder to tear, improve stats, speed, change color with mood or whim. And that doesn't even cover perks associated with named cores."

"Interesting," I replied. "Ladies, are you ready to pick some stuff out?"

"You know we are," Chloe whispered, and Mabel nodded animatedly.

"I don't want to be in the way. I'll be outside. Meet me out there when you're done?"

"Holler if you need anything," the clerk said, slumping back down into her chair and staring at her tablet.

I leaned in and whispered into Chloe's ear, "Don't go too crazy, but try and keep it below **5,000** Fres, alright?"

Shit! The clerk looked up, just as the number glowed to life between us, sabotaging my attempt to be subtle.

"Really?" Mabel asked, staring at the floating number.

178

"Certainly. Have fun. I'll be outside, checking the booths further down."

I turned and was about to leave when Chloe caught my wrist.

"Why are you leaving? You're paying for this stuff; don't you want to see how it looks when we try it on?"

"Oh," I replied, initially unsure how to respond. "Maybe Mabel wants to go first?"

The elf shook that notion away quickly.

"There, see. That settles it. Why don't you take a seat... right here?" Chloe said and dragged me over to a stool.

I didn't fight, despite my aversion to the notion. I'd never been a huge "shopping" fan, especially when it was for clothing. It was all the standing around and waiting for someone to change outfits, only to check it out, and start the process all over again. Although...

Chloe didn't waste any time in untying her top and pulling an arm through. My attitude immediately changed. Yes, I would sit here and watch the two beautiful women undress over and over again.

"I'll be at the front," the clerk said, pushed out of her stool, and pulled a curtain divider across, providing us some privacy. The elf murmured something about young, horny students, but I couldn't be sure.

Chloe stripped off her robe, revealing a rather skimpy, black thong and a matching lace bra. I immediately crossed one leg over the other and tried not to look too pleased.

I watched as she bent over to sort through a pile of garments, and intentionally shook her rear my way. I clicked my tongue and she laughed. Somehow it was even more erotic with Mabel present. Maybe it was the public nature of our venue or the voyeuristic element of having our relatively innocent elf-friend with us.

Mabel coughed after Chloe stood again, her boobs right in the elf's face. I shifted on the seat, thoroughly enjoying the show. The stool creaked loudly beneath me.

179

Chloe turned to track the noise and lifted a single eyebrow. "You just keep your hands to yourself during the show, buster. But you, Mabel, feel free to touch all you want," Chloe teased.

Mabel blushed hard, the color creeping over her cheeks and up her ears. But to her credit, she didn't hide her face or turn away. And then, to my surprise, she started to disrobe. I moved to stand up, fully intending to leave, but Mabel spoke first.

"Please stay, JD," she said, quietly. "Just don't stare."

"I won't. I promise."

"I want both of you to know," she said, cradling her top against her breasts. "I was considered trash back home, because of a nasty scar that never healed. The blood elves pride beauty above all else. Pristine, unblemished beauty."

"I didn't think I could hate those jackals any more than I already do," Chloe hissed. "Your body? Trash? What would we be?" she asked, turning to me.

I shook my head.

Chloe turned back to Mabel then, reached in, grasped her bunched-up clothing, and pulled. The robe slid down the young moon elf's legs, bunching up by her feet. Mabel gasped, covering her breasts with one hand, and privates with the other.

I was honestly so shocked by it all that I didn't turn away. But Mabel wasn't quite naked, though. She had her hand covering her... well, breasts. Most of them, anyway, and a rather strange-looking pair of underwear. The scar was another matter entirely. It ran from just below her left breast, and in a wide, half-circle to her navel. It was truly impressive. The kind of scar I would show off, or get a tattoo done over it for emphasis.

Mabel turned around, showing me her back, just as I finally managed to look away.

"Was it Emron?" I asked, my voice trembling. Just the thought of someone intentionally defacing such a beautiful young woman re-sparked my rage. Mabel didn't reply, which was all the confirmation I needed. The silence became deafening.

180

"Don't even think about it," Chloe said, as I turned to face her. Perhaps she was the anger, no, the murder in my eyes. But she needn't worry. I wasn't that stupid. No way was I going to confront him right then. No, I would grow stronger, and more proficient, and when he wasn't expecting me, I would pop in and knock his stiff, arrogant ass onto the ground. That was a promise.

"I just need some fresh air," I said and got up. "Don't worry, I won't go far." I memorized how she looked in that moment, long and lean, in that sexy black thong, and imprinted the image to memory. And before she could argue, I walked out.

The rage washed up inside me, trying to claw itself out from deep within. Chloe was a tease, a flirt, a girl far more comfortable with her body and her sexuality, but even she went rigid and quiet when Mabel's scar popped into view.

I went out into the bazaar. Two, no three stalls away before I realized how far I'd gone. I was moving, searching, but for what? Then it hit me. I... no, we needed to get stronger. The three of us. And we would need *stuff* to make that happen.

I started searching for crystal cores, beast cores, and magic books, grimoires, or ancient, banned tomes... anything that could teach us grandiose, freaking elf-humbling magic, but there was simply too much, and yet too little to see. At least, until I spotted an old man sitting on the ground ahead and to the right. He sat cross-legged, with a small rug spread out in front of him. I approached and bent low to consider his wares.

He looked up at me and then quietly gestured to his items in order—a piece of rock, a folded robe exuding mana, a small, nondescript book with a wooden cover, and lastly, a ring. I studied them all, and then looked at him. Strangely, he looked human. A human-human. Not a shimmering, poorly veiled copy, like Relina.

"Sir," I said as I knelt next to the old man.

His gray beard was at least twenty inches long, but his head was as bald as a marble. It even shone like one. A strange vibe radiated from the elderly man, one that led me to believe he was quite dangerous.

"What is it, young man?" he asked, closing his eyes.

"Are you from Earth?"

That question seemed to get his attention. One of his eyes opened into a slit, and then the other followed. His semi-scowl lifted as he considered me.

"You're from Earth?" he asked. "Now isn't that something? I didn't think I would ever see another human! Not in my lifetime. Thank the heavens! Thank the Lord!

There was a wisdom in his eyes that seemed to clash with... everything else about him. His unkempt beard and bushy eyebrows, his dirty fingernails, and his ragged clothing all conveyed the air of a broken, homeless man.

"I just got here a few days ago," I said, excitedly. "And I'm not the only one. There's a girl with me as well."

"Oh? Now that's peculiar," he muttered. "Two humans at the same time. That is quite unusual. Unusual indeed."

"How about you? How long have you been here?"

"Hah!" the old man laughed. "You have no idea, young man. I've been here for decades. Decades. A man... an old man quite at odds with this world. It isn't made for someone like me."

I nodded to be polite, but I really had no idea what he was talking about. He'd been here for decades? In reality, it looked like a hundred. And more, it looked as if the weight of the world was pressing down on his shoulders. His skin was deeply wrinkled, and his eyebrows were white as snow, but it was his posture. He was bent and stooped as if the ground was slowly but surely trying to reclaim him. I didn't understand what he'd meant by, "It isn't made for someone *like me*."

"What does that mean?" I asked. "Why are you at odds with this place?"

"I will not... cannot answer that question, young man. Unfortunately, you will have to figure it out for yourself. The story is too long, too personal, and most of it... I have forgotten, unfortunately. You are not alone here, that is what matters. Not yet, at least."

"What does that mean, 'not yet'?"

"I can only tell you this. You will not survive here alone. It is hard. Lonely. Demeaning. Every step between desperation and fear, love and hatred, betrayal and brotherhood. You have a long road ahead of you, young man, but don't make the same mistake I did. Do not try to walk it alone. Find someone to spend *this* life with. If I had, then I would not be the broken, hollow shell sitting before you. I would have realized my power and not been broken by those hoarding it."

"Did someone betray you? Was it the mistresses?" I asked, confident in what he would say. I felt the hatred pumping in my heart, fueled by the idea that blood elves had ruined lives before. That it wasn't just Mabel, and they were *the* villain in this new story.

"Betrayal," he chuckled, "The mistresses. All and none. Yes and no. It is these worlds. You will see. I used to rival the strongest of students, even the weaker mistresses. My power was significant. But power breeds enemies as quickly as anything. And a man alone with his power is an island. Do not be an island."

I listened to him, the lines on his face seemingly deepening as I knelt there. He spoke in strange riddles, but I could gather enough to interpret. I had already started to gather that being human in a place like Zenith set me apart, but not in the ways I immediately believed. Here, being different wasn't necessarily something the others would celebrate. It all tied into the story Chloe told me, about the two human warriors forming a bond to survive. The theme meshed too well with the broken man in front of me.

"Thank you for talking to me, sir. Thank you for the time."

"Time is all I have left, young man. And no hard feelings. But tell me, what is your name?"

I offered him my hand. "JD. It's a pleasure to meet you—."

183

"You can call me White. Or Old White, if you'd prefer. For some reason, I cannot remember my old name. That life... it is just gone."

"Okay, White," I said, the name feeling more than a little strange coming off my tongue. "I have to be honest. It is nice to see another human here."

He grinned and nodded.

"So, are you selling these?" I asked, gesturing to the items positioned before him.

"I am, or was. Maybe I still am, I don't know. I guess I don't have any use for them anymore, but it wouldn't feel right to let go of them for nothing."

"Your most prized belongings?" I asked, guessing the sentiment. He nodded and for the first time since we started talking, really looked at me. Not just into my eyes, but seemingly into my soul. My very being.

"Yes," he responded simply, and then held his hand over each in turn. As if feeling their embedded memories and significance. "Each one of these things is a treasure worth a million Fres. I assume that kind of money is beyond you, eh?"

"A little," I chuckled. "I'm really just looking around right now, trying to get the lay of the land. Plus, it doesn't hurt to find things I might need later and plan. To build towards."

"Why don't we play a little game? You tell me things... say, important events from the last four decades on earth."

"Sure," I said and moved to sit.

"And in return for that information, I will give you something as payment. Every time you come back to see me, we can have a little chat. You can roll a dice and I'll then give you one of the remaining items."

My eyebrows rose at his offer. It was more than appealing, but there had to be a catch, right? There was always a catch in a too-good-to-be-true situation. I considered the offer for a moment, his story spinning in my mind—regret, loss, love, and promise unrealized.

What would happen when all of his possessions were gone? Would he simply lay down and die? I didn't ask the question. Hell, there was no way I'd be able to form those words, but it weighed heavily upon me as I sat down.

"You're an interesting, young man," he laughed, "I saw the question birthed, saw your mind give it life, right in your eyes. You are wondering if I am going to die. Am I right?"

I know I couldn't hide my shock. Because he laughed.

A dark, simmering flame burned in his eyes suddenly, growing stronger with every heartbeat.

"Yes. I was going to. I was fully prepared to. But talking with you has changed my mind. And I thank you for it."

"I'm happy I could help, but tell me. You aren't prepared to give valuables like this away, are you? What else do you want? I mean, I do have money."

"Oh? And what is a burned-out old shell like me going to do with the money? Didn't you hear me? I want stories. I want to hear of home."

"You have to understand why that sounds odd to me. Money is everything nowadays. Parents would sell their children if the price were right. That's why it sounds strange that someone is willing to give up their most prized possessions in exchange for... stories."

"Hah, money he says. Money. What in the hell did money do for me back then? I had millions of dollars to my name when I got here, but I had nothing. Understand? I brought myself up from nothing in the academy to power and prominence but now look at me. I'll die with nothing, just like I came into the world. So, yes. I want stories. If that makes you uncomfortable, there is something else I can ask of you."

"What would you ask?"

"A quest, if you will. Does that interest you?"

Was I interested in a quest? Was this guy serious? All he was missing was a column of bright light making him stand out from

185

everyone around us and he would be my first, quest-giving NPC. Hell yes! Game on.

"What kind?" I asked, trying to hide my enthusiasm. I wasn't terribly successful.

"We'll talk details once you're a little stronger. Think you can handle that?"

I stuck out my hand, offering for him to shake it.

"You got yourself a deal, Old White. Unless it involves certain death, that is."

"Don't worry, young man. I will not put the only other human I know in danger. That's the last thing I'd want to do."

"I approve," I said, returning his smile. "Say, why 'Old White'?"

"Because of my hair," he explained, grabbing a thin lock of his white hair and pulling it around to examine in the light. "Now, how long has it been since they started calling me that? Ever since my glorious black mane turned into snow?"

He tossed his hair over his shoulder, sighed dramatically, and picked the folded robe up off the rug. Then he handed it to me.

"What would you like to know about? From home?" I asked, understanding well enough from my experience managing a bar, that when goods exchanged hands, so did the payment.

"Not now. Later. Take the robe and come see me when you've got some time to spare. Your friends are waiting for you." Old White flashed me a smile, then pointed over my shoulder, where I found the girls waiting.

I looked down as I pushed off to stand. I'd thought the robe was a dirty, ragged garment at first glance, but up close, they looked to be in pristine condition. I smoothed the fabric only to feel a surge of power shoot up my arm.

"Yikes!" I gasped, shaking out my hand, "what was that?"

"Something that will benefit you for a long time to come. A shortcut to getting where you need to be so you can protect those you care about."

"And you won't tell me anything about them?"

He shook his head and started gathering his belongings.

"When you come to see me next time, keep walking through the bazaar until you get to the end. If I am not there, ask around for me. Someone will know where to send you."

Remembering all the kung-fu movies I'd spent my life watching, I knew the highest form of thanks was to bow respectfully. So, I did.

"I'll come to see you in a few days after I get settled with classes."

"Remember what I said. Don't die alone," he whispered, reaching up to put his hand on my shoulder. "Take care of yourself. And your friends."

I clutched the robe tight to my chest and bowed again.

Then, before I could thank him again, the old man gathered his stuff and walked away.

"Hey, JD, who was that?" Mabel asked, walking up behind me. I turned to greet her, but snapped back around, thinking I could introduce them to the old man before he got too far away. But he was gone. Disappeared, as if into thin air.

"That's...Old White," Chloe replied for me. "I think."

"Yeah, he is. Anyway... what did you get?" I asked, spotting the merchant leaning out of her tent. She looked quite pleased.

"A lot. It cost us **3,000** for everything. You okay with that?"

"Did you get good value? If you did, then I'm okay with it." I honestly didn't know what a good deal was, so if Chloe and Mabel were happy, then by extension, I should be, too. I couldn't expect to learn everything in a day, right?

"We did. I'll show you what we got when we get back."

I smoothed out the robe in my hands again, surprised to see they were as white as snow now. I could have sworn they were black when they were sitting on his rug. Or had I just remembered wrong? I held them a little closer, excited to get them home and have a better look. Maybe try them on and explore their hidden power.

187

"What were you talking about with Old White?" Chloe asked. "Did he give you the robe?"

"Yeah. How well do you know him?"

"I know *of* him. But we've never spoken. The other merchants talk about him all the time. Evidently, he just sits there every day, and even when offered astronomical prices, he doesn't sell his stuff. Why did he give you that robe? What is it, anyway?"

"I have no idea, but it's full of mana. I can feel it when I touch the fabric. I've honestly never felt anything like it."

"I can feel it from here. It's pretty strong. Almost makes me jealous."

I flashed Mabel a smile, but she immediately looked to the ground.

"You okay, Mabel? Did you get everything you need? We've got more time to shop if you need anything else."

She nodded and flashed me a weak smile.

"Thank you. Both of you. I'm fine, truly."

"Aww! See how cute she is?" Chloe chuckled. "Jokes aside, you need to try that thing on when we get back. If it's what I think it is, you're going to be happier than a pig in mud."

"Hah, better that than giant cockroach guts," I laughed. "But let's be honest here. Making such a strong enemy the first time out in a dungeon dive is rather bad luck. Can we aim for a quieter trip out next time?"

"Oh? Am I too exciting?" Chloe chuckled.

"You're just right."

She laughed and threw her arms around me, so I pulled her in tight. I savored her warmth and smell, but mostly the sparkle in her eye. Sure, I'd had girlfriends before, but our relationships either never got serious or they ended abruptly over one reason or another. And usually with a bad fight. This time I'd give the relationship my full attention and make sure I wasn't the weak link. This time I would be the best version of myself.

Robes Maketh the Man

THE GIRLS WERE IN HIGH SPIRITS as we made our way back to our room. It looked like they had bonded over their shared shopping experience, and it made me practically glow inside. It was a great start to our new lives together and the promises I had made—to bring us together and keep everyone safe. Hell, at this rate, we were well on our way to becoming our own little family, and Chloe played a large part in that.

When we arrived, the collective mood sank through the floor when we all noticed a big, red circle painted on the center of our door. Mabel immediately started shaking. Chloe put her arms around the elf, and I moved in to investigate.

"He can't do shit in here. This just proves it, Mabel. He is lashing out, making this whole thing psychological, because he knows he can't touch you," I said and opened the door for them. "Get in."

"This is to let us know that *he* knows where we live," Mabel whispered.

I nodded. It was an "I see you," poke to make us feel those invisible eyes always weighing on our backs.

"Don't worry, we're here for you. All together. And it's not like no one knows where we're staying. Everyone knows we're in the VIP ward," I said and put my hand on her shoulder. My mind was filled with cheesy movie and television references, but one stood out above the rest. *The Three Musketeers.* "All for one, and one for all," I whispered, and she finally looked up at me.

"I like the sound of that," Mabel whispered.

I looked to Chloe, who shook her head as if saying, "Really, the Musketeers"?

Yep. I may not have been leveled up in this world yet, but my nerd powers were legendary.

"If he tries something stupid, we'll just report him to the headmistress," Chloe added, "You heard Scarlet. She's not going to put up with any of his bull shit."

Chloe's cheeks were red, and her eyes narrowed. She looked as mad as I felt.

It seemed some things were universal. People just couldn't let me be. Or my friends. It just made sense, really. It was like that for High School and college, why would a magical academy be any different?

"The thing that worries me the most is if he decides to send someone else to mess with us, perhaps someone attending Zenith. Are there any other...?" I fumbled, struggling with titles and words, "Any servants, family members, or other elves that we should be keeping an eye on?"

"Anyone with ears like mine," Mabel muttered. "The blood elves are highest amongst my kind, so his racial and familial leverage is great."

That didn't give us a lot to go by, in fact, it didn't really narrow down the field by much, especially if we had to worry about any elf at Zenith not named Mabel. *Shit!* But Mabel was right. He would use his racial leverage. Besides, royalty barely did things themselves. If he was going to act, he was going to get someone else's hands dirty.

"What about weapons? Can they draw weapons inside the dorms?"

"No, they can't," Chloe replied as she pushed Mabel into our room, "Weapon use outside the classroom and dungeon's is heavily restricted. The mistresses would know immediately. But that is not to say they can't harm us with their fists and feet. It isn't much, but we are already higher rank than most of the freshmen, so that should serve as a deterrent for a little while. Unless they leapfrog us, that is."

I followed the girls inside and closed the door behind me. I pushed and pulled, making sure it was closed and latched tight, but I still struggled with that helpless feeling. My apartment had been broken into several times, and as I'd learned, that vulnerable, weak feeling didn't go away quickly.

Chloe dropped on the bed and propped herself up on one elbow while Mabel looked away, obviously embarrassed. I figured she had a chaotic mass of things rushing through her mind, namely rooming with us, but I wasn't going to let her change her mind. We were her friends and family now, for better or for worse. We'd weather it together and overcome any hardships this place could throw at us. And then some.

"Mabel," I said, walking up to her. And when she refused to look up at me, I forced the young elf to meet my eyes. "Don't fixate on it, alright? What's done is done and it won't do you any good to sit and stress out about it. Even if you did go back, he'd target me for defying his will. Right?"

Mabel bit her lower lip and nodded, her hair falling to hide most of her face. She was beautiful but understandably haunted. Part of me could relate, especially if she felt like she didn't belong anywhere. I'd just have to show her how wrong that feeling was.

"So!" Chloe said, almost yelling. "What bed do you want?" she asked, pointing at the slightly larger bed to the right, the one she had been using, and then the one she was currently perched upon.

191

"I'll take the smaller one," she said, "but is it possible to put up something between us? I'm... not quite comfortable with other people watching me sleep."

"Yeah, we can get a room separator or something. Worst case scenario, I sleep somewhere else for a day or two until you get used to me. Does that sound okay?" I said. I wanted to show her that she would be respected and cared for in our shared space, even if I had to sleep outside for a day or two.

"No!" she said, shaking her head adamantly. "I don't want that. It's actually not about nudity. It's just that we moon elves are vulnerable while we sleep."

"Vulnerable?" I asked. "Like weakened?"

It didn't surprise me, but I also wondered what she meant. Personally, I fell into almost coma-like periods of unconsciousness, where I wouldn't hear an army march past.

"All moon elves are naturally strengthened by moonlight. When we sleep, and not under the open sky, we are in a weakened state. You see, our home world is tidal. One side is always in the sunlight, the other always in darkness. The blood elves discovered our weakness long ago... not that we are necessarily weakened by the sun, but by the moon's absence. They used that knowledge to enslave most of my kind."

"Shit," I breathed. And I suddenly hated the carrot-topped pointy ears even more. Wasn't there an authority to keep these imbalances from happening? A Star Fleet or governing body to keep one race from dominating another?

"You'll be safe when you sleep in here, Mabel. I am a decidedly light sleeper. I've got your back. And maybe once we've gotten a little stronger, we can capture a little bit of your homeland and recreate it on the wall. I have heard that gifted cultivators can create lifelike starscapes on the ceilings of their homes."

"My stars, that would truly be a blessing." Mabel's eyes lit up and looked genuinely happy for the first time in a long while.

"Good. Cause I love that shit," Chloe added. "Now, back to the sleeping arrangements. If we take the larger bed, you'll probably see and hear all kinds of things... like him snoring, or rolling out of bed, or you know, some other nighttime stuff."

"Wait, what? I'm taking the wall then. You're not kicking me out."

"And I gather the 'me falling out of bed part' will be you kicking me out?" I asked, reading between the lines. "Then we had better get a bigger bed because I am not a huge fan of sudden, nighttime falls onto a stone floor."

"Bigger?" Chloe asked, then brightened. "Maybe we could push the beds together? Huh? What do you think, Mabel?"

"Wh-what?" she stuttered. "Seeing me is one thing but—I'm not sure I can sleep in the same bed as a man."

"At least not yet," Chloe whispered.

"Okay... we don't need to push the issue for now. I don't want anyone uncomfortable with their sleeping arrangements."

Mabel slunk around Chloe, as the blonde held up her arms and tried to pull her onto the bed with her. Then she moved to the other bed and patted the mattress as if testing its softness.

"At least it's decent enough."

"And it shouldn't have many stains if you know what I meant! At least, not yet." Chloe laughed and I rolled my eyes.

She was incorrigible, and I understood where her reputation came from. She was a free spirit, relatively open-minded, and not afraid to voice her opinions. I loved all those things.

"I'll pretend that I didn't hear that," Mabel said, nonchalantly. "I gather I will have to infuse some mana into the mattress to make it more comfortable..."

"Will that work?" I asked, ignoring Chloe's continued efforts to be lewd, and instead joined Mabel.

"Most certainly," she said, brightening a bit from my interest. "Here, let me show you."

She pressed her hands down, flat against the mattress. Mana blossomed and immediately started to flow freely into the cushion. It started to rise and fill out as if it were an air mattress connected to a pump. "There," she said, pulling her hands away, "I infused just a bit of my mana, and as you saw, it spread out all on its own. I believe this one is Frexian wool, which is an okay mana-binding medium. There are better, softer ones available, but this will work."

"Frexian...wool?"

"It is a pack animal that—."

"Sorry, boring..." Chloe cut her off as she plopped down on the bed. "Ahh! This is so good! Do ours, too!"

"Okay," was all the elf said, before repeating the process on the other bed. Once done, Mabel laid down, and seeing as how Chloe was sprawled atop the other, I dropped down next to her. No sooner had my weight landed than she shot back up again.

"Umm, yes, you know, mana skills and magic spells can provide us with many quality-of-life improvements, so if there's anything you'd like help with, just tell me," she blurted and promptly scurried off to the kitchen.

"Geez, JD, run the poor girl off, why don't you," Chloe said, raising her eyebrows, comically. I didn't share the sentiment. If anything, I felt bad. Mabel obviously needed something, some extra sense of security we weren't yet providing.

"Hey, Mabel," Chloe called, jumping out of bed and following her to the kitchen. "How come we haven't heard about the quality-of-life things? Like puffing up a mattress or pillow with mana?"

"Well, that's because it is rare for anyone outside of service to use them. Not many elves teach them to their offspring anymore, because they consider them to be beneath them, or demeaning."

"Service? Is that like butlers and maids?" I asked.

"Don't ask that, JD. It's inconsiderate."

"I'm sorry..."

Mabel shook her head. "No, it is okay. He doesn't know," she said, her weak smile and quiet voice almost immediately quitting Chloe. She turned back to me, that haunted look in her eyes setting me back and tightening my gut.

194

"My kind was royalty until the blood elves enslaved us. That was eighteen centuries ago. We have been their property ever since. That means we are considered beneath even the weakest and worst blood elves—the criminal, the handicapped, even those born with no magical ability. No matter our talent or lineage, in the end, we are all destined for service... in one form or another."

"So, once you have finished your time at the academy, they would just take you back and force you to serve someone?" I asked, goosebumps spreading over my arms.

She nodded. "Yes. The family that owns my hereditary line... Emron's family, will re-stake its claim and collect. My mother tried to fight that fate, and it killed her."

"What about the academy? Can't you stay here?" I asked, fighting to control my temper. It didn't feel possible, that in a magical world, no, worlds, one race was allowed to simply own another. That an entire people could be born and never breathe free air.

"Stay as what?" Mabel asked, laughing bitterly, "A teacher?"

I nodded. "It isn't that crazy, is it? You could teach young zither players and support techniques. Surely the mistresses would help you. I don't know, maybe open a new branch or a sister academy? You could provide music during festivities and gatherings. We would do whatever it took to make it worth the risk for the headmistress."

She shrugged and sagged back against the cold wall, seemingly crushed by the horrible reality of it all. Her pale skin seemed to glow, as if by some unseen ray of moonlight. I watched her for a moment, marveling over her exotic beauty but also deeply troubled by the fact that someone could actually *own her*. Own her—a real, flesh and blood elf, with smooth, ice-cool skin, large, beautiful eyes, and lustrous hair. It didn't seem right. Not at all.

The nerd and the sexually mature man inside me clashed. If I were in a video game, and I had just unlocked a quest to "free the beautiful moon elf maiden", I wouldn't just earmark it for later. I

195

would set that shit on **active quest** mode and do whatever it took. *What?*

The words **[Active Quest]** appeared in the air before me. Mabel immediately noticed and sat up. Chloe did, too.

"What is that all about?" Chloe asked.

"I don't know. Uh, I was just thinking, that's all," I stammered, awkwardly, unsure how much to share.

"About what?" Mabel asked, and I realized I couldn't keep it to myself. No, I didn't want to.

"I was just thinking about Mabel's situation and how fucked up it is that this world allows one race to own another. Then I got thinking about video games and realized that if there was a side quest to free Mabel, I would deviate from the main story to complete that right away."

"Newbie to a magical world and you're already prepared to fight the system. I like you more and more with each passing minute. Just please keep something in mind," Chloe said, shifting to sit on the bed. "We haven't even started classes yet. Let's save those high-level ambitions for when we've gotten a little stronger, eh?"

"Chloe is right," Mabel said, quietly, "We will see what the future brings. I just might become strong enough to break my own chains. But I very much appreciate your support, JD. Thank you."

I nodded, humbled and angry. There was so much I wanted to do, to promise, but I knew better than to write checks my body couldn't cash. And they were both right. We'd just gotten here. I didn't have to like how the world worked, but until I gained some more strength, I couldn't expect to enact much change. I would have to learn to pick my battles.

"Why don't you try on your new robe?" Chloe asked, changing the subject. "The one you got from Old White?"

I nodded, eagerly. Besides, Mabel was uncomfortable with all the conversation about her people and their royally messed-up circumstances. I wouldn't exactly make it any better by dwelling and stewing on it.

196

I started to unfold the robe. It wasn't a robe. At least, not the white fabric I had been petting on our way home. The robe lay within that protective sleeve, its pearlescent fabric gleaming with a dull, white light as I pulled it free.

"Ah, nice. The gold and red threads are very subtle," I whispered, laying the garment out on the bed. It was impeccable, every stitch and thread meticulously placed. Strangely, the robe looked brand new. For something the old man undoubtedly wore through dungeon dives and sparring matches, I had expected ragged, stained, with more than a few mismatched patch jobs and mended cuts.

"That... it's so beautiful," Chloe muttered, petting the sleeve. "Put it on!"

I nodded and absently opened the robe, my fingers lingering on the smooth fabric. It was as smooth as silk, cool to the touch, and decidedly delicate. And yet, I gathered that it was much stronger than it appeared.

"Heavens! That is elven palmire!" Mabel gasped, then slapped her hand over her mouth. "So, sorry. I spoke out of turn."

"Out of turn?" I chuckled. "Mabel, we're friends here. We're all equal. But what is palmire?"

"It is fabric fit for royalty. All of Emron's clothes are made out of it. My people spin this fabric from the silk of lunar spiders. Once properly woven and cured, it is nearly impregnable. Even when torn, the wearer only needs to infuse a bit of mana to repair it. It is illegal for my people to wear it. This," she said, pointing to the robe on the bed, "is truly a kingly gift."

I listened and watched as a fire blossomed in Mabel's eyes, that small connection to her people's history immediately starting an inferno within her. Then I turned back to look at the robe. Why would the old man just give me the robe, especially if it was so valuable? Did he know about the tension between our little group and the blood elves? How could he?

"He only wanted stories as payment. Why would he give me something so valuable?"

197

"I can think of a few reasons," Chloe said, cutting in. "There aren't many of us here. From earth, that is. It is like I said before, humans don't amount to much here. Perhaps, this is his way of helping you break that trend."

"Exactly," Mabel whispered. "But wearing elven Palmire will show the others that you aren't alone, that someone with considerable resources is supporting you. With that in mind, Emron will be far less likely to openly call you out now. He will wonder who your benefactor is and will likely expend a great number of resources to find out."

I immediately thought back to the old man in the bazaar. He looked withered, haggard, and frail... hardly what I would consider a wealthy benefactor.

"Do you think Old White would throw his weight around if someone or something threatened me?" I asked, wondering out loud, "Does he have any weight to throw around?"

"I think we're going to have to admit that we just don't know. That is the thing about mana, isn't it? With the right knowledge and training, the weakest, most infirm man could contain unbelievable strength," Chloe said, finally pushing off the bed and approaching. "Those sound like tomorrow's problems. Right now, let's see what you look like in that, magus supreme."

"Magus? I'm a sorcerer now?" I chuckled. Chloe winked and immediately started undressing me. Right in front of Mabel. The elf moved to turn away, but Chloe snapped her fingers.

"Oh, no, girl. He watched you undress earlier. It is your turn now. It is only fair, right?"

The moon elf considered it for a moment and then smiled. "You're right, Chloe. It is only fair," Mabel said and settled onto her bed to watch. Although I did notice a touch of pink darken her cheeks.

"This model is the latest in human males. He comes complete with knobby knees, body hair, and I'd say about ten o'clock shadow," Chloe said, turning me around. She gestured to my legs, stomach, and chin as if she were a saleswoman demonstrating the strong points of a product. She poked me in the belly, to which I shamefully giggled.

Mabel laughed, the sound genuine and warm. "Oh, can he be trained? Can he do tricks?"

"I'm afraid these models come pre-programmed right from the factory. Complete with burping and farting protocols, lawn mowing **101,** and many optional upgrades available. Can I interest you in one of these bad boys today, ma'am?" Chloe asked, turning me around to face her.

"Oh, yes. Yes. But what is 'lawn mowing'?"

"Don't you worry about that now, ma'am."

I smiled and played along, mimicking pushing a lawnmower. Mabel laughed again and slapped her knee, that hollow look now replaced with real joy. Was it humiliating? Sure. But was it worth it to hear her laugh? Hell yes!

"Understood. Put that young moon elf down for **2** human males. She's got lots of grass to mow, ladies and gentlemen."

Then Chloe reached around and pinched my rear. And in a single, fluid motion, reached down and pulled her robe aside, revealing that her thong was gone, replaced by one of the soft, fabric undergarments I saw Mabel wearing. Chloe leaned in.

"You can pull it off with your teeth later," she whispered. "If you behave."

"If I behave?" I asked.

She nodded, mischievously, scooped the robe off the bed, and slipped my right hand into a sleeve, then the left. She tied the left flap to a loop on the inside, and then pulled the right side around me, tying it at the front. The robe abruptly tightened around my body, adjusting to fit my frame. Chloe gasped as it moved by itself and then laughed.

"What in the hell is it doing?" I asked, spinning around as the robe continued to change. The hem lengthened, as well as the sleeves, the stitching glowing with bright gold and red light.

"The robe is remaking itself to fit you!" Mabel cried, watching with obvious joy.

A sudden rush of energy washed over me, filling me with mana. I felt it tug and push on the pathways, widening and humming with new and awesome potential. And unlike my first experience, when Chloe burned crystals through my hands, it didn't hurt. If anything, it felt like a long-lost part of me had finally been returned.

"Did it... did you... just jump to rank **4**?" Chloe asked incredulously, her face frozen in a look of disbelief.

Mabel inched closer to the edge of her seat until she almost fell off. Her mouth opened wide, but it was several long moments before she spoke. "I think he just did," Mabel whispered. "I've been cultivating power for several years now and I'm barely into the third rank. You just started the other day, right? How have you elevated so fast?"

"I am rank **3**, but we had a...shortcut," Chloe said, but I gave her a hard look, cutting her off. I didn't necessarily think it was the best or safest time to share the story about our pairing, our dual cultivation. It wasn't that I didn't trust Mabel, but some things were safer kept close to the chest. And I still didn't know the whole story. I needed to know more about the people in Chloe's story and how it affected us moving forward.

"That is unheard of," Mabel whispered. "The jump from rank **1** to **2** is the hardest, and you both are already at rank **3**? How?"

The look in Mabel's eyes was equal parts wonder, incomprehension, and jealousy. But there was hope there, too. A spark had lit in her eyes. She knew we'd stumbled onto something.

"We've put a lot of time into it since arriving. I promise, we'll help you get there, too," I said.

"Really?" Chloe asked, pinching my arm. "Does that mean what I think it does?"

"What does it mean?" Mabel asked, turning between Chloe and myself, obviously confused.

"No. It's just..." I started to say.

"Wait," Mabel said, cutting me off, "I see. It has to be. You two...did it, didn't you? You forced a pairing and cultivated intimately."

Chloe groaned and nodded. Well, that escalated quickly. But I had to give Mabel credit, she seemed to take it really well.

"Mabel, I'll tell you why later, trust me," Chloe said, turning to the elf, then she looked at me. "JD, why don't you check your stats? Let's see exactly what that robe did for you and if we should start bowing when you enter the room."

I nodded, but frowned at her "bow" comment, then held up my hand and pulled up my stat window.

NAME: Heaven-Defying Palmire Robes (R4)
TYPE: Armor, Scaling
POWER LEVEL: 140
DESCRIPTION: Symbiote armor crafted from the finest Elven Palmire silk. Only found in the Elven kingdoms.
Infused by a rank **9** *named* Heavenly Tiger Core.
HEALTH: 200, **MANA:** 100
ATTACK: 40, **DEFENSE:** 40
MANA SHIELD: 200 + Deflection Perk

I was startled by the stats, but the growth was easy to understand. Scaling meant that it would go up with level, at least that's what it meant in games, so I assumed the same applied here. From my jump from rank **3** to 4, I gained **50** Health, **25** Mana, **10** Attack, **10** Defense, and **50** Shield stats from every rank. The robes were incredible, but they would only grow to be even greater if I could keep gaining strength.

Chloe and Mabel watched the numbers pop up in the air and fade away as I did the mental math. I watched them shift from admiration to excitement, and finally, jealousy. I put myself in their shoes. If we were playing a game and someone in my party picked up a drop like that, I would be jealous as hell. Unfortunately, this wasn't a game.

I had a feeling I had a deity looking out for me. If there were even beings like that in these magical worlds. Shit. I couldn't wait to see the look on Emron's face when I saw him again.

"Okay, girls. Wipe away your drool. Our next mission is going to be to acquire something good for each of you."

I pulled my stats up next and couldn't suppress a broad grin. I immediately felt more confident in my role as a tank, especially when we faced the boss monsters in our next dive.

NAME: JD, AGE: 24
WEAPON: Pen-Blade
CULTIVATION: Realm 1, Rank 4
POWER LEVEL: 300 (141)
HEALTH: 580, **MANA:** 240
ATTACK: 80, **DEFENSE:** 70
MANA SHIELD: 430

"What—in—the—hell!" Chloe hissed, her eyes wide. I suddenly feared that she would get mad, especially when her cheeks puffed out as if she were going to burst. Then she hollered and threw her hands up in the air! "Winner-winner chicken-dinner. That is awesome, right there. So not fair! But, totally awesome."

"Goodness! It must be infused with a high-grade boss core and have a scaling property, or it wouldn't have increased all your stats that much," Mabel whispered. "All of it across the board."

"Wait, can you not see the second part of the description?" I asked.

"Second part?" both asked in unison.

"We can only see the power level when we look at it," Chloe added, quickly.

"Well, it says that it has a *named* rank **9** Heavenly Tiger core."

Mabel stuttered, pointed, stuttered again, and then dropped onto the bed. It looked like she was going to cry.

Please don't cry. Please don't cry!

"Mabel, how does a mana shield work?" I asked, eager to change the subject.

"It is a bubble of mana that covers your body and absorbs mana-infused attacks, spells, and elemental damage. It won't protect you from a punch or a sword slash, however. That would require a separate perk."

"Would that be a deflection perk or something like that?"

"Yes... wait. It doesn't have one... does it?"

I nodded.

"That... is... valuable," Mabel breathed, "But don't let it go to your head. Perks like that are not absolute. If it is a *deflection perk* then there is only a chance it happens—say, only when weapon and attacker strength is below your shield level."

"Interesting. Who would have thought there could be such a system in place?" I mumbled. "Sure, there are all the other stats, but a shield that differentiates between attacks is something else."

"Oh, it is. Especially later on when you fight big and bad monsters. You'll see why it's important. Or when fighting another Student. That extra perk just might stop the one attack you don't see coming. The blade at your back."

"So, spells like his Air Slash would be absorbed by mana shields?" Chloe asked.

Mabel nodded. "Exactly. And the same with your fire mana-infused wave attack. What is it called again?"

"Flame Slash," she replied.

Mabel smiled. "Those attacks are actually very similar. With some more practice, you both should be able to create larger area-of-effect attacks. They will cost more mana but do more damage over a larger area."

"Speaking of mana and skills, how can I see them? I have no idea what it does other than start stuff on fire and use **7** mana."

"Sure. Let me just finish by saying that the amount of damage dealt will be first subtracted from the shield, and then your health points if someone or something were to hit you. They will cover this all-in class, of course."

203

"Right. The more we know, the better," I said, gently petting the sleeve of my robe. Then I caught myself. I was *petting* my robe. Wow.

Mabel noticed and smiled. "This is what I know," she said, yawning. "Not all body parts are the same. Every creature has a critical weak point, and it's usually the head. It can cause double or triple the damage, but it has to be pinpointed. Area of effect attacks won't do the trick."

I nodded thoughtfully, chewing it all over. It was disturbing how similar it was to video games. Or... then my thoughts locked in on Chloe's story. Humans had been recruited from Earth for a long time. Had people somehow gone back? Maybe used their knowledge of the towers to create video games? It made too much sense. I filed that question away into my [shit to think about later] folder, only to see the words pop up in the air.

"What were you just thinking about?" Chloe asked, with a smirk.

"I'll tell you later," I said, laughing. Mabel moved to speak but yawned, and then her stomach growled. Loudly.

"I am hungry and tired. Or maybe just tired," Mabel said and got up. "No, I am definitely hungry."

Chloe and I watched her stumble into the kitchen. My stomach rumbled then, too, not one to be outdone.

"What are we having?" I asked.

"Chorba. It's stew. Trust me, you'll like it. There are large chunks of meat, something that looks and tastes just like potatoes, and some hearty spices. It's kind of like chili, in a way. Come, boyfriend, try it and find out."

I nodded and Chloe pulled me into the kitchen. I pulled out a chair for her and she sat. I let my hand linger on hers for a moment and she looked up.

"Hey, you just called me 'boyfriend' back there?"

"Huh? What?" she said, blowing a quiet raspberry. "I think you're hearing things."

"Uh, I don't know. I've got rather good hearing, girlfriend." I cringed inwardly, realizing how corny and bad that sounded. In a split second, I had become the people I most hated in High School. The—look at us, we're in love kind, that had to always be hanging on one another, splattering the place up with PDA, and calling one another cutesy lovey-dovey nicknames. Ugh. No. Just no!

"You'd better get the food out and eat before..." Chloe said, trailing off.

I grabbed a container, instantly marveling at how the food was hot and steaming when I cracked it open. You would have thought that I had just scooped it out of a boiling pot. I sat opposite Chloe, while Mabel sat to my right, scooping food out into her mouth in impressive spoonful's. I scooted my chair up to the table and grabbed my spoon just as something hit my chair.

Chloe took a bite and chewed, her mouth turning up into a crooked smile. I felt her foot creep up and into my lap. Blood immediately rushed to my groin, and I shifted forward, pressing into her.

"So, JD, what do you think about Zenith Academy so far?" Chloe asked.

Mabel took a bite, smiled, and watched me expectantly. I scooped up a bite as she pushed her foot harder in, messaging it against my hardening member.

"I like it," I grunted, and cleared my throat. "I'm all for a challenge, but I don't think it's necessarily a friendly place."

"Oh, not friendly?" Chloe asked, shaking her head. Her foot immediately pulled away. I immediately cursed my choice of words.

"Not welcoming and not kind to humans," I said, trying to explain. "They don't like us for some reason, even though I don't think they understand us."

"It is what it is," she muttered. "I know only what I've read in the library and heard from other students. But something is going on. We need to focus on making good first impressions for a while. This school will have its clicks, like any other."

"I actually got a really good first impression, specifically when I was introduced to the VIP dorms."

Chloe winked and licked her lips.

"Yes. You all have been so nice," Mabel agreed and jumped out of her chair, and started scooping the food containers off the table. Chloe and I both started to protest, only to watch as the cutlery and napkins disappeared, leaving the table empty and clean.

"I'm off to bed," Mabel declared, "And so should you two. The first day of classes is tomorrow. So important to be rested up. Busy-busy-busy."

We watched the elf shuffle off into the bathroom and re-emerged a few moments later, face clean and wearing a nightgown. I stood, hooked an arm around Chloe's back, and pulled her into me. I bent down and kissed her hard, savoring her sweet, wet lips. She pulled into me, hands sliding up and down my back, the contact of her skin through my robe somehow enhanced. Her tongue met mine and then swept across my lips.

She leaned back then, pulling her robe down one arm, and somehow, shimmied completely free of the garment. It slid down to her feet, and she kicked it up onto the back of a chair. Mabel's bed creaked as she laid down, and Chloe leaned in, naked save that black, elvish underwear. Her breath was hot on my neck, her tongue tickling my ear before she spoke.

"Give the girl a few moments to fall asleep, then join me... if you can get that robe off, that is."

I watched her sweep away. She hooked a thumb in the strap of her underwear, gave them a pull, and then disappeared around the corner. A heartbeat later, the light in the bedroom went dark.

Cultivation of the Ancients

I MOVED INTO THE BATHROOM and washed up, scrubbing my face and brushing my teeth. I turned and moved back towards the bedroom several times but worried I hadn't waited long enough. I walked up to the bath and feared that I'd waited too long. What if Chloe was asleep, too.

Then her words struck me. *If I can get my robe off.* What did that mean?

I reached for the tie at my waist, but it was... gone. Cursing quietly, I followed the fold of the fabric up to my neck and stuck my hand inside, searching for the other tie. It was gone, too. My hand came free just as a small prompt appeared in the air before me.

DO YOU WISH TO HIDE YOUR HEAVEN-DEFYING PALMIRE ROBE?
[*YES / NO?*]

Startled, I chose yes and to my horror, the robe suddenly disappeared, leaving me standing there in the hall, buck-ass-naked. Seriously? Even my underwear was gone. I was keenly aware of wearing them when I'd tried the robe on. This was interesting, and I realized I would have to be careful about where and when I decided to take the robe off.

Immediately aware of my nudeness, and my still very-excited erection flopping around in the air, I ran quietly back out of the bath and around towards the bedroom. The light from the washroom went out as I rounded the corner and had to feel my way forward in the dark.

Shit! I just had to make sure I ended up in the right bed. Now, that would be awkward.

"Ouch, who poked me? And what is that…?"

"Oops. Surprise, Mabel, it's me. And I'm naked. Ta-da!"

My hands bunched up into the blankets and I felt someone shift. Then I heard Chloe whisper, "Get in."

I slid under the covers, pulling the blanket up and over me. I shimmied sideways until I found her. She was laying on her side, facing away from me. She flinched as my hand came to rest on her side, just above the curve of her hip. I let my palm drift down first, sliding effortlessly over her thigh, then back and up, giving her oh-so-shapely rear a gentle squeeze.

There was no thong to get in the way this time.

I felt Chloe's hand capture mine and she pulled me closer. I scooted on the mattress, until I molded around her, a big spoon finally reunited with its little counterpart. She turned her head and leaned back into me, her sweet and spicy smell filling my nose. I kissed her neck, letting my tongue trace a path up to her ear.

"I want you to take your time," she whispered, spreading for me and guiding my fingers slowly between her legs. "I want you to feel me. Feel all of me. Use your hands. Your mouth. Your tongue."

She kept her hand on mine, guiding it back, spreading her warm lips, deeper, pushing past the pearl of her clitoris, and stopped just short of sliding inside her. Chloe moaned, the noise turning almost feral as I teased my fingers in a small circle and then pulled them back, almost removing them entirely.

208

"Oh, you tease! You horrible tease," she groaned and let go of my hand. She reached back and grabbed my ass, squeezing hard.

It wasn't just my desire to tease her, however. I was genuinely worried about putting Mabel into an even more awkward situation. Nothing like moving into a new dorm only to have to lay in a strange bed and listen to your roommate's grunt and groan all night.

Chloe rolled a little further back, pressing even more weight into me. She seemed to know immediately what my hang-up was.

"It's okay. Just listen for a moment," she whispered, kissing my cheek, then my chin, and finally my lips. She guided my hand back and forth, pushing her hips into me to increase the pressure.

I lifted my head, and between Chloe's forceful, lust-filled breaths, I heard Mabel. She snorted and then snored quietly. The sound immediately put me at ease.

"As long as we don't start screaming, I think we'll be fine..." Chloe breathed.

I slid my hand forward, my middle finger, already wet with her arousal, sliding easily inside. Chloe bit off her words and moaned. I opened myself up to my mana as I eased my finger in and out, her sex contracting around me. I pulled back and eased in a second finger and she flinched, pushing her bottom back, grinding it against my throbbing erection. The contact—the soft skin, the heat, and the electric tingle she inspired made my heart hammer in my chest, the ache in my pelvis growing almost painful.

I pushed a bit of energy and strength down my arm and into my hand, infusing it with my sexually charged desire. My fingers practically vibrated in response, and I could tell Chloe approved. She spread her legs wide and grabbed my wrist, urging my fingers in as deep as they would go.

"Easy," I whispered, leaning in to bite her earlobe. Then I intentionally slowed down my movement. "You said you wanted me to take my time, remember? Just relax. Let's see how deep this rabbit hole goes."

She giggled quietly, but I wasn't sure if it was my touch or the bad rabbit hole pun. I meant our connection, our dual cultivation pairing, but my words didn't always adequately convey my meaning.

I did exactly what Chloe asked for, I explored her body, inside and out. I moved my fingers inside her, matching her natural rhythm. Then I switched it up, bending my fingers and moving in a circle, discovering every inch of her. I felt her energy blossom, the warmth of her body gaining intensity until it pulsed with tangible waves against my hand.

"I feel it. It is humming inside me. Can you feel it? Oh, god, JD, I want to feel *you* inside me. Make us whole. Make the connection," she begged, softly.

I could tell she was struggling to stay quiet, the urgent, writhing of her body saying what she couldn't with words. But that just heightened the experience—the danger of waking up our sleeping roommate, the forbidden nature of it. The profound burning in my groin wasn't going to go away on its own, as my body practically pulsed with need. But I knew what to look for now, how to focus on the swirling yang energy inside me. It was pushing outward, straining against its natural barriers and fighting to make contact with Chloe's yin.

I felt Chloe's energy push against my hand, forming an electric bubble between us. It was pulling on me, her yin moving like a living thing, seeking that previously established connection with my yang. The energy of our bodies was pulling us together, drawn like the opposite poles of a magnet.

And that was when she reached down and pulled my hand free. Chloe shifted, the bed creaking in response and her hand found my cock. The touch ignited a fire that shot up through my pelvis and into my chest, and when she pushed back into me, my almost painfully hard erection slid smoothly inside.

Inch by tantalizing inch we joined, the fiery energy swirling around in my chest responding. It pushed down into my stomach and then my pelvis. I pulled back and thrust forward, the bed

210

shaking in response. I drove into her again and again, the warmth and tightness of her body increasing, until I almost couldn't pull free.

She twisted just as our energies connected. Her back touched my chest and together we fell. The bed, the dark chamber, Mabel... hell, the whole academy, disappeared. It was just her and me, our bodies alight and connected in ways we could never understand or explain. I felt gravity shift, tumbling us in one direction, only to have it shift again. But it wasn't disorienting. Our conjoined energy swirled between and around us, encompassing our bodies in a supportive cloud or ever-shifting light and color.

"Achievement unlocked. We have to hold this as long... as... possible," Chloe whispered, throwing me a lusty wink. Then she kissed me, her lips and tongue brushing gently against mine at first but pressing in with increasing intensity.

Supported within our cultivation cloud, I pulled free, but only to bring us closer together. Chloe rolled and I slid over, her legs hooking behind me and pulling me atop her. I felt Chloe ease us together with her legs, but it wasn't just her. The churning cloud of colorful energy wrapped around my hips and forced me forward, sliding my cock right back inside her.

I eased forward, savoring how her tight body accepted me, and kissed her stomach. I pulled back and into her again, tracing my mouth up her body slowly. I ran my tongue between her breasts, kissing my way over to her right nipple. Then I took it into my mouth, teasing it with the tip of my tongue and teeth. I pulled my cock out and pushed into her again, the force binding us together eagerly pulling me towards my climax. I felt Chloe on the other end of that invisible tether.

Make it last... as long as possible, I thought, struggling to suppress that fire, the consuming need to give in.

Chloe wove her fingers into my hair, but as soon as I formed suction, she grabbed ahold. Her legs tightened behind me, and she pulled my head, breaking suction on her nipple and wrenching my mouth up to hers. I returned her kiss hard, her lips and hot breath fueling my fire. Our tongues met as the cloud of conjoined energies changed color around us. The sensation changed as well, the fire of lust shifting like cool blue enervating electricity.

"I don't know how much longer I can last," I grunted, pulling away for a breath. Chloe groaned and pulled me right back into a kiss. Our yin and yang would change one more time. I knew, it, somehow, even though I couldn't explain why. It was the pairing, the exchange. Chloe's energy was feeding something inside of me, I don't know, a weakness perhaps, or a deficit within my soul. And in return, my energy was doing the same to her.

Unable to resist any longer, I broke free from her kiss and rose. I shifted and hooked her legs at the knees, then lifted her hips for a better angle. I thrusted hard, falling into the pairing's simmering, electrical charge. Chloe's breasts bounced as I picked up speed, thrusting into her again and again.

"My, god. I can't. It's coming. Too soon. Have to... wait," she gasped, reaching down between us and grabbing my hand. Then she pulled it forward and wrapped her lips around my thumb and sucked.

Oh, my god, was right. She sucked hard, moaning and twitching her hips.

I felt my climax rise inside me like a runaway freight train, a force too great to ever stop. Then Chloe's resistance seemed to fall away, too. She clutched at my stomach, urging me on harder and faster. I leaned forward, grabbing onto her side with my free hand for better leverage. Then the energy shifted around us.

It changed from crackling blue to orange, bathing us in all the warmth and light of a perfect sunrise. Chloe's body spasmed around me a heartbeat before I tumbled headlong into my orgasm. The light around us brightened, pulsing and surging as I came, wave after crashing wave of stomach-cramping, ball-shaking ejaculation. And then with disappointing finality, our glowing cocoon faded.

I sagged forward, my face nestling between her heaving breasts. I was warm, slick with sweat, and so was she. But I had never felt more right in all my life. It wasn't just the afterglow of great sex, but that deeper connection. It felt like having a missing piece of myself returned, and finally, after waiting so long, being made whole.

I rolled free only to have Chloe snuggle up into my side. She kissed my shoulder and cheek, then I turned to meet her lips with mine. We made out for a while, as we both tried to hold onto that feeling we'd experienced at the very end... that sunshine-like energy. It felt like floating in happiness. If that was at all possible. While we'd been there, we had no troubles, no worries.

Chloe's hand drifted down my chest and stomach and gently wrapped around what we both discovered was my still very erect penis. Before I could even whisper a joke, she threw her leg over me, slid me inside her, and we started again.

Our yin and yang energies didn't blossom or connect that second time, nor did we manage to recreate our cradle of cultivational magic, but that didn't matter. We took our time, kissed each other, exercised our passions in every conceivable position, and by the time Chloe had her fourth orgasm, I was spent. Beyond spent, actually.

I sagged to the mattress and closed my eyes. I think I was asleep before that, but there was no way to be sure. My dreams started, as vivid and real as if I was still awake. To be honest, I thought that I still was, if not for the fact that I was in the tower's central, circular corridor, and Chloe was next to me. What else gave it away? We were clothed.

"Are you really here?" she asked, turning towards me. Her voice was distant, like an echo, despite standing right next to me.

"I think so," I replied. "If only we had a top to spin, heh?"

"Nice Inception reference," she said. "Do you want to know something? I thought I was dreaming of this place when I first arrived. It wasn't until the third night that I realized it was real. Every other dorm was full, but Scarlet kept saying she was still

213

looking. And I would have a roommate when she found 'the right one'. I kept expecting to fall out of bed or get shaken awake every time I opened the door to leave our room. So... strange."

"What do you think it means?" I asked, just as a gust of wind blew through the open space around us. It whistled, the sound tickling my ears. "Did you hear that?"

The wind swirled back through the open space, whipping around the wide support columns and picking up bits of dust off the ground. I couldn't remember if there had been wind in that chamber before. The noise echoed again from above. This time it was louder, and I could tell it was a voice—feminine but strong.

"It's a voice," I said, and Chloe nodded. She turned her head, holding her ear towards the drop-off.

"He is calling my name," she said, "he wants me to join him."

"Him? I hear a woman's voice."

She shook her head and looked up. I did, too. The tower's open core loomed, the floors spanning far above before eventually disappearing into a hazy layer of what looked like clouds.

"He really wants me to come to him. You seriously can't hear him? His voice is strong now, pulling on me, lifting up on me," Chloe said and rocked forward for a moment, as if unsteady. "I want to see him."

I watched her out of the corner of my eye and listened. The voice was louder, incessant. But the wind was too loud. Then it shifted and I heard a single, clear word.

"... JD..."

I turned just as Chloe stepped off the ledge and into the air. My heart leaped up in my chest and I lunged for her. Except, the ground fell away, and I tipped forward, the sensation of falling immediately flip-flopping my stomach.

SHARP CANINES

I SNAPPED AWAKE, flinching from the sensation of falling, only to find Chloe awake as well, fighting to extricate herself from the sheets. She finally flopped free and dropped back onto the pillow, then turned. I blinked away the sleep and caught her gaze.

"Did you…?" we asked, at almost the exact moment.

Yes, it turned out we had. She snuggled up and put her head on my chest, her mouth pulling into a smile. Then she turned towards me, her mass of tousled hair falling over her face. I tucked it behind her ear and planted my lips against hers.

"Well, then. Good morning," she whispered. "Last night was interesting."

"Morning," I yawned and stretched. When I finished, I found her still watching me, waiting. So, I asked the question hanging between us. "Did you know that would happen? If… that really did happen."

"Nope."

She swung her arm and leg around me and then started to softly rub against me. My heart started to race, and somehow, someway, I started to get hard again. How is that even anatomically possible?

"My goodness, how can you still be horny?" I asked.

"Me?" She looked at me, batting her eyes innocently.

Mabel snorted and promptly stirred. She sniffed and sat up. "It smells funny in here. Do you smell...?" she asked, groggily sitting up.

I turned to face the young elf and can admit that I stared. She swung her feet out to stand, bare naked and in all her elven glory. My eyes wandered up to her face and back down. She stretched, highlighting some impressive flexibility, then reached for the nightgown draped over the nightstand. It was only then that she seemed to understand that she was both naked and right in front of us.

I turned away as Chloe laughed.

"Shit, you don't know," she said, "Elves sleep naked."

"Why would I know something like that? I just met my first elves like... yesterday," I protested. Chloe pinched me and rolled, throwing off the blankets. Mabel's eyes widened at the sight of her naked body, but to her credit, she didn't squeal and run away.

"Speaking of which, why *do* you sleep naked?" Chloe asked.

Mabel shuffled around, evidently trying to put something on. Her panties maybe? I turned back to her when I heard weight settle on her mattress only to discover that she was still very much naked.

"This is stupid. You've already seen all of me, so why hide?" she whispered. "I can't be ashamed of my body forever, and if we are going to live together, we might as well get this over with now."

"Right on. I like that attitude," Chloe agreed, and then hooked her arm under my blankets and pulled them off.

"Shit..." I cursed and covered up.

"See," Chloe smiled, now we're all on equal footing. Mabel's eyes went wide, and she covered her mouth, trying to suppress a very innocent giggle. Being a little less comfortable about being naked in front of everyone, I lunged for the sheet and covered up again.

"We sleep naked for a simple reason," Mabel started, her eyes flicking suspiciously towards my mid-section, and then promptly moving towards the ceiling. Her ears actually turned red.

"Yeah. Pretty simple. Elven bodies, uh, they are different. We release our surplus mana as we sleep. If we wear clothes, the mana can become trapped."

"Trapped? I don't understand, can't you just reabsorb it when you wake up? What about the sheets, won't they do the same thing?" I asked.

"I could if I wanted to absorb a bunch of yuckiness," Mabel admitted, her face scrunching up. "But, no. Excess mana carries impurities away from the body, kind of like sweat. If it cannot disperse, the mana will evaporate and leave the toxins on my skin. That residue can cause skills and spells to fail or misfire. Besides, it is totally gross. So, yeah, we sleep... the pure way."

"That is interesting. There are so many things I have to learn. So, I'll just say it in advance, I'm sorry... for all the times I *will* say or do something stupid."

"It's alright, JD. At least you're respectful and aren't doing it on purpose."

Mabel sniffed again. "What *is* that smell? Did you two make food after I fell asleep?"

"No," Chloe chuckled, "JD and I had sex last night. A lot of sex."

"Oh," Mabel said and sniffed involuntarily.

"Does that make you uncomfortable? Knowing we were this close?" Chloe asked.

To my surprise, Mabel shook her head.

"Are you sure?" And to accentuate her point, Chloe reached under the sheet, grabbed my dick, and started stroking it.

Mabel shook her head again but refused to look at the sheet as it popped up with her hand. "You might find it weird, but moon elves are very free with their sexuality. It's just, and yes, you will laugh at this, we have become timid about nudity."

"... have become timid? So, you're not shy about sex, but you are shy about being naked? And you sleep in the nude?" I asked.

"Yes. As I said, you will find it strange."

"But you're naked right now? Doesn't that make you uncomfortable?" Chloe asked.

"You two aren't wearing clothes either. So, no. It is less weird. For my ancestors, this was the most natural state. They believed the moon's power could only be absorbed through the body. They would hold ceremonies, perform rituals, all directed at the moon. All were naked. It was the way."

I rubbed my face, eager for this strange conversation to end.

"So, what changed?" I asked.

"The blood elves. They are un uptight people, and that was before they conquered us. We knew they were uncomfortable with our traditions, our confidence, and natural beauty, but kept to ourselves and tried not to rub our traditions in other people's faces. It wasn't enough for *us* to know they disapproved of our way of life, our culture. They made it a point to outlaw most of our traditions after we lost the war. It went further. They use ritual scarring to deface moon elf maidens in the days before they come of age. Normally it is the face, sometimes the breasts, but others..." Mabel covered her stomach then, the large scar suddenly making far more sense.

My anger swirled as I latched onto a story I heard in community college. A classmate did a report on African tribes and how they would invade their enemy's territory. And if death and destruction weren't bad enough, they would physically cut the breasts off their women and mutilate them in... other ways.

"If they ban you from culture, do they not let you take a partner?" Chloe asked. "Have you ever been with a man before?"

A loud gong-like noise reverberated throughout the tower, interrupting before Mabel could ask Chloe's question.

"Shit! That is the one-hour chime. We need to get ready for class!"

218

We jumped out of bed and hurried to the bath. I waded into the steaming water behind Chloe and Mabel and watched as they immediately submerged, surfaced, and started scrubbing. I knew it was part of this world, beyond the magical and fantastical, just another example of the everyday cultural differences. Here, people were open and free, unabashed about their bodies. They bathed publicly, roomed with the opposite sex, and when the match was right, cultivated their power together. And there were elves.

I have so much to learn, I thought and started scrubbing.

We got cleaned up quickly, the bath filling with the smell of that special soap. It took us only ten minutes to get dressed, after which we sat down for a quick bite to eat.

"How is your hair already half dry?" Chloe asked, after taking a drink of tea.

I listened curiously between bites of my juicy hamburger. It was a small piece of home, and I enjoyed the hell out of it.

"Mana," Mabel explained. "Infuse some into your hair and then let it dry."

Another chime reverberated throughout the tower, nearly vibrating Chloe's teacup right off the saucer. We quickly finished, cleaned up our faces, and slipped on some shoes.

"We don't want to be late for our first class. So, we should go now," Mabel said.

We left our dorm and walked down the corridor, navigating through and around groups of meandering first-year students. The largest throng had formed ahead, ironically, between us and our classroom. A few were arguing animatedly as we approached, some were just talking, and others kept silent, but upon recognizing us, most parted to let us pass.

"Don't you love the attention?" Chloe whispered, but I couldn't tell if she was asking rhetorically.

Was it something we did or said? Or... then I realized it was *who* we were. I was wearing the robe from Old White, which practically crackled with power and awesomeness, and above that,

219

I had a girl on each arm. Holy shit. In this world, I was *that* guy. How is that even possible?

Students whispered and pointed. There were so many more of them than I remembered—three or four different types of elves, two dwarves, giants... boy, they were hard to miss, maybe twelve species of beast-men and women, a group of young, pink creatures that looked strangely like a skinny Buu from Dragon Ball Z, with the elongated head-tails. There were more beyond that. So many more hiding in our periphery. It appeared the other species had arrived. Let the games begin.

"This is going to be a really weird year," I said, leaning over to whisper to Chloe.

"You can say that again," she hissed back, nodding to a kid with scaly skin and crocodile-like eyes and teeth.

I'd never really been good with remembering things—names, birthdays, dates... stuff like that. So, I took it all in, enjoying the spectacle. We'd have many more opportunities to mingle, piss people off, and make friends. Maybe we'd stumble upon another crazy chick Chloe and Mabel could take shopping. That girl, whoever she is, can gladly have my spot.

Several elves stood in the doorway. And they weren't all the dickhead variety blood elves, either. Not wanting to look out of place, I sidled up to one of the darker-skinned elves. His ears were pointier than any of the others, and his skin a dirty, almost granite gray. He also didn't look particularly friendly. More the rabid junkyard dog kind, than the poofy family bichon frise. I turned just as more elves moved in, forming a line to block out other students behind us.

"Hey, look at this guy," one of the dark elves said. I'd played enough D&D growing up to recognize the traits. Now there wasn't much about his posture or physique that scared me, but if he pulled an onyx statue of a big cat out of his robes, I was prepared to turn tail and run.

I turned to the dark elf but kept an eye on the others with my peripheral vision. I tried hard not to stare, but damn, it was hard.

220

I wanted them to be the ones to start shit, but I knew how these scenarios worked. More times than not it was the person that retaliated that got in trouble, not the instigator.

Stay cool.

"You're doing a shitty job!" a blood elf yelled and kicked one of his darker-skinned companions. The poor sob sprawled on all fours. Everyone laughed.

"This place is more like High School than I ever thought possible," I mumbled to Chloe. She nodded and pulled in tighter to my side. Mabel was practically hiding under my arm.

The red-haired bully strolled right up to me, smiled wide, and put a hand on my shoulder. I looked at the hand, then back up at his face, that smug "I'm better than you" smile burning an instantaneous hole through my patience. Part of me wished that I had taken up boxing or karate after school. Curse my indecision.

He whispered, "Move if you don't want to end up like him."

Okay. So, I wasn't Chuck Norris. I wouldn't be taking them all on with my fists and feet, but I still had my natural gifts. And darn it, I could sarcasm with the best.

I shuffled to the side two small steps, Chloe and Mabel moving with me.

"Done," I said, smiling as I nodded. "Thank you for that reminder. Health experts do recommend that you keep moving throughout the day. It is the only way to keep healthy and avoid the onset of avoidable diseases like diabetes."

"Dia..." he echoed, turning a confused expression towards the closest elf. Oh, man, that look was satisfying. I was ready when he turned back to me.

"Yes. **9** out of **10** pediatrists agree. Diabetes is bad. You might have just saved our lives. I am eternally grateful."

Chloe sniggered next to me, and the blood elf turned his sneer her way. Then he seemed to finally notice my robes. His sneer morphed into a smile and was replaced by a frown before his face excreted that god-awful sneer again. He lifted his hand back up to my shoulder, dangerously close to where Mabel stood.

"How about you move that hand, guy," I said calmly, but my tone was as sharp as a knife. I was hot, angry, disgruntled, irritated... in a word, ill-tempered and well on my way to wrathful. It was the hateful, superior gleam in his eye, the condescending sneer, and my brain's insistence on replaying Mabel's story back in my mind. On repeat. With subtitles. I kept seeing that half-moon-shaped scar on her stomach. I couldn't *not* see it.

This prick *believed* it was okay to own someone else, that it was acceptable to cut and scar something pure and beautiful and outlaw their unique culture. I didn't think it would affect me so quickly, but shit, even their proximity was enough to threaten to send me over the edge.

"What the hell is this round-ear doing with Palmire?"

"What-in-the-hell?" the dark elf to my left echoed, grabbing my arm and rubbing the fabric between his fingers. "—shit! That is real Palmire."

I took a deep breath in and pushed it slowly out through my nose, fighting to control the heat and irrational anger telling me to punch him in the face. No, I wanted to Temple of Doom these guys, and give them one last fleeting glimpse of their beating hearts as they slipped into oblivion. Okay, yes, that would be an overreaction.

"Guy," I said, turning to the dark elf. "It's early, so I'm guessing you didn't hear me say it to your friend. But get out of my personal bubble. Bad... touch."

The dark elf turned fully to me, staring directly into my eyes. His were poison-green and his hair a matte silver. His robes were the same as those of his companions: dark blue with white trim and matching white stitching along the hem and the sleeves. He chuckled and tightened his grip on my sleeve.

"Oh? And who's going to stop me? Your patron?"

Chloe and Mabel pulled away just as I lunged forward and grabbed his neck. Then, channeling all my anger and frustration, I pushed him hard across the corridor and into the wall. He hit with an audible *oof.*

222

The dark elf scrabbled against me, slapping my face and chest, clawing and fighting to pull my hand free, but I held firm. One of the perks of dishing out slippery, sweating mugs of beer night after night is the strong grip, I guess.

He snarled and bared his teeth, then hissed. His sharp canines caught the light, the sight and sound sending a shiver up my spine. He almost looked like a vampire at that moment, mixed with an angry snake.

"That is enough!" a strong and resonant voice rang out from behind me. I looked over my shoulder only to find Mistress Scarlet floating, cross-legged on a freaking broom. How in the hell was that possible or normal?

"Let go of him, JD. And the rest of you, make room if you don't want to get kicked out on your first day of class!"

The crowd spat, groused, and whispered, but turned away from the mistress. I tightened my grip on the dark elf's throat and prepared to shove him violently into the wall, but Chloe stayed my hand. Scarlet dropped nimbly from her broom and moved towards us, only to have a dark elf step in front of her, blocking her way. She smiled pleasantly.

"Move, young man."

He didn't move.

Scarlet smiled, and with just the smallest flick of her hand, and a flash of red mana, sent the young elf flying back and into the wall. He hit with an impressive *crack* and bounced to the floor, blood seeping from his head.

"Does anyone else see fit to test my patience this morning?" Scarlet asked, that haunting red light inhabiting her eyes. "You all know what is expected of you. You sat in the cafeteria and listened to our charter rules. Do not misunderstand me when I say, your race may open doors and extend you privileges on your worlds, but it means *nothing* here!"

The students murmured and moved, more than a few of them turning to stare at the young elf lying bleeding on the floor.

"Your spot at Zenith Academy is not a right, but a privilege. You useless maggots *will* show respect to your elders! You *will* carry yourselves with decorum. Or, you will promptly find your happy little butts headed home, with the imprint of my broom on your rears. Am I clear?"

The group of blood and dark elves pulled back from the entrance, gathering their friends as they moved. I suppressed a gleeful smile as the other elves followed suit, eyes down, feet dragging against the ground. They were all obviously scared of Scarlet. Good. My not-Chuck Norris grade fighting abilities would have only gotten me swarmed over and beat up. Now that would have been the wrong way to start my first day.

"Move aside!" a voice rang out. "Move! Aside!"

The throng of students parted for a surprisingly diminutive figure.

"Come on, get out of the way!" he yelled, his massive voice at odds with his surprising lack of size. The man was roughly three feet tall, with hands and feet that looked too large for his body. He wore a pair of spectacles on the tip of his nose, the light gleaming off his balding pate.

He stormed over to the group of elves, and was, I noticed, the only one I had seen so far not wearing a robe, but black trousers and a flowing, cotton shirt.

The small man grabbed the silver-haired elf by the robe. At his stomach, mind you, as he couldn't reach any higher than that. Then he noticed the young man on the ground, specifically the wound on his head. He cursed under his breath.

He released his hold, crouched down, and placed his hand against the wound, and started whispering under his breath. A warm green and yellow aura spread from his hand to the wound. I watched in amazement as the blood flowed right back into the sizable gash, and it closed, without a hint of a scar or bruise.

"Thank you, Zafir," Scarlet said. "If I had known you were so close, maybe I should have hit him a bit harder. It is always a pleasure to see you work your magic."

"Hah, Headmistress, you flatter!" Zafir laughed, good-naturedly. His chest bounced with the sound, again his voice so much larger than seemed possible for a person his size. "I'm just glad he's easy to patch up. The last fool took several days to mend."

"If only they learned," Scarlet said, covering her mouth with the back of her hand, stifling a rather witchy cackle.

"Yes, well. Now, if you'll excuse me, I'll get back to the infirmary. Maybe you can swing by for a coffee and some pastries later? I've heard some interesting things."

"Perhaps," Scarlet said, noncommittally. "I will see you later."

The dark elf groaned as Zafir helped him off the ground, then they moved together down the corridor. The mass of students piled in again, whispering and chattering, eager to see what had happened and to whom.

"Enough gawking! Get inside and pick a seat! Now!" Scarlet snapped as the portal glowed to life, filling the doorway. I watched as students passed through, five wide, before disappearing.

"You want to wait or go in right away?" I asked the girls.

"I want a good place," Chloe whispered and pulled me forward. "Come on!"

"I want to sit in the last row," Mabel added. "That way I can see everyone and everything."

"Alright, then. Here we go. Let's hope classes are better than the welcoming committee." We waited for a pair of dwarves to pass through the portal and walked after them, a wave of cool, blue light washing over me.

An Introductory Seminar

WE STEPPED THROUGH THE PORTAL and not into a classroom as I'd expected, but into the rear of a cavernous auditorium.

Chloe and Mabel pulled me forward, my eyes drawn forward and down. Over forty rows of seats sprawled downwards, leading to a wide and richly appointed stage. Rich, red curtains hung at either side, tied off by large, braided gold ropes. Bright pillars of light illuminated the space, but as I tilted my head up and back, I struggled to find a source.

That was when I noticed the auditorium's full scale. The girls and I moved out from beneath the balcony, the ceiling looming easily...**150 feet.** The number popped into the air before me as I considered the distance. *Points for that,* I thought, appreciating that I wouldn't necessarily have to wonder about things like that anymore.

Not one, but four rows of balconies hung above us, the highly-polished dark wood gleaming in the bright spotlights. Students hung over the railings of all four tiers, pointing excitedly about the room. Chloe and Mabel pulled on my sleeves, urging me towards a seat, but I was too enamored by the space, the sheer size and majesty of it. Hell, I had to take it all in, but in sections—the gray granite slab walls, the large tapestries hanging on both walls. They matched, gently rippling blue fabric with a bright, stylized sun in the middle.

"Find your seats, please. We would like to get started!" a loud voice boomed, all around.

"This place is crazy..." I whispered, turning slowly and struggling to get my brain to absorb everything around me.

Mabel pulled me around and to the side, just as another group of students swarmed in from the portal. They would have run me over, surely.

"Come on," she said, "First-year students and non-nobles can't sit on the ground floor. We have to find seats on the balconies."

I followed the girls around to the left. We made our way to the far wall and up a set of stairs. Elaborate, bronze lanterns hung from the walls on either side as we climbed up, reached up to the landing, and continued. Chloe jumped out through the doorway onto the first balcony but reappeared quickly.

"It is all full. Keep going up," she said, obviously winded.

We continued up the stairs, trumping up flight after flight. I thought I was in decent shape, but the auditorium proved me wrong. I think we were halfway to the second balcony and my calves were on fire and I could barely breathe. Luckily, Chloe and Mabel both sprinted out through the door and didn't reappear.

"Okay... good. You go on... ahead and I'll catch... up," I panted, sucking more wind than was probably necessary for a man my age. *My age? Twenty-four and out of breath struggling up the stairs.* If only I had worked less and worked out more.

Narrow tables stretched the entire length of the balcony, seemingly hewn from a single slab of rippled marble. Wooden chairs, made from the same, polished dark wood as the stairs, railings, and banisters, featured overstuffed green cushions. I followed Mabel in towards empty seats, counting the rows of tables.

227

25. *Thank you, magical world. Damn, twenty-five rows of tables, easily a hundred feet long, per balcony.*

Magic. Holy mother of whoever came up with the place. It was freaking spectacular.

Mabel dropped into an open seat, and I flopped into the one next to her, and then Chloe sat to my right. More students passed around us, but Chloe pushed several chairs away, creating a bit of extra space between us and the others.

"This place is freaking intense!" Chloe whispered, leaning in. "How many people can it hold?"

I was about to say something stupid, but Mabel cut me off.

"Two..." she started to say, only to have the number pop up between us.

2,000.

She watched the number disappear, her mouth pulling into a frown. "Plus..." and she waited.

500.

"... in nobility," she finished, swatting irritably at the number. "But they have space reserved below on the ground floor. Evidently, they don't like stairs."

I watched the elf lean forward and look down towards the stage.

"How will we hear what they say, or see what's on the board? It is so far away."

"Don't worry. Everything in here is amplified through mana," she said. "Trust me, you will see."

I turned to flash her a smile but found her watching the podium intently. She looked nervous. Like a kid on the first day of school. *Shit.* We were kids on the first day of school. It all started to sink in. I was going to learn a form of magic!

Scarlet appeared on the stage then and moved smoothly to the podium. She settled in behind the lectern and summoned a glowing orb. It danced and floated through the air around her. Large, magical cards appeared around her next, white paper

228

catching the light as they floated in a circle. I couldn't see or read them, per se, but could just make out red, painted symbols.

"Greetings, students. It's good to see all of your bright and enthusiastic faces this morning. Welcome to your first day at Zenith Academy. I know you are anxious to get your studies underway, so let us start the first class of our introductory seminar: **The History of This World.**"

The title of the class didn't pop up in front of just me. It popped up in massive, glowing letters before the whole auditorium.

"Hell yes," I whispered. "Now we're talking!"

Scarlet chuckled and somehow, I gathered she turned to look right at us. Had she heard me? If she was magnifying her own voice, did she have a way of listening in on every student in attendance? Damn, the thought was eerie. But then again, my new robe practically glowed, there was that.

Scarlet moved out from behind the lectern and clapped her hands, the auditorium falling silent. An enormous hologram appeared in the center of the room, floating high above her. It was an image of a planet, covered in blue oceans, sprawling landmasses, several that dwarfed the Euro-Asian-African continents, even when put together. I saw clouds and polar ice caps. But it wasn't earth. I had studied a globe enough in school to know that much.

The image rotated and froze, the central, largest landmass on display. It slowly zoomed in, forests, mountains, rivers, lakes, and cities, all appearing. It was devastated, ruined, burned, and twisted... all save for one: an enormous, walled-in city centered around an impossible, monolithic tower. It stretched toward the heavens.

"Is that—wait, is that this tower?"

"Yes," Mabel whispered back.

Chloe dropped a hand under the table and grabbed my thigh, squeezing tightly. My hand covered hers. Warmth radiated from her into my body, accompanied by a part of her feelings.

229

"Now, why did we start here?" Scarlet asked, but it wasn't a question she expected anyone to answer, it was just a statement. "The reason is simple. Many of you, thanks to your birth, family, or race, already know about our world and what this tower is for, but for the others…"

Scarlet paused, allowing the hologram to continue scrolling through images of the burned and crumbling wreckage surrounding the massive wall.

"… for some, the truth is hard to grasp. To absorb. Some fall into denial. While others have even tried to take their own lives. It is too dramatic a shift from the reality they knew. It's for those that fall into the latter category that this class exists. So, please listen carefully."

The image shifted again, and a seemingly endless number of red dots appeared all across the continent, then they spread to the others. I saw small dots, barely noticeable from our distance, while others were large.

"**Beasts**!" Scarlet said, the single word appearing in the air above the hologram. It echoed off the ceiling high overhead, the ground at our feet, and every table. "An untold number of them. They have taken every city within a thousand miles of us. Every village. Every town. Overrun, their buildings torn apart and burned, the people killed. This tower, our tower, was created using the lives of thousands of cultivators and millions of crystals and cores. The sacrifice went deeper. So much deeper, but we will save that for another class. Once constructed, the tower saved this dying world. And thanks to its existence, the continent now looks like this."

The red dots disappeared from around the tower, along with several other smaller regions. They were slowly replaced by large, blue dots. The image zoomed in on one of them, and a smaller city came into view. The walls were tall and sturdy, like the ones surrounding the tower, and manned by hundreds of armed men and women, patrolling, and keeping watch.

230

"We have reclaimed three cities over the course of a century. Our plan for the next hundred years is another five, and that is where you all come in. After you have studied, trained, passed all of our tests, and become more powerful than you've ever thought possible, your **true journey** will **begin**. The term of **service** is **50 years**. For that term, you will fight the beasts on this continent. You will clear out their infestations, hunt their brood mothers, fathers, and kings... their savage and primal monarchs. Through your power, we will reclaim this world!"

"Fifty years?" I whispered, the number rattling around uncomfortably in my head.

"Yes," Mabel whispered, leaning in. "I am the seventh generation of my line selected. But for elves it is different. We live for centuries, even a millennium if careful. I am over two centuries old in human years, but to my people, I am considered a young adult... just out of my teens."

I snorted and barely suppressed a cough.

"Two centuries?"

She frowned and nodded.

"What? What's wrong?"

"Sorry, it's just..." I paused, trying to put my thoughts into words. "It just caught me off guard. I didn't know you lived so long. I thought that was just something they made up for movies and stories."

Scarlet snapped her fingers, the sound filling the space like a crashing gong. It wasn't just the sound, but I felt it, like a blow to the head. The auditorium immediately fell quiet again.

"As for the cities we have liberated, they are under constant guard. By whom? By thousands of cultivators, all graduates of the tower's many academies. Yes. I know the question you all want to ask. The answer is farmland... the one thing we cannot create here."

She stopped, picked up a glass from the table that hadn't been there a moment before, and took a long drink. I was starting to put the picture of my new world together. *Starting to.* But things

231

still didn't make much sense. If there were already so many high-grade cultivators here, why take in people like me? People with zero knowledge or cultivation abilities? Especially since there were races, like Mabel's moon elves, that already understood what was happening and why.

"You all come from different worlds and planes. Some are heirs to kingdoms, future queens, emperors and empresses, warlords, or peasants chosen through divination. Others were at the right place at the right time. None of that matters now. We all share one thing in common: as long as you are here, you... your life, belong to us, the academy. Nothing can change or supersede that."

Scarlet snapped her fingers and the hologram changed back to the worldview. A single green dot appeared on our continent, just where the city had been. Then it panned further out, revealing two more towers on other continents.

"Every continent has a tower, and every tower can grow warriors... some better, some worse. Yes, there is competition to be the best. But at the end of the day, we all fight for the same thing: a tomorrow. So, now I ask you all a question. Why are we using you, students, to fight this war?"

Hundreds of hands shot up. But none appeared to be on our balcony. I twisted around, anxiously waiting to hear the answer.

Scarlet nodded toward one of the more human-looking species.

"Thank you, Headmistress, you have my greetings. We are here to earn the privilege to keep the powers we get here. If we were to drop out of the academy, graduate, and then desert from the fight against the beasts, we would wither and grow weak. Students earn their power through the fight."

"Exactly!" she snapped. "We give you power, but you have to earn the right to keep it, otherwise everyone would just take the powers home, wouldn't they?"

"If we *could* go home in the first place," I muttered, shifting uncomfortably on the seat.

Scarlet looked right at me, and this time I was sure she could hear me. *Ah, shit.*

"Some races can't go back... even if they want to," Scarlet said, her eyes sliding from me and back to the others. "Their people, their societies, are incapable of accepting anything beyond what is already *known*. And that is why their worlds are barren of mana or any kind of magic. If they were allowed to return, they could take over whole worlds. So, what I say next is for those individuals."

I felt Chloe's grip on my leg grow tight, and although Scarlet didn't look directly at us, I had the distinct feeling that we were the only three people left in the cavernous auditorium.

"When those people finish their 50-year service, they are presented with a decision. Do they join the academy, go out into the city and live out their lives, or do they stay in the army as a distinguished veteran? There is another option, although I do not like speaking of it. If they do not fancy those options, they can present themselves to the tower, and allow it to strip away their power and memory, and then send them back."

The holo of the planet disappeared and then lit the place up again, showing five different kinds of creatures.

"Moving onto beasts," Scarlet said, her tone brightening, "They are separated into five different categories. "First are the **Mundane**. They can vary in size and power, but the one thing that ties them together is that they possess no elemental affinities or special powers."

The first category zoomed in and spread out across the auditorium. Creatures ranging from ordinary rabbit-like creatures to dogs, wolves, bears, snakes, and even one that looked like a giant gorilla.

"The second category of beasts are the **Magics**. They possess an elemental affinity to one element and are generally much stronger. Don't be fooled by their size, as the magical beasts can be much smaller than their mundane brethren, but also much stronger. They can be of any element."

233

The image changed to another, showing off more beasts, but with vastly different traits. Some had flaming heads, other hooves made from ice, bodies of steel, or tree bark-like skin.

"The third category are **Fero** beasts, referred to as savage, by most. These creatures possess at least one special trait or elemental affinity. They're usually anywhere between the sixth and twelfth rank."

"Now those look scary," I muttered, watching the images flip through. Most were at least the size of large trucks. And although I told myself size wasn't everything, especially in this world. But in this case, they were truly awe-inspiring. I didn't know how I would approach fighting such foes.

"The queen we faced was a magicis," Chloe whispered, "But she was quite weak. Same with the cockroach. He was slightly stronger but in the same category."

I nodded, knowingly. It was hard to understand just how strong something *could* be after only diving into the weakest dungeon a single time. Sure, I was looking forward to seeing more, but from a safe distance. Like those flaming and ice-covered monsters. If only I had a phone with me so I could snap a few selfies. Now wouldn't that be all the rage?

"We've come to the fourth category," Scarlet said, drawing my attention back down to the podium. "The fourth category are the **Regium** beasts... the so-called king and queen ranked beasts. Don't be fooled. Anything can have the words king or queen in their name, but that doesn't necessarily mean they are in this category. For example, you have the Ape King, who actually belongs to the fero category of beasts. King and queen-ranked beasts are extremely strong for their stages and can appear on every floor of a dungeon. Even on the first one."

"Are they supposed to be boss beasts?" a voice rang out just below where we sat. "Or am I wrong?" It belonged to a tall, broad-shouldered woman. A giantess. Her fiery red hair was pulled back into an enormous ponytail.

234

"They can be bosses, but it's not exclusive. Just the other day several students killed two second-category bosses inside our local dungeon. If the creatures had been rank **3**, the students would have died horrible deaths."

Several students sitting near us glanced our way knowingly. Shit. It appeared the news traveled fast. Keeping secrets at Zenith would be difficult. I kept it in mind for the future, as people coveted treasure and glory above almost everything else.

"Hah, would serve them right for getting into a fight before classes even began!" a student shouted from below.

"Hush, child," Scarlet snapped. "If you had even half the balls the girls showed during that battle, you wouldn't be speaking now. Or brains for that matter, to learn when it is appropriate to speak."

A chorus of laughter reverberated throughout the auditorium. I leaned over the edge and looked down, confirming the voice had come from a group of blood elves.

"Serves him right for trying to piss on us," I muttered.

Chloe's hand squeezed hard on my leg as she moved her chair over next to mine, then leaned her head against my shoulder.

"I'm not usually a PDA kind of girl," she whispered. "But it feels good to have something... err, someone familiar around. Know what I mean?"

I turned down to stare into her eyes and smiled. She was right. It did feel good, and not just because I was in a strange place, surrounded by strange people, customs, experiences, expectations, and... well, everything. Okay, so not completely. But mostly. Chloe had most of the things I'd been looking for in a girl... ever since I had been dating. It was almost like someone, or something screened us and put us together. Had they?

"Something of note about the king and queen category," Scarlet yelled. Her voice washed over us again like a gail wind, blasting the student's idle conversation away.

"That is better. Today is your one chance to acclimate to this academy. Starting tomorrow, idle chit-chat during a professor's time will not be tolerated. Now, as I was saying, king and queen beasts are normally somewhere in the second or third realm and have at least two or three specialties. They can also possess dual elements in some circumstances. A prime example is the Frost Giant Ymir. He is in the third realm and has three specialties, but all pertaining to his affinity for ice."

"How likely are we to face the third or fourth type of beasts in the dungeon?" another voice asked, but much further down and closer to Scarlet.

"Highly unlikely," she replied. "Once you hit the fifth floor you will encounter the occasional third category beast. On the tenth, there is a chance you will stumble upon a king or queen at full strength. However, and this is important, so listen up," she said and held up a finger. "That does *not* mean that they can't push through to the lower level. If you see one. Run. They won't be as strong as they would be on the upper floors, but they're still frightening and likely well beyond what any of you could handle."

"Thank you, Headmistress," the same voice said. Scarlet nodded and flashed the young man a warm smile.

"This feels like a natural time to move onto the fifth category of beasts. Those are **Ancients**, beasts that have lived for decades, even centuries, depending on the species. They have grown and evolved their way to the top of the food chain. Just like you, there are male and female varieties. The former are hunters without equal, beasts of cunning and unequaled hunger. Meanwhile, the latter are usually brood mothers, though do not let the term fool you. They are likely equally strong."

She stopped, allowing the glowing image to change. A beast appeared, massive, and... well, I didn't know how to describe it. It looked like a mammoth, but without all the fur. It had large tusks, though. And it walked on two legs and had arms like a man. How did I know the last part? Because it held a gigantic hammer.

"Shitballs," I whispered. "A weapon?" Chloe clucked her tongue next to me, and Mabel whistled quietly.

"As you can see, they are not your run of the mill, stick a fork in it and be done, beast. Brood mothers are territorial. They and their young will stay in a region and defend it, violently. Obviously, you can avoid conflict with them by simply avoiding their territory. But if you stumble into their midst, expect a fight."

"Just imagine going toe to toe with that," I whispered. "Shit, I get goosebumps just thinking about it. That hammer looks big enough to flatten a house!"

"Shh," Mabel hissed. "Things are getting interesting."

I rolled my eyes and shut up but leaned further into Chloe. Mabel wasn't wrong.

"Does anyone have any questions so far? Good," the headmistress asked, but continued before anyone could speak. "**Behemoths**. The sixth final category is the most dangerous. Their power level does exceed those of their ancient kin, yes, although not by much. Their main danger comes from their ability to form and control beast waves. They are extremely aggressive and smart, and usually have more than two elemental affinities and special traits. Just the mana alone they exude is enough to kill a lesser man."

"Mistress!" a female voice rang out far to my right. "Is it true that they can take on a humanoid form?"

Scarlet mulled over the question before finally nodding.

"That is true. But in reality, most beasts above rank four can take on a roughly humanoid shape. With that said. They radiate impure mana, so it is easy to spot them... to the trained cultivator-eye, that is."

"So how do we fight them?" the same red-haired girl asked. She flexed her giant muscles, but it didn't have the effect I think she was trying for. Laughter echoed from the blood elf contingent directly below us.

"Leave it to a giantess to ask," Scarlet laughed. "To answer your question: ridiculously hard. You would need to expend large-scale magical skills, which would require quantities of mana and crystals you do not possess. Even then the probability of killing a category six, five, or even a strong four is small. The beasts could simply expel their life force to protect themselves. Some would

237

purge mana into toxic clouds, likely killing anyone foolish enough to remain close."

"Then how *do* we kill them?"

Scarlet smirked as she looked right... we were sitting behind the giantess, after all.

"You go in hard and fast, get up close and personal, and without wasting time or energy, cut their hearts out."

The girl seemed to notice the mistress looking past her and she turned, staring right at me. Her deep blue eyes reflected the light, shimmering like the ocean. And she had a pretty face, too, with a splash of freckles across her nose. Physically, she was imposing, however. Her shoulders were broader than mine and had arms a bodybuilder would be proud of. I couldn't be sure, but judging from how she sat in her seat, she was at least a head taller than me. Her clothes caught my eye, just as those around her turned to stare as well. It was a bodysuit and seemed to shimmer.

"You carved the boss's hearts out, pretty boy?" she asked.

"We certainly did," Chloe snapped. "Both of them. Cut them right out!"

The girl snorted, shook her head, and turned back around. Scarlet's eyes lingered on mine for a moment longer before looking away. Murmurs broke out as students started chatting animatedly, but a single snap was enough to quiet them down again.

"Are there any questions?" Scarlet asked. "I know this has been a very basic overview, but your individual classes and books will go over everything in more depth. This is not a typical school. We do not have curriculums that waste your time with information you don't need. No. Here we will only teach you those things that will help you become stronger, and help you survive out there." She pointed to her right, indicating the world beyond the tower. "You don't even have to attend. You can hunt beasts in the dungeons and become stronger like that if you're sure of your abilities."

"Mistress?" Mabel asked, suddenly raising her hand.

238

In typical fashion, most of the auditorium turned to track the voice and stare. And seeing how we were huddled together, they stared at us too. "What if a high category monster would spawn inside the dungeon?"

"Ahh, now that's a good question. See, some seven decades ago we had an incursion inside the tower. A category five formed a beast wave and somehow, using mana manipulation we still don't understand, bridged all the dungeons together. Then it unleashed its wave on the tower. Hundreds of students died that day. We managed to defeat him in the end, but the cost was great."

"Shit," I muttered under my breath. "Inside the dorms."

"And what about the rifts throughout the tower? Were they invaded?"

It took a moment for my noob brain to catch up with Mabel's question. Our pocket dimensions used for storage were rifts, but in a way, so were the many extra-dimensional spaces. The bazaar was likely one, too. If beasts had managed to infiltrate the tower, that means they could have breached those areas as well.

Scarlet shook her head. "Thankfully no. When the tower was breached, we were able to deactivate most of the portals, effectively sealing off those areas."

"Most?" Mabel asked, catching on faster than me.

"The beasts hit so hard and fast, some portals were immediately compromised. And since those areas are located on different planes of reality the people located within them had no means of escape. Those areas physically connected to the tower... places like the cafeteria or the armory were hit the hardest, however. It was a day these academies will never forget."

"Were you there?" another student asked from far across the room.

"I was," Scarlet said, her voice catching. "It was a rare behemoth, a particularly old and strong one at that. It was in the third realm, somewhere in the middle around rank 6. The cursed thing swept the first floors in minutes, sending thousands of smaller beasts down the stairs and lower floors. That wave alone contained

239

tens of thousands of category ones. We only managed to hold them back. We fought for hours after that... room by room, passage by passage, clearing everything up to the seventeenth floor."

"That has to make her what, seventy? Eighty?" Chloe whispered. "She doesn't look a day older than my cousin. How does that work?"

"Really? She has been cultivating for a long time. Mana makes you age differently. You two are the worst," Mabel muttered. "I'm trying to listen!"

"Sorry," Chloe mouthed as her hand moved up and down my leg.

"Me too," I whispered. "The listening part."

Chloe rolled her eyes and shrugged but didn't remove her hand. I didn't mind. and subtly slid my hand into the fold of her robe and slowly hooked a finger inside her thong. She practically purred.

I looked back down at the headmistress just as a student asked a question. I didn't hear what they asked, only Scarlet's rather clipped response.

"Yes, you can use the bathroom. Go. Does anyone else need to go potty before we continue?" she asked, tapping her heel impatiently against the stage.

"This place might be more like home than I realized."

240

CATCHING UP WITH THE BASICS

MORE STUDENTS GOT UP and trickled out for a break and I watched Scarlet track everyone with her eyes. If looks could kill those students wouldn't necessarily die, but damn, they just might get frozen alive or catch some strange and incredibly painful illness.

"Okay. We'll go ahead and jump back into it. The others can get caught up later," Scarlet yelled. Her voice immediately cut through the idle chatter. She walked out from behind the lectern and moved forward to the edge of the stage, stopping a moment to smooth a crease out of her tight, black robe. And then she looked up right at me again, that strange and haunting red glow in her eyes somehow visible even through the bright spotlights.

Something twisted in my guts, then deeper. Every time she looked at me, I immediately struggled with the feeling that she was analyzing, waiting for, or maybe even hoping for something. Did she have ulterior motives? A single question remained unanswered. Why was *I* specifically recruited for Zenith?

Chloe mentioned she'd waited to be paired with a roommate while they *searched* for the right one. But why? And what criteria had I met?

As if sensing my troubled thoughts, Chloe squeezed my leg.

"So? What did you think?" Chloe asked.

"About?" I whispered back.

"Last night," she bent in closer. "It was different. More intense. Almost as if it momentarily transported us someplace different. I think we need to do more research, see how far this connection goes and why."

"I'm up for that kind of 'research' any day," I whispered back as Scarlet hit the table with her open palm.

"Oh, she looks mad," Mabel whispered, wringing her hands.

"Now, we will move on to **Cultivation Basics.**" The hologram appeared before us, depicting a glowing warrior, crouched in a fighting stance.

"When it comes to Martial Arts Cultivation, the body becomes both your weapon and your shield. Fundamental forms compromise the basics but elevate in complexity, difficulty, and destructive potential as strength and mana integration increase. Body Tempering is perhaps the single most basic and important achievement for those who fight with bare fists and foot."

"What about the mana-infused skills, Mistress?"

"Good question. It would seem obvious that a punch is not a powerful attack when compared to a beast that can tear through steel and stone with its claws. But that is where you need to let go of what you think you know and open your mind to several new truths. First: the stronger your body becomes, the more damage it can sustain and inflict. It is your base. If it cannot withstand the recoil of your attacks, it will break. That goes for casters, too. Mana backlash from a magical spell could kill you faster than your opponent."

Two martial artists started fighting on the hologram, throwing punches and blocking. They sparred for a good twenty seconds, then the fighter on the right performed a hard roundhouse kick. The fighter on the left blocked, and even though his arm crumpled from the blow, the attacker's leg shattered. The class groaned sympathetically.

242

"This example is exactly what I mean. A tempered body doesn't just withstand weapons and high-level skills, but it can turn defense into offense. We won't go into that in more detail here, as hand-to-hand combat is taught by special instructors in our sparring classrooms. If you're not into martial combat, then there is always..."

I watched as Scarlet hiked up her sleeves and thrust both hands into the air. A wild, searing column of fire erupted from her left palm, while a shower of ice leaped from her right. She angled her hands inward, bringing the contrasting elements together high overhead. The ice melted but doused the fire, releasing an impressive cloud of steam.

"That would be handy, especially if you're in the mood for a little sauna time," I whispered. Chloe chuckled and shook her head.

"That sounds hot and sweaty," Chloe chuckled. "I like the sound of that."

"It would be a great way to decompress after rigorous training."

"You two are driving me crazy," Mabel hissed. "You're radiating so much sexual energy, it's not even funny. Do you know what that does to elves? We are incredibly sensitive to those kinds of vibrations."

I mouthed, "I'm sorry," just as Scarlet spoke again.

"So! What did you just think of my little trick? Did everyone like that impressive light and fire show?" Scarlet asked, her voice several times stronger than it was moments ago. "Let me show you again, slower, and in practical steps."

The headmistress stuck her palms in the air again, mana flushing out and over her palms. The magical energy pooled and then abruptly flashed brightly.

"Did you see that?" Scarlet asked. I pushed the mana up and over my hands. You will be able to feel it, like ice water covering your skin. Once you have enough pooled, simply mold it into what you want it to become. Mana is like clay, and your mind, the tool. Shape it."

The mana burst into an arcing, flashing bolt of lightning, and connected both of her outstretched hands. It formed a ring that kept expanding and growing larger until it leaped high in the air. Small, dancing bolts flashed off the arching ring, crackling and superheating the air around her. A gust of wind ripped across the stage, billowing Scarlet's robe as it swirled and spiraled around her. The wind hit the lightning circle, flashed bright, and morphed into a bright circle of flames, a raging inferno that spread out in all directions. A circle of mana appeared, containing the fire into a perfect sphere.

"That's high-tier magic," Mabel whispered. "Just look at the control! That's incredible! She isn't just powerful, she is gifted!"

As someone who, up until a few days ago thought that card tricks and sleight of hand were the most magic I would ever know, I just agreed simply that it was super-impressive. Then again, if someone walked up to me and made a quarter actually levitate off their hand, I would probably giggle uncontrollably.

This? Watching Scarlet mold and bend mana to her will was freaking amazing, Merlin-level shit. Truly.

My heart stirred with the thought of being able to command magic like that myself one day. Sure, I could already use some skills with my pen-blade, but that felt like a completely different zip code from shooting flames or lightning bolts out of your hands.

"And that is that," Mistress Scarlet said, her billowing cloud of flame abruptly going dark. "One of the most important stats you need to have as a **Magic Cultivator** is **Mana**. Everyone gets mana as basic stats, but only those at a higher **Realm** can upgrade their mana circulation through practice. For those that don't know, that is simply the speed at which your mana regenerates. For most cultivators, it is equal to **1%** every five seconds. If you are working out the math in your head, that means it will take approximately **8** minutes to regenerate your mana stores."

I followed the numbers as they appeared in the air. Then Scarlet took a sip from her glass and straightened her robe. I noticed that it didn't lay right on her body, not since the powerful gust of wind rolled over the stage. A lace garter flashed into view on her thigh as she fought to fix the garment.

"Think you can learn those spells, too?" I asked. I reached for the armrest to her chair and accidentally grabbed her knee. Mabel jumped.

"Y—yeah, I think so..." she stuttered.

"Why is this important?" Scarlet asked, cutting in and rescuing us from further awkwardness.

"Because you can't cast beyond your level?" a student shouted.

"Right but also wrong," Scarlet responded. "Technically you can. But you cannot cast high-tier spells if the demand exceeds your mana count, and if you have to constantly wait for your mana to refill before casting again, then I'm sorry to say it, you're useless as a **Magic Cultivator**."

"She's so right," Mabel whispered. "If only I had a true magic-based affinity."

"Isn't it something anyone could learn?" I asked curiously.

Mabel shrugged. "They can, but it takes much more effort and a lot of time. Not to mention the items you would have to purchase. Crystals aren't cheap, and neither are the ingredients used for magic cultivation. In that same time, a person could make much more progress along with their natural affinity."

"But with us, you might find that it is easier," I whispered, and her eyes narrowed. She watched me for a second, turned back to listen to Scarlet talk about support magic, and then turned back.

"What do you mean?"

"As it stands now, you can't do much in a battle aside from snare enemies, and maybe once you've learned, provide buffs for Chloe and me. What if you started picking up some offensive magical cultivation? We could work on your mana regeneration rate and your total count. Then, during a fight, you could still support, but also throw some of that awesome destructive mana magic around."

Mabel watched me for a long moment. As if waiting for the other shoe to drop.

"You mean that? I ask because the cost would be high," she said. "I'm much more useful in a support role, though."

I nodded. "Of course, I do. Why wouldn't I? We're a team, aren't we? If one of us grows stronger, then we all do as a result. I want you to be able to defend yourself, against any enemy." I finished speaking and watched her eyes, having held back so much. I wasn't even talking about beasts at the end, but the blood elves and their wretched ways.

"So!" Mistress Scarlet continued. "What is the second most important stat for a **Magic Cultivator**?"

"Attack!" a girl from somewhere on our balcony called out.

"Exactly! As far as stats go, yes. But that is relatively straightforward. I want to talk about another skill that is as important to you magic users as Body Tempering is to martial fighters. Let's talk about **Mana Tempering**."

"That's one of the four holy beginner skills, right?" a giant from several rows below asked. He was bald and broad-shouldered, looking every bit the powerlifter.

"Exactly. We already showed you two of them: **Mana Charge** and **Mana Discharge**, but to keep confusion to a minimum we will save that part of training for your classroom time. You'll get to learn them from your teachers."

Scarlet's fingers snapped again, and the hologram changed to that of an aerial view over what looked like a battlefield. I thought it was a movie at first, but as it zoomed in, I realized that it was real life... likely sometime in the past.

"If you look here, you'll see that magical cultivators are situated at the back since they have long cast times and are more vulnerable. That's why Mana Tempering is so important. It helps you shape the mana to your will faster. But it isn't just about speed. Tempering will allow you to forge stronger spells with greater elemental effects. That way, you know that every bit of mana you throw forth will do the most damage possible. Mana tempering is great for spells, yes. But not all of them, mind you. Take into consideration that it is a process and will not work on minor skills, especially those that have an instantaneous cast time."

I listened, not knowing how everything pertained to me. But decided right away that I would throw myself into every lesson of every class with all of my attention and focus. If I was going to fail in this new world, it wouldn't be for a lack of trying.

"I have that scroll," Mabel said, out of the blue. "I will share it with you."

"Aren't scrolls single-use?" I asked, unsure if my elf friend had mind-reading abilities. Because that would get awkward quickly. I have a relatively dirty mind.

"No, I have a spare one. I will show you how to use it later."

"Next is **Cultivation Crafting**," Scarlet said and the students below us started yelling and heckling. I couldn't tell if they just didn't have any respect for the crafter school, or they were just being dicks. But Scarlet's eyes immediately flashed red. Okay, so they were...suicidal.

"Show the headmistress some respect, you...!" I yelled, but the red-haired giant girl from below cut me off.

"Will you shut up!" she boomed. The rowdy crowd immediately went silent.

"The next student that speaks out of turn will find themselves hanging upside down in my closet, naked, and covered in leeches," Scarlet said, her voice dropping to a cold and deathly whisper. Yet, we all seemed to hear here just fine. Then she turned to the giant girl and me in turn. "Thank you."

"Scary woman," I whispered. "Hot, but scary."

"Pfft, so am I!" Chloe chuckled, her voice so low I could barely hear. "And yes, she is. Got to give credit where it's due."

I shut up, afraid she might hear us and focused on what she'd say next.

"**Cultivation Crafting** is straightforward. Crafters are a class that supports us from the backlines, similarly with the **Magical Cultivators**. They create, test, and equip traps, snares, weapons, and specialty armor for warriors and hunters. They help the rest of you restrain beasts, win fights, and survive those battles you probably should have avoided. They are not fighters, but good crafters are more valuable than a dozen warriors. Do not let big-headed martials tell you otherwise. Pick crafting as your specialty and you, too, can learn to make weapons like this. Besides, all the weapons you received during your tryouts were made by crafters. Remember that."

Scarlet pulled a small crossbow from... somewhere in her robe. It had what looked like a magazine on top, and yet the whole weapon looked barely longer than her hand. She opened the magazine, pulled out something incredibly small, and held it up.

"This is a magical capsule. It is crafted with rift magic to store one hundred bolts. Depending on the skill of the crafter, they can be poisoned, explode, freeze on contact, or deliver a measured electric charge."

The headmistress placed the capsule back inside, lifted the crossbow toward the ceiling, and fired, just as a massive ball of ice appeared high above her. Two bolts flew straight into the target, erupting into impressive, fiery infernos.

"That looks like it came from a dwarven crafter. They're obsessed with creating small, portable weapons. They're usually insanely powerful, too," Mabel said, quietly. "I've never seen one like that before. My uncle got his hands on a dwarven poleaxe, though. It was enchanted with ice. Every time he grabbed it, the blade would frost over. He tried to recharge it with his own mana and it kind of blew up in his face. He was one of my favorite relatives."

"Was?" I whispered.

"It killed him. Blood elves don't allow us to have weapons like that. He couldn't take it to a smith or a crafter for work, so he tried to do it himself. When it blew up, it killed him and took half of his house with it."

I let out a long breath, envisioning what it would feel like to hold such a weapon.

"I'm sorry. That must have been pretty hard."

She nodded, that hollow look returning to her eyes.

"If we had access to such a weapon," I replied, "Well, just think about the possibilities."

"It's not as simple as pulling the trigger, JD," Mabel said, "Those shots are infused with potential. The wielder still has to use their own mana to fire them off, guide them, and initialize the destructive potential."

I nodded. It all came down to mana, in one way or another.

"Do you want one?" I asked. "I mean, think about it. It could help deal sustained damage from a distance while you support. If you're in the back, you have a better chance to spot weaknesses. And it is a means of defense, as well."

Mabel nodded and pursed her lips as if falling into deep thought.

"Last but not least, **Beast Mastery**! The primary function of a beastmaster is control and taming, but also absorption of their power. A beastmaster can extract beast cores and absorb them. When you consider that more powerful beasts, and this depends on their realm and rank, can possess anywhere from three to ten cores, all possessing potentially elemental-based mana. A beastmaster will know how to handle, store, and best use those cores. Interesting? Well, you'll love this. Beastmasters can actually equip beast cores and use their power to supplement their own. Remember our motto when it comes to mana—waste not, want not."

Scarlet summoned an honest to God beast right there on the podium. It wasn't big, probably close to six feet tall, with an oddly monkey-shaped head and face, short legs, and long arms ending in clawed hands. Now that I thought about it, the thing almost looked like a Gorilla but with a thinner, smaller build.

"This is a **Clawback**! I can control a dozen of them without issue, and you can, too... if you opt into that specialty."

"What about the other specialties? Can they equip beast cores as well?" asked a large, broad-backed young man.

"As long as a cultivator has the necessary proficiency and their body is adjusted accordingly, yes, anyone can do it," Scarlet replied. "But it won't help a magical cultivator when you consider those equipped cores will negate any mana tempering or other beneficial skills. And speaking of skills, **Beastkin** can take this one step further. With the right power, they can transform their bodies into the shape of a beast they have an affinity for. Or... as I said before that they can take this one step further, a beastkin of high enough level can actually temporarily absorb a beast's core and take their shape."

That news interested me, and I suddenly wondered what beastkin were, exactly.

"Headmistress," I called out, genuinely interested in hearing more about what beastkin were, exactly. But somehow, the connection between my brain and my mouth went screwy, and something completely different came out. "Ugh, what's the highest rank beast any of the beastmasters have in this... place?"

What? What's the highest-level beast? Why didn't I just ask her if Pokemon are real?

"Oh, JD," Scarlet said, her tone and posture saying more than her words. It was as if she was saying, *"I had such high hopes for you"*. "I can safely say the most powerful beast contained within this tower is above rank 6 of the second realm. Now, does anyone else have any equally smart questions they want to just yell at me? No? Good. Moving on."

I tried to melt back into my chair, heat blossoming on my face and neck. The crowd didn't say anything. Hell, they didn't even heckle. That would have been better, as they just glanced at me over their shoulders.

"Now, the last thing we will go over today is a rundown of the tower and its available facilities. This is going to be a lot of information, and you will probably want to take notes. I will give you a minute to prepare."

The auditorium erupted with chatter as Scarlet took a seat, picked up her drink, and took a few sips.

"I can't wait until we're done," Chloe muttered. "I'm already stiff as hell and this chair isn't doing me any favors!"

"Your own fault," Mabel whispered. "If you would have gotten some sleep last night and didn't let him be all over your...breasts."

"What...wait... what did you just say?" Chloe asked, sitting forward and almost laying across my lap. "Since when is it a crime to have big tits? And besides, yours aren't much smaller! Were you just putting us on this morning? Were you awake last night, listening to us?"

"Of course, I was awake," Mabel replied, calmly, and folded her arms over her chest. "How am I supposed to sleep through all that groaning, moaning, and bed creaking. I didn't want to embarrass you."

"Oh, boy," I groaned and leaned back, rubbing my face.

"Embarrass me?" Chloe snorted, "You're adorable. We tried to be quiet for you."

"Can we not have this conversation here? This isn't the place," I protested.

Just then Scarlet got up and clapped her hands. The commotion in the auditorium died down immediately.

"Dorms! There are two types of... yes, I know. It sounds stupid to talk about them, but you would be surprised by how many students we find trying to sleep in the corridors. So, listen up. Every student is registered in the academy's magical system, and there you will remain until graduation. Twenty percent of the dorm capacity is assigned to the first years, twenty to the second years, fifteen to the third years, fifteen to the fourth years, and the rest are for holdovers. The second type is the special dorms. Some refer to them as VIP dorms."

251

She paused and the holo changed, shifting from the insides of the ordinary dorms, which looked nice, to a dorm just like ours. We immediately drew several nasty glances.

"Twenty special dorms are given to first-year students, thirty to second, forty to third, and fifty for upper classes. They must be earned either through deeds or for the cultivation of a rare or promising affinity. Another way to become part of a special dorm is to get invited to their party. Unlike ordinary dorms, special dorms can grow. Add another room. Or two. Fancy a gym, or a second bath? Maybe a kitchen or a sex dungeon. Maybe a sparring room or a beast pen? Whatever it is you want, you can upgrade the rift inside accordingly. The requisites are written on your door from the inside. The tower grants permission, although entry is fueled by your mana."

"Ahh! So, we can have a bedroom of our own?" Chloe whispered, excitedly.

"Privacy would be nice," I agreed. "It would be nice to expand the space, especially if more people join our small group. I like the idea of a sparring room, too."

"Someone like me?" the red-haired giantess asked, having turned around in her seat.

"Maybe, if you prove yourself in battle," Chloe said.

"Have you ever seen one of my kind in battle before?"

I listened to the two girls talk but didn't respond. And honestly, I couldn't deny that I was intrigued and kind of wanted to see the giant girl in action. She looked like she could swing a mean sword or ax.

"Enough!" Scarlet yelled from the podium and before I could move, curse, or even lean out of the way, a flash of lightning tore off her hand and struck all four of us. It didn't hurt much, but it stunned me momentarily and worse, sapped all of my mana. Poor Mabel. She hadn't even been talking and she was hit, too.

"Thank you for helping me make that point. We will talk about classroom etiquette later. Now, how about we get to the second matter?"

252

I cursed through clenched teeth as Scarlet shot us a smirk.

"Cafeteria. Every Saturday and Sunday the food is on us. We decided to change it slightly to give you the sense of being able to take two days off and rest, study on your own, or do whatever it is you youngsters do where you're from. Lunch and dinner. That's it. Lunch is at twelve, while dinner will be served promptly at six in the evening."

"What about breakfast?" a tall student asked. He looked more alien than any of the others, with a long, slender neck, and oblong head. "Isn't breakfast the most important meal?"

Scarlet promptly ignored his question and forged on.

"Violence on the grounds will not be tolerated. The only exception is in the arena. If you want to fight, go there. Anyone caught intentionally causing bodily harm to another student will not only have it repaid on them personally, but they will risk expulsion and banishment. Bullying is discouraged. The mistresses and other teachers have enough on their plates and cannot afford to babysit you. However, I will say this. Preventing someone from **cultivating** or **progressing** is tantamount to violence in my eyes and will be dealt with accordingly. Regardless of who you or your parents are. This is not home. You belong to us now."

Murmurs resounded throughout the auditorium, but no one dared protest. Hundreds had been present when she threw the blood elf into the wall earlier, and if they hadn't witnessed it personally, chances were someone would tell them the story. I immediately wondered if the blood elves would retaliate. Would they be bold or foolish enough to strike back against the headmistress?

"As is our tradition, we will host our first battle festival when the midterms arrive. Over the first week of term, the academies will host in-house duels to determine their top five freshmen. The week after that, those five will face the top five of other Academies. This will continue until there is a single victor. That victor will receive the praise and acknowledgment of their peers and the academies, as well as a treasure trove of crystals, cores, gear, and more."

I squeezed Chloe's hand and she squeezed it right back. We were going to do whatever it took to win those duels and get our hands on those prizes.

"Next! Classes! They'll be held each morning. A single block is one hour. One class block is required, but beyond that, extra is available. After that, it is expected that all students self-study, put those lessons demonstrated in classrooms to practical use through sparring, dungeon hunts, and reading. Make sure you pay attention and put in the effort because no one here is going to carry you."

Scarlet stopped and looked around the auditorium. The students were already antsy, shifting, and preparing to leave. I was no different. I liked the idea of minimal class time. It would mean we had that much more time to practice and get our hands dirty!

"Allowance and Dungeons! Everyone will get **10x Rank 1 crystals** per week for cultivation purposes! If you feel confident in your abilities, go dungeon diving! Three of our students received boss cores in there just last night! Freshmen! On their first dive. Who knows? Maybe luck will favor you as well, and you can find yourself the recipient of one hundred times your allowance from a single dive. Know this. After your first three months, the allowance stops. Not just that, but you will need to start paying *us* tuition. This is how we finance the next freshmen class."

"Who got the cores?" a proud blood elf asked, rising from her seat to look around.

Scarlet's head slowly turned toward us as a grin made its way up her face.

"There will be plenty of time for introductions later. I'm sure you will meet JD and his two friends when they have the time."

Not likely, I thought and watched as the blood elves all mouthed murder my way. I blew them a kiss and sank a little further into my chair.

"As for the dungeons, there are fifty floors. They gain difficulty evenly, which should help minimize the guesswork on

254

what you will be facing when you make a jump. Every beast that lives on a certain floor will have a boss. The floor's boss monster must be taken down to move to the next floor. Take your time and be patient. Most of you won't proceed further than the second floor this year but do your best."

"Headmistress," Chloe called out and pushed out of her chair. "What about older students? We can't possibly compete with them for kills."

Scarlet nodded slowly. "Starting this morning, no student over rank **5** can enter the first floor, rank **6** the second floor, and so on up to the fifth floor. From there on out it's every man for themselves, but keep in mind, they might take it personally if they find you attacking a boss they want. We will not interfere unless your life is at risk, though."

"They're forcing you to form a holy trinity," I chuckled.

"What's that?" Mabel asked.

"It's a way of playing games. See, you have a tank, you have the support, and you have the damage dealers. I'm both a tank and a damage dealer, you're a pure supporter, while Chloe is a sort of damage dealer as well. We need a pure tank or a healer type."

"Oh? I can learn to heal after I do magic cultivation. Even the zither has buffing skills. I will need to learn them first."

"We'll talk about that later," I whispered as Scarlet clapped her hands together.

"Now, the most important thing of all. Parties must be formed. No less than three people to start. Choose wisely, as you will not be allowed to leave the party until the year is over or... unless you die. Once joined, the party will give each member a **10%** bonus on your stats, and you will receive the other's bonus as well. Max size is five, one for each of the specialties. A total of two specials can be added to any given party, bringing the total to seven members. If you join a special's party, you will automatically be transferred to that dorm. Make sure you have enough room and resources to maintain the party. And lastly, for every party member and their every cultivation rank, you pay a rank **1** crystal per week. Do you want the bonuses? Work for them."

Now that was a chunk of information that made my day. I'd be able to share **10%** of my stats with the girls and would in turn receive some of their power as well.

"Lastly!" Scarlet snapped, seeing things were already descending into chaos. "This tower is a bastion and stronghold, but the city around us is still very much a war zone. You will find the benefits extended to you here will not follow you there. They see your life as privileged, one they can't afford. Their hatred and dislike are wrongly placed, but you must understand the death and hardships they have faced. Within the city, there are five districts. Each district belongs to a cultivation discipline, so keep that in mind. Families run most of these areas, so be mindful of where you go and with whom. You may not be welcome everywhere in the city."

"Is that politics?" a young man asked as Scarlet got up from her chair. "I thought in a world which faces extinction people would be less hungry for... weak power, focusing less on biases and prejudices and more on seeking true power, like cultivation."

"You are right. But people are stubborn, and many choose to live with their delusions. If there are others to protect them, why would they bother growing stronger to do it for themself? If their parents, and their parents before that hated blood elves, then so should they, right? It is not the way things should be, but unfortunately, it is the way our world is. The world outside is dangerous and confusing. Stay inside the tower and don't cause your seniors any trouble, at least for now."

I nodded subconsciously, trying to picture the outside world in my mind. Were the people out there like those I saw in the bazaar? Were they free from glamours out there? If so, I immediately wondered what they all looked like, how they spoke. There was a whole new world to explore... new worlds, rather, and I couldn't wait to take it all in.

"That is enough about politics for now. Remember, tomorrow is an off day. Use it to prepare for the start of classes the day after. Let us take a short break and then we will talk about the disciplines and where you all fit in."

DEMONSTRATION

"TAKE A BREAK, GO PEE, maybe get something to drink!" Scarlet yelled when no one moved. And then everyone was moving at once.

I didn't have to pee, nor was I thirty, so I just sat back in my chair and let it all wash over me. I turned to Mabel, the moon elf bouncing in her chair and humming under her breath.

"Mabel," I said, turning to her. "There is something that has been... perplexing me about this place. Well, not just one thing. The whole place is beyond everything I've ever known and dreamed of. But the prompts, ugh…" I paused, struggling to put my question into words. So, instead, I showed her. "**Magical Cultivation**."

True to the world, the word popped up between us, glowing for a moment in the bright auditorium.

"That," I said, pointing at the word before it faded. "Why does that happen?"

"I can see why that would be confusing," Mabel said, the word reflecting in her large eyes. "I hear that is why people from the mundane worlds are rarely recruited. Well, that, and the fact that once they are indoctrinated to our magical system, the results

258

can be very unpredictable. My people have dwelt in magical worlds for millennia."

"What do you mean by unpredictable?" Chloe asked, leaning across me to join in.

Mabel shrugged. "I don't know. It is just what they say. But personally…" she said, pausing to watch the group of blood elves as they reappeared in the auditorium. "I have heard stories about the towers, and that they changed the nature of not just mana, but the worlds they are connected to. I am not old enough to know what it was like before them, so this is just guessing on my part. The prompts, as you call them, *are* the tower. It doesn't create mana but regulates and controls it. Before them, I believe cultivation was much more unpredictable, or raw. Some, born with more sensitivity to mana, could probably acquire a great deal of strength and power quickly. Others struggled to gain an understanding of the basic principles. Those people that have been living in worlds controlled by the towers for so long. You two have not. Anyways, it is just what I think. In most cultures, it is not considered acceptable to discuss it openly."

"Okay, let's get back to your seats and be quiet," Scarlet said, her voice booming over them.

Could that be the answer to Chloe's doubts? I wondered. *Are races like the blood elves afraid of our cultivation potential, because we aren't a known commodity?*

"I know we've gone over a lot so far. We will not have time to go through it again so, if you have questions, ask your teachers during class. We are moving on."

She turned back to the glowing hologram, and it changed again. The different disciplines appeared, each dropping into a particular fighting stance. I perked up. Now, this was the thing I was interested in most. Maybe it would help me decide my specialty.

"The disciplines. **Weapon Cultivation, Martial Arts Cultivation, Magical Cultivation, Cultivation Crafting**, and **Beastmastery**. The blade, fist, magic, forge, and claw. This is the

259

foundation of our world. And as we know, without a good foundation, there is no cultivation."

The image shifted to a man and a woman holding a sword and a spear. They bowed to each other and then started sparring, deflecting blows, and counterattacking.

"**Weapon Cultivation**. It's as simple as the name suggests. The main focus in this branch is twofold—weapon style and form. The idea is, a weapon is an extension of your body, therefore we gather as much mana as possible, infuse it into our bodies and merge it with the weapon. Eventually, a strong weapon cultivator will unlock their **soul sea.** Then, it can be linked directly with the weapon, making what was two—cultivator and weapon, into one."

"Mistress?" a young girl called out from one of the front rows. "What is a soul sea?"

Scarlet eyed the girl and nodded, evidently happy with the question.

"Think of it as an awakening of your ultimate mana potential. All cultivators possess a pool where we store collected mana. Despite our arrogant beliefs, that pool will always be finite. Unlocking your soul sea is to tear the very nature of your pool, folding it into space beyond space. Done properly, a soul sea can potentially hold an infinite amount of mana. But that is far down the road for you all. We are talking about **2nd Realm** cultivation."

The girl hunched over her lap, frantically scribbling notes as the headmistress spoke.

"And how do we expand our bodies' mana capacity before that ability is unlocked?"

"By ranking up in cultivation. It is automatic, but the more you ingest mana into your system, the larger the pool becomes. Now, if you have any other questions, I would direct them to your professor in your **Basic Cultivation** class."

"Sorry, Mistress. Thank you for taking the—."

"No need. That is why this seminar exists," Scarlet said, waving her off.

"Now, where was I? That's right, I was at the soul sea. Now, the main thing to note here is that **Weapon Cultivation** can be done with *any* weapon. Yes, the weapon size, skills, and style might be different, but the **Mana Infusion, Mana Dispersal**, and **Mana Discharge** will all function in the same way. Those are the foundational elements for that discipline. Our weapon cultivation professors are masters of countless weapons and styles, so listen to them."

The fighting man and woman in the image stepped back, holding their weapons ready before them. Their weapons started glowing—the man's spear blue and purple, and the woman's sword yellow. A wall of earth appeared between the two as the man's spear cut forward. The wall shattered, absorbing some of the spear's energy, allowing the woman to deflect the blow with ease.

"Shit, that's so cool!" I laughed and caught myself. "Sorry," I whispered and sank back into the seat. Chloe elbowed me, while Mabel just chuckled uncomfortably.

"I'm glad you find this so amusing, JD," Scarlet said, looking up at me. "Is there anything you would like to add? Or perhaps you would like to join me down here for a live demonstration?"

I froze. "Headmistress? Don't you think it would be better if you used someone more…competent?"

"Are you calling yourself incompetent?" she teased.

"Go," Chloe whispered, "show those stuff pricks what you can do."

I tried to sink into my chair and out of sight, but that didn't work. More faces had turned to stare at me, watching and waiting.

Do it. The old you would have bitched out. Make this time different.

"No, not incompetent. Headmistress," I replied, "I'm coming."

I got up and steadily moved to the end of the row and then down the stairs. They seemed to go on forever and my shaky legs didn't do anything to help. By the time I got to the bottom, my palms were sweaty, and my heart thundered in my chest. At least

I didn't fall and kill myself on the way down. That would be just my luck.

Scarlet waited up on the stage, standing just before the podium, a poorly veiled smirk on her face. I mounted the stairs and made the mistake of looking out into the crowd. The bright lights hit my eyes and nearly blinded me. But I could still see the students. The crowd didn't look this big from above. Shit, my knees went weak, and I almost went over.

"Good job, JD, you made it down here alive," Scarlet said, a piece of parchment appearing in her hand. It was yellowed and heavily worn.

"Take this skill and study it. You have five minutes. We'll wait for you. Then you can show us if you are as good with your fists as you are with your mouth." The crowd groaned and hissed, some even snorted and clapped. I felt my cheeks and ears grow hot.

Very nice, JD. Very nice.

"Thank you, Headmistress." I accepted the parchment and stepped back.

I stared down at the new skill, scanning it in the bright light. But it wasn't just *the* skill, there was a lot of theory, notes, and movement diagrams drawn below.

"That is quite the robe, young man," Scarlet whispered, under her breath. "I'm glad you met him. Let's talk about it later. I've got some things to tell you… about him and the robe."

"That's very much appreciated," I whispered without looking up at her. I was trying to focus on the skill, and not think about her unreasonably tight robe, or the bright lights, or the laughing, snorting, pointing crowd, too.

"Here, go inside the rift and study. These cretins do not understand courtesy. Plus, I want to see you perform at your peak, not fail miserably because a few thousand students made you nervous."

She drew a chorus of chuckles and laughter, but they didn't bother me. I wasn't worried about what they thought, only about how I could prove myself by succeeding. If everything I'd heard so far was true, power was everything. There was nothing I could say to change their minds.

I walked through the small portal next to the podium and found myself standing in a small square room. It was barely twenty paces in length and width. A small chair sat in one corner, with a spindly table next to it. An antique oil lamp sat atop the polished wood, glowing brightly. Besides a rug, there was nothing else in the room.

"At least I have enough room to move around."

I walked over, turned the oil lamp up, then sat down in the middle of the rug and stared at the parchment, reading over the text first.

SKILL NAME: Mana Discharge (B)
TYPE: Basic, Mana, **RANGE:** 10 paces
DESCRIPTION: One of the *Foundation* skills used in all disciplines. This skill is used to attack an enemy with a burst of mana. Knockback, stun, blind, and physical damage.
BASIC: +40 Attack on mastery, Damage: *Attack x 1.25*, Mana: 25
ADVANCED: +80 Attack on mastery, Damage: *Attack x 1.45*, Mana: 40
MASTER: +160 Attack on mastery, Damage: *Attack x 1.8*, Mana: 60
NOTE: Mana Discharge can be used with or without a weapon.

I scrolled over the wall of text and smiled. So, this was going to be the first skill that I'd learn all by myself. But how?

Luckily, I was *normally* pretty quick on the uptake. It helped that I was an artist myself and used to not only looking between the lines but trying to find ways of breaking something down into its base components. I immediately noticed that there were two stages to the attack. First, the mana had to be charged. Then, simply... or, it sounded simple, discharged.

"Okay, if I am a magical attack, consisting of two parts, how do I work? Two parts..." I whispered, turning the parchment and examining it from different angles. I let my vision go fuzzy and held it out at arm's length. Then the parchment started glowing and abruptly tore in two.

"Oh, shit. That did something," I said, as the words and images shifted and moved to the left piece of paper, while new ones appeared on the right sheet.

My eyebrows rose and I considered giving myself a high five. So, she'd planned for this to happen.

SKILL NAME: Mana Charge (B)

TYPE: Basic, Mana, **RANGE:** 1 pace

DESCRIPTION: One of the *Foundation* skills used in all disciplines. Mana Infusion is used to gather mana into a weapon or the body and then use it to either attack or defend against attacks.

BASIC: +20 Attack, +50 Health on mastery, Charge Time: 5 sec

ADVANCED: +50 Attack, 100 Health on mastery, Charge Time: 4 sec

MASTER: +100 Attack, 200 Health on mastery, Charge Time: 3 sec

The first skill looked easy enough to master, essentially considering what I had already gone through, burning the crystals through my hands. I simply had to focus on the mana. So, I did.

Mana bubbled forth inside me, immediately answering my call. I gathered it in a ball and then started to spin it clockwise, the magical energy swirling in the palm of my hand. I fished my pen-blade out of my rift, and carefully brought the tip of the weapon to the glowing ball of light. The bladed tip started glowing with a white and light blue swirling mass.

A message appeared in front of me.

YOU HAVE ACQUIRED BASIC MASTERY OF: MANA CHARGE
ATTAINED BONUS: +20 Attack, +50 Health

I brandished the pen-blade before me, its tip glowing with that bright light. I used my imagination to construct a beastly enemy before me... trying hard to imagine it with a full, effective loin cloth...

The second sheet of parchment showed the discharge as a simultaneous release of mana, focused into a direction of focus. I closed my eyes and gathered another charge of mana, but this time funneled it directly into the weapon. The swirling mass gathered at the tip of the pen-blade and remained there, pushing outward. And then, in a rather anticlimactic poof of light, dissipated.

"Son of a nugget," I cursed and stomped my feet. "No tantrums. Bad, JD. Bad. Focus, dummy. It is all about the focus."

I sucked in a breath and pushed it out, then tried again. I gathered the mana once more, formed it into a ball, and forced it into the pen-blade. The weapon hummed gently, and again, the mana dissipated in a poof of light.

"Okay. What-in-the-hell? How can I keep the mana in the damned blade—err... maybe," I stopped mid-rant, just as an idea popped into my mind.

I once again gathered, shaped, and forced the mana into the tip, but before it could dissipate, I formed a second ball that encircled the first. Most of the second ball disappeared, but a small barrier remained... one that held the first ball in place. I grinned but kept from celebrating prematurely. There was only one chance, and I had to make it slowly. Carefully, I remolded the mana ball glowing on the pen-blade... specifically, so it would discharge straight ahead. The next time, I would do it while forming the energy, but I had to start somewhere.

"Beginning magical cultivator. Boom!" I shouted, and swung the weapon, releasing the gathered energy. A thin shaft of bright light shot out of my pen-blade and struck the far wall. It exploded in an impressive ball of heat and sound.

YOU HAVE ACQUIRED BASIC MASTERY OF: MANA DISCHARGE
ATTAINED BONUS: +40 Attack

The room abruptly melted away and in a flash of stupidly bright auditorium lights, I found myself before Scarlet. I shielded my face and looked at the headmistress. And to my surprise, her eyes were wide with amazement, shock, or both.

"I pulled you from the crowd to teach you a lesson, Earther, but it seems the joke's on me. You just acquired **Basic Mastery** in a few minutes. I wanted to make sure you listened, to provide an example for all the other first-year students if you hadn't. Thank you. I needed this rather pleasant surprise."

"No. Thank you," I said, stowing the pen-blade back into my rift. "I appreciate you taking the time to instruct me one on one. I'm sorry if I was disruptive up there. Everything here is still so... different. There are moments when I struggle believing that I am truly here."

Scarlet snapped her fingers and my mana recovered, the magical energy flowing over and into me. It almost felt like someone had poured a bucket of icy water over me. I looked up to the girls and smiled. Chloe waved excitedly while Mabel covered her face.

"Now, why don't you show everyone here what you just learned. If you do good, I'll give you a parchment of the single most powerful basic skill, **Mana Dispersal**. Deal?"

I nodded and bowed. "Thank you, Headmistress. Where do I... who do I... use it on?"

"Who? Me, of course. Go on, hit me with your best shot," Scarlet said, taking two steps away and turning to face me.

266

"I'm not... so sure about that," I said, uncomfortable with the notion of attacking her.

"Come along. My mana shield can withstand a nuclear explosion from your world. A little mana discharge will be a drop in the bucket." She nodded and smirked at me, her eyes barely visible under the wide brim of her witch's hat.

Little? Drop in the bucket? I thought, squaring up with her. I'd always thought it was a strange phrase, made all the stranger coming from a magical professor in a magical academy currently wearing a witch's outfit. *Fine...* if she wanted me to hit her, I would oblige.

I lifted the pen-blade, summoned, and focused my mana, then stepped in, directing my discharge at her shield. A fist-sized beam of fiery light hit an invisible barrier surrounding her, exploding on impact and scattering heat and bright particles in all directions. Some of the students gasped while others cheered. The snooty nobility section didn't do much other than glare my way. At least the small group I got to know earlier... I'd have to start calling them something special.

"Good enough?" I asked as I lowered my weapon. She nodded and turned to face the students.

"See, this is a perfect example of what we call 'wild cultivation'. This young man here has no experience and extraordinarily little practical understanding of what he is doing, but he has a good basic instinct. And using his mind, innovative thinking, along with some instincts, he came up with a way to shorten the process."

Scarlet turned back to face me and *poof* another parchment appeared in her hand. To my shame, I flinched. But I didn't scream. And I wasn't naked standing in front of the whole school. So, at least I still had a portion of my dignity remaining.

I nodded, smiled, and accepted the parchment. But she held onto it for a moment, studying me, her bottom lip pulled between her teeth. I felt like prey being watched by a hungry lion. I glimpsed a bit of that red aura in her eyes just then... a not-so-subtle reminder that I was no longer in Kansas, and Scarlet was indeed not an ordinary, if entirely human, woman. But that begged the question, if she wasn't human, then what was she? And was her *pleasing* appearance just a glamour designed to appeal to my baser instincts?

If I can't trust my eyes, then what can I?

"Thank you, Headmistress. I'll do my best to surprise you every day," I said, as she finally let go, then caught myself. "Pleasant surprises!"

She eyed me for a moment longer and then laughed, the movement making her breasts bounce against the tight fabric of her robe. Had I overdone it? Had I made a promise I would later forget? Had I just signed up to be the next contestant in the game "who wants to get locked in Mistress Scarlet's secret sex dungeon so she can feed on their life force to maintain her immortality"?

Is that it? Is she some kind of succubus? I wondered, my comic book-inspired imagination latching onto every possibility and running.

"Alright, JD!" Scarlet said, waving her hand before my face and breaking me from my thoughts. "You can return to your seat. I need to finish up with the basics."

She didn't even wait for me to start moving before the image on the hologram changed to two martial artists again.

"Chloe's either gonna be pissed or excited," I whispered as I made my way up the stairs. She waited for me with a grin plastered on her face. Good, excited.

"You gotta teach me that shit, okay?"

I sat down and put my arm around her, pulling her in for an embrace.

"Whatever you want. As long as—."

The red-haired giantess suddenly hissed my name. "JD! If you get any cool skills for a martial artist, let me know! I'll make it worth your time!"

"Sorry, they're only 'one-time use,'" I replied with an apologetic smile. "But I will help if I can."

Chloe slapped my leg. "Get in line," she hissed back. "Me first!"

Scarlet continued her lesson, but I could feel her impatience... if gazes could slowly bore a hole clear through a person.

"Enough. It appears I have taxed your patience. Take a break. And while you are at it, get all of this chatty-chat-chat out of your systems. I will not tolerate it when we get back," Scarlet yelled and with a flick of her wrist, the lights dimmed.

"I'm not gonna lie. I kind of can't wait to get back to the room so you can show me how to do that mana discharge," Chloe said.

"So! I'm Skadi!" the giantess laughed, appearing out of the gloom ahead of us, and slapped her hand, palm down, onto our marble table. She had walked up to our balcony and shimmied between the handrail and our table, all without me even noticing.

"I think we should be friends," she said, "Because I would like to go out with you to hunt shit. With me in your party, we would be formidable."

"Skadi, huh?" I asked. "JD, Chloe, and Mabel. We have a room in the VIP dorms."

"Oh, yeah. We all know who you are and where you are staying," she laughed. Her grin was infectious. Not to mention the sparkle in her remarkably blue eyes. "I wouldn't ask you otherwise."

"So, say we take you in," Chloe started, sliding her arm behind me. "We're tight on space and beds as it is, right now. What would you bring to our little party?"

Skadi abruptly leaned forward, the angle giving me an unobstructed view right down her... giant-sized cleavage. "I hear you Earth men like gals with big..." she reached up, hooked a finger inside her neckline, and pulled it down a little more. Damned sakes. She was bigger and taller than me, but that didn't mean I couldn't appreciate her finely chiseled figure and... assets.

"Oh, god," I muttered. "Where did you hear that?"

269

"Umm," she muttered, "I don't know. I just heard it. And I know how things work around here. You find the people that will give you the best chance to stand out, then you do what it takes to fit in. Simple."

Mabel stirred beside me, and I looked over to find she had covered her face with both hands and was shaking her head. Right. This wasn't going very well.

"Scarlet's almost done with her tea," Chloe hissed under her breath. "I don't want to get hit with another lightning bolt."

"Thank you, Skadi. We'll talk about it. Okay? Your offer is giantly…Uhm, greatly appreciated."

"Yeah, yeah. Whatever. I'll catch you outside in the hallway. Just remember. Assets." To emphasize she flexed, showcasing some impressive arms.

Skadi abruptly turned and made her way back down the narrow gap between table and handrail. I couldn't quite banish the image of her bright eyes, wide smile, and almost unrealistic breasts. I mean, they were proportionate. *But damn!* If she was gambling on me being a "boob guy", she'd guessed right. Was it normal to daydream about getting naked with a giant girl?

In this world, I don't think that is weird at all.

I quietly slid down into my chair, to hide my tightening robe.

OLD WHITE'S LEGACY

SCARLET TALKED THROUGH FOUR MORE tea breaks, stunned five more students—none of them us, thank goodness, and finally seemed to be winding down. Honestly, by that time, I was nodding off and in serious need of a break.

"And that is why we don't pee in the passageways," the headmistress said, specifically looking at a furry-eared group of students to our right. I chuckled quietly, Mabel joining in.

"So, what do you want to do next?" I asked, stretching in my chair. "I need to catch up with Old White. After that, I think we should all absorb the first core." All three of us. Together.

"I'll set it all up before you're back," Mabel said, stretched, and then pulled her robe down as it hiked up her legs. From what she'd said about the process, it sounded involved and... intimate. While absorbing the core, we three would be connected.

"Want me to come with you?" Chloe asked, leaning on my shoulder. "I could use some distraction, and a walk sounds nice. I've been sitting so long, my butt feels flat."

I understood the truth of it. Ever since the giantess, Skadi, approached us about joining the party, Chloe had practically hovered over me.

"Oh? Are you worried Old White is going to hit on me?" I asked, poking her stomach.

"Hey! Of course, I am! Why wouldn't I be? And if he doesn't, that Skadi gal surely will. Did you see those shoulders and muscles? Hell, even I think she has beautiful eyes."

"Yes. Impressive. The muscles, that is," I added as Chloe grabbed my thigh and squeezed.

"How about—?" she started to say, but I pulled her into me, smashing my lips into hers.

I drew out the kiss longer than necessary, her tension melting away. It was my way of saying, "don't worry about me, I won't let the creepy, old man do anything bad to me. Oh, and the giantess isn't an issue."

"I'll be quick. Don't worry," I said, jumping out of my seat. I knew Chloe had a reason to be jealous, to be worried. There was something that set us apart from the other races at Zenith... something that either made us a target or perhaps a weak link. Until we figured it out, we would have to be careful of who we let into our circle and our dorm. At least she had Mabel.

"Oh, before I forget, here is your weekly allowance," Scarlet's voice boomed throughout the auditorium. I slapped my hands over my ears, as her voice continued to rattle around inside my skull.

Small pouches appeared on our desks. I opened mine and grinned, as the auditorium's bright lights glimmered on a sizable pile of crystals. I watched students empty the contents of their pouches into their hands, counting and ogling the crystals.

Yes. She said everyone would get ten crystals per week. But did I get more because she called me out and I delivered? Or was it something else...? I couldn't help but think about that almost feral, hungry look in her eye.

Don't be a sheep, JD! They always get eaten.

"Payday... boom!" Chloe yelled, tossing the bag of crystals up into the air and catching it. "Go have fun with your super old guy friend. I mean, I'll just do... whatever while you're gone. Maybe I'll lay around, pining over you, or maybe I'll find someone to entertain me." She cocked a single eyebrow at me.

"You wouldn't!"

"Wouldn't I?" she asked, running a fingernail down my chest. "You'd probably best not be away too long, lover."

Chloe pushed up onto her tiptoes, kissed me, then grabbed Mabel's hand and pulled the elf down the aisle and into the stairwell.

"Wait. I need to ask the headmistress about the formation we need to use," Mabel protested, just as they moved out of sight.

I followed them into the stairwell and made it two flights down before the giantess, Skadi, appeared through a doorway and jumped in front of me. She hooked an impressively powerful arm around my waist and guided me out the door, around the corner, and into the hall. It was almost like she had been waiting for me.

"Aren't you aggressive?" I asked, shrinking a bit in the girl's shadow. "I don't mind assertive women, but you are quickly approaching stalker territory."

"My people are direct—literal in pretty much every way, JD. Wait, it was JD, right?"

I nodded as I wiggled free from her hand.

"You already know it is. Just like you already know what dorm we live in and probably everything else about us."

"Well, you're not wrong there. Anyway, to give you a proper introduction, I'm Skadi Medvarna. I'm the heir to a kingdom. It is mostly ruined, but I will rebuild it once I'm strong enough and have ascended to the throne! Maybe even with your help?"

"That is optimistic," I said, "Glass half-full. I like it. I mean, I've never helped rebuild a kingdom before, but it sounds like it could be fun."

"Oh? You like me?"

"I didn't say that. But I don't dislike you. How about that?" I asked.

She frowned.

"Listen. This is nothing personal... I'm just the kind of guy who avoids answering my phone if I know a telemarketer is calling, and when I would go to a used car lot, I would intentionally sneak around the salesmen. I don't like being pressured or *sold* something. Girls where I'm from aren't usually so open and direct. So, I apologize if I get a little defensive."

"I don't know what any of that means," Skadi laughed, moving in a little closer. "But I like you. You're funny. That isn't common amongst the men of my people. They are serious. All the time. And I like to laugh."

She shrugged and crossed her arms over her ample chest. Her body bristled with muscles, but somehow, she still managed to look feminine—curvy where it mattered, and soft in others. She noticed me checking her out and patted my shoulder playfully.

"Do you like what you see? I think you are nice to look at, too. I think we should mate, but only if you agree to my terms."

"Hey, stop blocking the whole entrance!" someone yelled, a host of other voices joining in. I didn't even realize that we'd been blocking traffic.

I hooked Skadi's arm and pulled her out of the way, intentionally not turning back to see who had complained.

"Wait, mate? We don't even know each other!"

"Why would we need to know each other?" Skadi asked, her face scrunching up in confusion. "For my people, this is simple. You think I am attractive. I think you are attractive. Good. We lie together. End of story."

"Uh, wow. That is simple. Like... way simpler than I am used to."

"Yes. Don't worry. I would be gentle with you."

I shrugged, at a loss for words.

"Good. It is settled then."

274

"Wow," I snapped, finally breaking from my shock. "Nothing is settled. I am in a relationship with Chloe. And there is Mabel in our dorm, too, and she doesn't even have her own room yet. I gotta say, adding a third lady to the mix only sounds like trouble."

Skadi harrumphed and dropped her fists to her hips.

"You are... what is the saying? Overthinking this. I can share, you know? I don't mind. My people love physical interaction. We love life... drink, food, and mating, especially when it makes for sweaty, loud time. And if you are worried that I am a dirty girl. I am not. I wash very often."

"Right," I said, once again struck dumb.

"Accept me into your party and help me progress. In return, I will lend my strength and fortitude to your party. And when you are in the mood, we can lay together. Or stand. I am incredibly open to new things. What do you say?"

I shrugged and tore my eyes away, only then realizing I was staring at her chest.

"I'll tell you what. I will think about it, princess. The girls have a say in everything we do, so it wouldn't be fair to them to decide without them. I hope you understand."

"Sure, sure! I'll be around the dungeon lobby all day tomorrow. Come find me. While you're there, you can see what real power looks like!"

She patted me on the back, the force jarring me forward. Then she strolled away. My eyes naturally fell to her shapely rear, no doubt aided by her strange bodysuit. Sure, she was pleasing to the eyes, and I assumed she was a class that we needed, but her straightforward nature and complete nonchalance about sex actually set me back. Me... and I was the one that had sex with my new roommate literally the first day we met. Okay, maybe I was approaching this whole thing from the wrong angle.

My old life hadn't always been easy. I struggled to establish a career for my art, pay my bills, find a girl that would tolerate my quirks and sense of humor... and above issues with career and money. But here? I had a sexy, crazy-in-all-the-right-ways Earth girl convinced that the only way for us to survive was to connect our life energies... through sexual contact, a disturbingly shy but ground-breakingly gorgeous moon elf with self-esteem issues as a roommate, and now a freaking royal giantess with the physique of a pro-level bodybuilder casually asking me to mate. What in the serious fuck was going on?

Was it because of my power? I snorted and laughed out loud at the thought. I'd never had anything resembling power. Or perhaps the robes I wore? If they thought I had a powerful backer, that might make sense.

My brain snagged on that thought. Old White looked the part of the unassuming, frail old man, but things were not always what they seemed. And this world had tons of magic.

I made my way to the bazaar and luckily found the old man sitting in the exact same space as before. He scooped up his sellables the moment I stepped in front of him, and with surprising agility, rose to his feet.

"Come with me."

"Where are we going?" I asked, distracted by the colors, smells, exotic things, and people of the bazaar. It felt like there was something new to see every time I turned or closed my eyes.

"To drink some tea. There's a very nice little spot just outside the tower. I see things more clearly there."

My heart skipped a beat as I realized he was talking about *leaving the tower*. The thought, the concept, felt weird. Like— despite the fact that everything I had seen, tasted, felt, and done the past few days was in complete opposition to everything I had ever known and believed, somehow, I had come to accept most of it. Now I had to move beyond the protective walls and open myself up to a host of new things.

"How do we get there?"

"Easy," he smiled. "We use a portal scroll. It will connect the bazaar to the outer world. Come on, just follow me through."

He pulled a scroll from his rift and unfolded it. A trickle of mana ran from his palm and across the parchment before the sheaf erupted into a cloud of light and a portal appeared in front of him. He walked through and I hurried after him. I reached the light, struggling with equal parts excitement and fear. This was it, my new world.

The light faded and I found myself standing on a rooftop. Several buildings rose to my right, roughly pagoda-shaped. I recognized the style from mangas I had read, but also a comic book I penciled a few years before. It was a kung fu story of revenge, where a warlord was betrayed by his people, then miraculously reincarnated into the body of a dying man locked in a prison cell. I finished every page, only to have the publisher go belly up before we could publish it. I drew similar towers in that project— hexagonal structures covered with balconies and cool dragon-inspired architecture.

Old White had already taken a seat and waved for me to join him, but I walked over to the edge and looked out over the city instead. It was huge. No, the word huge was far too small for the sight. Gigantic was much more fitting, as it seemed to stretch as far as the eye could see.

The tower was to our right, hulking over us like a dark colossus, an impossibly tall construct of dark stone. It was at that moment that I understood its true scope, as it stretched through the clouds and towards the distant stars. I saw no windows, balconies, or doors... no indication where one floor ended and another began. It looked alien, a building beyond the ability and imagination of mortal men.

I turned, taking in the rest of the city. A tall wall surrounded it all, easily fifty-feet-tall and incredibly thick. It looked sturdy. No, a concrete wall enclosing a freeway looked "sturdy". This looked beyond durable, and I doubted even a tank battalion could blast their way through, especially since a shimmering dome covered the entirety of the city.

The skyline consisted of hundreds of buildings. Some that wouldn't have looked out of place in a city on earth, and others, well let's just say, I wanted to study their strange architecture up

277

close one day. Beneath the sprawling pagodas and high-rises sat a sprawling number of siheyuan. They were courtyard homes, walled in on all sides. Most close enough to see consisted of multiple buildings, and I immediately wondered if it was for multiple families, or were those smaller dwellings designated for people like Mabel, and her family.

"Is this world no different than the old one?" I whispered, but the old man heard.

"Yes and no, young man. Different, yes. But the same, no."

I immediately wanted to ask the old man why he was talking like Yoda but turned to consider him, and in the light, he did resemble the small alien a bit.

"No matter where you go, certain unfortunate truths will follow. Rich and the poor, strong and the weak. They may wear different faces, speak different languages, but the motivations are disappointingly similar. That is primarily why I holed up in the tower. I was simply not able to live out in the world any longer."

I nodded but turned back to the city. It was such a fantastic mashup of things I recognized and others that looked incomprehensible and alien. I wanted to explore it, but moreover, I wanted to believe it was above the failings of the world I'd left behind.

My slow pan locked on a place just inside the large wall. It looked like a market with countless parasols, each one a different pattern and color. They turned high above the booths and stands. Men, women, and children roamed around buying and selling, trading goods, and services. It made me think of the bazaar but in a much larger scope and the benefit of open air. The thought drew my gaze skyward again.

I looked past the lazily drifting clouds, the flocks of migrating bird-like creatures, and looked to the stars. They sprawled like twinkling dots on a navy-blue blanket. Then a planet resolved from behind the clouds. It was striped in swirling layers of tan, red, and blue, with a thick ring revolving around it. I felt my mouth fall open, the sight immediately tearing open my insatiable sense of awe and wonder.

The tower had been one thing... fantastical and new, but this? It was like a fact finally clicked into place in my brain... I was in an alien world. A place very much not earth. This was my new home.

"Sorry, Old White," I said as I finally broke loose and looked away. "I think it just got real. That I am really here." I held the railing as my legs got a little shaky, the realization, or perhaps my hunger, stealing their stability.

I turned back and stared out over the wall next, interested to take in the lay of the land. Grassland sprawled as far as the eyes could see, with forests and mountains in the distance.

"So, we can see them approach," Old White said, appearing next to me at the railing.

"That makes sense," I said. "But don't you think that it would already be too late even if we see them several miles out?"

He shrugged.

"It is not just about 'seeing' them," Old White explained. "We have magical devices that can sense the tremors from their movement. We also have scrying glasses, much like binoculars from back home. They provide a very good look from as far as five miles away."

"I see," I replied. "And to see that far out, I imagine all the trees had to be cut down?"

"Unfortunately, yes. A waste, if you ask me. But a cost they were willing to pay to prevent the loss of more lives. Now come, come. Let us sit, have a drink, and talk. I believe you owe me something."

"Oh," I chuckled, "Yeah, I do. Double, actually."

"Double? And why is that?" he asked, settling into his chair.

"The robe is excellent. Better than its power, though, is its ability to catch people's attention. People stare at me, and wonder who my big backer is."

"And do you?"

279

"Do I what?"

"Have a big backer."

"That is the question I have been asking myself since I met you in the bazaar. I think you are better equipped to answer it."

"Hah, I like you, kid. I really do. So, how about that drink first? We can have them bring a platter of snacks while chatting and drinking."

I settled into my chair as a woman approached. She appeared to be in her mid-forties, modestly dressed in a black dress, with her hair pulled up in a bun. And... she wasn't human. She walked around our table, drawing closer and I realized she wasn't covered with a glamour.

Her hair was thick, coarse strands, not the silky sheaf I originally thought. Her skin was rough as well and covered in tiny, opalescent scales.

A race of beastkin? I wondered, making a conscious effort to not stare.

"Miko!" Old White said, greeting her warmly.

The woman bowed low and held out a tray.

"What can I get you today?"

"The same, but double. I have an especially important conversation to have with my friend here, so can you make sure no one comes to the roof? Just for a little while?"

She nodded and pushed the tray towards him. White pulled a large crystal from his rift and set it on the tray. She flashed us both a smile and disappeared back through the doorway.

"Was that a rank **3** crystal?" I asked.

"Sure was. This place is pretty expensive, but I'm a regular... so I can make my crystals stretch pretty far. I did Miko a favor a long time ago and her memory is particularly good."

"Long memory, huh? Yeah, so you want stories, right? About earth?"

"Ahh, yes. I think every good relationship starts with honesty; don't you think?"

I nodded.

"Good. Well, good," the old man said and stared absently up at the tower for a long moment. His eyes were so heavily lidded that I started to wonder if he perhaps dozed off. Then, when I was about to clear my throat, he sat up, coughed, and started.

"I've been living here for almost two centuries now. I didn't tell you earlier, as I was afraid the news might scare you away. But yes, I have been here a long time. The last thing I remember from Earth was the British army attacking Washington and burning the capital."

"Oh," I replied, quite taken aback. "I have a confession to make. I'm horrible with history."

"History isn't just what fills books, my boy. You have your own history, as do I. That history can be just as important as what stuffy men in wigs do."

"That is a good point," I said, and immediately thought back on my years in school. Honestly, I'd spent most of my time in history class doodling in my notebook, thinking about how to land a job with Marvel or DC. Drawing comics was the only thing I really wanted to do, so it's all I let in.

"They burned the capital, but the war ended in a stalemate. No one won and no one really lost, save for the indigenous people. The British went home, and the colonials rebuilt."

"Oh? Returned home? Without victory? I thought we would surely win," he laughed. "So, what came next?"

"They started building railroads. Trains and stuff, you know?"

He nodded.

"Didn't think they'd become popular."

"Well, they did. Very much so. People pushed west. I think they called it 'manifest destiny' or something like that. Then there was the Texan war where they left Mexico and wanted to join the US. A war between them and Mexico, then one between the US and Mexico, and... well, now that I think of it, most of our history is war," I muttered. "Revolutions, multiple world wars, and cold wars, too."

"Cold war? Was that battle waged on the icy, snow-covered plains? Who fought in that conflict? And who won?"

Miko walked onto the roof then, expertly using mana to balance four trays at once. She lowered them onto our table one at a time, bowed respectfully, and left.

"So, it was like this..."

We spent the next two hours talking. Firstly, we covered World War I, about which I turned out to be more knowledgeable than I realized. It turned out the Captain America comic books helped quite a bit, especially when we made it to World War II, Korea, into Vietnam, and started talking about the Cold War, which he was disappointed to find out wasn't named for the icy battlefield or even the time of year.

"Once you start cultivating, you activate more of your brain," he said with a grin. "You see, I can recall everything I have done and seen since hitting the second realm. And when I say recall, it's to the smallest detail. The way her hair was done, the perfume she wore, the way she smiled at me when we sat here at this very table. Those details are all deeply ingrained in my mind... which is also why I was ready to give up on this life."

"Wait, you really were planning on killing yourself?" I hissed, leaning forward over the table and almost knocking over our bottle of liquor.

"I did. But not anymore. You see, there haven't been many humans in this place. You and the girl are the first I've seen in at least a decade. Maybe more."

"Was it a lot of bad things?"

He nodded, a sorrowful, hollow look inhabiting his eyes. Then he downed the rest of the amber liquor in his glass. I didn't know what it was, but it smelled and tasted strangely like bourbon.

"Too many friends died. Too many of them fell. And while I was strong enough to survive, I also wasn't strong enough to save them. That is the true curse of cultivating in this world. When I was younger, I was adamant about becoming a powerhouse, while most of my friends were simply content with just getting by. I

282

didn't push them. Didn't help them reach the apex of their abilities. Don't make the same mistake I did, JD. Keep your friends close here. Push them to become stronger, faster, and better. You will think that you will always be around... always be by their side. But it is a lie. Make sure they can fend for themselves. This is a mad world, JD."

I slumped further into my chair, mulling his story. Then I lifted my glass, took a long pull, and considered my situation. He was right. I couldn't be everywhere at the same time. Nor could I expect to realistically keep Chloe and Mabel out of every dangerous situation.

"I need to share everything with them. Mabel and Chloe... and whomever else I bring into our party. Even and equal," I said, thinking out loud. Then I poured another couple fingers of liquor into my glass, took a drink, and sat up in my chair.

"Good. Yes. A good start," Old White said.

"I want them to become as strong as me. No, stronger. Because it is mad to think we will never have to worry about each other. Right? They will always worry, and so will I."

"You got there rather quickly, my boy. It took me a very long time. Good. Now use that knowledge as your foundation. Build upon it. Think of your friends as family or clan. Go from there."

Silence fell over our table for a long while after that. He didn't speak, and I was too busy formulating plans to get Chloe and Mabel as strong as possible, as fast as possible. A random thought fired off in my brain, and before I could stop myself, I spoke.

"Say, did you ever get married... here?"

He nodded and looked away, his vision and mind seemingly firing somewhere far off in the distance. Then I realized what I had just asked. I already knew he'd lost everything, meaning everyone. Also meaning *the one*.

"Two in fact," Old White whispered, suddenly. "Both loved me but hated each other, though they came to tolerate one another. It was a mess, I tell you. I left one at home to go save the other. She was in danger, and by the time I got there, they were already overrun by beasts. I never found her body, but I did find the tracks. They circled right back to the town, and our home. I lost them both that same day."

I closed my eyes and clenched my teeth, almost able to feel his sorrow, his grief. Shit, that wasn't something any man was supposed to feel. Or remember, especially as vividly as if it happened the day before. In that way, cultivation sounded like a curse.

"I'm sorry, Old White. I truly am," I whispered, unsure of what else to say. Not much could be said in such a situation, especially since it had happened such a long time ago and he'd obviously come to hate himself for it.

"The core embedded inside the robe you are wearing came from that beast's partner. It was him, the Heavenly White Tiger King. I tracked him, set up my ambush to perfection, and yet, he still escaped. I ripped his Queen's core out. But I never managed to find him after that. The only solace I have is that his partner paid for my murdered wives."

"Please forgive me for asking," I said, feeling every bit the shit stuck to the bottom of a boot. I made him bring it up, think about it, feel it all over again.

"No forgiveness is needed, young man. But here, I want you to take this stone."

He handed me a fist-sized piece of…what looked like glowing rock. It was round, smooth, and pulsated with enough energy to make the hair on my arm stand on end. It felt strong, really strong.

"What is this?"

"It's called a **Breakthrough Pill**. I took seven cores and a great deal of mana and concentration to create, but I never ended up using it. Why?" he asked as if talking to himself, "Partly because it was far beneath the grade I needed. You could even go as far as to call it a failure, for me... but not for you. For you, I think it will be immensely helpful."

"I can feel its power."

"Yes. Take that power, use it, make it your own. Use it when you hit rank **seven** and it should help you break through to... another rank or two. Maybe more. I don't know. It is hard to tell."

I nodded my thanks and pocketed the pill, still unsure of what I did in my previous life to warrant such help here. The pill radiated and vibrated inside my rift, almost like a cell phone left on vibrate. Or more accurately, a drill slowly boring a hole into the fabric of my interdimensional storage space.

"When can we meet again?" I asked, "I feel a lot more information bubbling to the surface inside. I think you'll like to hear about football and American politics. I'm not sure which one is bloodier, though."

"Get settled into your classes first," he said. "Remember what I told you. Keep those girls close. Push them. Help them get strong. Besides. I'll need some time to digest all of these dwarven cask spirits."

"Dwarven cask spirits?" I asked.

"Well, they surely wouldn't call it whiskey," he sniggered and upended his glass. "But that is essentially what it is. The elves make it, too, although they add fruit. Different beast. Makes the hangovers much worse."

I grinned and nodded. Old White was a strange dude, but he seemed like a good man. A man who had lost everything and was still clinging to life, despite it all.

"How about at the end of the week?" I asked. "That will let me get the first week of classes out of the way. Get settled into a routine. Is that alright?"

He nodded. "Yes. Ask around the bazaar for me. Now that I'm not selling my legacy anymore, I'll be harder to find. Whatever the case, you can use this talisman to contact me," he said and handed me several business-card-sized talismans with symbols scribbled on top. "This will take you to wherever I am," he added and piled five scrolls onto the table. "Keep in mind, it is customary to make contact first. You just might teleport next to me in the bath, or while I'm on the crapper. You wouldn't like that."

285

"Thank you for everything you've done for me. I promise I'll pay you back one day."

"Bah!" he growled, waving me off. "Start by going back to your girls and meeting me at the end of the week. I want to hear all about the first week of classes, and specifically, what discipline you pick. I like our little talks. And, ugh, maybe next time you could bring one of the girls with you. I am just a lonely old man, after all."

"I'll try, but I can't make any promises," I laughed and pushed out of my chair.

I knew Mabel likely wouldn't be interested, though Chloe might. If I pulled on her heartstrings a little beforehand. Hell, maybe all it would take would be to mention that we are meeting a friend for a drink.

I bowed respectfully to the old man, almost falling over in the process. Damned sakes, dwarves knew how to make some strong spirits. Then, after a few steadying breaths, staggered through the new portal, and back into the tower.

QUEEN CORE

THE WALK BACK TO THE DORMS was...a heavy one. His words weighed heavily on my mind, and the liquor just made it worse. He'd lost the two people he loved most in the world on the same day. How much strength did a person need to keep on going after that?

I abruptly stopped, having reached our door without even realizing it. I steadied myself against the frame and took in a deep breath. But I didn't go in. Instead, I turned left and looked down the passage. Scarlet's room sat at the far end, a shiny name plate riveted to the wall just above the door.

I swallowed, made my decision, and strolled towards the door. I knocked before I could change my mind. The portal activated and an invisible force pulled me in and through. I immediately found myself standing in a large, luxurious place. The living room was easily fifty paces across and decorated with nice rugs, dark wood-framed furniture, silk privacy screens, and glowing lanterns. It was an incredibly vivid, exotic style that hinted at equal parts Japanese and Chinese influences.

I stepped forward onto a tatami mat and looked to my left, where an entire corner was filled with dozens of larger pillows.

287

Then I noticed the Cat. Or rather, cats. The first was pristine white, and the second was dark brown and a lighter black. The white cat glowed purple while the darker one glowed red.

A divider sat to my right, partially blocking my view of the next room. I stepped forward and caught sight of Scarlet sitting on a balcony. One that appeared to look out onto the city. Considering I hadn't seen any balconies from the outside, I found this more than a little surprising.

"Don't be shy, JD. Come sit with me," Scarlet said.

I moved around the corner, stepped over the darker of the two cats as it tried to rub against my leg, and walked out onto the balcony.

Scarlet sprawled in a wide, comfortable-looking chair. I greeted her with a smile, then my gaze crawled over her body, and I immediately looked away. She was wearing something that looked like a kimono, although it more accurately resembled a negligee, with lace, and material that seemed far too thin and sheer to cover much of anything. It honestly didn't help that she had kicked her feet up onto the handrail, letting the incredibly short garment ride all the way up to her hips.

I heard her clamp something between her teeth, and then draw a breath, before I caught a whiff of pipe smoke. I studied the city, putting all of my focus into finding the rooftop I had just shared with Old White.

"You are too cute, JD. Don't be embarrassed. You come from a world that is very uptight about the body, form, and sexual reproduction. Things here are much looser. You will learn, in time."

I turned slowly, just as she pulled a pipe from her lips. A cloud of orange and red smoke surrounded her, slowly dissipating into the cool air. Her long dark hair flowed freely over her shoulders, some reaching down past her hips. My gaze followed the line down to the just-visible strap of her panties—red, the color catching my eyes and holding on. She reached down and subtly

288

pulled the dark silk of her garment up a little more, revealing even more red lace.

"Do you like them?"

I nodded, the stupor from my liquor somehow deepening. I very much wanted to see more. No, all of her.

"Shit, you're beautiful," I muttered before I could stop myself.

"Yes. And thank you," she said, reaching up and pulling at her neckline, teasing me with a healthy glimpse of creamy, flawless skin and supple breasts.

I shook my head, trying to dispel the sudden and almost overpowering lust that came over me.

"Don't fret, young man. It isn't you, at all. But this," she said, holding up her pipe. "This is a special blend, one laced with a substance that makes it oh so difficult to tell lies. So, now is the time to ask your questions." She pulled the pipe to her lips, drew a healthy breath, and exhaled that strange, colorful smoke. "I can only tell you the truth."

"So that was involuntary just now? What I said?"

She chuckled. Her voice was almost as melodic as Chloe's. Almost.

"You only said what was truly on your mind."

I took a seat on the chair across from her. She set the pipe onto an ashtray, pulled something from her rift, and before I knew it cards were floating around her, white talismans with red symbols painted across their white faces.

"I have no idea why I'm here," I said, honestly. "I was in the hall, thinking about some things, and then just felt like seeing you. I think I want to thank you for everything you've done so far."

"You are welcome. And that is…everything?"

"No, not really. I'd—like to—pursue an intimate relationship with you." I heard the words slip off my tongue, the thoughts, the secret yearnings behind them, but I couldn't fully rationalize why I said it.

"Hah! You young men—all raging passion and fight. I love it. I thought I caught a glimpse of that hunger in your eyes."

I nodded stupidly and then shook my head, trying to clear away the cobwebs ensnaring my mind. I mean, yes, I'd fantasized about Scarlet on several occasions. Shit, I'd fantasized about Salina as well, when she showed up in my bar to recruit me for Zenith. I was a healthy, sexually active, red-blooded male. And I knew what I liked.

"Don't fight it, you can't escape the effects. It will only make them worse. But since I am under its effects, too, I will tell you this. I see a strength in you, one I find incredibly attractive. Relationships are not forbidden between mistresses and students, but I have to consider your safety." Scarlet smiled, reached down, and pulled the hem of her short robe back down over her red, lacy undergarment. Then said, "Come back and see me once you've hit the second realm. I would like to redress this conversation then."

"Thank you, Headmistress," I replied and made to stand.

"There isn't anything else? I could swear you'd want to know more."

"Why are you helping me? Helping us?" I blurted, sinking back onto the seat. The truth was, it was just the tip of the iceberg of my piled-up questions.

"Oh, the reasons. I supposed you won't accept, 'because I like you'. But, in truth, I like your fighting spirit. You see, I was a lot like you when I first arrived here—out of my element, and at odds with almost everyone and everything. I worked my way up every step and now I have some power, some control, and I intend to use it to help those that struggle as I did."

"You helped Chloe, too. You led her to the texts with information about... dual cultivation. Why? What is Chloe scared of?"

Scarlet chuckled, but there was no mirth to the sound. She picked up the pipe, put it to her lips, and took a long pull.

"It is not some grand conspiracy if that is what you are asking. But I gather you probably already know my answer, especially if Old White told you his story. You and Chloe come from a mundane world, one deprived of magic and its effects. You have to understand, certain races view you as beneath them. That unlocking the cultivation potential in someone like you is blasphemy to their cultural or spiritual beliefs. At the very least, you are a waste of usable mana. It is true, this world is a dangerous place. But for people like you and Chloe, the enemies will not always come from straight ahead, but also from behind."

"Then what about the blood elves? Or the others? Why are they allowed to... how can we...?" I stammered, the effects of Scarlet's pipe smoke giving my anger additional fuel. "Is there anything I can do to keep them from getting to Mabel? To protect all of us from them?"

Her expression changed, and for the first time since meeting her, she looked sad.

"Once she graduates, nothing, JD. Unfortunately, they will reclaim their rite of ownership and take her back. At that point, there is nothing you or I could do. Except... well..." Scarlet said, drifting off.

"Yes? What is it? Tell me, and I will do it."

"You would have to buy her. And that is only if they allow it."

My heart sank. I was prepared to do whatever it took to gather strength for us all, to build us all up, but what she said meant that it wouldn't matter. That I could perhaps help keep Chloe and Mabel safe while we were at the academy, but could enact no meaningful, long-term improvement for our loveable moon elf.

"I won't let them have her," I growled, my knuckles popping as I balled them up into fists. "It isn't right. For one person to own another. I'll stop it, no matter what it takes, even if it costs me my life."

"Good!" Scarlet said, abruptly pulling her legs off the railing and sitting forward in the chair.

I'd been so prepared to argue, to fight back as she told me how out of touch I was, or how it wouldn't matter, how I didn't have a chance. But she reached out and grabbed my hands and looked happy. No, more than that. She looked excited.

"Yes! That is precisely what I wanted to hear. For starters, keep being honest with yourself and stay true to that goal. If you can do that, then I will help you. I'll keep helping you, and I'll provide as much protection as I can without showing favor. Prove them wrong. Just like I did. But keep this one thing in mind. The academies do not have unlimited power. Races like the blood elves have collected a great deal of power beyond these walls. That power gives them status, and reach, but also protection. Do you understand?"

I nodded. It meant they could get away with murdering other students and Scarlet likely couldn't do anything about it.

"Stay true to that goal," Scarlet repeated and snapped her fingers.

I felt a pinch in my guts and then I found myself standing in the hallway, staring at the shiny name plate above her door. My heart raced and I immediately spun on the spot.

What in the hell just happened? Had it been a dream? Or did I hallucinate the entire conversation?

"Fucking hell," I cursed as I stumbled back down the hall. I put my palm on our door, pushed a little mana forth, and the portal opened. But just like with Scarlet's room, something grabbed hold and pulled me in. I smelled something unfamiliar as the room materialized around me—spicy and strong, but not unpleasant. At the same time, it wasn't exactly something I would smear under my nose, either.

A hand shot out from the darkness to my right and grabbed my wrist, then they pulled me into an embrace. The portal behind me closed and I blinked, my eyes struggling to pierce the darkness.

"What are you... doing?" I asked curiously. "I feel assaulted. Are you going to rob me?"

Chloe leaned in, her breath on my neck. "What would you like me to take?"

"Everything," I whispered back and when she leaned in to kiss me, added, "But leave me with some cheese whiz and a stack of crackers. I need a snack."

"You!" she snorted, and playfully punched me in the arm. "Come on, we're getting ready."

Chloe pulled me forward as my eyes finally adjusted.

The dining table was gone. Replaced by a large, round circle glowing on the ground. The light-blue light ebbed and flowed, pulsing with the same rhythmic dance as the portals. The ring rotated slowly clockwise. A second glowing ring appeared, hovering in the air over the first, rotating in the opposite direction. Three half-moons sat on three sides of the formation, all an equal distance apart, with multiple lines connecting them and shooting towards the center.

"Is this it?" I asked. "Is this the formation you were talking about?"

"Sure is!" Chloe said excitedly. "She's just finishing up and then we can start."

I nodded and dropped onto a nearby chair, watching Mabel, whom I hadn't even noticed crouched in the shadows, add several more glowing lines before she stood and stretched.

"If mistress Scarlet is right, this formation should be good for at least five uses, but depending on the cores, it might erode faster."

"But you could make it again if we need to, right?" I asked.

"This one was expensive as hell. It cost me over..." She paused.

"How much did it cost you? If it is the money, we can always work harder to earn more."

"I don't want to say," she whispered. "It's my personal gift to you... to our party."

I pushed out of the chair, put an arm around Chloe, and held the other out for the elf. She took a hesitant step forward, but then froze, as if unsure of what to do.

"Come on," I said. "We won't bite, Mabel. Parties are allowed to hug. Aren't they?"

Chloe did the same and held out her arm. Mabel nodded and moved in slowly, her gaze cast down.

"I'm sorry. I'm just not used to people wanting me around," she whispered. "A moon elf's place in my world is to not be seen or heard."

"You won't have to feel that way any longer, Mabel. At least not as long as I'm alive. You're our friend and part of our party, our family," I said, trying with every fiber of my being to believe it. Sure, things could change. We could stumble on some good luck and put in a lot of hard work, but if what Scarlet said was true about them taking her back, then I couldn't waste any time.

"Not quite yet. It won't be official until we put our names on the party agreement. You should invite Chloe first, as she was here before me. Then me. We'll accept and bind to this dorm, with you as the party leader."

I nodded but waved for her to join us. She dragged her feet and bit her lower lip, but finally gave in and joined us. Mabel sank into our arms and I pulled her close, Chloe smashing us all together. We stood there for a long while, Mabel eventually putting her arms around us and returning the embrace. It was a small step, but it felt monumental at the same time.

"Mabel?" I whispered as she moaned contentedly, her cheek pressed against my chest. I sounded like she was getting ready to fall asleep.

Chloe pulled her head away and smiled.

"Yes?"

"How do I make the party?"

"Oh, right. You just have to press your index finger against the person's forehead and ask them if they would like to join your party."

"That's it? Wasn't there a document Scarlet handed out? What is that for?"

"It's just the rules," she explained.

I broke free of our tangle of arms and placed my index finger on Chloe's forehead. She crossed her eyes to watch. "Chloe, will you join my party?"

Nothing happened. Then the girls fell into a raucous fit of laughter.

"He fell for it!" Chloe said, gasping for air. "Sorry, JD, we just had to! Don't blame her, it was all me."

Mabel looked away, but her shoulders bobbed as she joined in.

"So, Scarlet's scroll isn't just the rules, heh?" I muttered.

Mabel finally turned and nodded.

"I'm sorry, JD. I shouldn't laugh."

I pulled the party scroll from my rift and immediately pushed some mana into the parchment.

"Just remember. This will come back to haunt you both when you least expect it," I said, looking to each in turn. Then the scroll opened and text appeared.

PARTY CONTRACT ACTIVATED.
USE A DROP OF BLOOD TO SIGN THE
CONTRACT.
AVAILABLE PARTY SLOTS: 5/5

I pulled out my pen–blade and jammed the tip into my thumb. It broke the skin and blood trickled down onto the parchment. My name appeared first. James Wright.

YOU HAVE ESTABLISHED AN OFFICIAL PARTY.
STAT INHERITANCE: 10%
FOR NEXT RANK: 0/10

"Wait, what? You're a James?"

"Yeah," I muttered. "Forget about that and just call me JD."

"Sure thing, lover boy. I mean, JD."

"The more important thing is that message," I said, pointing at the parchment. "What do we need to do to get up to the second rank? I want to see that stat inheritance go up!"

"Sacrifice ordinary cores. We need to sacrifice ten of them for the second rank, but I don't know beyond that."

I took a breath to ask Mabel what it meant to "sacrifice a core" when a prompt appeared before me.

PARTY UPGRADE REQUIREMENTS & BONUSES
RANK 1 REQUIREMENT: --, BONUS: 10%
RANK 2 REQUIREMENT: 10, BONUS: 15%
RANK 3 REQUIREMENT: 50, BONUS: 20%
RANK 4 REQUIREMENT: 100, BONUS: 25%
RANK 5 REQUIREMENT: 250, BONUS: 30%

"Look at those," I breathed. They both nodded.

"That's...impressive. But the number of cores. Shit. You really need to think twice before starting a party, huh?" Chloe mumbled.

But she was right. There were downsides. If people left the party, it would negatively impact those that remained. And then again if you had people who weren't willing to add cores, then the party would stagnate and not grow stronger. I pushed the doubts aside. This was the way I was going to help us get stronger. The way to protect Chloe and Mabel.

"You next," I said, holding my pen-blade out to Chloe. She pushed it aside and pulled her own sword out. She followed my lead and let a drop of blood fall onto the parchment. Her name appeared as Chloe Sullivan. She didn't strike me as a Sullivan, but I wasn't going to tease her for it. Sure, we were all about that goodhearted fun, but this felt serious. Profound.

Mabel was next. Unlike Chloe, she accepted my pen-blade, pricked her finger on the tip, and let a drop of blood fall just below Chloe's name. Mabel Karash.

"Party," Mabel said to no one in particular. "You guys should open it as well."

"Party," I said, following her lead.

NAME: James (JD) Wright
CULTIVATION: Realm 1, Rank 4

NAME: Chloe Sullivan
CULTIVATION: Realm 1, Rank 3

NAME: Mabel Karash
CULTIVATION: Realm 1, Rank 2

It didn't show much information, but I didn't need much at this point. And now, thanks to our party status, I could follow their progress. Two small bars appeared next to the names: a red and blue bar. They were full.

"Health and mana bars? More things that make this feel even more like a game," Chloe chuckled. "Shit, what would my gaming buddies back home say?"

I laughed. "It is weird to think the life inside me is represented by that little, red bar."

"You really are at the fourth rank already?" Mabel whispered. She stared at me with equal parts jealousy and approval.

"Speaking of which, how about we get to cultivating? I want to use the Queen Core and see if we can all get a boost."

Mabel pulled away and crossed her arms over her chest.

"Do I have to join?" she asked, her voice tight with panic.

"It's not like we'll be doing anything awkward, right? We'll just sit in a circle and absorb mana. I mean that sounds pretty low-key to me," I said.

"You don't know," Mabel chuckled, "We have to be naked and... holding hands. From what I hear, quite a bit can travel back and forth between people in the formation. It can be quite intimate."

297

"Sounds like fun!" Chloe laughed.

"Please, don't think it is just about you both seeing me nude again. As I said, we moon elves are at home in our natural state. But it is what you might feel, or see, while we connect. I'm not sure I want to share... some things."

"You have to learn to trust us, Mabel. We're all in this together now. And that will only work if we learn to accept one another... flaws and gifts. I only see you," I said, then reached down, took her hand, and gave it a firm squeeze.

"Yep. All in this together," Chloe whispered and untied her robe at the front, then slid it down to the ground and kicked it away. She was left in just a strikingly blue thong. "Mabel, whatever it is, I still got your back, girl. Just promise me that you won't judge me too harshly from what you see of me. Cause I did some stuff I ain't proud of."

"Really?"

"Yep. But I got myself here, dang it. The world can kick you, but that doesn't mean you have to let it keep you down."

"I like that," Mabel sniffed.

"Perfect," Chloe said, clapping her hands. "Let's get this show on the road. I'm hungry. Again."

"Yeah, same here." I decided then that I would tell them about my conversation with Old White later.

Chloe moved forward and immediately started helping Mabel get undressed. I wasn't entirely sure if she needed it, but she didn't appear to have much choice. Her robe fell away, leaving the delectably curvy elf standing in just a pair of rather frilly white, silken panties.

"Mabel, you rebel! Ruffled panties?" Chloe gasped, leaning forward to flick the oversized ruffles.

"Yes. They are my favorite. Do you like them?"

"Oh, you bet I do!" Chloe said, turning away and throwing me a subtle wink.

"I have another pair..." Mabel started to say.

"Actually, can I just have these? I love the color," Chloe said, and before the elf could protest, she hooked her fingers inside the frilly undergarment and pulled them down her ankles.

"Yeah, okay," Mabel said, lifting her feet and stepping clear.

"Here, hold these, dear," Chloe said, stuffing Mabel's panties into my hand. She mouthed "burn them" and then she proceeded to pull off her own.

"I guess I'm next," I muttered, and pulled up the prompt. I selected [yes] to storing the heavenly robe, and pop I was naked, too.

"Wow!" Chloe gasped and did a double-take. "What in the... holy shit. Did you just make your robe disappear?"

"Yeah," I said, wishing that I hadn't. "It turns out I kind of have to summon and store it. Evidently, you can't just pull on a robe like that."

"Awesome. Now I want one even more. But you really gotta make sure you're not in public when you store the right item, heh?" she said, and her gaze flicked down to my midsection. Her mouth pulled up into a sly grin. "It seems you're as excited as we are, to ugh, cultivate today. Heh?"

I rolled my eyes but tried not to fall into her trap. What could I do if I was a healthy young man in his prime? I didn't need much to get my blood circulating.

"Yes. I am very excited, too. I think this will be fun..." Mabel whispered, and looked right down at my awkwardly stiff dick. It wasn't like I had a trapper keeper to hide behind. She actually giggled. Then looked up, met my gaze, and in a surprising move, looked right back down.

"So, what now? We sit in each of the three half-circles?" I asked, eager to move the proceedings along.

"Yes. Once we're all seated, you need to put the core inside the center circle, and we all join hands. The formation should do the rest."

I took my spot and the girls sat to either side. They joined hands as I pulled the core from my rift, set it gently into the designated circle, and took their proffered hands. A sudden surge of energy released from the core, billowing into the air. The formation seemed to snare it, keeping it from dissipating beyond a shimmering dome.

An intense and sharp pain spread all over my body as if a thousand tiny daggers were cutting into my skin. I felt the girl's mana reach out to me, and I responded, allowing it to course through my body. I pushed my own forth, forging the connection and effectively binding us all together. The girls gasped as a wave of mana flooded through our connection. I felt Mabel tense, her fingernails biting into my palm.

A wave of hot, turbulent energy grew between our palms, and before I knew it, it fired up my arm and tumbled me back into darkness. I flipped head over feet and landed, the ground bending beneath me. Light peeled open the world around me, and I found myself in a massive room. The walls were made of black stone, the mortar shimmering silver in the torchlight. Gilded paintings hung from thin, silver wire, depicting elves in armor, frilly dresses, and strange, uncomfortable-looking suits. They all had greyish skin and fire-red hair.

"No! Try again, worms," Someone screeched behind me.

I turned to find an old female blood elf in a simple, red robe standing over a line of moon elf girls. They looked young, no more than adolescents. Although, I had no idea how that translated into years. The blood elf towered over the girls as they each lifted a sizable platter before them, the trays covered in glimmering, crystal glasses. I approached, studying the faces, their strain obvious at supporting the weight.

"No noise. No shaking. No grunting," the blood elf screamed, the girl closest to her flinching at her voice. I stopped, frozen to the spot. The blood elf mistress swung what looked like a yard stick, the flat slapping hard against the back of a girl's calf. The sound alone was enough to cause me pain.

300

"You will serve, and when you serve you will do it without noise, without shaking, and without grunting. Pain is no excuse for weakness!"

I watched the one moon elf girl as she strained, a bright line having appeared across the painted skin on her leg. But there was something in her face, her eyes that rang so familiar.

"Did you hear me, worm?" the blood elf screamed. "I can practically smell your pain, your weakness. It is wretched!"

"Yes, Matrona."

Mabel? I thought, finally putting it together.

"And up!" the old woman said, turning and continuing along the line. "At our banquets, you will hold your platters up so civilized elves do not have to stoop or bend. Civilized, unlike you worms."

The blood elf snapped her short whip in the air, the crack so loud it made all the girls jump. Together, they hoisted their plates up high, the collected glasses clinking together.

"I hear noise!" And she cracked the whip again.

Mabel grunted and whimpered, and powerless to help her, I watched as her tray tipped and several of the crystal glasses fell. They hit the stone floor and shattered loudly, the pieces scattering in a cloud of glittering dust.

The other girls in line gasped, pulled their trays down, and backed away, leaving Mabel alone above the broken finery.

"Wretched worm!" the blood elf screeched, then batted the platter out of Mabel's hands, sending the rest of the glasses to shatter on the ground. "You will pay for that. Lift your smock! Do it now!"

I watched as Mabel started to cry, then with trembling hands, lifted her simple, stained smock to expose her legs.

"Higher, worm!"

The smock went up, the girl's belly coming into view.

"Wait. Stop!" I cried, moving to grab the old woman, but my hands passed clean through her. She pulled a short, hooked knife

from her belt, the edge wickedly sharp. The blade gleamed red in the firelight.

"If you cry out, I will only cut deeper," the blood elf hissed, and brought the knife into Mabel's stomach, the tip easily parting her moonlight-colored skin.

I was tumbling upwards next, and I found myself right back in the formation, that energetic, hot sensation pushing out through my chest and moving down my right arm, towards Chloe.

Mabel squeezed my hand tight, grimaced, and then gasped, "I just ranked up. I'm rank 3!"

I smiled, despite the cold pit in my stomach, the lasting image of the blood elf crone putting the knife to my beautiful friend's tender skin. I couldn't help but look down, just beneath her breasts, at the puffy scar marring her otherwise unblemished skin.

Chloe tensed next, a vice-like pressure squeezing our hands together. A long moment later, her eyes shot open, and she looked at me. She saw something, I could tell that much. But what?

The absorption steadied as it coursed through all three of us. I could feel it, every strand of mana that wove circles around us, carrying bits and pieces of memories, emotions, dreams, and feelings we'd tried to hide from other people.

The mass of mana was too large for our bodies to absorb at once, so it pushed through us, bonding with those hidden parts and carrying them on to the next in line. Over and over again. I saw Mabel's lifetime of abuse, pain, and loneliness. But I saw it in flickering fragments as if I was watching a movie through rapidly blinking eyes. Chloe's life was there, too. I saw a rundown home, bare cupboards, and holes in shoes. Then, police cars, foot chases down alleys, and finally, a seedy strip club, where men with greasy hair tried to buy more than she was willing to sell for a dollar at a time.

I felt my body stiffen and muscles expand, my skin gaining both elasticity and strength. A new rush hit me from all sides at once and the pressure increased. My yang energy responded, swirling, and then joining the mana flow. Mabel and Chloe's yin energy joined, somehow flowing in the opposite directions. Then their collective yin hit me all at once.

I grunted and swore as my veins widened, an entirely new path burning straight from my heart to my head, and another down to my groin. It was short, but the pain was brutal, almost as if someone was pounding foot-long nails into my skull, chest, and groin. I wanted to stop and scream, to curl up in a ball, but knew if I lost my concentration the girls wouldn't just not benefit from the experience, but the resulting bounce back could harm them. Some distant, deeply seated part of me knew this part wasn't normal... wasn't just part of the process. Perhaps it was because Chloe and I had already paired, and had already forged a deeper, more meaningful cultivation bond. If it benefited Mabel, too, I would gladly bear the pain.

"I'm... close!" Mabel hissed again through clenched teeth. "Just a little... more!"

The power coming from Chloe was several times cleaner and more powerful than that from the elf, who was losing a lot of it in the process. Maybe it was all the toxic memories bonding with the mana, her doubt, or her fear. Hell, maybe it was all of it.

Skin cracked and sinew tore where my muscles expanded, but then grew back together. I felt a staggering wave of weakness roll through me, and I almost blacked out. Almost... but not quiet. I sucked in a breath, set my jaw, and focused.

A sudden shockwave shook the formation from inside as we all ranked up and the last of the core's mana was absorbed. The formation cracked, the glowing lines flaring brightly, and then it all exploded, the force knocking the furniture over and leaving us gasping for air. I sagged forward, sweat dripping off my nose and chin, that familiar black mess stuck to my skin and the floor beneath me. It was cold as ice and covered both girls.

"Just look at the impurities," Mabel said, trying to pick a piece loose from her knee. And yet, while I was struggling through the shared recollections of their struggles, their pain, and hardships, she

303

was smiling. And not just an "I'm pleased" smile, but of the genuine "grade-A" joy, variety.

"Let me gather it in my rift." I watched as she formed a ball of mana, and then slowly pushed it over her body. It grew, changing color as it absorbed the dark mess. Then, before I could move, it swept over Chloe and me, cleansing away not just the dark muck, but the sweat and dirt we had accumulated over the day.

"Wow. So that is a useful trick."

"Useful when one is responsible for looking and smelling clean, but never given the time, clean water, or clothes, to actually bathe," Mabel said.

I frowned, again struggling with another pang of anger. Then I watched Mabel collect that dirty ball of mana and store it securely in her rift. Okay, strange. But heh, if that was her thing, who was I to stop her? And maybe she had a valid use for it. Perhaps a poison for certain fire-haired elitist pricks?

"Shitballs," I muttered, struggling with a momentary swelling sensation in my core. It felt like I needed to burp, but worse. "All this mana feels like it wants to get out again."

Mabel nodded. "It needs to be stabilized."

"How does someone…" I groaned, pushing against my belly, "go about doing that?"

"Many different ways, for many different people," she said, surprisingly calm. "Meditation, forced single-point concentration, weapons training, or sparring, while some couple to stimulate the pleasure receptors. If you know how to force it and find the right method for your body, the mana will stabilize much faster. Trust me, you do not want to continue upgrading without making sure the foundation and the previous ranks are strong and stable."

"What do you mean?" I asked as I laid down on my back, unable to sit anymore.

"Picture a bucket full of water. That bucket is your body, full of mana. What would happen if you threw a glass or another bucket at the one that was already full?"

"It would knock it over or make it spill."

She nodded. "You only maximize your stat upgrades if you do it properly. Not too fast. Those who... I think the saying is, cut off the corners, end up weaker than they began."

"It's close enough," I said, throwing her a smile.

Chloe rolled over, a mischievous smile spreading on her face. "Did you feel that last wave?"

"I did. Both of your yin hit me like a runaway freight train," I grunted.

"I think we all just reaped the benefits of our dual cultivation," Chloe whispered.

"Ohh?" Mabel's ears perked, visibly. "I wondered what that was, I got tingly all over like butterfly wings were touching my skin.

"So, how are we going to stabilize this new rank, because I'm ready for some food and then bed?" Chloe asked.

"I know a way, but I will need JD's help," Mabel said.

"Just tell me what you need! But after, it is pizza and beer, if we can find some... with an all-night Lord of the Rings marathon."

"What is pizza?" Mabel asked.

"Oh, you are in for such a treat!" Chloe giggled and clapped her hands.

BRINGING THE PARTY TOGETHER

I ROCKED FORWARD onto my hands and knees and met Chloe halfway, kissing her forehead before pushing onto my feet. I teetered for a moment, the room seemingly tipping around me. But thankfully, it stabilized.

Chloe giggled and followed suit, then Mabel.

"Weird, the ground feels spongy," Chloe laughed and tipped sideways into me. I caught her, and then helped Mabel, who almost fell back onto her butt.

We got dressed and Mabel gathered us in the bedroom. She had us sit on the larger of the two beds, forming a triangle, hands linked, not unlike in our formation.

"Okay, this is called 'single point concentration'. JD, are you ready?" Mabel asked.

"I am."

"You are an artist, so this is perfect for you. We are all going to close our eyes, and then I want you to walk us through drawing your favorite thing, step by step."

"Okay. Yeah. Let me see." The request took me off guard at first because I honestly hadn't practiced my craft for a while. The long hours at the bar and my resounding lack of success left me with very little motivation and artist currency. I was bitter, more than anything.

"I am thinking about a castle…" I started, but Mabel squeezed my hand.

"Good," she whispered, "Now walk us through its creation, from the very first step to the last. Help us make it real, too!"

"I have my simple grids drawn, and then I identify the horizon. The foreground is flat, and covered in trees, ugh, tall ones…" Chloe squeezed my hand next, providing me just a bit of added support. I took a cleansing breath and pushed it back out, sending as much of the shaky weakness with it as possible.

"Picture tall, straight pine trees, with full boughs of green needles capped with just a hint of snow. A red cardinal sits on the closest branch…"

"What is that?" Mabel asked.

"A bird," Chloe whispered back, "A really red bird."

"Okay."

"Those trees form a dense grove, but behind it, rising high in the air is a castle. I start with straight walls, forming several tall, cylindrical towers, topped with cone-shaped roofs…" And it all flooded back then, the techniques for straight lines, shading, stone and glass textures, all of it.

I'd drawn primarily comic book superheroes because that was what the studios wanted, but my first passion had always been castles and fantasy landscapes. I'd filled an entire notebook in High School with doodles of Moria, Rivendell, and Mordor.

I built the image in my mind, and it came alive in startling detail. In a way, my imagination never had before. I brought the girls with me as we walked through the trees, the smell of pine and wood smoke wafting in my nose. We stepped out into the clear and beheld the castle, the sun rising majestically behind it.

I don't know how long the experience went on, but by the time I opened my eyes again, my arms ached, and my back was sore. But to my surprise, that uncomfortable 'full, pseudo burp, I might need to throw up' sensation, was gone. I only felt a glowing well of power deep inside, stable and ready for use.

We didn't find pizza in our food inventory, a fact that left all of us a little salty, especially Mabel, as Chloe had established some profound expectations. But we settled on some hot beef sandwiches and fries.

Mabel opened up even more as we ate, talking about the stabilizing experience, the castle I painted in her mind, and her newly achieved rank. In fact, I don't think she stopped talking the whole time we ate. By the time we cleared away our dishes, Chloe was almost falling asleep in her chair.

"You know, if we keep up this pace through the whole year, we won't just become a lot stronger, but we might just die from fatigue," I said, propping her up.

"But just think about all the upgrades to your stats," Chloe said, and I helped her over to the bed. She dropped dramatically to the mattress. I was curious to see what the queen's core had done for me, so I snapped open my status window and studied the changes.

NAME: JD AGE: 24
WEAPON: Pen-Blade
CULTIVATION: Realm 1, Rank 5
POWER LEVEL: 480 (141 + 33)
HEALTH: 739 (+69) MANA: 326 (+41)
ATTACK: 109 (+9) DEFENSE: 99 (+9)
MANA SHIELD: 565 (+45)

I looked to Chloe, who was flat on her back, her stat window glowing above her. Mabel was sitting on her bed, studying hers, too.

"Do you have stats inside brackets as well?" I asked once I closed the status screen.

"Yeah, I do," Mabel said as she played with a stray lock of hair. "I got them the moment you added me to the party. And I gotta say that I like the way they look."

"Me too," Chloe added. "And the bonus is quite nice. I think we have a better chance of not being torn apart now. And... I can cast my skill two more times."

"Who knows what kind of party I would have been invited to, if I was at all?" Mabel whispered. "If I hadn't met you, that is."

"So, what do you guys want to do next?" Chloe asked, her eyes already closed.

"Really? You look like you're ready to drop. I say sleep. It's been a long day," I muttered. "Besides. We're off tomorrow. We can get up early and do another dungeon run. How does that sound?"

"Hey, before you fall asleep, there is something I want to ask both of you," I said as I sat on the bed. Chloe rolled over onto her stomach, so I rubbed her back.

"Is this about that giantess chick that talked to us during the seminar today?" she grunted.

"Yes," I said, as Mabel crawled under her covers. I watched her shift and shimmy, before dropping her clothes onto the floor.

"Can I be honest?" Chloe asked.

"When aren't you?" Mabel said, giggling.

"Fair point. But yeah. She intimidates me a little. She's like six foot six and two hundred and eighty pounds. It looks like she eats elves in her protein shake every morning."

Mabel's eyes went wide, and she pulled the covers up to her nose.

"She's just joking, Mabel," I said. "But seriously. I get the feeling that all the other students out there are busy recruiting the best and brightest of every discipline into their parties. This might just be our make-or-break moment."

Chloe turned to better face me. "Okay. Then we have to ask, is she a good fit because she wants to be in our party or because she is the best potential fit. Mabel, what do you know about her people?"

Mabel pulled the blanket back down. "The same things everyone else does. They are big, strong, straightforward, highly resistant to mana-based attacks, and are stacked with physical bonuses."

"That does sound like the ideal tank for our group," I said, honestly. And it had nothing to do with her sparkling eyes or outrageous bust. But secretly, those earned bonus points in my book.

"Okay. So, point for willingness to join," Chloe grunted, "I'm fine with it, as long as she cleans the Mabel-protein shakes out of the blender."

"What would we need beyond that?"

"It depends," Mabel said. "We could add a true magical cultivator, or perhaps another fighter... one who specializes in ranged weapons. You know? A bow or javelin. Something like that. But that will depend on what additional skills we can gain. Because I am support, I won't have much value beyond that aspect unless I can *truly* support us all. I need to round out my skill set."

"That is a good point. You only have one skill, right?" I asked, forcing the conversation into that direction. I forced the matter of our giantess-friend to the back burner. After all, if I made a decision they weren't completely onboard with then I undermined the integrity of our whole group.

She nodded. "I do."

"How do we get new skills? Are they all earned? Or is there a place where we can purchase or trade for them?"

"There are merchants that deal in skills at the bazaar, but you need to have something they would want in trade. And we don't have anything worth trading."

"Anywhere else?"

"The Dungeon lobby," Chloe added. "The sisters have beginner skills, but they're pricey. Like thousands of Fres expensive."

310

"Let's start there then, and if that doesn't work out, we'll hit the bazaar. Alright?"

"Sure," the girls responded together.

"Think about the fifth member and we'll talk about it again tomorrow. I want to get our party squared away as soon as possible."

"Easy, turbo. Why the rush. We don't even have our first class until the day after tomorrow," Chloe said.

"I know. But I am going to push this thing as hard as I can," I said, Scarlet's words still ringing around in my head. If races like the blood elves really viewed us as trash and knew they could get away with something violent, then there was very little reason for them to wait. If anything, they were more likely to try something soon before we formalized our entire party and gained strength.

"If we don't fill out our party and get stronger as fast as possible, we can't really help each other stay alive. That is the reality of our situation. This is more than just bullies." I turned to Chloe. "You said it yourself. Humans don't amount to much in this world. If they survive at all. I don't know about you, but I don't want to end like Old White—alone and broken. Emron and the other blood elves are going to test us. If we fight them, Scarlet will come down hard. And neither can we force them to leave us alone. Our only chance is the good old-fashioned nuclear deterrent."

"Nuclear deterrent?" Mabel asked, cocking her head to the side.

"They are really big bombs where we are from. The idea is, someone isn't going to attack you if they know that you can launch equally big bombs at them. It would be mutual destruction," Chloe explained.

"Bombs? Those explode, right?"

"Precisely," Chloe said, mimicking a mushroom cloud with her hands. "When you put it that way, I agree. Let's go nuclear, baby!"

311

Chloe rolled over and closed her eyes. Mabel was asleep just a few moments later. The room filled with the sound of their slow, rhythmic breathing as I pulled the table and chair out away from the wall. I positioned it so I could see them both sleeping. Then I rummaged through the closet until I found some spare parchment. I didn't find any pencils, only a quill, and some ink.

I knew I wouldn't be able to sleep, not with my almost runaway thoughts and emotions. So, I used the one tool I had neglected but desperately needed. I drew.

SECOND DUNGEON DIVE I

I AWOKE THE NEXT MORNING in a tangle of limbs. Chloe had rolled over at some point and practically pushed me off the bed. I cuddled in close, in what would become a night-long fight for survival. I was sore, and not entirely sure if it was from ranking up or from her elbows and knees. She really was a fearsome sleeper.

We ate, bathed, and got dressed, then set out. The hallway was crowded with other freshmen, most heading in the direction of the bazaar. The throng split in half before us as we approached. Most of the students were indecisive about where they wanted to go or how they wanted to spend their time. That was fine. We had a plan.

No one hassled us on the way, so we took our time getting there. The dungeon lobby was crowded, easily a hundred students sitting, talking in crowds, or just milling around. Thankfully, I didn't recognize any faces, or red or silver hair, in the crowd.

"It is weird, no one seems that motivated to do anything except stand around," I whispered, leaning into Chloe and Mabel.

"There is no rush for them. This is a requirement by their people, their families... gaining strength is not needed for their basic survival. As long as they don't pick any fights they can't win or step on the wrong toes while they are here, there is relatively little risk," Mabel said.

"Must be nice," I mumbled, as we walked up to the counter, and the waiting twins.

"Good..." Belma said.

"Morning," Selma finished.

Okay, that is creepy.

"Hi there," I chimed.

"We've got a few questions," Chloe cut in.

"Oh? What's that?" Belma asked, leaning in on her elbows and eyeing us both. A strange gleam burned in her eyes. On its own, it wasn't that odd, but with her expression, it was a tad unnerving. Yet another reminder that although most of the people here looked like me, that didn't necessarily mean they *were* like me.

"Two things. I'm interested in some beginner skills. I'm sure you ladies could hook us up with some of them," Chloe continued, thankfully. She didn't seem as disturbed by the twin's strange, almost manic look.

"What's the second thing?"

"Where can we upgrade our weapons?"

"And here I thought you would be offering us more steak," Belma muttered, rubbed her stomach, and sighed dramatically. "I guess we could help you, but what kind of skills are you looking for? And for whom? We need to know the discipline."

"For the three of us. Anything that can help, at this point."

"I hope your coin purse is bulging," Belma said, pointing at me. "The cheapest pen-blade skill costs over **50,000** Fres and you'll have to talk to the mistresses. They hold specialty skills for certain weapons. Or you could search for them in the Bazaar. There might be a few merchants with pen-blade skills sitting around, collecting dust, but it is such an underused weapon, I wouldn't count on it."

"Why don't we take care of Mabel first?" I asked. "What do you have for her?"

"I can offer her skills in three categories: Heal, Buff, and Debuff spells. I have a Heal spell that costs **1,500** Fres. As for Buff spells, we

314

don't have anything that she can use, right now. The buff spells and skills start at rank 6. We do have some debuffs, however. Ooze, Debilitate, and Malice."

The words and numbers flashed before us, and it quickly became too much. I closed my eyes and simply listened.

"And what do they do?" I asked. Judging from my experience with games, buffs were normally game-changers, especially if you could stack their effects.

"Ooze slows an opponent down, Debilitate lowers their attack ability, while Malice drops some of their defense. The higher the skill level, the better the effect."

"How much are those?" Chloe asked.

"We would part with them for 1,500 Fres each. You still have your card, right? We'll take crystals, too."

I nodded. "I do. But I also have some rank 2 crystals. Interested in those?"

"Oh?" Selma chimed in for the first time. "How many?"

"I've got 5 of them. How much can you give me for each?"

She licked her lips as she thought, but then she pulled her sister aside and whispered something. The two went back and forth several times before walking back over.

"We'll give you **5,000** Fres for one, and **11,000** for two. We don't need more at the moment."

I pulled two of the stones from my rift and moved to hand them to the sisters. Skills meant so much more to us than money or crystals at that point. They could mean the difference between life and death, and it wasn't like we had bargaining power, so we could always haggle over price later.

"If I take all...?" I started to ask, only to have Chloe pull me aside.

"They're swindling you," she said. "Each of those crystals is worth easily **10,000** Fres to the right buyer."

I flashed her a grin and pulled her in for a kiss. "But that is only if they are willing to pay for it, right? No amount of crystals will do us good if we're dead."

315

She shrugged and nodded. "You're right. But you need to realize these people love to haggle. They live for it and will never give you value unless you are willing to push for it. Trust me. They want to buy your crystals. Demanding a fairer value will not alienate them."

I looked down at the crystals still clutched in my hand and thought about it for a second. I realized she was right. I was so willing to not make ripples, to blend in, that I was going to give away something of major value. I gave her a wink, turned back to the sisters, and openly placed the crystals back into my rift.

"What? Are you going back on the deal?" Belma asked, pulling the four pieces of parchment back towards her on the counter."

"No, but our deal is not yet concluded. Can I see what you have for Chloe next?" Her expression changed, that gleam returning to her eyes. "Hmm, let me think." Belma and Selma moved as one and held their open palms out towards Chloe. "Yes, she is a…" Belma started.

"Sword Aura user," finished for her. "They are rare, and unfortunately, there are not many skills available for them. The best way to grow in that particular specialty is to buff her stats. I would recommend the Lion's Roar and the Stalwart skills? That's about it... for what we carry, anyways. Come back once she hits the 8th and 9th ranks, however. Then, we can do business."

"Those skills, the Lion's Roar and Stalwart skills, how much are they?"

"They are **2,000** Fres each."

"Understood," I said, silently tallying my money up in my head. That would leave me with **1,000** Fres left. If I accepted their reduced offer for my crystals, that is. And the last thing I wanted was to leave us with zero money. "What kind of Magic skills do you have?"

"Why? You do not have a magical user in your party."

"Because I'm asking. Do you have anything fire-related? Any fire spell, even the weakest one."

Belma pursed her lips and pulled out two pieces of parchment, then placed them in front of me. She pointed at the first and held up three fingers, then at the second, and showed five.

"What? They're **3,000** and **5,000** each? What the hell do they even do?"

"This is a very basic [Fireball] spell, and the other a [Summon Fire Elemental]."

"I'll take both," I said and didn't break eye contact.

"With the two spells, that will bring your total to 18,000 Fres. But you don't have enough credit left on your card. So, are you trading the crystals or not?"

"Hold on," I said, opening my rift and fishing out the coin. I set it on the counter, and both of the sisters frowned and crossed their arms across their chests.

"Credit. We don't like accepting coins for goods. It is too much... counting."

"That is a bit hypocritical of you, don't you think?" Chloe asked, "I mean, you are the ones that gave us the coin in the first place."

Mabel shifted uncomfortably behind me, but she didn't say anything. I'm sure she had already begun imagining those delectable skills she'd been craving disappearing back behind the counter. And if I was right, she'd likely spent all of her money to buy the ingredients for our core formation. I owed her big time.

"Our shop, our rules, younglings. If we say we don't want coins, that means we don't want coins. There are lots of you first years to do business with," Belma said. She moved to push my crystals towards me, but I reached forward and put my hand over hers, holding it in place.

"Hold on. We're still negotiating."

"We are?" Selma asked, eyeing my hand touching her sister's. "Because it just sounds like arguing to me."

"What else do you want?" Belma asked.

"Equipment upgrades," I said.

Selma whistled. "Costly stuff. And I'm not giving you shit for free."

I frowned. "We're not looking for handouts, just fair deals."

"A weapon upgrade skill costs **10,000** Fres, the skill upgrader costs **7,500**, and the spell upgrader another **7,500** Fres. Each is single... use... only. Only."

"What?" I exclaimed. "That's highway robbery!"

"What is a highway?" Belma asked.

"Take it or leave it!" Selma snapped.

Freaking elves! I took in a deep breath and let it out again, cutting myself off from saying something stupid.

"Can I upgrade their weapons as well?"

"No. Only if you give them the parchment to use. One-time use. So that is three weapons, three upgrade parchments."

I studied the testy elves for a moment and ran through all the calculations in my head. Working at the bar helped, as I was used to mentally rattling out tabs without the use of the register or a calculator. It didn't make sense to buy only one weapon upgrade when realistically, all three needed it. I could always purchase those after our run if we brought enough in with loot. In our situation, another spell upgrade was probably more beneficial.

"I've got **18,000** Fres wrapped up in buffs and spells, plus I want another **22,500** Fres in skill and spell upgrades. That is **40,500** Fres. Now I've got credit and coin, plus five juicy, rank **2** crystals in my possession worth at least **10,000** Fres each. You said you needed two of them. Why don't we meet in the middle and say I give you all my credit, plus the two crystals, and still owe you two thousand in credit after our dive? By my math, that is you two getting great value for your goods. We get what we want, you ladies sell some stuff, and neither of you has to dirty your cute, little fingers counting coin. Deal?"

Selma and Belma looked at one another, then turned away and quietly whispered together. Chloe put her arm around my midsection and squeezed me.

"Fine! Fine! Deal. But you owe us... **4,500** Fres!"

"In ingredients. Not credit," I said, and shook Selma's hand. She squeezed so hard my knuckles popped.

"You sure drive a hard bargain, don't you, mister human?"

318

"It's a pleasure doing business with you, ladies," I said and scooped the sizable stack of parchments off the counter.

I shook my head and stared at the far wall. No one was there so it was the perfect spot for us. "Come on, give me a minute to gather my thoughts."

"So... what's the deal with this waiting?" Chloe asked after a good minute passed. "Did I miss something?"

"I thought someone was going to be down here, that's all," I said, coming clean. If Skadi were here, waiting as she said she would be, then we could have settled the issue of adding her to our party. I had to consider that something came up.

"I'm adding a cost of **1,000** Fres to your entry!" Belma yelled after us.

"Sure thing, Belma! Thank you! You're a gift from above!"

Chloe laughed. But Mabel stared at us as if we had a screw or two loose. Beyond that, most of the people standing around the tavern were now staring at us. We made for the portal and stopped just as a young man cut us off.

"Hey, a giant girl was waiting for you. She said she was going to do a dungeon run with you guys today," he said. "I guess she'd been down here for a while but decided to go in with some randoms."

The young man was a beastkin, with the overall body and face of a human, but with hairy, round ears and clawed hands. Several tufts of fur covered his wrists and ankles, even parts of his legs and arms. He looked like he belonged in a 1980's horror film.

"Who did she go in with?" I asked.

"I don't know, man. We just ended up waiting at the notice board together, so we chatted. Good luck finding her."

He turned and walked off. Strange.

"What was that all about?" Chloe asked.

I shook my head. "I don't know. She said she wanted to do a dungeon run today and that's it. I figured if she was here, we could also talk to her about joining the party."

"No, I mean she seemed capable, but what's with him telling us that? Do you think she might have gotten herself hurt?"

319

"Come on, how about we run through the first floor. If we run into the party she's with, maybe we can ask."

"Yeah, sure," Chloe said, but I struggled to read her emotions. I still couldn't tell if she wanted to add Skadi to our group, or if she just wasn't thrilled about our party growing, period.

The portal spewed out a gust of mana that pulled us in and before we knew it, we stood on the other side of the gate where the familiar jungle greeted us.

"Come on, let's sit over there," I said, pointing at a lone log. "Learn your skills quickly and test them out before we go."

The girls nodded and took a seat, then I pulled out the parchments and handed them out. Then I went through the rest. I paused, with the fire ball and summon elemental in hand, then pulled my pen-blade out. The parchments contained glyphs; forms drawn to symbolize that particular spell. I'd had a theory brewing since our last time out and needed to test it.

The pen-blade was more like a real pen than it was like a real sword. And it connected with my mana, but moreover, my will. It created things, the air slash, for example, from a combination of my will and mana. If that logic stood true, then in theory, if I knew the right formation to draw, then I could create the fireball as well, even if I wasn't a magic cultivator.

I got up and moved away from the girls, just to be safe... especially since fire had a way of pushing beyond boundaries. They looked and watched quietly as I studied my parchment. I read the theory, the power, and form, but used my artistic experience to break the glyph down into segments that I could recreate with the pen-blade.

According to the parchment, mana flowed into a fireball differently than any of the other skills. First, it formed in one's palm, then condensed toward the center, but instead of releasing the mana, the cultivator pulled on the mana, compressing it into the tightest, most condensed form possible.

"Shit. It's like the power stroke on a car's engine. The mana is poured into your hand like gasoline into a cylinder, then the hand compresses it, just like the piston, just before it ignites. I can do this,"

320

I whispered as I focused mana into a ball. That was the easy part, and even slicing a third off and pushing it outward wasn't hard, but when it came to compressing it, that part wasn't so easy.

Sparks danced in my palm some fifteen minutes later. I was making progress and needed just a last push. Thinking about what I did during our battle with the queen and the fly, I held the pen-blade in one hand and the parchment in the other.

"Fireball," I said, and recreated the glyph in my head, stroke by careful stroke.

The glyph appeared in the air before me. I set the pen-blade to work, drawing from the top right to the lower-left corner, flipped over the trajectory, and went back around again, then toward the upper left corner, ending there. Each stroke glowed to life as the pen-blade infused it with life, and as I connected the last lines, a ball of crackling fire appeared in my hand.

SKILL NAME: Fireball (B)
TYPE: Basic, Mana, RANGE: 20 paces
DESCRIPTION: One of the basic elemental spells.
Highly versatile yet destructive in the right hands.
BASIC: +30 Attack, +20 Mana on mastery, Damage: Attack x 1.55, Mana: 20
ADVANCED: +60 Attack, +40 Mana on mastery, Damage: Attack x 1.75, Mana: 25
MASTER: +120 Attack, +80 Mana on mastery, Damage: Attack x 2.0, Mana: 30
NOTE 1: Attack goes up/down by 50% depending on elemental affinity
NOTE 2: Fire Ball can cause debuffs that cause fire damage to target

I first cast a Fireball and then an Air Slash right after, but it didn't do much. It wouldn't work the way I wanted it unless I figured out how to properly combine them. Every try cost me 27 mana, but I was far from able to do what I wanted. At least for now. Perhaps I just had to learn to combine the two glyphs, in essence, merging the two skills.

I drew another fireball, and held it in my hand, then quickly scribbled out a small whirlwind of air. Only after the air attack stabilized, did I merge the two together with a single, decisive swipe of the pen-blade. Fire and wind blossomed together into a spiraling inferno that struck a tree and set it ablaze. A small chime sounded, and a screen popped to life.

ADVANCED AIR SLASH MASTERY UNLOCKED
BONUS STATS RECEIVED:
MANA +50

Attack was one of those stats that everyone loved more than any other, but in this world where we needed to pay for skill and spell use with mana, getting a mana boost was perhaps even more valuable. Fifty points would allow me to cast several more attacks. Or, as I had just learned, chain several more together.

"Did you just cast that fireball without having to master the skill?" Chloe asked, moving in from her perch on the log.

"Yeah. I think so," I said, the parchment still clutched in my hand. "But there's something I just don't understand..." I paused, unsure how to broach the topic. Then I decided to just throw it out there and see what happened. "Every skill I've learned through the pen-blade so far immediately goes up to Basic Mastery right away. Without me even having to do it more than a few times. Any ideas?"

"What in the hell are you on about? I've used my Sword Aura over thirty times since getting here and I still haven't achieved Basic Mastery!"

"I don't think it's about how many times you use it," Mabel added, thoughtfully. "It's more like how good you are at using it. Or, if you think about it this way—how innovative. In this case, JD mixes and combines skills, which usually isn't an easy thing to do. Plus, he is an artist, so he already has the muscle memory and the creative side down. If you put it all together, the pen-blade just works for him."

322

"Not fair," Chloe muttered. "What about me? How can I do the same?"

"I don't know," Mabel replied honestly. "My people used to have what we called moon dancers. They were the pinnacle of the blade arts. It was as much a dance as it was fighting, and so the name went. But to become a moon dancer, an ascending elf had to first master every form and technique. It was like, learning the ugly stuff before they could learn to make it beautiful."

Chloe placed her hands on her hips. "That just makes it sound like I need to spend the next 20 years practicing just to get as natural with this," she said, holding up her impressive blade, "as he is with that." She finished by pointing at my pen-blade.

"Well, that just makes me feel bad," I said. "I don't think Mabel is trying to make you feel like you aren't good with your weapon. But I think she is right. I have worked with pen, pencil, charcoal, and knife since I was eight. All that time I was training my body to handle this." I tossed the pen-blade and caught it. "I mean, if anything, I got lucky. If my affinity had been for any other weapon, I think I would be screwed."

"Dammit. Why didn't my parents force me into baton twirling or kendo, instead of volleyball," Chloe said, but changed her grip on her sword, and smiled.

"You're a natural," I said, slid forward, and kissed her on the cheek. "You throw magical sword-fire better than anyone I know.

"Thanks."

"Do you two need more time on your skills?"

"We're already done," Mabel replied, then stretched.

"We were done before you even cast your first fireball," Chloe added. "These skills were tailored toward our classes and affinities. So, it was easy peasy."

"Slap hands!" They both obliged me with a high five.

"This slapping hands thing is weird, but I like it," Mabel laughed.

"At least you didn't hit his pen-blade," Chloe laughed back, "You never know what might happen. Hell, he could accidentally paint your clothes off, or something."

"Can it do that?"

"I don't think so. Although…" I said, pausing. "But seriously. I'll get around the affinity barrier as long as I have the skill parchments. And I seriously doubt air slash is supposed to be a pen-blade affinity skill."

"When I think about your weapon, I'd imagine skills that would allow you to paint monsters to appear," Chloe said.

"Oh, oh. Or maybe paint larger, danglier balls onto monsters! Stuff like that," Mabel added, excitedly throwing me a wink.

"Gross. That is gross, Mabel. Did you have to bring that up?" She nodded, laughing with Chloe.

But they were right. A pen was supposed to create things. And the only thing holding it back was the wielder's imagination.

"So, what now?" Mabel asked.

"Practice before we commit to anything serious," I replied. "I need to get the hang of my new skill and we need to understand what Mabel's skills do and how they work in a support role. You, too. I'd like to see the difference in your fighting with and without buffs."

"Alright then," Chloe replied cheerfully as she pushed off the tree log. "Lead the way, tank."

"Hah, I'm far from a tank," I chuckled. "But looking at my stats, I'll work for now."

We left our sheltered nook and made our way onto the forest path. The trees greeted us like old friends—large, shadow-throwing, and creepy friends, actively hiding things that wanted to murder us. But still… friends.

"I'd love to get a giant-sized person adept at hand-to-hand combat into our party to take over this tank roll," I said, as we rounded a colossal tree. Honestly, it was probably ten feet wide, at the base.

"But you've got the highest defense and the highest health, so you're the tank by default," Chloe said.

"Keep your distance as we move, miss damage-dealer. We never know when—."

I didn't see the beast or hear it, but I did feel the tentacle strike me. And then I saw the prompt glow to life in the darkness.

Mana shield has sustained 2 damage.

"And to think I almost panicked. Where the hell did that bastard come from." We backed up, fanning out, with me in front, Chloe behind and to the left, and Mabel further back and to my right.

The plant thrashed its tentacles, hitting me several times, before pausing as if to say, "my dude, why can't I harm you?"

"It came from the shadows," Mabel said, pointing to the spot where it had appeared.

"Thanks, Mabel. I was asking rhetorically." I sent an Air Slash at it, immediately. The blade of wind hit, cutting it into two messy halves.

"I don't know what that means. Rhe-tor-ical."

"I think it's a question designed to emphasize a point, more than to actually get an answer. I don't know, I could be wrong," I said and walked over to the plant to pick up the loot.

ITEMS RECEIVED:
Venus Lorana: 1
Core crystal Rank 1: 1
Fres: 73

The loot itself wasn't anything to write home about, but if we stayed in here for a while, it could eventually add up. Good farming.

"I already know what you're thinking, and yeah, I'm all for it," Chloe laughed. "You just keep the damned bastards away from us and we're good!"

I gave her a thumbs up. Yes, I would keep the beasties away from them, as long as my mana shield held up and my body didn't fall apart.

"We need a bigger beast or monster to test our new stuff on," I replied as we continued down the path. "And feel free to stay back and let me deal with the pesky shit."

Three Venus' died by my hands first, and then another two before we even made it down the first valley and back up the next hill. I stopped and turned back to the girls.

325

"How far along are you willing to go?"

"Wherever you want," Chloe replied.

"We aren't even ready to go to the 2nd floor," Mabel said. "I'm not confident in our powers, at least not yet."

She was right. Technically. "Why don't you two decide on the route. I'm content to go wherever you want... as long as there are beasties to fight."

"You just call out for a map, and the current map of this floor will pop up."

"Now you tell me," I said, not quite happy this news hadn't come up before. And it made me wonder what other things there were I had yet to discover. "Map."

A bright light split the dark forest as a map appeared right in front of me. It was rectangular and large, almost as tall as it was wide. It depicted a living maze, swaying from side to side. The reality of that moment sank in. I had just pulled up a freaking mini map!

I studied it for a moment. Six large red dots appeared, with a black outline, and three smaller ones just like them. Other than that, there was nothing. The dungeon itself was a mess and almost resembled a creature from nightmares, a corpse with sewn-on appendages that stretched far and wide. Alright, I was being overdramatic, but there were quite a few rooms. One would easily get lost without a map.

"Chloe, you've been here before, right? Not just with us?"

She nodded.

"I did a small run with other freshmen, and we learned some of the basics, together. Why?"

"I just want to make sure I know what I'm looking at. The smaller dots are creature-type bosses, and the large dots are dungeon bosses?"

"Heh, you're smarter than you look, and yes, you're right. There are six bosses in total, but they could technically be mini-bosses or real bosses. How many do you see?"

"All six. But what are they?"

"We met two, right? The Venus Lorana Queen, who is a plant-type boss, then the Hulker Gargantua, the cockroach-like thing. There's the Mutated Swapper Fly that we also killed, the Three-Horned Viper

King, the Leech Queen, and then the final floor boss is the Gorilla King."

"Weakest to strongest?" I asked, not liking the sound of some of the names.

"Venus Lorana Queen, then the Mutated Swapper Fly, the Hulker Gargantua, Leech Queen, Three-Horned Viper, and finally the Gorilla King. But we're set when it comes to weaknesses. You have fire, I have fire. It works on all but the last two, against which it works without the weakness bonus damage. And all the variants can spawn as mini bosses as well. Just like they did last time."

"Effective means that it does 50% more damage," Mabel added quickly.

"Yeah, I saw in the spell description. The Fireball description I mean." She nodded knowingly and flashed me a smile.

"Thanks, Mabel. Chloe, tell me something. Are the zones where they're supposed to appear the same? Or are they random? Meaning, do they spawn in the same place every time?"

"They appear randomly, but if it's a small dot, it's one of the three weaker variants, and if it's a big one, it's one of the two big guys. Luckily, the zone boss always stays in the same room."

"In that case, we'll head straight for the first smaller boss. A bigger one is not far from there, according to what the map says. So, if one fight goes well, we can jump into another."

She shrugged. "It's the first floor, so nothing in here is terribly strong. Chloe and I are rank 4 and you are rank 5. We're in the same party and we're using the Solidarity formation. We got skills, and some basic gear, so there is really no reason to fear them."

"That sounds like 'game time' to me," I said, "But let's not push our luck. Things are just starting to look up for us."

SECOND DUNGEON DIVE II

WE PROGRESSED STEADILY through the forest, killing venus loranas, flies, other insect-like creatures, and even some snakes. There wasn't a ton of enemy variety, but everything we did stumble across all proved susceptible to fire, and ironically, our blades.

I stopped some thirty minutes in and checked our progress on the map. The zones were much larger than they looked originally, and I struggled to determine how much time we'd need to cross the first one. We'd lucked out our first time in, evidently, as both mini bosses had spawned within the first zone.

A crossroad lay ahead. The left path led up and around, in a rather roundabout way to the floor-boss room, while the one on the right led to a second room with a smaller dot. Several flies appeared from the treetops, while a small swarm of venus lorana crawled in from the underbrush. I formed us up, putting me in front, then moved straight at the first venus. I put the pen-blade to work, forming a single, strong slash. It hit, cutting through vines and body easily. That first plant died and went opaque.

Two flies dive-bombed us, but as they plummeted in, I heard Mabel's zither come to life. Snares blossomed in the air, catching the flies and pinning their wings to their bodies. I double-slashed, cutting the two down with ease. Chloe cut to my right and slashed through two of the remaining venus. That left two flies. Ready for a little practice, I started drawing the glyph for a fireball, only to watch the flies abruptly turn and disappear in the trees. I let the glyph fade away, unfinished.

"Does it make sense to pursue them?" Mabel asked.

I shook my head. "No. Don't waste mana. We're here for bigger fish."

"I don't think there are any fish-shaped beasts in this dungeon," Mabel explained. I knew she was trying to be helpful, but wow, I needed to either stop using earth-based colloquialisms or get her up to speed.

"It's just a saying," Chloe explained. "When fishing, it just means throwing back a smaller fish in favor of trying to catch something bigger."

"Oh, I get it. That makes sense. I think…."

I looted the corpses, finding several crystals, some fres, and we moved on.

"We should do this every day," I said. It wasn't something the girls would like to do, but if this was standard loot, then we would be foolish to not milk it for all it was worth.

"Yeah, about that," Chloe chuckled. "It doesn't matter how many crystals you have, but if you don't take the time to properly absorb the mana and let it settle, you'll never get a chance to use it. We will have to take days off, sometimes longer. At least that's what I read in the library."

"Oh?" I asked, checking my map. Considering everything else she'd learned, I couldn't discount her opinion. "Did you find any skills in the library?"

"I wish," she said, shaking her head. "They're smarter than that. They don't keep the good stuff lying around where just anyone can learn it. Anyone in a position to pass along that kind of meaningful knowledge is selling for top dollar. All that's left in the library are history books."

"We'll have to talk to the headmistress about Mabel and I getting access to the library, right? I'd like to spend a little bit of time there as well."

I took in a deep breath and led us around a bend in the path. A sizable puddle of water came into view and looked very out of place. I put my hand up for the girls to wait and moved in for a closer look. A vine struck out and lashed around my leg, then another joined in, and a third, all slithering and constricting around my body before I could even react. I tried to slash with the pen-blade but stumbled and fell over, the vines pulling me off my feet and into the water.

I splashed and fought, the puddle not actually a puddle, but an incredibly deep and dark hole. Fear washed over me, and I panicked, kicking and clawing to bring my head back up to the surface. The vines tugged me down, into the darkness, towards something I couldn't quite make out. It moved, opening and snapping back together, sharp, silvery teeth glinting in the light from above.

I cursed, a stream of bubbles erupting from my mouth. I kicked and struggled just as a bright, golden thread appeared in the water, synching down around two of the vines. The constricting force loosened just enough for me to break my legs free. I kicked and gained some distance, only to have the vine around my left arm pull tight.

Unable to focus, I swung the pen-blade down, jamming the tip into the vine as hard as I could. Cloudy, black sap blossomed in the water. I brought the blade back and jabbed it in again and again. It finally released and I pulled for safety.

My head broke the surface and I gasped in a spluttering breath. Mabel was there, her hands held out, her mouth moving. I didn't even hear what she was saying but grabbed ahold and together, I managed to crawl free. Mabel kept pulling and I didn't understand why until I toppled atop her and turned.

A mass of grasping, twisting, and hungry vines erupted out of the water, thrashing and reaching for my legs. Chloe jumped across, bringing her flaming sword up in a single, violent cut, and effectively severed the groping tentacles.

"Heal," Mabel whispered.

I rolled over and pushed my way to my feet, but the severed tentacles pulled back into the water.

"Why did you just waste... mana on a heal? I'm not... hurt."

"Because you were poisoned. Didn't you feel it?" Mabel replied. "You were glowing green, and this Heal can also nullify poison and some other debuffs. Only minor ones, but still."

"I see," I muttered. "But my robes are... never mind. They're already drying and repairing."

"What? You're shitting me!" Chloe hissed. "That's so cool! I want one too! Get me one next!"

"Then thank you," I chuckled, still fighting to catch my breath. "It was just a puddle. I mean, I almost drowned in a damned puddle just now. Who does that?"

I opened my status window to confirm the Poison and see if I'd lost much Health. I was full, but I caught sight of a few negative statuses before they dropped off the screen. Shit. The name of the beast... whatever it was had been on my screen, but I didn't have time to read it before it disappeared.

"It was a monster. Not quite a venus, but something similar. The dag-gone thing didn't even drop any loot. Unless it isn't dead..."

"It was a trap, Mabel. It was a trap monster," Chloe explained.

The elf lifted an eyebrow as if to protest, but she didn't take the bait. "Yes. But it only matters that JD is okay."

"Yes. I'm okay. I'll just have to be a little more careful about our surroundings from here on out."

I turned back to look up the path, then brought up my mini map. The next room was relatively long and thin, the path leading directly to a prep-chamber and the big boss beyond that.

"The path looks pretty straight. Let's take a break before we move in. I'd like to let my mana replenish before we take on a potentially big fight. I don't want to get caught with my pants down."

"Why is that a bad thing? Can I see that?" Chloe chuckled. "Please?"

Before I knew what was happening, Chloe moved in close, worked her hand into my robe, and grabbed ahold of my manhood. I frowned.

"Chloe, really? In a danger zone? As much as I like the attention, this hardly seems like the time."

"Don't you think that's hot?" she whispered, her touch and proximity sparking an abrupt rush of blood and heat to my pelvis. "I bet Mabel wouldn't mind keeping watch, so we could take a little break. I'll bet she'd watch us, though."

I was cold and still relatively wet, so my trouser weapon was a little... shrunken. Sex was honestly the last thing on my mind.

"Oh, she definitely would mind!" Mabel snapped. "You're not getting any if I'm not getting any!"

"Okay. This is getting out of hand. This is hardly the time, girls," I said. "Chloe, if you're that 'lonely' later, I'll give you all the attention you can handle."

"Deal!" Chloe said. "And just so you know, I have this fantasy of getting freaky on a boss corpse!"

"That is really gross!" Mabel spat.

"Well, what is one of your fantasies?" Chloe asked. "Tell me one, so I can tell you how gross it is."

They continued back and forth, so I retreated to a fallen tree and stared out into the distance. I didn't want to break them up, especially if this was some odd form of girl bonding. Or maybe this was how they both dealt with stress? Perhaps Chloe got horny when things got tense, or Mabel grumpy? Who was I to tell them their methods for coping were wrong? I didn't want to be "that" guy.

Once we'd rested, and the girls got their "interesting" conversation out of their systems, we continued up the path. We came upon and dispatched another dozen venuses in a short amount of time, stopping to loot their bodies before continuing on. We followed the path down into a valley, but when we reached the top of the next rise, a shimmering, blue wall came into view.

"The first boss is in there," I said, pointing and confirming with the map. "Here is our strategy. Mabel, you use your snares to immobilize, but save your mana for debuffs. Keep it slowed and weak, that's the main priority... beyond staying safe and alive."

"Sure thing. I'll prioritize the two of us, then the boss, and then you."

"I don't like hearing that,'" Chloe protested. "Yes. Killing the boss is important. But not more important than the three of us walking out of here."

"Don't worry. If it's slow, then that just makes my job a little easier... you know, not get hit!" I said, reaching in to pinch her butt. "Sacrifices need to be made. If anything, Mabel's mana has more value in weakening the boss than it does supporting me. I'll be fine. Trust me."

"Okay. But you can't expect me to not worry. Cause, I'm going to worry. But what do you want me to focus on?" Chloe asked. She stood with her hands on her hips, as if daring me to disagree with her.

"Your job is key. We need you to take care of the ADDS, or the so-called additional mobs. If we're distracted by the boss, they are even more dangerous."

"ADDS!" she whispered. "Yeah, I'll take care of the small fry."

"Good. Once they are gone, you help me, alright? With our newfound skills, I'm looking forward to seeing what new and more powerful combinations we can come up with."

"You know, you're not a half-bad party leader," Chloe snickered.

"Half bad? I was only shooting for one quarter. So, that makes me an overachiever, right?"

She leaned in and kissed me. "Just a little. You can show me how bad you can be later." Then she gave me a healthy smack on the rear, propelling me down the path.

We spread out and made our way carefully towards the glowing barrier. Once we were close enough to see through, I pulled up behind a thick tree trunk and scouted ahead. I immediately spied a large but relatively open space, rimmed by thick forest and broken by several large boulders. I didn't see any water, so that was good. One trap per dungeon dive felt like too many.

If it followed us here, I needed to know where I could fall back. Understanding the layout of a battlefield was one of the first keys to victory. With that thought, I pulled up the map and gave it a quick look, just to make sure there weren't any hidden chambers I didn't know about. Wouldn't it be a nice surprise to see a new swarm of flies or other pests come in just as we engaged a larger, far more deadly enemy?

I stopped again just before passing through the shimmering wall. I pulled the map back up just to confirm, as I couldn't see anything moving inside. The map still showed a red dot in the next room, and it was even moving.

"Chloe: You need to get inside to see the monsters. You won't be able to see them from outside the room."

"Mabel: Wow, this is so cool! Wish I'd known about this earlier!"

I turned around and put my hands up as if to ask how.

"Chloe: Say the word 'Chat' and you can use the party chat. Just speak to the chat system and we'll see what you're saying. You don't need to make much noise for it to pick up your voice."

Another first. A chat. How am I just hearing about this now? I thought, pushing aside the irritation.

Sure, the chat didn't feel that important, until I actually thought about it. No, who was I kidding? This was as important as...anything really. We could warn each other, we could communicate from afar, and we could chat when in different rooms or zones. We could continue to strategize and identify weaknesses in real-time, during a fight. That was huge!

"Chat."

A new window appeared, small and translucent with bright blue edges.

"JD: Can you hear me?"

"Chloe: Hah! See? Easy!"

"JD: Cut it. What was that about going in? Do I need to enter the next zone to see the beasts and boss?"

"Chloe: I think so. I remember hearing other students talking about it. They want to keep the special zones a surprise... so, no peeking! We'll be right behind you. Don't worry!"

"JD: I'm not worried, just annoyed that I am finding out about this chat thing like, right now!"

"Chloe: Oh, right. Sorry."

"JD: Yeah, let's work on minimizing the surprises!" I stopped and took in a deep breath as I readied myself. "Wait until I give the go-ahead."

I took in another deep breath and stepped through the shimmering wall that separated the rooms. The space beyond was roughly shaped like an inverted crescent moon, but without the sharp edges. A dozen small venus plants moved slowly, ambling as if without purpose. The queen sat in the middle of the space, silent, her form gently bobbing from side to side.

The space wasn't empty, as it had appeared from the outside. Trees, shrubs, and viny plants filled the space between boulders, providing cover for us if we needed it. But also, a hiding spot for other beasts, as well.

Next time don't look through the magical boundary and formulate a plan. Wait until you understand what lies ahead. Got it.

"JD: It's the Venus Queen. You can come in. Let's get this done."

"Chloe: Coming."

"Mabel: Me too."

335

"Really? Do they really need to reply separately?" I whispered, readying my pen-blade. Once they appeared behind me, I checked the queen for her stats.

NAME: Venus Lorana Queen
TYPE: Zone-Boss
POWER LEVEL: 500
HEALTH: 2,000, MANA: 500
ATTACK: 100, DEFENSE: 100
WEAKNESS: Fire, Sword

"JD: Not too bad. Only 2,000 health. We can whittle that down pretty quickly. Just make sure the ADDS are gone, Chloe. Mabel, are you ready to start?"

"Mabel: Yeah, we're ready."

The moment she stopped talking, Mabel shot a Slow debuff at the Queen, followed quickly by a Malice, and finally Debilitation. I rushed in, not waiting for Chloe to start cutting away at the smaller Loranas.

I started drawing the first glyph in the air just as I saw her Sword Aura light up the shadows. Red-hot searing flames erupted from the blade and cut across the clearing. I didn't need to see the wave of fire to know Chloe had gotten stronger. I could feel the heat, see its bubbling, blistering potential arcing and scorching the damp air.

I changed directions and quickly scribbled a whirlwind Air Slash, the twirling gust of wind catching her flames, and immediately merging into our hallmark flaming inferno. It enveloped several smaller venus plants and caught the queen, instantly setting two of her tentacles aflame. It shrieked and thrashed, pounding the burning appendages against the ground as the smaller ADDS died. They simply leaned over and died, their color and fight bleeding away.

SKILL USED: Air Slash x 3

MANA USED: 30
DAMAGE DEALT: 117
DAMAGE DEALT: 114
DAMAGE DEALT: 228.
CRITICAL HIT!

"Hah! Look at that damage!" I cried in triumph.

"That's because I'm so strong!" Chloe laughed.

It matters not, JD. Do it when it counts, I thought, summoning the glyph for a fireball in my mind.

"Fireball," I said and scribbled the formation in the air, focusing my mind on moving, shaping, and giving the right-sized ball of mana life. I finished the last line of the glyph as I compressed, the mana bursting to life. Then I pushed it forward, striking the queen's side. The attack hit square in the side, her pale, puffy flesh singing black and catching fire.

SKILL USED: Fireball
MANA USED: 20
DAMAGE DEALT: 193
BURN DEBUFF INFLICTED
DAMAGE DEALT: 47
DAMAGE DEALT: 45

The damage was good and consistent, both attacks having lowered her health to around 1,400 points. Still, it was just a start, and this creature was a boss for a reason.

I dodged to the side as a massive tentacle rose and came right down at me, the spiny appendage hitting hard and tearing large clumps of ground away in the process. I jumped over a smaller rock, cut behind a tree, and wove my way back around, keeping out of the plant's reach.

The queen's burned outer 'skin' burned off in large swathes, exposing a pulsing, soft interior skin. She lashed out again, nicked Chloe with a tentacle, and then hooked a tree, as she tried to grab

Mabel. The tentacle jerked back, ripping the tree right out of the ground. Okay, I didn't remember her doing anything that impressive before.

She threw the tree at me, and then immediately started to hop and dance, spewing globs of green goo in all directions.

MANA SHIELD SUSTAINED: 27 DAMAGE
MANA SHIELD SUSTAINED: 21 DAMAGE

"It's a debuff! Get out of its range!" Mabel yelled. I looked up and saw I was only ten paces or so from the edge and backtracked, running as the green acid ate into my shield, leaving me with a mere 93 points as I lunged out of the area of effect.

A warm green glow enveloped me as Mabel cast her healing spell. The corroding damage dissipated, and my shield started recovering at a rate of 1% every second. I got back to my feet and ran around the targeted area, but the acid rain was subsiding. Still, I didn't want to risk it and flanked the queen as the last of the flames went out.

I checked its health and grinned. It was down to 997 points. Elemental debuffs were insane. I'd need to invest some resources and time to improve them. If we made it out alive.

Chloe sent out a wave of flaming sword aura that cut deep into the lorana queen, eliciting a strange, chortling shriek. I rushed the monster and struck two times, using simple, but hard slashes. The first two strikes hit her lower half, one cutting off a number of her legs, while the second and a third follow-up hit puffy interior flesh and tentacle. Her movements were already sluggish compared to the previous battle, but not entirely from damage. Mabel cast another Slow, stacking the effects, and giving us the upper hand.

A tentacle slammed down and despite her reduced speed, I wasn't able to get completely out of the way. I deflected some of the blow with my pen-blade, but my mana shield took the brunt. I staggered to the side just as another Sword Aura slash cut into the queen, tearing through one of her last tentacles and splashing her body with charring fire. I sent two more air slashes at the flames that were spreading along its right side. The wind picked up and spread the fire all around, eating away at the newly-formed vines, the flesh, and the root-like legs.

"Shit, that looks painful," Chloe muttered as she stood next to me, her sword held ready.

"Better her than us," I said, watching as her last tentacle fell off in a burning pile. It wasn't just that. It was her whole body. The fire spread too quickly. "Fuck! If it keeps burning there won't be a corpse to loot!"

I charged in, Chloe catching on quickly. We ducked in and around the flames, identifying any spot not on fire, and started stabbing and cutting. Its tentacles were gone so it didn't have any to defend itself with, and under the storm of our desperate blows, the Venus Lorana Queen finally died. As soon as her last HP was expended, the flames died away and her corpse turned opaque.

I sagged against my knees, breathing heavily. I considered my arms. The fire had not only singed my arm hair, but it had burned it clean off. I looked over at Chloe, who threw a hand on my shoulder and used me for support. We smiled together, still working to catch our breath.

There was nothing more exhilarating than putting your life on the line and coming out on top. Yes, it still felt like a dream, a wild fantasy, but I knew right then and there that I would get extremely comfortable in this lifestyle.

I put my hand out toward the queen and looted her.

ITEMS RECEIVED:
Venus Lorana Queen: 1
Vine Ring: 1
Thorn Ring: 1
Venus Lorana Queen Ink Pouch: 3
Core Crystal Rank 1: 22
Core Crystal Rank 2: 7

"We got two rings. I guess every bonus helps, right?"

"Oh? Two rings?" Chloe asked, a hint of surprise in her voice.

"Yeah, here. Look." I held the rings out for them to inspect.

NAME: Vine Ring
TYPE: Accessory, Ring
POWER LEVEL: 1, **SLOTS:** 1/4
DESCRIPTION: Ring made from Venus Lorana Queen's vines
STATS: Health + 40, Mana + 30, Defense + 10
NAME: Thorn Ring
TYPE: Accessory, Ring
POWER LEVEL: 1, **SLOTS:** 1/4
DESCRIPTION: Ring made from Venus Lorana Queen's thorns
STATS: Health + 40, Mana + 30, Attack + 10

"Well, won't you look at that," Chloe chuckled. "It's as if they prepared the rings for the two of us."

"Yeah, I'll take the one with the defense," Mabel said, boldly stepping forward and holding her hand out.

Good. I'd been waiting for our moon elf friend to start showing some confidence. And she was a major reason why we'd earned this loot. And what more, the stronger the girls were, the less I'd have to worry about them during battle. And... the easier things would be for me!

"I agree. Here," I said, handing Mabel the one with the defense stat, the Vine Ring, and then offered the Thorn Ring to Chloe. She grabbed it excitedly and slid it onto her finger.

"Hell yes!" Chloe cried out. "My first equipment! Bucket list item checked off!"

I smiled, watching as they held their hands out, showed off their rings to the other, and compared stats. It was like a nerdy Christmas morning, and I loved every moment of it. They were genuinely happy, and so was I. Then I turned my attention to the items I felt were geared more towards me—the ink pouches. I pulled one up and read the description.

NAME: Venus Lorana Queen Ink Pouch
TYPE: Upgrade Material
DESCRIPTION: Ink Pouch taken from a Venus Lorana Queen.
Used in upgrading certain weapons—Pen-Blade and the Quill-Blade.
STATS: +10 Attack from rank 1-5

This was quite a surprise. I had no idea that this was how upgrading the pen-blade worked, but—right, the twins. I would probably need to cash out 10,000 Fres for the skill. Still, at my current stage, 10,000 for + 30 attack was a small price to pay.

"So, what now?" Mabel asked when she saw I'd finished reading about the pouch. I grinned.

"I was just thinking about these boss rooms," I said, casually pulling up the mini map. "Is there any information about special boxes with rare or better loot being found after the bosses were killed? You know, just like in games?"

Chloe shrugged and Mabel just looked confused. I had to remind myself yet again that she didn't understand what games were. To us, it was something we played on a system or PC. To her, it was real life.

"You want to search this place? I mean it's a damned jungle," Chloe asked after she looked around. I shook my head and turned back toward the exit, but stopped, changing my mind.

"Let's make sure."

I made my way toward the entrance, then slowly started skirting the walls. Strangely, it wouldn't let us move into the brush. There was an invisible wall that wouldn't let me move past it. At least until I made it to a far corner, one where the wall bent inward and let me walk around a large tree. Behind it was a small wooden chest, one that blended in very inconspicuously with the foliage around it. I bent over and ran my hands over the surface. The wood was worn, pitted, and dry.

"JD: There's a chest here. Move over to the entrance so you can run if need be."

"Chloe: What kind? Is it gilded and glowing, filled with glittering, sparkling gems, and diamonds?"

"JD: I just eye-rolled, in case you were wondering. Be right there."

I pressed my hand against the chest and a prompt struck me.

ITEMS RECEIVED:
Core crystal Rank 1: 20
Core crystal Rank 1: 10
Fres: 15,000

I was left with mixed feelings. Treasure chests were things from legends. After discovering one, I was hoping for something along the lines of getting a dragon egg, or epic gear. No, I shouldn't look at it like that. I got crystals and a nice pile of Fres. Considering it was free, that was a hell-of-a-deal.

I walked back to the girls, unable to hide my stupid grin. Mabel loved the news, immediately jumping on the spot and clapping her hands. Chloe just watched the elf and smirked. She shared my sentiment. Still, I could see a glimmer in her eyes. She was totally a loot girl.

"What now?" I asked. "Do we go back?"

"I agree with what you said early, about not pushing our luck," Mabel replied. Oddly, they were on the same page.

"I agree. Let's go home. I'm hungry, dirty, and wouldn't mind a little downtime. We've got classes starting tomorrow as well."

I nodded and pulled both girls in for a hug. We stepped out of the small area and into the larger zone, just as a group of students walked past us. They were all armed, deep in conversation, and thankfully, hadn't spotted us.

"They're gonna get themselves killed," Mabel whispered. "Isn't the bigger boss room in that direction?"

I nodded.

"It is. Do we try to warn them?"

"I dislike needless death," she whispered and clutched her hands together against her chest. The solemn, worried look in her eyes was convincing enough.

"You're right," I said and ran after them. "Hey! Wait up!" I yelled as they made their way around a corner and out of sight. I kicked into a faster run and yelled again as they came back into view. They finally heard and stopped.

"What do you want?" one of them asked, a larger, broader beastkin. He had the body of a human but the head of a bull and arms to match it. It wasn't just him, actually. The entire group were beastkin.

"One of the bigger bosses is in the room ahead. I just thought I would warn you, so the boss doesn't catch you off guard."

"Hey, aren't you that JD dude? The one the headmistress called up onto the stage to help demonstrate that beginner skill?" one of the smaller in the group asked. She looked half-human, half-feline. I would guess a lynx. Her pointy ears ended in dark tufts, and I found that I very much wanted to pet them.

"Yeah, that's me. I'm here with my party. We just took care of a zone boss and were heading back outside when we spotted you."

"Oh? So... what's your play? Trying to hog all the glory?" the bull-man asked. "You warn us off of the danger only to slink in after we've gone and then make the kill?"

"Ugh, not exactly," I said, stifling the urge to sigh and turn around. "I don't want to see people die, that's all. As I said, my party and I just had a good battle of our own."

"Well, thanks for the warning, tough guy, but I think we'll try our luck," the bull-man sneered. "We all need this shit to work, so... yeah. You go do whatever it was you were doing."

The girls approached quietly behind me. I could hear them, just over the raging heart in my ears. It might have been the lingering effects of our fight, or the way the beastkin looked down at me, but my anger threatened to run away.

"Alright," I said, sucking in a calming breath. "Listen. We're just trying to be friendly and helpful. Would you like us to stay close by in case you get into trouble? We won't interfere with your kill. The only way I'll step in is if you really need us."

He narrowed his eyes and studied me, flexing his impressively muscled arms.

"You stay clear of our little battleground, and yeah, we're good. Hell, you all might even learn something."

He turned around and his group followed him forward. All except the one lynx female. She smiled, threw me a quick wave, and then hurried off after the others. I disliked doing it, but I let them go.

"Chloe: Leave them be. They're too proud to admit they need help. Probably too proud to give up, too. The best we can do is offer up a silent prayer."

"Mabel: I agree, don't push them. We might have to end up fighting."

I growled and silently cursed their stupidity. I watched the last of their group disappear behind a copse of trees. I had to realize that they were just as desperate to gain strength as we were. That they didn't have families with money or a strong backer.

"JD: I feel sorry for them, but let's not ask for trouble. If they want to have a go at it, then let them. We've got more important things to worry about."

"Oh? What's that?" Chloe asked as we turned toward the exit.

"Like weapon upgrades. I found some ingredients I could use to add +30 attack to my weapon."

"What? That's so not fair! You always get the good stuff!" she protested, but then stopped and frowned. "I've kind of been a bitch today, haven't I?"

"Just a little bit," I admitted.

344

"Not at all. You have been an excessively big bitch today! Like the biggest I have ever seen." The moon elf clapped her hands and beamed, and then I knew she had no idea what she'd just said.

LET'S SHAKE ON IT

IT TOOK US ABOUT AN HOUR to get back safely. We were in no hurry at that point and had plenty to talk about. Sure, mini-bosses were still alive, prowling the dungeon, but we would have to fall face-first into one of their mouths, with our hands tied behind our backs, and let it eat us... and I didn't foresee that happening. Besides, we ran across several other groups of students, all out searching for their first taste at glory. Truth be told, it felt a bit crowded, and that tarnished the excitement for me.

"There isn't quite the same sense of danger with all these other students roaming around," I said as we stepped in front of the portal. "We'll need to focus on getting to the second floor next. This place is going to get busy once a thousand students start popping in here regularly."

"That will never happen," Mabel said. "See, even the floors are rifts... pocket dimensions. The bosses and mini bosses won't spawn in each instance and are instead shared, so if it's killed in one, it's dead in the others. But the ordinary beasts and monsters spawn so everyone has something to kill. Oh, and it is possible that we would never spawn in the same version of the same dungeon floor more than once."

"Okay, now that's interesting," I whispered. "Then that means we don't have to worry about people stealing our loot."

"Exactly," Chloe added, inserting herself into our conversation. "You know where else they won't bother us? Our room. I want to go home."

"Home?" I asked. "Oh, yeah. Right. I think it is all so new, that I am still trying to wrap my head around the fact that this place is our home."

"It does take a little while, I know. I'm just starting to get there myself," she chuckled and hooked her arm around mine and pulled me along. "Let's go."

With Mabel in tow, we exited the portal and entered the tavern, making our way to the counter where we waited for our turn to speak with the twins.

"You're back," Selma said.

"Hopefully with our money... in ingredients," Belma finished, her eyes narrowing on me.

"Do you want it all at once?"

"Of course, we do! What do you think this is, a bank?"

I snorted, more entertained by their attitudes than irritated by it.

"Okay, but you asked for it." I started pulling the corpses out one by one. Chloe and Mabel helped me stack them up, those strange, little square-shaped crystals quickly building before us and the sisters. I counted as we went.

Belma appeared to the left of our growing stack, and Selma on the right. Their eyes grew wide as they hissed back and forth to one another. I couldn't hear what they were saying, but I was fairly sure it had something to do with steak. Whether it was for them or to sell, I didn't know.

"So, we have a total of 71 venus loranas, 24 vipers, 11 hulkers, 23 swapper flies, and a single venus lorana queen. But not a mini boss, no, we got a zone boss this time!"

"Well? What do my favorite wheeling and dealing ladies think?"

"Oh? We are your favorites now?" Selma chuckled. "Care to stick around until our shift ends to show us why?"

Chloe went rigid next to me. "Sorry, girls, but we've got plans," she said, then added, "He's spoken for."

"Truly a..." Selma started.

"Shame. You should learn to share," Belma finished.

"Well, I already share my room and my bathroom with an elf. So, let's not go crazy!"

Selma started to laugh, her shoulders bobbing animatedly, while Belma just watched me, quietly.

"... and moving on," I said, "Can we get this transaction done?"

"Fine, fine. You are no fun, JD," Selma mumbled as Belma started inventorying the corpses and their condition. Seemingly annoyed by the simple act of counting, the elf pulled out a scroll and activated it. Most of the crystals turned from light green to yellow. A few glowed orange and others red, while only a select few appeared dark green. The queen, oddly enough, was light green.

"Is that their quality?" I asked curiously.

"It is," Belma replied. "I don't usually stoop to divination magic, as it costs me 1,000 Fres per use, but you apparently felt the need to put every beast from the dungeon onto our counter at once. This is quite the haul."

"We were motivated today."

"I'd say." The parchment abruptly changed, glowed brightly, and she scooped it out of the air. "We are prepared to offer you **6,400** for the loranas, **2,900** for the vipers, **1,300** for the hulkers, and **1,800** for the swappers. But this beauty here, oh my goodness. The usual price for a zone boss in this state is about **20,000** Fres, but I'll bump that up to **22,000** considering its size. Plus, the meat is mostly intact, which is a rare treat for this one."

"How much for all the steaks."

Now it was her turn to purse her lips and frown. "I'll give you another **15,000** if you leave the meat."

"I'll leave the meat in exchange for the forgiveness of my **2,000** Fres debt. Deal?"

"Agreed. Coin or on your card?" Belma said.

I nodded, happy that we were haggling pleasantly now. I had bigger goals in mind. Specifically, the **500,000** Fres for the next level of service and goods. If my mental calculations were correct, which I was pretty sure they were, they would be depositing **59,400** onto my card.

"Card, please. I already have enough coin from the monster drops."

Her mouth pulled up into the first smile I'd seen on her for a while.

"Very well."

I handed her my now empty card, and as soon as she swept it across a stone tablet, I could feel it gain weight and substance.

"Is there anything else you would like to barter for today?" Belma asked. "Since you're already here and all."

"I want one of the weapon upgrades...skill? Perk? Whatever it is. Before I buy it, tell me how it works. For my pen-blade in particular."

I'd talked myself out of buying the weapon upgrade before we went into the dungeon, but I wanted to see how it worked, and more importantly if it was worth the investment. If it paid off, we could purchase more before our next dive.

"Quite simple," she replied casually. "You need to gather the necessary ingredients, activate the Forge Skill, and simply follow the instructions. It is relatively foolproof."

"Alright. I'll take one. And also, a round of drinks, please."

"Hah! Libations!" Selma laughed. "Let's see if you can hold your booze. First drinks are on us."

I looked around the room and found an empty table near a pillar and thankfully, by itself. We walked over and sat down, and I immediately dug in and activated the Forge Skill. A new window popped up, showing a single box on the left side, and several stacked together on the right. Weapon appeared above the single box on the left, with Materials showing to the right.

I pulled my pen-blade out and pushed it into the left slot. It disappeared, a glowing, pen-blade-shaped icon appearing in the left-hand box. On the right, an image of an ink pouch appeared with a 0/1 just below the image. I pulled a pouch out next and placed it there.

DO YOU WISH TO UPGRADE "PEN-BLADE (R1)" TO "PEN-BLADE (R2)"?
[YES / NO?]

I pushed [Yes] and was immediately overcome by a strong and borderline uncomfortable sensation. It immediately felt like pain but shifted into something almost orgasmic. Pressure grew in my chest until the pen-blade icon popped in a shower of bright, glowing particles. The pressure promptly dissipated, and the screen updated. My weapon no longer showed as R1, no, now it was R2.

NAME: Pen-Blade (R2)
POWER LEVEL: 11, RANGE: 5
ATTACK: 10

I hurried up and did it two more times, upgrading the pen-blade to rank 4. I checked it again and was surprised when I saw that range had increased a little as well. A barely noticeable white glow covered the pen-blade. One that extended several inches past the tip of the blade.

NAME: Pen-Blade (R4)
POWER LEVEL: 42, RANGE: 6
ATTACK: 30

"Wow, baby," I whispered, watching the stats increase.

"Why is it glowing?" Chloe whispered. "That looks so cool!"

"It really does," Mabel added, practically shouting excitedly. "Can I touch it... hold it?"

Chloe snorted. "Really? You want to touch it?"

"What?" Mabel asked innocently.

Selma arrived then, carrying a tray of drinks. She set down the first glass, leaned in, and noticed the glow as well.

"Oh, that looks mighty fine!" she said and stared at the pen-blade. "Ingredients like that are quite rare. A lucky find, truly."

I nodded and put the blade away after several more people glanced our way. I know it wasn't a good idea to flaunt sparkling, valuable things in my old life, and it probably rang just as true here.

I picked up one of the three glasses and took a healthy drink. It was sweet but strong. In a way, it almost tasted like Jägermeister. I swallowed, felt, and tasted the burn in my throat, and blinked.

"Not so fast, you!" Selma scowled as she pushed the glass away from my mouth. "You're supposed to savor it. Not gulp it down like some drunken tavern whelp."

"Sorry, I've been on a dry spell," I said, swallowing again. I'd drank my fair share of bourbon and whiskey before, so the gut-burn wasn't unexpected. But this was next level as if the drink was glowing and pulsing inside me. I turned to Chloe. "Do you feel that, too? Are my insides on fire?"

"On fire? No," Chloe said, braving another tiny sip. "I also didn't chug mine. But yeah, my insides are really nice and warm right now."

"It is a sipping liquor," Selma explained, her hands dropping to her hips. "Perhaps you three should take your glasses with you. Put them in your rifts and drink when you get back to your room. The last thing we need is for you to stagger through the wrong portal and fall off a mountain, or down a dark shaft. Scarlet does get grumpy when students die."

"Off a mountain?" Chloe asked, quietly setting her glass down. Selma smiled, crookedly.

351

"Yeah. I like that idea. In the safety of our room," I agreed and promptly stowed my glass on a shelf in my rift. "Come on, girls."

Chloe snuck another couple of sips, spilled some down her chin, and then giggled as she opened her rift. She noticed a nearby table of students watching her, leaning into one another, and whispering. Ironically, most at the table were blood elves.

"Is there a problem?" she asked, her voice rising.

The other group just started whispering louder, one even lifting an arm to point at Mabel. Chloe turned as Mabel finished a sip, and I noticed it, too. The moon elf's ears were red. Hell, they practically glowed. Chloe spun back on the group.

"Ugh. Let the girl drink in peace and mind your own fucking business!" she snapped.

"Let it go, Chloe. Let's just get the hell out of here."

I took her hand and pulled her up to stand. She didn't protest, but she didn't look away from the other table of students, either. I guided Chloe and Mabel out before me, then intentionally walked by the table of rude elves.

"Red ears on elves are highly distasteful," a blood elf said.

"Gross," another added.

"Almost as bad as a mixed company. Like sitting with humans," added a third.

Chloe bristled and tried to stop, but I pushed her towards the portal chamber.

I stopped and leaned in between two of the blood elves, resting a palm on the table and intentionally letting my fingers touch the food on their plate. I looked around at the group, sizing them up, then pointed at the young male elf directly across from me-the one that had called us "mixed company."

"Dude, you've got an enormous booger hanging out of your nose. Honestly, it is huge. That is totally gross." Then I wiped the sauce from my fingers on the closest elf's shoulder, smiled, and walked away.

I heard the commotion at the table, the one elf practically falling over in his effort to cover his face. The other was trying to wipe the food off his robe. They'd probably curse or hex me. Something like that. But it was totally worth it.

I walked out and into the main corridor and in a stroke of incredibly bad luck, walked right into another group of damned blood elves. I sighed and tried to move around, only to have them step sideways to block our path.

"Really?" I asked. "Do you think we can skip the games today? I'm not really in the mood."

"What games?" the one with the most hair asked. I recognized him immediately. He was the prick that made it known that Mabel's family belonged to his. Interesting.

"I don't remember your name. Blondie? Captain Big Hair? No, I remember, Grumpy McSnottypants, right?" I said and nodded towards his hair. I wasn't sure if he knew what blonde meant, but if bullies were the same here as back home, I knew he'd take his name-sake trait very seriously.

His eyes narrowed and slid toward Chloe, then finally landed on Mabel's.

"I'm here to take you home, Mabel," he said, not falling into my trap. "It's bad enough that you haven't realized your place by now, but to slum around with these mundanes. Really? For one born into the gutter, I didn't think you could stoop any lower."

"Mundanes?" Chloe growled, visibly bristling.

"Haven't you figured it out yet?" the blood elf asked, turning on her.

"What's that?" she asked, snarling.

"Your kind don't belong here. Your kind isn't worthy of this place or the power it wastes on you. You are fleas, biting and sucking the lifeblood of greater people."

"Oh, shit!" I laughed, unable to hold it in any longer. "I mean, I gathered that you red-haired, nut jobs were some arrogant, stuffy bastards, but holy crap did I underestimate. You've got your size-5 My Little Pony undies pulled so far up between your cheeks, you're practically tasting cotton. We might not have magic oozing out of every pore where Chloe and I come from, but we've figured out by now that it isn't okay to own other people. We've also... generally, figured out how to not be pretentious douche bags. So why don't you do yourself a favor, and step-the-fuck back? Mabel isn't going anywhere with you."

The blood elf's eyebrows rose, practically disappearing into his hairline. Two of his brutes stepped in and around him, one even going as far as to put his hand on my shoulder. I slapped it away and pushed him back. He stumbled and tripped over his friend's foot, drawing several chuckles from a quickly gathering crowd.

"Do you honestly think you can deny us, here? You... and her? I was giving you more credit than you deserved when I called you fleas. You are flea's excrement," he said, then moved right up to me, and leaned in between Chloe and me. "Have you ever stopped to ask yourself why there are only two of your whole pathetic race here? Hmm?"

"Ascal, don't," Mabel said, her voice strong as she pushed up between Chloe and me. I beamed inside, proud that she'd finally found the strength to stand up for herself.

"No, it is okay, Mabel. Look at him, he's practically dying to tell us something important. Besides, you are a legal member of our party now. Which means you don't go anywhere until our training is complete. You were saying, Bernard?"

His lip twitched as I intentionally screwed up his name. It appeared I was finally getting under his skin.

"It is no secret, really," Ascal said, brushing off his sleeves as if shaking off my insult. "The Great races take pride in these academies and the defense against the beasts. That pride means we will do whatever it takes to protect the world from beasts and mundane threats. One way or another, threats are dealt with. Cleansed. But you don't have to worry about me. I'd be the laughingstock of my family if I attacked lowly creatures like you. I don't want to tarnish my reputation, my 9th rank."

354

"That is quite the accomplishment," I said and clapped mockingly. "It must have taken you a lot of time and resources, right?"

"It did," he said, airily. "So how about this? You duel against one of us. If you win, I'll leave you be for a whole year. I trust that will be enough time for you to learn elves and…humans don't match well. And that some, like Mabel, are better owned than befriended."

"Enough of this," Chloe growled at my side. "As long as he's the same rank as JD, he'll take him on!"

That hadn't exactly been my plan A, but Chloe's temper had a way of changing things. You know what, good. I liked plan B better anyway. Beat a blood elf's ass, keep from dying, and hopefully get those pricks off Mabel's back. I would show them that our party wasn't to be fucked with.

"I'm ready to go, Bernard. You choose any rank 5 carrot-top and I'll take him on." I moved to pull my pen-blade free, thinking we would fight right there.

Ascal grinned and tapped the guy next to him, the one I threw on his ass.

"I think you two will prove to be an equal match. Now, how about one of the guardians comes and takes us down to the first floor? We have a duel to fight."

A tall beastkin warrior appeared in a flash of light and mana, then nodded first toward Ascal and finally at me.

"You are the two parties involved in this dispute?" he asked, his voice resonant and deep. To say he was all-business was a gross mischaracterization. And when a trickle of his aura filled the air around us, it became immediately clear that we were far outclassed. Ascal didn't appear as fazed as I was, however.

"We are, Guardian. We've agreed to a duel. One in the arena."

"And what is the bet?" the guardian asked. "State it clearly."

"If I win, Ascal and his friends will not harass or attack us for a year."

"I see. Your words have been recorded. And you? Please speak clearly."

"Yes," Ascal drawled, dragging out the word unnecessarily. "Seeing we haven't been teleported down yet, why don't we make a little extra wager? Just to spice things up?"

The glint in his eye set me back.

"Like what?" I asked. He watched me, his tongue stuck between his top lip and gums as if caught in deep thought.

"A card with **50,000** Fres and... how many equipables do you have?"

"Two," I said, only counting the rings. Even if I lost them, they appeared to be something we could easily replace."

"Type?" he asked curiously as his eyes roamed lazily over me. "Rings."

"And are you interested in wagering them?"

"I am if you match."

"Good! Delightful!" Ascal laughed. "I will wager two of my items which will be randomly pulled off my body, in the unlikely case that you win."

I stuck my hand out and he jumped back as if I was about to attack him.

"Humans seal a deal with a handshake. Give me your hand. Squeeze and shake mine, or there is no wager."

"You what? Disgusting. Brutish! Why would I want to soil myself by touching you?"

"Shake on it or no deal." I stared him down. His hand slowly moved in, and I grabbed it, then squeezed just hard enough.

"An agreement has been made! Let the death duel begin!"

"Umm, what? Death... duel?" I asked. "What's that with a death duel part?"

"The blood elf Ascal invited you to a death duel. You agreed," the guardian said, his voice now tinged with a hint of anger. "Do not waste my time, human!"

Ascal clapped his hands excitedly and he leaned forward, his mouth pulling up into an exaggerated smile. I groaned and turned toward the girls.

"Give me your rings. I need every health point and stat boost I can get my hands on."

Mabel slid her ring off and handed it to me, then Chloe, who looked at me with a mixture of fear and anger.

"I didn't…or I wouldn't…I'm so sorry," she whispered, tears forming in the corners of her eyes. They rolled down her cheeks and carried a trace of black eyeliner with them, staining her cheeks and chin. But before I could say anything, or even reach up to wipe them away the guardian put his hand on my shoulder and the world upended. The next thing I knew, I was standing on a bright ring, hovering perilously over what looked like a bottomless pit. Ascal's buddy stood directly across from me. Well, shit. That wasn't what I expected at all.

"I'll give you the first hit," the elf snorted. "Come on, hit me!"

I watched him for a moment and tried to bring up his stats, but most of it was blocked. All I could see was his power level: **638**. Damn. That was a difference of almost a hundred points between us. Not good. Not good, at all.

I quickly equipped both rings and pulled out my pen-blade. Without waiting for him to go back on his word, I activated a skill I had been practicing since our introduction seminar. Mana Charge. The elf stood still, watching me, but I didn't delude myself. He wasn't just waiting. Somehow, he was already casting or preparing some attack or defense. Because no one was that stupid.

I leaped at him once I'd counted out the four seconds I needed and feigned an attack. He jumped toward me, then changed direction and slid left. Since we were equally fast, I tracked him with my left hand.

SKILL USED: Mana Discharge

357

MANA USED: 25
DAMAGE DEALT: 213

The attack fired off and connected, striking his side, and sending him skidding back on the arena floor. I didn't wait for him to get up and sent two, quick air slashes his way. The attacks were fast but didn't hit with any real power. Maybe he had an elemental defense? I cut in again, forcing him to spin, jump, and dive aside. At least I could keep him on the defensive.

The blood elf landed, fell to a knee, but kicked back up with surprising speed and violence. A shockwave erupted from him, and I barely jumped back and out of the way. He flew at me then, his fist glowing with a pulsing blue aura. I ducked the first blow and slashed in a counter, connecting with the back of his left knee almost entirely by luck.

DAMAGE DEALT: 92.
CRITICAL HIT!

The good old weakness game. Except fighting an elf wasn't the same as fighting a beast. This opponent was constantly moving, watching me, and calculating, working to identify my weakness and strike that killer blow. I couldn't afford to give him an opening.

The elf came in, kicked, and punched, which I ungracefully dodged, but it had all been a feint. I spun back around just in time to see him discharge his attack at where I was, not where I had been. The surge of mana hit me right in the chest and exploded outward as my shield barely held.

MANA SHIELD SUSTAINED: 317 DAMAGE

Shit. Compared to mine, his mana discharge was beastly, and I realized Ascal had duped me. There was no way this kid was my level. I couldn't afford to take another discharge like that, or I would be done for. I rubbed my side, where a cramp was forming. The elf didn't lunge or attack, giving me a moment's reprieve, but I had no idea how to approach this fight. I was lacking skills, but more so, I was lacking experience fighting an opponent that knew how to fight back. What in the hell had I been thinking?

"Are you already giving up? Will it be this easy?" the elf snickered and pulled his robe aside to reveal his right shoulder. Four ritual scars ran down toward his bicep. "Do you see these?" he asked. "One for every person I've killed in here already. You'll make a nice addition."

"The hell I will," I cursed. "Fuck you..." My mind went blank, and for the first time in my memory, I was left without a witty comeback or insult. "Come and give me your best shot!" I'd do down in a blaze of my own glory if need be.

I formulated my plan quickly and immediately put it into action. I readied a fireball. It formed in my hand quickly. Just before I released, my pen-blade scratched out a familiar glyph... the mana pooling, forming, and instantly taking shape inside me. The elf set his feet, charging his mana, just as I let the fireball fly.

The gust of wind ripped forward next, hitting my fireball, and exploding to life, entombing the elf and most of our glowing platform in a fiery inferno. I charged in, moving as close to the raging flames as I could, slashing frantically at his open back. It was instinct. Cut. Stab. Survive.

"You cursed—you wretched little—human!" the elf roared and surged forward, his foot streaking out of the fire and catching me in the side. I stumbled back and rolled, the blow knocking the wind from my lungs. I skidded to a halt only two steps from the edge and pushed to my feet, still struggling without success to draw breath. I wordlessly slashed and sidestepped, catching his incoming leg. It struck his boot and sent him on his ass, flames still raging, burning his robes, hair, and skin. I launched another fireball and hit his leg, scribbling out a gust of wind that spurred on the flames.

He chuckled. The bastard really chuckled as if nothing was going on. He was burning, the air tainted by the smell of burning hair and skin, and he was laughing.

"We're going to make Mabel watch as we clean your bones for trophies," the blood elf snarled. My hesitation melted away and I plunged my blade into his guts, finally breaking his shield and drawing more of his health. He finally seemed to notice. Using what little mana I had left, I created another fireball and shoved it right into his face.

SKILL USED: Fireball
MANA USED: 20
DAMAGE DEALT: 197

The fire blasted away most of the skin on his face and scorched his eyes, the impact knocking him to the ground. He rolled over, limbs limp and body still smoldering. I froze. Then tucked my foot under his side and nudged him. He didn't move. Shit. Did I just kill him?

The realization crashed over me like a cold, smothering wave. Goosebumps popped up on my arms, cold sweat immediately coating my neck and face. I watched the blood elf, expecting, no, hoping he would breathe or shift. Do anything. But he couldn't move. I killed him.

"What...did I—do?" I mumbled, turning on the spot. "No. They tricked me! They made me do this, knowing someone would die! But it was supposed to be me. They were planning on it being me. What now? What happens to me now?" I spoke out loud, trying to calm my raging thoughts and make sense of what just happened.

The guardian appeared in a brilliant flash of mana.

"Loot him, just like you would a monster in the dungeon. Whatever he had in his rift and on his body now belongs to you. Once you are done, this duel will be complete."

My hand moved on its own, hovering over his body, trembling in time with my raging heart.

ITEMS RECEIVED:
Mana Fist Skill Scroll: 1
Mana Surge Ring: 1
Core crystal Rank 1: 109
Core crystal Rank 2: 37
Core crystal rank 3: 2
Fres: 23,928

The arena floor disappeared from beneath me and I found myself standing next to Mabel and Chloe, the noise and commotion of the passage not there one moment and surrounding him in the next.

Chloe spoke, grabbing my arms but I couldn't make sense of her words. I looked to Mabel, but she just shook her head. Strong hands clamped onto my head and turned my neck. Chloe was there, in my face, her gaze pulling on mine. I looked to her lips, and a word finally made sense.

"Okay?" she asked. Then I strung it together.

"I'm... yes. I am okay. I just wasn't ready... for that." She came forward and hugged me, Mabel joining at my side.

I turned to find Meran standing just a few feet away, his face a mask constructed of the purest hatred. A white light struck him three times and he gasped.

"As per the duel's agreement, you have received a 50,000 Fres card and two random items Meran wore at the time you... shook hands.

"No, wait!" Meran hissed. "I took them off before the duel even began! You can't take things from my rift! My family will hear of this! Give it back! Give me back my birthright!" the blood elf lunged for me, but the guardian slammed his fist into the elf's guts and knocked him low with a single blow.

"You may go, human. No one will dare touch a victor of the arena in my presence."

I nodded, grabbed the girl's hands, and quickly pulled them past the crowd. It wasn't just dozens of students anymore, but two, three times that. They filled the passage, pushing each other out of the way and shouting at us. Word had spread fast.

More than a few had red hair, so I figured it wasn't wise to linger.

DEALING WITH ISSUES

I DIDN'T STOP OR SPEAK until we were back safely in our room, with the door closed and sealed behind us. My heart was still racing, and an uncomfortable lump was perched in my throat and my hands were shaking. I paced in the bedroom, then I moved to the kitchen, rifled through our food, couldn't focus long enough to decide on something to eat, then paced back and forth into the bathroom.

I don't know if it all became real, but something had changed. Perhaps it was the stakes, or maybe it was the way my fire and pen-blade burned and split his skin—a real, flesh and blood person. An elf, sure, but still, he wasn't some beast manifested into a dungeon. I hadn't just hurt him. I killed him. That thought burned inside me like a simmering, toxic lump.

Mabel and Chloe watched me, hovering just beyond the kitchen as I made my way back in and dropped on one of the sofas. I pulled my leftover drink from my rift, pressed it against my lips, and took a sip. I didn't want to think about the fight anymore— the sound of his voice as he died, the smell of my fire burning his hair. Hell, the surprise and horror in his eyes.

The girls sat down on either side of me but didn't speak. After a minute or so, the silence had become deafening, and I couldn't take it anymore.

"Did you... could you... see us fight?" I asked.

"Yeah, we saw everything. I think everyone saw it. It was projected in the center of the floor," Chloe whispered. "I'm sorry," she added quickly. "I'm really sorry, JD. We had no way of knowing they would make it a life and death match!"

I lifted my arm and she immediately scooted over, snuggling in. The warmth of her body, the closeness, it helped. Mabel snuggled in from the other side.

We sat there in renewed silence for a while. I picked up my glass and sipped, working through my chaotic thoughts.

"I thought I was going to die... after he hit me. There was no way he was my rank, not the way he moved and struck. I panicked a little, kept thinking about you two, everything I'd seen, and all the stuff ahead of me I would never get to experience. It was death. I knew I was going to die and felt powerless to change it."

"We... they... should never have put you in that position," Mabel whispered.

I stroked her hair and hated the fact that she felt guilty, that she would feel like she put me in that position. It wasn't fair. Not even close.

"It wasn't you, Mabel," I said, quietly. "I meant every word I said. It isn't right—how they treat your kind, how they treat you. Hell, I hate the way they talk to you. Then, it was also what he said about Chloe and me. We're from a mundane world and that makes us no better than shit on their boots. They just came right out and said it, that they kill whomever they don't feel are worthy of a place in this world."

"It is what Scarlet was trying to tell me," Chloe said.

I nodded. But hearing something wasn't always enough to make it real. Sometimes you had to have your face rubbed in it. Or in my case, have someone try to jam their fist through my chest. Now I had to come to terms with an even more terrifying

364

fact. We were living in a world inhabited by people that seemed to want us dead.

"How many of the races agree with Ascal? How many of them actually want us dead?"

Mabel shrugged. "It is hard to tell. Maybe all of them... maybe none. The blood elves are especially hateful and have many allegiances. But most of those relationships are based on fear. I imagine some would respond very differently to you if they were not under the blood elves' influence."

Our dorm room fell silent again for a long while. I tried to wrap my head around the day's events and what it meant for our lives moving forward, and judging from their body language, Chloe and Mabel were doing the same thing. I had played video games since I was a kid, and judging from our conversations, so had Chloe. They were usually all violent. I drew comic books, which normally centered around heroes in a variety of genres. But one theme resonated throughout—one hero or a group of them, fighting diametrically opposed villains. The overall theme throughout—violence.

Those were tropes, and the stories usually skewed perspective against the antagonists and towards the hero. But things in the real world were much grayer. Motivations weren't always so cut and dry, and I knew next to nothing about the blood elves or the other races. Perhaps I needed to do some research before we had any more deadly run-ins. Perhaps I could find a way to parlay and avoid more duels.

"I thought you were done for when he hit you with that skill," Chloe whispered. "What was that?"

"It was a special kind of mana discharge. One called mana fist," Mabel responded. "It has a comparatively long charge time but is devastatingly effective."

"And thanks to my duel with Ascal's friend, we have it now," I said and pulled out the skill parchment he'd had in his rift. "I'm going to learn it so I can protect myself if someone else comes too close or blindsides me again."

"It's a hard skill to learn," Mabel whispered, "but I can help you."

"Good," I nodded, still struggling with that hollow, sour feeling in my gut. I wanted someone to pop into existence before us and say "surprise. The whole thing was a big joke. Congratulations, you passed the test". But I knew better. Somewhere, a blood elf mother was learning that she would never see her son again. Sure, he'd killed people, and they seemed like rather disagreeable people, but who was I to play executioner? And who was I to judge an entire race based on the actions of a few? I had to consider that I was dealing with a sect or fanatical group of zealots. There could be perfectly reasonable blood elves out there, somewhere.

But *he* was dead. My thoughts came full circle. Shit, I'd never even been around a dying person before. Save for my grandma, and she passed before I could even get to the hospital.

"Say, what was Ascal screaming about some heritage?" Chloe asked. "I don't want to sound insensitive, but Ascal kept screaming about it."

"I don't know," I said and immediately opened my rift. One item, in particular, stood out—a shiny bracelet, made from light, silver metal. It was studded with small, red gems, set flush with the surface. I picked it up and held it before us.

NAME: Heritage Bracelet (R5)
TYPE: Accessory, Bracelet, Scaling
POWER LEVEL: 155, SLOTS: 1/2
DESCRIPTION: Bracelet that feeds on the owner's health during battle. When active, it improves the attack power of mana-based attacks by 3% for every rank.
CURRENT BONUS: 15%
HEALTH: 100, MANA: 200
ATTACK: 50, DEFENSE: 25
MANA SHIELD: 300

"This is…quite the treasure," I whispered, unable to take my eyes off the stats. Sure, they were lower than my robe, but this was just a bracelet.

"No shit," Chloe muttered. "You are on a lucky streak getting the good stuff. Although let's hope you don't always have to duel people to get it."

"Hold on. There are two more things. Another ring and…oh, look at that," I said as I pulled out a pair of boots.

NAME: Elven Aspire Boots (R1)
TYPE: Armor, Upgradeable
POWER LEVEL: 115
DESCRIPTION: Elven Aspire Boots made with protection and amplification in mind. The boots amplify self-buffs by 20%.
HEALTH: 100, MANA: 50
ATTACK: 30, DEFENSE: 50
MANA SHIELD: 150

"These are for you, Mabel. The special stats look like they were made for you."

"Oh, oh, oh! Thanks!" She launched herself across the sofa and landed on top of me, excitedly plucking the boots from my hands. She rolled back over into her spot, ripped her shoes free, and pulled the new boots on right away. I immediately felt a rise in her power level, an almost static-like tingle from her that made the hair on my arm closest to her stand on end.

If I'd worn them, they probably would have provided me a stronger individual bonus, but I couldn't exactly buff others. If the overall strength of our party was important, then they had far more use on Mabel's feet, especially with all the new buffs we'd just purchased. And thanks to my recent duel, we now had a large target painted on our backs.

"And let's see the last item."

NAME: Mana Surge Ring
TYPE: Accessory, Ring
POWER LEVEL: 115, SLOTS: 1/4
DESCRIPTION: A ring made by elven smiths. It uses 10% more mana when casting spells but amplifies the spell's effectiveness by 20%. The amplification works with: Healing, Buff, Debuff, and attack spells cast by the user.
HEALTH: 50, MANA: 100
ATTACK: 20, DEFENSE: 40
MANA SHIELD: 200

"That's quite the treasure, too," Mabel whispered. "These boots have made a world of difference. Both the duration and effectiveness of my debuffs rose! As well as my healing ability!"

"At least one good thing came from this fight," I mumbled. "Not that I'd want to do it again. I made it out based almost entirely on luck and dirty fighting. I can't expect to be able to replicate that every time."

"Never say never," Chloe said and leaned in to kiss my cheek. "You won a duel. Yes, you had to kill someone, but it isn't that different from historical duels on earth. He'd killed before, he was trying to kill you, and you effectively defended yourself. They took the element of choice out of the equation for you. Don't beat yourself up about it. All you can do is learn from it and try to navigate yourself onto a different path next time."

"You're right," I mumbled. "It is hard to shake the idea that I didn't just beat him, but he is dead because of me. It feels so utterly... final."

"I don't think it gets any more final than that," Chloe whispered and snuggled in close. "And I know it's a bit selfish to say, but I'm really glad that you're the one that is still here." I nodded but didn't respond.

"Okay. Here is what we're going to do. Let's get your mind onto other things. First? How about something to eat? Then we can get cleaned up, rest, and recover. We've got a big day ahead of us tomorrow with first classes."

Just the mention of food affected me. My stomach rumbled and Chloe pulled away.

"Well, okay. Evidently part of you agrees with me. That is a start!"

"In that case, I'll take two hamburgers," I said, sitting up.

"And he's back, folks," Chloe said, jumping up and then helping me off the sofa. We made our way to the kitchen and settled around the small table. I opened my rift and pulled forth two small packages. I opened the first, a palm-sized hamburger sitting inside, steaming as if it had just come off the griddle. Okay, magical duels, not so much fun. But the food? Loved it.

We finished eating without much chatter and then bathed. The mood was still somber, no doubt negatively impacted by my sulking. I scrubbed myself clean, spending several moments removing a large patch of dirt before I realized it was a bruise. I watched Chloe and Mabel talk quietly as they got clean, both respecting my need for space and time. It endeared me to them even more, their ability to sense my struggles and the insight to let me work through them on my own. It worked.

I replayed the duel in my mind over and over, but also the conversation with Ascal before it. His words, his hateful glances, all changed the duel's result in my mind. He'd set out to kill me long before that run-in in the hall. For whatever set of circumstances, they wanted me dead. In hindsight, I had only ever had two choices—die or fight.

I made a decision then, and it proved to be one of the best I'd ever settled on. Ascal's friend sealed his own fate, not me. He'd known the consequences of accepting a duel and knew only one of us could walk away. That was on him and his friends, not me. I could only control what came next, those things I could make informed decisions about. And the ramifications would be severe. We were talking about the death of an important elf.

369

Chloe and Mabel finished their quiet conversation on the other side of the tub and Chloe got out, pulling a towel around her body and leaving.

"It's pretty late," Mabel said and left as well.

I rinsed, pulled myself out of the bath, and dried off. Then after brushing my teeth, I pulled on some clean shorts and a t-shirt and dropped into bed. Chloe wasn't there and a moment later, the lights in the bedroom went out. Then the kitchen, until the only illumination came from the bath, a distant and diffused glow. I closed my eyes and willed my troubling thoughts away, hoping I could manage a dreamless night.

Someone padded into the room a few moments later and I heard something scrape angrily against the ground. She grunted and it scraped again, my bed jolting as something collided with it.

"What are you doing?" I whispered and rolled over, half-sitting up to see what was going on. I felt someone's weight settle onto the bed and reached out, only to discover Mabel's bed had been butted up against ours.

"Shh," she whispered and tentatively laid down right next to me. I knew it wasn't Chloe right away. Mabel just smelled different, and beyond that, she felt different, too. It must have been the engrained magic, the subtle tingle of her slightly different energy as it reverberated off her body.

Mabel lifted the blankets and slid under, her body pressing up against me. Her head came to rest on my shoulder, her right hand on my chest, and her leg draping over mine.

"Where's Chloe?" I asked, keenly aware of her breasts pressing against me, but more, the warmth between her legs bleeding through my thin shorts.

"We talked," Mabel whispered, "This was her idea. Please don't push me away. I want to thank you, in my way. You're the first person who has ever defended me, sacrificed anything for me. Words can't express my gratitude. I need to show you." Her breath was hot, tingling my ear as she hovered so tantalizingly close. But it was more than the academy's special soap. Mabel's

370

smell, her warm breath, mixed with that subtle energy to form an almost intoxicating aura.

I turned into her, meeting her lips as she leaned in. A spark blossomed as our lips met, the electric tingle shooting down and into my arms and legs. Her kisses were hesitant at first, light and gentle, but I returned them with equal pressure. I brushed her curtain of wet hair back and hooked it behind a pointy ear, then kissed her a little harder. She tasted sweet, like ripe apricots, or peaches. No, it was strawberries.

There was something about her smell and taste. It cycled and changed, moving through all the sweet things I'd loved. It jogged memories loose in my mind, stimulating not only lust by nostalgia, as well.

I tasted her lips, savoring her almost candy-like sweetness. She leaned in a little further, gaining confidence and brushing her tongue against mine. I rolled fully into her, working my left hand over her firm breasts and down her side. She squirmed and giggled as my hand slid over her ribs and around to her back. Her skin was the softest thing I had ever felt before, supple, warm, and in the darkness beneath my blanket, glowing with the faintest, blue light.

Mabel kissed me harder then, any hesitancy bleeding away, a lustful, hungry moan growing in her throat. I felt her hand work its way down my shirt, inside my shorts, and over my swollen erection. The tingle I felt before was nothing compared to what happened below my waist. Just a brush of Mabel's soft palm against my member made it jump and ache, the light shorts suddenly struggling to contain me.

"As slaves, we were not allowed to choose partners. When we came of age it was forced upon us," Mabel whispered, her mouth pressing right up against my ear. I felt her tongue brush against my skin, hot, electric impulses firing through me in response. She wrapped her hand against my throbbing cock and slowly stroked it down, lovingly releasing her grip and easing down over my balls and cupping them. "That is why I want you to know that I choose you, JD. You actually see me for who I am. Not as a thing, or a

371

possession. I want you to see, feel, taste, and possess all of me. Yes, I choose you."

I tried to pull her in for another kiss, but she was up, the blanket thrown free. She hooked her fingers inside my shorts, and I lifted my hips, helping her as she pulled them off. I watched her kick her right foot over to straddle my legs, her skin glowing like a beautiful moonrise, and then leaned forward, lifted my aching member, and slowly, accepted me into her mouth.

Her lips slid over my head, her tongue and mouth warm and wet as she eased her head down. I laid back onto the pillow, almost undone by the subtle vibrations emanating from her body. I very nearly came then and there from the wave of pleasure she sent up my body.

Mabel took as much of me as she could, my swollen tip hitting her throat, and she pulled back. Cupping my balls, she rocked forward again. I grunted and groaned, struggling and failing miserably to stay quiet. The elf picked up speed, bobbing her mouth up and down, the pressure from her tongue and suction almost more than I could take.

"I can feel your yang energy," she gasped, after pulling free. "It feels like sunshine on my skin. So hot. So alive. I'd never imagined it to be so strong."

I hooked her hands and pulled her forward, desperate to be closer, to make good on her request to see, feel, and taste all of her.

Mabel rolled onto her back as I pulled my t-shirt free and threw it onto the floor. She spread for me, and I eased between her legs, the smell of aroused elf washing over me. It wasn't what I'd come to expect, but heady and sweet, like fragrant wildflowers in full bloom. If it was possible, she smelled like magic.

I kissed her passionately, worked down over her neck, then down between her breasts. I kissed each of her perked nipples, her body writhing beneath me as I took the right one into my mouth and gave it a healthy suckle. She moaned and clawed at my head and shoulders as I moved over to the left, licking her soft, sweet skin. She moved her hips, trying to angle the head of my cock to her opening, to satisfy that growing need and push me inside her. But I pulled back and worked my way down, fondling her perfect breasts as I traced a line of delicate kisses over her stomach. I didn't bypass her scar, that blemish she viewed as a flaw. I kissed it, tracing it with a finger, then afterward, with my tongue.

Mabel was practically vibrating off the bed by the time I came to her hips and ran my tongue down between her legs. Her lips were warm and wet, and I parted them with my tongue, favoring the pearl of her clitoris and back up. She clutched at my hair, grabbing ahold as I explored her sex. Her smell grew stronger, but it only served to spur on my drive. She really was sweet and smelled like flowers, the hearty thrum of her yin energy blossoming out of her every pore. It washed over me, curving over my skin like creeping moonlight as it sought to pull me down, working to bond with my life energy. I kissed and favored her as long as I could manage, her moaning an escalating song of need before the pull of our opposing energies was too strong to ignore.

I straightened, shuffled forward on the bed, and guided my erection between her legs. My swollen head parted her and eased inside, her canal dangerously tight. I rocked forward with my hips, easing as deep as it would go, before pulling back and plunging yet deeper.

"All of you. I want to feel all of you," Mabel whispered over and over. Her feet hooked behind my butt and pulled me in, urging me to thrust deeper still.

I worked into a rhythm, thrusting gently into her, but struggled. She was so tight I could barely hold back my climax. Finally, with an extra little push, Mabel gasped, and I slid in all the way. The moonrise glow of her skin increased until she practically shone beneath me. Everything became swirling color and heat, blasting away my inhibitions. I worked my hands up her soft stomach and over her bouncing breasts as I pulled back and rocked in again and again.

"Love me, JD. Please love me," she whispered.

373

I grabbed onto her hips and drove in as hard and as fast as I could. The heat intensified as I managed to push my mass of red yang energy down to where our bodies met. The cloud of white energy engulfed it immediately. Unlike with Chloe, the energies didn't just entwine, mingle, and feed off each other. But my yang merged with Mabel's yin. They became one, gaining strength and taking on an entirely different color. The resulting explosion of energy hit us at the same time and toppled Mabel into an orgasm I felt, heard, and saw. Hell, I'd be surprised if our whole wing of dorms didn't hear.

"My goddess!" she screamed, spasming around me. I watched her whole body shake, the sweat glistening on her stomach, chest, and face. The heat continued to churn, her body clenching against my cock, her legs wrapped too tightly around me to move otherwise. I savored her joy, the obvious pleasure, and silently wondered if it was the first time she had been allowed to not only experience it but enjoy herself.

A few moments later, her legs released, and she fell limp to the bed. Her skin still pulsed with that cool, inner light, as if ebbing and flowing with the beating of her heart. The bed creaked as Chloe crawled on. I pulled free of Mabel, the elf cooing quietly and gently rubbing her body.

"All right, you two have no idea how hard that was to listen to," Chloe whispered, slinking over Mabel, and even stooping in to kiss her glowing skin. "The sound, the energy pouring off you, but mostly…" she kissed Mabel again, the elf wrapping her arms around her and pulling them together. "The smell," Chloe gasped when they pulled apart. "My god, Mabel. I thought you two were chewing bubble gum, but now that I'm closer, you smell like cherry pie, fresh out of the oven, and ice cream. I am so horny right now. What is it with your smell?"

"Like I said. We moon elves are sexual creatures. When aroused, we emit smells and tastes that appeal to those we wish to attract," Mabel said, and kissed Chloe back, "I think you… smell good… too.

374

Chloe kicked her leg up and over Mabel, and they laid together, breasts to breasts. They kissed again, the elf's skin glowing brighter again in response. Not to be ignored, I moved forward and picked up the bottom of Chloe's robe, pulling it up to expose her muscular rear.

Well, hello there, I thought, running my hands up over her hips, then eased my cock, still wet with Mabel's arousal, into Chloe.

"Oh... JD. Hello back there," she moaned, as I pushed in up to the hilt, pulled back out, and pushed back in hard. I thrust into her, the sound of skin slapping against skin growing stronger.

Chloe kissed Mabel, then traced a trail of love pecks down her neck and over her breasts. The elf gasped and the two girls squirmed together.

"I'm starting to like our room and board situation... very... much," Chloe moaned, reaching back to play with herself.

I slowed, pulled out, and eased back inside Mabel, the elf shivering in response.

"I'm starting to like our room and board situation, too... two?" I said.

"You tease," Chloe breathed, "You horrible, horrible tease."

Getting Started

I AWOKE SOMETIME THE NEXT MORNING in a tangle of limbs. Chloe was to my left. Her right arm was wedged under my pillow and her right leg overtop me. Mabel was on my right, her face wedged in the crook of my arm and her left leg hooked over Chloe's right leg.

A distant, reverberating gong sounded all around us, somehow vibrating out of the tower's stone walls and floors. Mabel snorted awake while Chloe tried to sit up, nearly taking my pillow, and my head, with her in the process.

It took us several, sleep-dumb moments to untangle and pull free.

"I'm up... I'm up," I grunted, as the strange gong sounded again. "What is that?"

"The tower," Mabel yawned. "From now on it will wake us up every day classes are held."

"Well, isn't that handy," Chloe said, and promptly pulled her pillow over her head.

A short while, some baths, and fresh clothes later, I was sitting at the kitchen table, picking through the food in my rift.

"So, have you decided?" I asked Chloe. "You're doing weapon cultivation, right?"

She nodded. "Yeah, that's the plan. "And you?"

"I don't know. I was thinking of magic and martial arts cultivation first. I want to strengthen my body and my magic powers. But I can see benefits in almost every discipline. I've never really been a good person at making choices."

"Hah, yeah, you're quite the unconventional fighter, aren't you?"

"Unconventional? Yes. But I think that might just help me out here. I have a feeling it will help me when going up against other cultivators. They won't know what to expect," I muttered. "Also, I don't think I'm a good tank. I know you don't like Skadi's pushy nature, but unless you have any other recommendations, I think we should recruit her to the party first thing. Otherwise, that leaves me upfront, taking the brunt of the attacks."

"Which isn't a place I want you to be," Chloe said, immediately. "It's not that I don't like her pushy nature, so please don't think that. It's just... well, she intimidates me. The muscles, the boobs, all of it. If I have to share you with someone, I want them to at least be feminine. She's kind of a brute."

"And you don't have to share me with anyone if you don't want to. Last night, that was..."

"Amazing," Chloe breathed. "She shrugged and let out a sigh. "Mabel is sweet. She's beautiful. And she genuinely needs us. Plus, phew. I don't know if that is how all elves are, but man, she is like a walking aphrodisiac. I was originally worried about keeping you away from her... but I think now it might be me you have to worry about. I messed around with a few girls in college, but it never went anywhere. But wow. Elves."

I laughed. "We'll have to see if she can..."

"I can what?" Mabel asked, appearing from the bath.

"See if we can get any sleep at all with us sharing a room," Chloe said and threw her a wink.

"Do I need to leave? I'm so sorry. I didn't mean to..."

"My god, you are too adorable," Chloe gasped, jumped out of her chair, and wrapped Mabel in a hug. "You're not going anywhere. You're one of us now. But yes, you sultry minx, some nights JD and I are going to need to get some sleep."

Mabel blushed hard, her ears turning red, but sat down and joined the conversation.

"Listen," I said, "I don't want to push anyone into anything, but sooner or later we'll need more people, especially if we want to explore the next dungeon and get our hands on more loot. Plus, I imagine having more... and stronger party members will help keep certain groups from harassing us. I know Ascal promised to leave us alone for the year if I won the duel, but I don't think we'll be safe from reprisals. If anything, he'll use other groups to get to us indirectly. Zebras don't change their stripes."

"I agree," Chloe said.

"What is a zebra?" Mabel asked, leaning forward over the table.

"It's a sort of striped horse," I explained.

"Oh. We have those where I am from. Some have wings. They are very pretty and very magical."

"I want a unicorn. Are those real?" Chloe asked.

"Maybe..."

"Find out and let me know," Chloe turned from Mabel to me. "If you find your giant girl, talk to her. Otherwise, maybe we'll meet some candidates during class? I just...don't know. If she says yes, can you have her not do all the flexing around here?"

I nodded. She was right. We didn't necessarily need to settle on anyone... but we didn't have all the time in the world, either. If we waited too long, the most desirable party members could be gone. We had already become infamous, so that could be good and bad.

"And Mabel? You weren't here when I asked Chloe, but what's your verdict? What discipline have you decided on?" I asked. Mabel's expression pinched and she looked down.

Oh shit. She still hasn't decided.

378

"I don't know," she blurted, finally. "I just need time to think. Yes. Just give me a little quiet time to think."

"Okay," I said, "yeah. No pressure here."

I left Mabel at the table. First, I went back and tidied up our bed, but a thought struck me as I straightened to look around. We'd talked about adding party members but hadn't bothered checking out the dorm upgrade system. Well, I mean, we didn't have enough crystals before, but now? It couldn't hurt to look, right?

I immediately moved to the door, where an A4-sized piece of parchment hung on the wall. I touched it and a menu popped up. It displayed the requirements needed to upgrade our dorm to the second level. We needed 150 rank 1 crystals. Beautiful. I currently had over 200.

DO YOU WISH TO UPGRADE THE ROOM?
[Yes] – [No]

I selected yes and found myself staring at three new layouts. Our current setup was the most basic... two rooms with dividers. One room was separated into a sleeping area, while the other in a kitchen and seating area. The second room was the bathroom.

"Now this is interesting," I whispered as I eyed the new options.

Two choices drew my interest. The first added a new room that we could use as a separate bedroom. It also expanded the room I was currently standing in, making more room for the kitchen, dining area, and living room. The second option would also make the grand chamber larger, but it would also give us an elevated loft that looked down on the first floor. It looked much more ideal, in my opinion, as the girls and I could easily use the elevated loft for privacy while keeping the closets and furniture where they were.

I decided to go with the second option and accepted the changes. To my surprise, a bright light filled the room, forcing me to shield them. It only lasted for several seconds, but then a strange

379

chime resounded all around. I opened my eyes and looked around. Our room, as if by magic, had changed. The two beds we'd pushed together the night before were gone, now replaced by new living room furniture.

A massive sofa sat in a corner with a large coffee table. Two recliners sat in another corner with a smaller but taller coffee table between them. I walked towards the longest wall, where a window now broke the expanse of stone wall, a sunrise view of the city visible beyond. The kitchen was now a real kitchen with a table for four, cupboards, fully stocked cabinets, and an iron stove. A sink sat opposite. A partition separated the entry to the bath. The closets were there now, providing us a dressing area. And ironically, there were four doors now, not two.

And above it all, set high on the wall was the loft, accessible by a ladder chiseled into the stone wall itself. It sat above eye level, but I could clearly see a wide, wood-framed bed, nightstands, and dressers. Pictures hung on the wall, illuminated by glowing candles set in wall sconces, and another window.

"No longer a cave! We have two windows, and all that for 150 crystals, huh?" I whispered.

"Hey! What's with the blinding lights and the shaking floor?" Chloe yelled, "And why is it so dark?"

I poked my head around the corner, but they weren't around the kitchen table anymore.

"Huh? What just happened?" Mabel asked, appearing from behind a closet door. A moment later I heard something bang inside another closet and Chloe emerged. "What the hell? We're at the kitchen table one moment and in a closet the next. What did I miss?"

"Ta-da!" I said, holding my arms out to show off the space.

"Did we just get transported to the penthouse? Shit!"

"Did you upgrade our dorm?" Chloe asked, scoping the place out.

"Are you happy with the changes?"

"Hell yes!" she laughed as Mabel crawled up the ladder to the loft. She tested the bed's softness, ran a finger over the dresser, and stopped before the window.

"You've—this is so beautiful!" Mabel finally said, finding her voice. "I love the view. And I can see the moon now when I sleep. Goddess be praised!

"How much did it cost?"

"**150** crystals for it all. I wasn't going to spend it, but I figured something good needed to come from my duel. So, here you go."

"Okay. I can't argue with that," Chloe said "Besides, we'll be staying here for a long time, so why not try and make it as comfortable as possible? If we get any new members, we'll certainly need the space."

"Ahh! Just look at that marble countertop!" Mabel echoed, now behind us in the kitchen. "And this wooden table! Is this mahogany? It is a very luxurious import from earth! So impressive."

I chuckled, watching the elf dash about the dorm room, inspecting, giggling, and touching everything. It was like Christmas morning. This moment right here was worth all the hardships Mabel had suffered through, and hopefully would provide a stable base for the ones before us.

"Should we skip class today and just do dungeon runs?" I asked, abruptly. It wasn't just the prospect of having to face the repercussions of my duel, but also... Okay. It was almost entirely the duel. I didn't want to see how students reacted. Would they stare? Whisper?

"Where are you going with this?" Chloe asked.

I took in a deep breath and put up my best smile. "I think we should skip most of school and just do dungeon runs. We could get the basics from the mistresses and then keep on doing our own thing."

Chloe considered it for a moment, and judging by her expression, she wasn't completely opposed. But Mabel shook the notion away immediately.

"Not a good idea. Not good, at all," she said. "The royals are already far ahead of us. The best way to keep us all safe is to go, make good with the teachers, and learn."

"Right, but we need an unconventional approach, Mabel. If we just do what the others are doing, then we will never catch up. You know that, right?"

"There is nothing conventional about these academies," she responded right away, her voice stronger than I'd ever heard it. "Look at what you two have done in just a few days. Look at your robe, JD. Yes, you will learn what everyone else does, as they learn it, but what you do with that knowledge is what will ultimately set you apart... or not. I know you don't want to go because of the duel. But it will only get worse if you avoid them. Trust me, they will only see that as weakness."

I didn't rock back on my heels, but her blunt honesty did set me back. And she was right. Yes, I was scared to face Ascal and the other blood elves again. Yes, I wanted to just avoid the whole situation.

"Yeah, okay. I'll admit it. You're right. But I have a feeling that true strength is gained not in the classroom, but in the application. I want to maximize my time practicing. I think we'll find that a little time in the classroom and a lot of time putting it to practical use might just be best. Is that a compromise you can live with?"

"I think JD is right," Chloe added, then leaned in, putting her hand over Mabel's on the table. "Think about it. Who is stronger? A warrior with a head full of knowledge he kind of knows but cannot do very well? Or one that has mastered a dozen forms and techniques?"

"Mastery is always going to triumph," Mabel admitted.

"Preach to the choir!" Chloe cried. "Let's get educated today!"

Another gong reverberated through the tower.

"That is the **15**-minute warning. We should get moving. I want a good seat for the first day of classes," Mabel said.

We finished getting ready then and left our dorm with five minutes to spare. I walked out onto the circular corridor to more activity than I'd seen at the academy. Large groups of students stood at the classroom entrances. Having decided we'd start with weapons cultivation, we stopped behind the largest group of students. Elves, dwarves, giants, a rather large group of alien-looking creatures, and dark elves waited for the professor, Leona, to arrive.

And she arrived in style. A bolt of lightning struck the ground before the portal, flashing bright and knocking back the closest students. The professor appeared from the center of the light, her long, red hair and tight, black kimono blowing in an invisible, soundless wind. A glowing blade appeared before her, floating in the air. Leona grabbed it, twirled it around, and artfully slid it into a scabbard in her left hand. As she did, a gust of wind swirled up around her, billowing her gown and showing off a rather racy, black undergarment. I must have been staring because Chloe jabbed an elbow into my ribs.

"Her, too? You were with two girls... one of them a smokin' hot elf, for a good portion of the night, and now you're ogling one of the mistresses," she hissed in my ear.

"I can't help it. I just appreciate the female form," I whispered back.

"But they're all old!"

"They don't look old..." I said, appraisingly.

"Alright, my dears!" Leona said, the magical wind dying down. "I hope you liked my introduction because it is going to be the only weapon twirling, dancy-dancy, show off crap anyone does in this class. My class is all business. Weapons are not toys. And in our discipline of cultivation, we take the art of killing very seriously."

WEAPON SOUL

WE PASSED THROUGH THE PORTAL and into a massive, dojo-like space. There were no chairs or seats, only tatami mats surrounding a central, bamboo sparring floor. Stone pillars circled the outside of the space, while long, richly-colored tapestries covered the walls. As I walked in and studied them, the calligraphy glyphs shifted on the fabric closest to me. One moment it was covered in foreign symbols, and the next I could read it perfectly. *Evade.*

I turned to the next down the line. ***Defend.*** And they continued around the sweeping space. I turned to find Leona studying me, then she smiled and addressed the class.

"Take a seat." She gestured around the room. Students formed groups and formed up on mats. But at least a hundred students were left milling around by themselves, talking to established groups, or shyly standing out of the way. I pulled Chloe and Mabel to the far side and settled on an empty mat, a few stragglers settling in around us.

"Glad I'm not one of them," I whispered. "Would suck to sit alone. I wonder if they are even with a party?"

"What would you do without me?" Chloe chuckled and leaned in. "I know you want to rescue everyone, but don't go inviting the entire class to live in our dorm. It's not big enough, and I'm not *that* social."

"Quiet down! The chit-chat happens in the passageways. When you are in this classroom, you will listen," Leona snapped but didn't look our way. Most of the murmuring and whispering died down. "Today we start with the basics. For those of you not instructed, pay attention. For those that *think* you know what you are doing, pay attention. Trust me when I say, most of you have no idea what you've signed up for. To give it straight, look around you. These tapestries are everything to weapon cultivation. Posture. Evade. Guard. Strike..." and she went on, all the way around the room.

She abruptly snapped her fingers once done and a piece of parchment appeared in front of every single student. I plucked mine out of the air and read it, immediately grinning. It was yet another skill. Yes, it was simple... a foundational skill, but I had to start somewhere.

"This is where it all begins, the ground floor of your weapon cultivation journey. Today you will learn how to connect your weapon to your soul. It sounds simple, but trust me, it is not. Nor is it something everyone *does* do. If you want to develop your skills and gain an understanding of your weapon's true potential, this is the first step. This will make your weapon into something more than just forged, shaped, and tempered steel. It will make it into an extension of your will. Your weapons will become as much a part of you as hands and feet. Never forget that!"

I looked back down at the skill. Weapon soul. How... odd. Even odder was the fact that you could bind a weapon to your soul, but who was I to judge? This world was more fantastic than I'd ever hoped.

"Weapon soul. Remember that name well, as once you learn the skill it will become a part of you until... you die. Your weapon is your lifeline in battle. Never forget that!"

Leona looked around the dojo and motioned for one of the loners to join her. I didn't know what his race was called, but I thought he looked a little like skinny Buu from Dragon Ball. But the mean, evil one. His skin was purple, with a single, antenna-like appendage on top of his head. It curved back, angling towards his body where it ended in a sharp point. He appeared to be completely hairless, as well, so his body glistened in the light. He wore a sleeveless shirt and silken pants.

"What's your name and race? I've never seen one like you in our academy," Leona asked.

"We're the Mabiju, Lady Mistress. As for my name, I go by Nergal in your tongue."

"Right, Nergal. Summon your weapon."

He nodded and plucked a spear from his rift. It had a wicked, triple edge on one side, and a scythe-like serrated blade on the other.

"That thing is so cool!" I whispered to Chloe. But my voice carried way better than I intended and Leona's eye snapped up to me.

"Okay, fine. Second volunteer. You too, JD. Come here... since you're so excited."

I cursed quietly and tried to think up an excuse, anything so that I wouldn't have to be another professor's guinea pig, but nothing came to mind. So, I got to my feet and walked over to the center, bowing my headfirst to the professor, and then to the Mabiju, Nergal.

"Greetings, Mistress Leona. And to you, Mabiju Nergal."

Nergal studied me for a moment, but then imitated the motion, drawing some chuckles from his people. His face grew dark, but he didn't respond or look their way.

"Good. You have restraint. That is a good start," Leona said, her voice barely audible. Then she turned back to the class and spoke louder. "Now! I will show you all just once how to activate your weapon soul! This is a skill that requires more focus than skill, so pay attention to the process."

386

She held out a longsword in front of her and mana quickly pooled in both of her hands. She pulled one hand away from the blade and pressed it to her chest. Mana sprouted from her hand still on the sword and grew towards the hand on her chest. A matching tendril appeared from her body and met the other halfway.

"What you see is only half the equation here," Leona said while concentrating. "I am pushing the mana, and thus my will, towards the blade but I have to guide it. That is why focus is so important. I am recreating this sword perfectly in my mind, every nick, hammer mark, discoloration, and scratch in the leather. If it is not real in your mind, it will not be real in your heart. Show your mana where to go and let your heart bind it."

The sword started to glow, an almost ethereal overlay of light covering it from tip to pommel, which quickly solidified and disappeared. The mana tether surged brighter, changed from blue to green, and then blinked out. It looked so simple. Shit. I would have this skill in the bag and be dungeon diving within the hour.

"I will assign you numbers now," Leona said as she snapped her fingers. Smaller pieces of parchment appeared in everyone's hands, except for Nergal and me. "Numbers **1** through **200** will stand and spread out across the dojo, leaving five paces of room between each other. Once the first student finishes creating his weapon soul, number 201 will stand and take his place."

I was happy to see both Mabel and Chloe had moved in close. Good. Either Leona placed them there, or she didn't prevent it. Either way, I was more comfortable with them nearby.

"Begin!"

I studied the skill parchment.

SKILL NAME: Weapon Soul (B)
TYPE: Basic, Mana **RANGE:** 1 pace
DESCRIPTION: A foundation Weapon Cultivation skill. It allows you to connect your weapon to your soul and allow it to start absorbing mana.

Once learned, you can never lose your weapon as it becomes a part of you.

BASIC: *+50* Attack on mastery

ADVANCED: *+100* Attack on mastery

MASTER: *+200* Attack on mastery

I immediately followed the skill's instructions, drawing from Leona's example. The pen-blade went out in my right hand, while my left went over my heart. It didn't look or feel difficult until I started channeling my mana. I pushed it to both hands, then noticed a thin thread appearing between my palm and the hilt of my weapon. My hands shook as I tried to push the mana into the pen-blade's hilt, but the tendrils moved, evading, and spinning like slithering snakes.

"What in the shit biscuits?" I muttered. "Why is it moving... so much?"

"Because you haven't anchored your mana. You're trying to catch the blade without having anything to hold it. Like I said, build it in your mind. Make it real," Leona whispered, her mouth surprisingly close to my ear. "I shouldn't tell you that because students *should* figure it out themselves, but Scarlet told me to...push you in the right direction."

I quietly nodded my thanks, then turned toward the girls and started anew. Two mana balls spun in my hands, and I used the right to create an anchor in my chest. The thread between me and the pen-blade became slightly thicker, and I could see it better, but it still felt off. Basic things were easy, right? Wrong. I had been arrogant to think I would master the skill so easily.

"Don't be that guy," I whispered under my breath, and started recreating the pen-blade in my mind. I used my tactile contact and my artist's imagination to help build my mental image, piece by vivid piece.

I pushed the mana from my chest toward my heart, forming a thin line that bore into my skin. Shit, it hurt like a bastard! But I bore down and pushed through as cold sweat formed on my brow.

A wave of lightheadedness washed over me as the mana tickled my heart, and then it went even deeper, wrapping itself around my beating core over and over again, winding on it like a ball of yarn. My eyes were watering, and my body was shaking by the time that first part was done. I was also having difficulty breathing. I lifted my left hand and pressed the mana into the blade's hilt, creating a lasso and grabbing it by force, then started pulling it in toward the other half.

A calming hand landed on my shoulder. I jerked my head around only to find Nergal standing beside me, a trickle of calming mana flowing from his hand and into my body. The energy was foreign and strange, but oddly soothing and helped keep me on my feet.

I straightened my back and brought both hands together, wrapping the mana in a knot and then tugged at the weapon's soul. It sprung forth from the pen-blade and protested, just like an angry bull, but I refused to give in. A classroom full of students was watching me, I could both see and feel their attention. I refused to fail!

I redoubled my focus on my mental image, using both my mind and my will to pull the pen-blade spiritual double towards me when a rough hand touched my back and helped me focus. A rush of unfamiliar, alien power hit me, and I was as focused as ever.

The soul finally separated from the weapon and floated before me. I pulled it toward my heart and tightened the line. The knot suddenly broke but the mana quickly reformed the bond. A peculiar, calming sensation washed over me as the pen-blade finally touched my skin and started entering my body. Inch by inch, the weapon disappeared inside me, until finally, my ears popped, and it was gone.

YOU HAVE ACQUIRED BASIC MASTERY OF:
WEAPON SOUL
ATTAINED BONUS: +50 Attack

I let go of all the mana and my legs immediately went limp. Thankfully, Nergal caught me and lowered me to the ground. The alien averted his gaze as if embarrassed and stepped aside.

"Thanks, dude," I said and held my hand out. "I really appreciate your help."

Nergal stared at my hand, the ghost of a frown pulling the corners of his mouth down.

"Sorry. It is a human custom," Leona explained, appearing behind him. "They shake hands when they want to thank or greet someone." Then the mistress pushed Nergal toward me. He moved stiff-legged but shook my hand once and let go again.

"It was my pleasure both seeing and assisting in the process, human JD," he said before turning and moving away. I watched him pick his way through the crowd, before settling into a spot and pulling his own weapon from his rift.

"Strange fellow," I muttered under my breath as I got to my feet and stretched.

"You made it look so easy," I said, as Mistress Leona turned towards me from another group of students. "Focusing on the blade wasn't that hard. Neither was guiding the mana. But trying to do both at the same time? Now that was difficult."

"You show impressive focus," she said, nodding approvingly. "You can now use your weapon soul as a skill. It is expensive and hard to upgrade, but it will improve the more you use it. Before you know it, your attack will soar. Why don't you try it out as you wait for your friends?"

I bowed, turned, and spotted the girls. I didn't want to interrupt their studies, so I hit Chloe up on chat.

"JD: Did you see? I did it? It's harder than it looks."

"Chloe: You're not joking!" Then I watched as her mana disappeared and she slumped. Both girls immediately walked over to me.

"You good?"

"Yeah, sorry. This is my first time doing something like it," Mabel replied. "I think it might be the crowd. Too many people around. I just need to find a quieter spot and try again. I don't want to stay here all day."

"You heard the elf!" Leona snapped. "Get back to it! I don't have all day, either! This is a simple but powerful skill. Don't make it more complicated than it is. I would like you all to have this mastered quickly, so you can spend the rest of the day practicing it and gaining experience."

I guided Mabel away from the crowd—most had gathered when I was completing my weapon soul, and remained, as Leona was nearby, and they wanted or needed help. We found a quieter spot near a column, and I sat on a mat, with my back to the stone. Mabel's questions tumbled forth as soon as we were away from people.

"Did you picture your weapon in your mind in black or white...?"

"Did it hurt...?"

"Why were you shaking so much...?"

I chuckled and answered her questions one at a time. Mabel and Chloe wanted to try it again, but only after I demonstrated what the skill looked like.

I focused on the skill, activating it. A window appeared, similar to the weapon upgrade panel but featured two different slots. The one on the left was already filled while the one on the right had an icon of a crystal. Not the crystal cores we got from monsters, mind you, but of a different shape and composition. I focused on it and a pop-up almost hit me in the face.

NAME: Spirit Gem
TYPE: Upgrade Material
DESCRIPTION: Gems grown in areas with an incredibly high spiritual concentration.
They are mined deep underground and can only be extracted using a high-grade source of mana.

An angry shout snapped my attention away from the window. I quickly looked around, spotting a mabiju at least two heads taller than me standing over Nergal, his weapon raised. I turned right, not spotting Leona anywhere. So many students were working on their weapon soul skill, the vast majority of the students hadn't even noticed the rising conflict.

Shit. Why is it always me?

I snapped back to Nergal. Several other mabiju stood behind the weapon-toting brute, threatening Nergal. I groaned and got to my feet just as Mabel spoke.

"Mabel: I'm done. I got it, JD. I got it! How far along are you, Chloe?"

"Chloe: Almost there. Just need to pull the soul in."

"JD: He helped me, now it looks like he needs a little something in return. BRB."

"Mabel: Wait, what is JD doing?"

"Chloe: Oh, come on! Can you avoid trouble for like one day?"

I immediately set off for Nergal.

"I got it," Mabel gasped, and I heard the girls fall in line behind me.

I stepped in behind Nergal and put a hand on his shoulder— a subtle but undeniable reminder that he wasn't alone. He suddenly looked much taller than I remembered, which made his bigger counterparts look even bigger. Shit, we really were the smaller race.

"Nergal, my man! Need a hand with your weapon soul? Or have you already banged that one out? I'd love to see yours in action if that is the case."

Nergal turned, his strange, alien eyes narrowing on me, but recognition swept in quickly. He moved to shrug my hand off, but I kept it there on purpose.

"What do you want, little creature?" the largest of the brutes sneered. "Can't you see that I'm talking to my...old friend?"

392

"Your old friend?" I asked, refusing to back down as the three moved in and tried to appear even larger. "Customs must be different for our people, but we don't normally stand over our friends and talk down to them. Maybe I'm wrong, but it seems like you're trying to intimidate my new friend here. Can't we all work together to create some badass weapon souls?"

I really wasn't looking to interfere, or God forbid, start another fight, but the way the bigger guy stood over Nergal set me off.

"Nergal is small and weak. You, little creature, are even smaller. Nergal is mabiju. You are not. Move aside."

I moved in next to Nergal, reaffirming my place aside my new friend, and stared up into the bigger alien's eyes. They were dark blue and without noticeable pupils. Okay, creepy and intimidating. I didn't have a huge body of work with which to judge, but I imagined he wasn't one of the prettier examples of his race.

"Chloe: Please don't. I'm already tired and one duel is enough stress for one lifetime."

"Mabel: Yeah, come on, JD. Diffuse the situation. Please."

I turned and glanced their way.

"JD: What coincidence, 'diffuse' is my third, middle name!"

"Chloe: Oh, boy."

"Guys, I think we got off on the wrong foot. How about we all come together to share a few mugs of..." I started to say and turned back only to catch a fist right in my face. My vision snapped red, my head snapped back, and I staggered from the blow. There might have been Tweety Birds circling my head, too, but I couldn't see them through the bright lights.

MANA SHIELD SUSTAINED: 83 DAMAGE

"Hah, I haven't been punched that hard since my second year at Sisters of Mercy Catholic School. Mary Catherine, now that nun could throw a punch," I laughed and wiped some blood from

393

my split lip. There was no way for him to know that I'd just said he hit like a girl, but I appreciated it, damn it!

He pulled his hand back for another blow, but Nergal flashed into motion. His rift opened, his arm darted in, and a spear appeared, all in the batting of an eyelash. He dropped his right foot back, twirled his spear, and jammed the bladed tip through the brute's wrist as it came forward. The larger mabiju growled and pulled back, blood splattering from the wound. Several drops hit my robes, but the fabric self-cleaned.

"You don't need to fight my battles, human!" Nergal snarled, dropping into a fighting stance. "Don't think we're friends just because I was...friendly to you."

I pulled my pen-blade out and threw him my warmest, "I don't care that you don't want me as a friend, but you're stuck with me" smile.

"You just tell yourself that all you want, buddy. I took a face-punch for you, and you drew blood for me, I think we're more than just potential friends. I think we just moved into BFF territory. Next thing you know, we're gonna be playing D & D together, eating pizza, and drinking beers."

"I don't know what any of that is," Nergal said, turning to me.

"Challenge accepted," I said, just as a peel of thunder shook the room. Leona appeared, her longsword held out in between us and the mabijus. They were ready to kill, but seeing the frightening professor, they immediately backed down.

"What are you doing?" Leona raged. "I leave the classroom for two minutes and students are already trying to gut one another."

"This trog struck my Earth counterpart, JD. I have the right to defend those around me, if they are in need," Nergal said.

"Is this true?" Leona asked, turning on the taller mabiju.

To my surprise, he nodded. "The little creature interfered with our matters."

"Chloe: This isn't what diffusing the situation looks like."

394

"You four will take this grievance before Headmistress Scarlet," Leona decreed.

"No. I will not wait!" the brute growled. "I invoke the Rite of Retribution!"

"Vegar, that rite cannot be rescinded. Are you sure?"

The big mabiju nodded and stepped forward, his wounded wrist having already closed. *Magic.*

Leona narrowed her eyes as the class shuffled quietly around us. A pinprick dropping might have sounded like a car wreck.

"You both understand what that means?" Leona looked to Vegar and then Nergal.

Vegar nodded. "I do. I want to fight him right now!"

"Nergal, you accept?"

I held my breath, hoping that my new acquaintance would wise up and shake his head. I only wished that I had the chance to share my experience first. But Nergal nodded.

Damn it!

"Alright, by the Zenith bylaws, Rite of Retribution is in effect. No one is allowed to heal you. To intervene, except to provide a merciful death-strike. Everyone, stay here and practice. Nergal, do you want JD and his team to serve as your witnesses?"

"I will," I said, replying before he could speak. I was worried he'd say otherwise. "His witness, his second, whatever capacity he needs, I am there."

Nergal bared his sharp teeth. But I wasn't sure if that was a sign of acceptance or argument. Leona just nodded, so I didn't question it.

"Vegar, will your group accompany you as witnesses?"

"I demand healing! No one should start a fight wounded!" he protested.

The bastard was right. His wrist had closed over, but it still had to hurt like a son of a gun. Then again, it was his fault. A bum wrist could cost him more than just his pride, but his life.

"When the rite of retribution is called, the duel will start right away. No one is to equip, trade for, or steal items or weapons. The rite says you fight the way you stand. Both of you."

Leona nodded toward the portal, but Vegar seemed reluctant to move. Afraid even. Served him right.

"Move or I will cut you down where you stand! I gave you the chance to back out of this, and you refused. As your adjudicator, I must declare the winner," she hissed.

"Fine!" he roared, his voice almost deafening. "I will finally get to kill you, half-blood! The shame of my family, bastard-cousin!"

Oh, so that's what it was. A family feud, huh? Great. Just what I needed. And there I was trying to be cool like I could defuse the situation. Who knew how long this powder keg was set to blow.

A wave of light and heat washed over me, and suddenly I found myself standing in front of a ring. To the right was the group of fairly aggressive mabijus.

"The Rite of Retribution ends only with final blood. Final! Now, begin!" Leona shouted, her voice reverberating through the arena.

Nergal faced down Vegar, both holding identical weapons, though the larger mabiju's weapon was easily a foot longer.

Nergal didn't hesitate. He was smaller, perhaps weaker, but he was fast and decisive.

Nergal shot forward and ducked under an awkward, sidelong swipe from Vegar, deflected a follow-up, dove left, and drove his spear right at the bigger opponent's chest. Ice erupted forth as the tip connected with his shield, encasing the larger fighter in a coffin of ice. It only lasted for several seconds before exploding in a cloud of intense flames.

Vegar came in, aggressively swinging his weapon—hard cut down, swipe up, sidelong sweep, and followed immediately by a single-armed jab strong enough to drive through concrete. I marveled at Nergal as he ducked, twirled, and jumped over each attack, moving with the grace of a dancer.

396

Vegar snarled and redoubled his efforts, cutting, swiping, and stabbing, but his attacks had already slowed. The big mabiju narrowly missed hooking my new friend, only to have Nergal spin around and jump back, swinging the scythe–like side of his spear down, and separating Vegar's wounded arm at the elbow.

Seemingly indifferent about his abruptly shortened arm, Vegar swung his spear around, letting forth a billowing cloud of flame. Nergal dodged as best he could, but the flames blossomed too quickly. His mana shield caught the brunt of it. He stopped, slammed the haft of his spear into the ground, and showered the area in frost, dousing the flames. Nergal turned the spear on Vegar, peppering him with the last shards of pelting ice and cold.

Vegar dodged sideways and tried to catch him with fire again, but Nergal feigned a second attack, and lunged in low, only to intentionally pull up the spear short, kick around in a summersault-like move, and stab at Vegar's rib cage on the other side. Honestly, I struggled to track his movements, I couldn't imagine how Vegar managed.

The attack was nothing special or flashy, just good old-fashioned mabiju muscle thrusting well-honed steel. The bladed tip passed clean through the mana shield and plunged into Vegar's side. The big mabiju staggered and dropped to a knee. Nergal pulled his spear back and immediately swung the weapon violently around, screaming as it cut through his opponent's neck. Vegar's head tipped and landed with a meaty thud on the arena floor.

RITE OF RETRIBUTION IS COMPLETE: NERGAL WINS!

I'd never thought about it earlier, but I tried to peek at Nergal's power level. It was over 9,000! No, wait. It said **900**. My eyes were playing tricks on me. But shoot. I had wanted to throw in a 'finish him!' remark, but he really didn't hesitate. That head rolled faster than a basketball downhill.

Leona walked over to Nergal, bowed, and whispered something into his ear. I couldn't hear what she said, but I did notice that he glanced over at us, before nodding. When she was done, Leona walked to the center of the arena.

"Witnesses! You have been a party to tower justice. I, as this rite's adjudicator, declare it complete. If any of you are asked to present a witness for this match, only speak the truth. If you speak falsely, you will face the tower's retribution. Do you understand?"

"Yes, Mistress," I replied.

That familiar and strange 'pull your stomach out through your mouth' sensation kicked in, and we were abruptly standing back in the classroom. The mass of students immediately stopped practicing and turned to us. Eerie. Leona turned on Nergal.

"I want you to take the rest of the day off from classes. I see most of you have already managed to open your weapon soul. But don't think of this as a vacation. I simply don't want you all disrupting class anymore. And hey," Leona said, moving in closer to me. "Nergal is...much like you, JD. Probably more like you than you realize. He's a loner who has had to get by on scraps... if that. This is his chance to make something out of himself and drag his family name out of the gutter. He could become a great ally."

I nodded. "I like him," I said, honestly. "And thank you for... standing up for us. There isn't much to keep the royals and high-born from just pushing anyone they don't like aside. Meaning, down a mineshaft or off a mountain"

"More times than not they're the ones that pass, so you'll have to either get used to them or find a way to coexist. As for Nergal, he'll be detained for **24** hours, but once he's free, he'll seek you out. You saw him in action, but for your party, you will not find a more natural fighter."

Leona smiled, nodded, and then we were teleported out into the main corridor.

"Okay. That needs to stop or I'm definitely going to barf," I groaned and tried to get my bearings.

"Did she just force someone onto our team?" Mabel asked.

398

"I wouldn't say forced, but I think she is strongly recommending it."

"Did that battle scare anyone else?" Chloe asked. "From what I could feel they were an equal match, but that Nergal fellow was faster. I like him. But, man, I don't want to fight one of them. I got a little motion sick just watching them twirl and spin."

"That was kind of dumb, you know?" Mabel whispered. "I know you like to stand up for people, but it is different here. Sticking your nose into the wrong argument in the academies can just as easily kill you. Vegar could have killed you before Leona even stepped in."

"But he didn't. By my reckoning, I'm undefeated. Lucky as hell, but undefeated."

Mabel rolled her eyes and turned away. "I just want you to take this seriously. You come from a small world, but here, we are grains of sand. The tide could wash a thousand of us away and the world beyond the tower would hardly notice."

"I get it, but yeah. It's kind of been one of the only things I've thought about since getting here. I joke to keep it from bothering me. I do take it seriously. Believe me."

"Thank you," Mabel said, turning back.

"So, we just got kicked out of classes for the rest of the day. I guess that makes the whole skip and dungeon dive decision a whole lot easier. Where to first?" I asked.

Chloe asked, "Where are you taking me?"

"Well, I was thinking of scouring the bazaar. Maybe we could spend a little money, do a little shopping. You know? See if we can find anything useful."

"Mabel? You in?"

The elf considered us for a moment. "How long are we staying?"

"An hour? I don't know. It could be more or less. We'll see how things go. I just kind of want to check out the stuff I didn't get to see last time," I replied.

"Yeah, sure. We can circulate mana and recover. And eat. I'm hungry again."

"You take his right arm," Chloe said as she hooked her arm from my left side. Mabel grinned and took my right as we made our way along the mostly empty circular walkway.

PREP WORK

THE BAZAAR WAS PRACTICALLY BUZZING with activity. I marveled at how it always seemed busy, but more so, always fresh and new, with shifting colors and smells. It felt like I stepped into a different space every time we visited.

We made our way in the bazaar, looking and yet barely paying attention. There was simply too much going on all around us, and while mixed with the excitement from class, it made it a little hard to focus. We'd almost made it all the way to Reline's small store before I truly realized how far we had gone. The peculiar woman stood out front, stacking what looked like rolls on a shelf.

"Hey, Reline," I said.

"Oh, greetings! I was wondering when you three might darken my shop's doorstep again."

"Got any sweet snacks for us? Stuff from earth?"

"My sweet little Chloe. Best be careful with the sweets. They will go straight to your belly and thighs."

I watched as Chloe's smile turned upside down and she stiffened, so I put my arm around her.

"I don't think she'll need to worry about it, not with all the running around we do!" I said, trying to divert the conversation. Then I addressed the shopkeeper directly. "Reline, can you pack us up a bag of sweets to go. We'd like to have something to nibble on while we make our rounds?"

"Consider it done!" she said, her mouth pulling up into that strange, exaggerated smile. "Here you go." She pulled a paper bag from her rift and handed it to Chloe, and then another one for Mabel, who nodded her thanks.

"Thanks," Chloe said but muttered something under her breath. The shopkeeper either didn't notice or didn't care, she just watched us with that strange, stretched smile. Then, abruptly turned and walked back into her tent.

The weird will never get old around here... I thought, then said, "Moving on," and pushed the girls ahead. Chloe continued to mutter but pulled her bag open and started snacking. She pulled forth something that reminded me of chocolate, popped it into her mouth, and chewed.

"Tasty?" I asked as we slowly made our way down the path. We passed the last food stand and moved into the clothes district.

"Yeah, they're good. Almost like caramel or something. Makes me wonder if my teeth are gonna rot."

"Do you two feel like enjoying those snacks and looking at clothes while I scour the third district?"

"Mind?" Chloe asked, hooking an arm around Mabel's midsection, and pulling her in close. "After last night, you might want to be careful about leaving us alone for too long."

"You'd better behave yourself," I said, giving her *the* look and an upraised eyebrow.

"Me?" Chloe asked, holding her hand to her chest with a mock look of outrage. "I am practically a saint. Practically..."

"Okay, well why don't you find some crippled children to heal while I'm gone. Mabel, can you keep her out of trouble?"

"Can anyone, really?" the moon elf asked. Chloe grabbed her sides and tickled her, I laughed, and we separated.

I checked my wallet and found it sitting at just under **65,000 Fres**. I knew that wasn't a fortune in this world but compared to what my checking account had back on earth, it looked good.

It took me about ten minutes to get to the spot where I met Old White the first time. He was nowhere to be seen. Not that I'd come to see him, mind you, but I had been thinking about the old man quite a bit, especially since my chat with Scarlet.

I picked my way through a couple of tents and open-air shops, looking for everything and nothing at the same time. It struck me odd how few peddlers there were. Barely twenty people had set up on the walkway, under the various archways, or against the walls. They unrolled rugs like Old White, selling seemingly random items. I walked along, perusing, but didn't see anything I needed or wanted.

I approached a man seated under the large, stone arch, his head bowed in rest or meditation. He looked up as my shadow fell over him. White streaked his dark, brown hair, and yet he didn't look that old. Perhaps forties. Hell, I'd seen much worse from much younger...friends back home. Friends. The idea hit hard... that those people, that life, were behind me.

"Greetings," I said, cupped my left first with my right palm, and bowed. "Might you have anything of use to a new student?"

The man studied me for a moment, then looked down and gazed quietly at his displayed items. It was several long moments before he looked up, shook his head, then pointed towards the end of the peddlers' row. I followed the gesture and immediately stuck on his robe. It was of good quality.

The next two down the row wore nice clothes as well. And yet, the further I went down the line, the poorer the sellers looked. I finally stopped at the last spot and stared at the goods. The seller was a young man, somewhere in his thirties most likely. His robes were tattered, dirty, and torn. Beyond his clothes, he didn't look healthy. His eyes were sunken and his skin sallow, both nostrils red and irritated.

403

"Hello," I said, cheerily. "Is there anything you could sell to a first-year student?"

He perked up at the sound of my voice and looked up, then stood. He mouthed something, before pointing to the ruined stub where his tongue had once been.

"You can't talk?" I asked and pointed toward my own mouth, imitating speech. He nodded and then used a stick to point at several items. Stacks of parchments were lined up neatly, making five piles. I knelt in front of him and leaned in to see what they were.

His hand shot up and he showed me three fingers.

"Three thousand Fres?" he shook his head and cupped his one hand. "Three crystals?" He nodded animatedly. "So, you want three crystals for each parchment?"

He opened his mouth and he tried to speak…the noise was strangled and unintelligible. I took that as a yes and picked one of the parchments up. **Weapon Upgrader**. Next to it lay a **Skill Upgrader**, and next to that one lay the **Spell Upgrader**.

I pulled out **24** rank 1 crystal cores and handed them over. The sickly peddler counted out three spell upgraders, three skill upgraders, and three weapon upgraders and placed them in my hands. I quickly stored them in my rift, a bit of buyer's remorse kicking in as I watched him pocket my cores. I only had 70 rank 1 cores left, which meant that I'd need to watch my spending.

I rummaged through the fourth stack next, only to find the same skills the twins were selling. They wanted Fres, but this guy wanted cores. It was handy in case I ever needed a skill and was out of money.

I picked the last stack next and found several low-grade spells and skills that Mabel and I could use. One of them was **Ice Shard** and the other **Cutting Sound**. He lifted his hand and showed me a two on the spell, and a two on the skill.

"They're both low-level, right? I want the cutting sound for a zither user. She's in the first realm."

He nodded, smiling.

"Do you have anything that someone with a mana sword could use?"

His face screwed up in thought for a moment and he picked up that last stack. He rummaged through the stack and pulled a skill out. **Mana Flash**. He showed it to me, mimicked swinging a sword, then held his hands up before his face, as if blinded.

"How much?" I asked, "And is it a beginner skill?" He held up three fingers and then nodded. "So, she can use it in the first realm?" He nodded again. "Alright, here you go."

I handed him seven more crystals and he bowed.

"Do you have any gear? Any armors or accessories?" This time he shook his head but pointed at another man sitting across from him and to the left. "Thank you."

I made my way over to the peddler he'd pointed out.

"I see you've done some trade with our mute friend over there," the man said as I approached. "He's a good lad, but dumb. He sits here day in and day out selling other people's stuff."

"Where I'm from that isn't so strange. I think it is more bizarre to see people peddling their own goods. Or, to have them not made in some factory overseas. I'm not really interested in why he's doing it. All I care about is finding beneficial items. Beginner items preferably, since I'm not that wealthy. Not yet at least."

"You're wearing Palmire and not wealthy? I've heard some stories in my day, but that... hmm?"

"Not a story. Just the truth," I replied, trying to remain respectful, but his attitude had already rubbed me the wrong way. His robes were in a decent state, and he looked cleaner than most. He also sized me up quickly and spotted my robe... so I had to consider there was more to him than his simple, humble appearance indicated.

"Alright. Then I've got nothing for you. Sorry. Move along."

"Thanks for your time," I said, as heat rushed to my face.

I turned my back to him, looking around as if searching for the other peddler's goods. But it was more to give me a moment to calm down, and not say something I might regret. A small part of me expected him to apologize, or stop me, but he just sniggered and straightened the items on his rug. *Fuck.* The whole encounter could have gone differently, starting with me, but I refused to grovel and beg.

I walked down the line, intentionally looking back his way, but the peddlers grew progressively nicer, their clothes of better quality. Their trinkets, bobbles, and finery glimmered expensively in the limited light. I could have asked for prices, but I knew they all heard my exchange with the rude peddler and didn't want to embarrass myself. If nothing else, I'd walk away with new skills.

I left the peddlers' market and noticed the girls sitting on a bench just inside the clothes district, quietly chatting and watching me approach.

"Now that is just rude," I said, dropping down next to Chloe. "You can't just stop talking about someone when they sit down."

"Pfft! Sure, we can. Girl privilege."

Mabel giggled and her ears flushed pink. Oh, boy. It must have been something naughty. Well, two could play at that game.

"Guess who bought you girls new attack skills? I'll give you... one guess."

"Oh, oh! What did you get me?" Chloe asked, clawing at my shoulder, but I intentionally turned away from her and towards Mabel. "Tell me, tell me!"

"Pfft, as if I'm telling you!" I retorted. "Boy privilege."

Chloe growled, the noise eerily similar to an angry cat.

"I was thinking of modeling some new underwear for you tonight. Oh, well. I guess not."

"Maybe Skadi can show me hers," I whispered and got off the bench. "What do you think, Mabel?"

"Oh, don't pull me into your messed-up little game."

I turned back to Chloe, who watched me through narrowed eyes.

"New undies? Sexy ones?" I asked.

"Maybe," Chloe whispered. "What did you get me?"

406

I opened my rift and slowly pulled all the scrolls out, handing Chloe **Mana Flash** and the upgraders, then gave Mabel her scrolls. Her guarded expression melted away.

"When are we going to try them out?" Chloe whispered, cradling and petting the parchment.

"Wait, is this really an attack skill?" Mabel asked. "I get to learn an attack skill? I do? I do?"

"Damn straight. I want you to be able to defend yourself. You will need to get a little stronger, mind you. The guy sold it to me for a song and a dance, so I couldn't pass up the opportunity."

"Ohh," Mabel giggled, clapping her hands. "I wish I could have seen your dance. I so love song and dance."

Chloe groaned quietly next to me, but I didn't have the heart to correct the elf, so I smiled and promised to show her sometimes.

"Why are we still sitting here? I want to test my new attack out!" Chloe said. "Get up! Come on!"

It felt good to see them happy. There wasn't much I could do for them, but the things that I *could* do, well, they would have to make up for those I couldn't. They devoted themselves to me, so I'd have to give back in equal measure.

It was half an hour before we were back in our room, but we managed to get in a quick bite. Tidied up our room and prepared to head out, gambling on the idea that most students were still in class. I hated standing in line or standing around, only to have people stare, so the timing felt perfect. There was one thing I needed to do first, though: learn the **Ice Shard** skill, so we didn't have to find a quiet place in the dungeon again. That last trip had been a little rushed.

I pulled the parchment from my rift and started to read.

<u>SKILL</u> <u>NAME</u>: Ice Shard (B)
<u>TYPE</u>: Basic, Mana, <u>RANGE</u>: 30 paces
<u>DESCRIPTION</u>: One of the basic elemental spells.
Highly versatile yet destructive in the right hands.

BASIC: +30 Attack, +20 Mana on mastery, Damage: Attack x *1.4*, Mana: 20

ADVANCED: +60 Attack, +40 Mana on mastery, Damage: Attack x *1.6*, Mana: 25

MASTER: +120 Attack, +80 Mana on mastery, Damage: Attack x *1.8*, Mana: 30

NOTE: Attack goes up/down by 50% depending on the elemental affinity

NOTE: Ice Shard can cause debuffs that slow or freeze the target.

There was a small depiction of mana flows that had been absent in the skills I got from the academy and the dungeon twins. Were they withholding that information on purpose? Or was it just a new-to-me element of a different kind of skill? I decided to try it out and see for myself.

I closed my eyes and held my right hand out, palm up. Mana started gathering and spinning together into threads, just as the parchment required. They knitted together until it formed a glowing ball. The trick with creating ice over fire wasn't in the amount of mana or how tightly I packed it together, but instead pooling it and then inverting it, to create a vacuum inside the shell. At least that's what I gathered from theory.

I tried again and again, pooling mana, creating the threads, and forming the ball, but inverting the pressure proved more complicated than I realized. I worked at it for half an hour, then a full hour, without a break. Chloe and Mabel worked through their skills together, but finished before me and settled onto the bed to watch. I didn't mind. They were quiet and didn't distract.

It failed again and again until I finally realized my error. It wasn't the amount of mana, but the direction and rotation of the mana threads that formed the ball.

I rewound the mana, and the pressure inside grew accordingly, then, I inverted the pressure. The heat and potential immediately shifted, forming into ice on my palm. I launched the ice shard at

408

the portal door. It exploded like a grenade, peppering the entire space with finger-sized chunks of cold, sharp ice. One hit Chloe in the ass, another bounced off Mabel's arm and got stuck in her hair. Being the unlucky guy, I took a piece right between the eyes.

I staggered back, grunting and laughing. I didn't know if it was funny or painful, just yet.

"JD! What the hell are you doing?" Chloe cried and jumped around, swatting at the cold, wet spot on her butt.

I rubbed the red spot between my eyes and surveyed the damage. Ice shards covered... everything but were quickly melting into puddles. Mabel hid beneath the pillows on the sofa.

"Sorry. I was trying to figure out this ice shard skill but think it's more of an ice grenade. Are you okay?"

Mabel slunk off the sofa, held her hand up and a green glow washed down Chloe's body, healing her. Since it hadn't even broken skin, the damage couldn't have been anything serious, but she was putting on an act so I would feel guilty. I immediately pulled her around, knelt, and kissed the spot.

"There, I kissed your booboo away," I said. "Before I almost killed us all with ice, did you master those skills?" I slapped her ass and jumped away before she could retaliate.

"Umm, master them? Hell, no. But we learned them," she said.

"And managed to do it without harming anyone else," Mabel added.

"Oh, snap!" Chloe cried, and held her hand up. The elf didn't hesitate in dishing out a high five.

"I feel attacked," I said.

"Good. Then we're even."

"So, spells are harder than skills?"

"Yeah, they are," Mabel chimed in. "Spells are harder since they have greater potential. You can create new spells by combining them with elemental affinity. Like your air and fire. But if you try to combine fire and ice, it won't work. And skills, well, they're just that. Skills. You can't do anything special with them. You activate a skill and then you use it."

"Okay. So, that's the difference. And what about you? Did you learn your skill? It was a skill, right?"

Mabel nodded. "Yeah, it was a skill. Only you got a spell this time. And yes, I'm ready. We can go any time you want to. What about you, Chloe?"

"Yeah, I'm good to go. As long as our fearless leader is thawed out, dry, and ready to go, I say we roll out."

"Sorry, I wasn't listening," I said, "I was staring at your pretty ass. Do you think maybe we could cast a spell over it so other guys can't see it? I don't want them checking you out. I'm just a jealous little boy at heart."

"Hah! Did you hear that, Mabel? He basically just called me 'his'! And to think that before I came here, hundreds of men watched me dance, mostly naked on a stage."

"Okay, whatever," I said, waving her off. "Let's all go dungeon diving in thongs, then."

Mabel laughed loudly but caught herself until Chloe chimed in.

"Aww, you'd be so cute in one!" Chloe chirped and jumped me, hooking her legs behind my back. "I fucking like you, you know that? I can't say I love you as it's too early, but shit, I don't want to ever be without you. I think I finally found a guy with *enough* of a sense of humor."

"Hey," Mabel said from behind her. "I like him too, you know? In fact, I met him first... so, that means I have dibs. Is that the word humans use?"

"Whoa, now. Hold your horses, elf girl. Before last night you weren't claiming dibs on anyone. Now, after one rowdy tussle, you're all in on my man here?"

"I don't know what a tussle is, but if you're referring to our coupling last night, then yes," Mabel protested. "I like human men more than elves. They're...weak in bed. They refuse to take charge and be flashy, and fancy. I like a lover that just gets to the point."

"And here we have a male specimen that likes to get to the point!" Chloe whispered, lifting an eyebrow at me. "And speaking of getting to the point. I feel like killing some stuff! Our dungeon awaits."

She hooked Mabel by the arm and quickly pulled her out through the portal. I couldn't help but appreciate their enthusiasm... both for me, and the dungeon-diving distractions of our new world.

We moved directly towards the dungeon portal, emerging into a relatively empty tavern. I couldn't help by smile. I had to be honest, crowds weren't really my thing.

"Hey there, my favorite first years!" Belma said, looking up from a thick, heavily bound book splayed open on the counter.

"At least they are your favorites," Selma said, refusing to turn.

"Hey there, our favorite twins!" I called back and waved. "Well talk to you after. Is that okay?"

"No worries. You can pay when you're done."

"Thanks!"

In all honesty, I was still a bit pissed about my last encounter with them. And it wasn't just their prices, but also that their scrolls seemed to come with far fewer instructions than others. So far, I'd paid more from them for spells and skills that just proved harder to learn. Logic told me that since they were likely to be one of the first to sell to new students, they should be selling parchments with more direction, not less.

We stopped at the portal, and I checked for available formations. They were the same as last time, but that wasn't necessarily a bad thing. I'd take *15%* to attack and *10%* to defense any day.

"Are you girls ready?"

Mabel and Chloe both turned to me at the same time. They nodded, and together we activated the portal and stepped through.

411

Third Dungeon Dive I

THE FIRST THING I DID when I regained my senses was to open the map. Five large red dots hovered in the same places as our last visit. The queen was missing, however, which struck me as odd.

"When we come through the portal, are we joining a new instance of the first dungeon floor?" I asked.

"Maybe. I mean, I'm not sure," Chloe replied, her brow wrinkling.

"I'm not sure either. Why?"

"I've got a hunch," I replied and closed the map, then opened it again. The queen was missing, but a boss was present. The very same one I'd tried to talk that other group of students out of fighting. "Chloe, why don't you buff up and try your new skills. I think we should go somewhere special this time."

"Yeah, sure." I watched her cycle through her buffs, a green, glowing ribbon spiraling around her, then a blue one. She pulled her blade out, then activated her new skill.

Chloe crouched, brought her sword over her shoulder, and focused. Mana surged in her hand, through the handle of her weapon, and in response, the blade glowed gold. She sucked in a breath, stepped forward, and brought the sword down. Except, she disappeared before the blade could drop, and reappeared five paces out in a violent release of spiked mana and cutting steel.

I blinked several times, trying to ward off the afterimage burned into my vision.

"I'd hate to be on the receiving end of that strike. You looked good."

"You can be on the receiving end of something else later," she said, playfully snapping her teeth at me.

"Me next," Mabel said, pushing past Chloe and into the clearing. She readied her zither and traced her fingers along the strings, playing a beautiful chord. Then her fingers went to work, and a violent melody erupted from the instrument. Mana surged through her arms and into the air, a tree nearby exploding in pieces of jagged, splintered wood and shredded leaves.

"Hey! That's even cooler than *my* skill!" Chloe hissed. "Not fair!"

"Wait until you see mine. Stand back, alright?"

The girls took a step back as I created a shard of ice and launched it, the frozen shard hitting the damaged tree with a thud. It felt, looked, and sounded rather anticlimactic, despite the chunk of ice being a good twenty inches long and ten or so thick. But I had an idea and needed to test the theory.

I quickly formed another ice shard, but this time with my left hand, and pulled my pen-blade out of my rift. I imagined a whirlwind, slashed out the glyph into the air, and then combined the two. The wind picked up the ice, instantly fragmenting it into tiny, sharp, cutting fragments. The whirlwind slammed into the tree, the icy fragments ripping it to shreds until it had been reduced to a pile of what looked like mulch.

My eyebrows rose. Even if the damage from a small ice shard was a fraction of the larger piece, I would be multiplying damage by hundreds, no, thousands. Especially if I launched the attack into groups of monsters or enemies. Those that couldn't get out of the way would be shredded.

When I looked around, I found the two staring at me.

"Mr. Pen-Blade," Chloe whispered. Mabel snorted to add emphasis.

"Hey, I didn't choose the weapon affinity, okay? It chose me," I said, and nodded toward the tree wreckage. "It's fortunate for us as a party that the weapon skills merge so effectively with other abilities. But don't worry, we'll get you flashier stuff when we're stronger."

"Ugh," Chloe muttered. "It's not *just* about being flashy. And I don't know if it is *you* or the pen-blade…but you're so good at combining these things."

"Like I said. 'Artist'." I pointed to myself. "I have more than a leg up. You'll get better. Trust me. Come on."

I started walking and the girls fell into step, quickly pulling up beside me. We were several minutes in, and still hadn't seen a single monster. I was already getting antsy. Usually, we'd have fought several groups of them by now. We made it to the crossroads and turned toward the boss but still, nothing. I stopped and considered my map. We could turn and take the other leg south, which would take us to another smaller zone and another big boss.

I looked back at the map, then ahead, and back. My heart started to pound in my chest and sweat formed on my brow. I had no idea what was going on or why I was feeling so weak. My legs started to shake and my hands grew sweaty. It was something… a worry, no, a doubt. I was sure of it. My body was trying to tell me something.

"Isn't that the boss room where that group of beastkin was headed the other day?" Chloe asked, pointing toward the shimmering wall ahead.

"It is. And I have a suspicion they're probably dead in there. I think we spawned inside the same dungeon instance."

"Wait, what?" Mabel said, putting her hands up. "What are you talking about? That isn't supposed to be possible."

414

"I'm not sure either, but I think this instance is either bugged, pardon the pun, or someone is playing games with us."

"What's a...pun?" Mabel asked. "I've never heard the word before."

"It's something from our world... world play between words with multiple meanings, usually," Chloe replied. "But that aside, are you sure? Because that doesn't sound like a small deal."

"Sure? I'm not even sure that this isn't a dream, and I won't wake up in my undies having fallen asleep in front of my TV again, but I do have a nagging feeling. The only way to know for sure is to press on."

"Okay, but you're not going in there alone again," Mabel said, stepping forward. "If something's going to happen, then it's happening to all of us."

I nodded. She was right, especially now that they were stronger. We had a far greater chance of survival if we fought together.

"Alright. The same tactic but stay further behind. Please. You keep each other safe first and then me. We bunched up too tight last time. We can't let a potent area attack affect all of us at once."

"Agreed," Mabel whispered as her arms wrapped around me. Chloe joined immediately and we all held one another. I kissed their foreheads as we all separated.

"Let's go be dungeon-diving legends!" I said, throwing them both an equally nervous and excited smile. I didn't know if I wanted to giggle or pee myself. Maybe both.

We stopped right in front of the shimmering wall separating the two zones. As before, we couldn't see inside, so we had one option: get in there. Nothing would change unless I walked in, so I readied my weapon and stepped through. The transitional tingling filtered over my skin but was quickly replaced with a punch in my guts, knock you down, and scream in your face- welcome to the party realization as a massive, coiling form moved off in the distance. It was big. No, huge.

"JD: Holy shit! What in the hell is that thing?" I cursed in our party chat so they could read before walking in.

"Chloe: What thing? What are you seeing?"

"JD: Huge ass snake! But you can come in, it's far away."

"Mabel: Coming in now."

Chloe appeared first, but Mabel popped in right behind me and ran into my back. They turned forward, saw what I saw, and yelped. I couldn't look away from it, the size, the rippling muscle, and gleaming scales... the sheer violent potential.

NAME: Three-Horned Viper King
TYPE: Zone-Boss
POWER LEVEL: 640
HEALTH: 2,700, **MANA:** 500
ATTACK: 110, **DEFENSE:** 120
WEAKNESS: Fire, Sword

It was a monster in its own right, probably around forty paces long with a body that was as thick as a minivan. Glistening dark green scales covered its body, ending in a strange cobra-like shaped three-horned head. The middle horn was longer than the ones on the side. It was strange seeing a snake with a horn. Almost as strange as picturing a unicorn, honestly, as I couldn't imagine a serpent using it to gore its prey.

"Hey, what's that over there?" Mabel asked as she tugged at my sleeve. I turned away from the snake and followed her arm. The beastkin were still in there, huddled behind a rocky shelf for protection. They looked to be alive from what I could tell at a distance, but beyond that, I would be guessing. Several questions immediately tumbled forth in my mind.

Had they been in here, fighting this entire time?

How in the hell were they still alive, if that was the case?

Did they at least manage to score some loot or new abilities along the way?

"And... if they couldn't defeat the viper king, why didn't they just retreat?" I asked, speaking out loud the last thing that ran through my head. Heh, it's just how I worked.

"I don't think they can," Mabel whispered in response. "I sense many things, monsters hidden in the tall grass. Easily a score of them. Maybe twice that. It is hard to tell."

"Shit," I breathed, scanning the space. The tall grass surrounded the beastkin, filling the space between them and us. It was probably why they hadn't retreated.

"There's not much we can do but work our way forward and take care of the ADDS as quickly as possible. But if we get that viper's attention, it could be all over for us, too." Chloe looked at me, a sudden sparkle shining in her eyes.

"They're hiding in the grass. Grass burns." She stretched her sword arm.

"I like how your mind works. Give me a second to figure out how to use my fire elemental. Then we'll take care of the snake."

I pulled out the last skill parchment and studied the contents.

SKILL NAME: Summon Fire Elemental (B)
TYPE: Summon, Mana, **DURATION**: 60 Minutes
DESCRIPTION: Basic Summoning spell to create a Fire Elemental.
BASIC: +50 Health, +30 Mana on mastery, **STATS:** User x 1.1, Mana: 50
ADVANCED: +100 Health, +60 Mana on mastery, **STATS:** User x 1.4, Mana: 70
MASTER: +200 Health, +120 Mana on mastery, **STATS:** User x 1.7, Mana: 85
NOTE 1: The summoned Fire Elemental lasts for 60 minutes or until killed.
NOTE 2: The user's stats are multiplied with a modifier depending on mastery.
NOTE 3: Summon stays active for 60, 120, and 240 minutes depending on mastery.

To my surprise, all I needed to do was to be of the fifth rank and embed mana into the scroll itself to bring the fire elemental to life. So, I did. The scroll glowed and heated up in my hands, then just a few paces ahead a bright burning ball appeared. Arms and legs poured forth, liquid fire bubbling and searing the air, tendrils of flame arcing out and charring the ground black.

Once fully formed, the elemental looked like a bunch of molten lava rocks arrayed so that it took a vaguely human shape. Arcing, dancing fire connected the individual pieces of its body, save for the largest piece, which I guess you would call its torso. Red-colored mana burned around and inside this seemingly hollow piece, the heat making the eyes set within the stone skull glow.

"Can you hear me?"

It nodded its stony head but didn't speak. I wasn't sure if it could.

"It's kind of cute," Chloe muttered. "I so want to squeeze it but I'm afraid it will burn me."

"Really? You want to hug a fire elemental that's made of magma rocks?"

I chuckled at Chloe's response, but then remembered my spell upgrader. I activated the skill and immediately saw a window appear. All my skills were listed, and strangely all greyed out except for the elemental. I chose the skill and got a new pop-up.

CRYSTAL SACRIFICE TO ADVANCED MASTERY: 0 / 100
NOTE: Core Crystal Rank 1 = 2 points, Rank 2 = 5 points, Rank 3 = 25 points

I checked my crystal stash and nodded. I had enough crystals, but the girls might get pissed if I upgraded it just like that, without asking.

"Before we take this thing on, I think we should upgrade it. It is gonna cost us **100** crystals. Any objections, especially if this thing keeps us alive?"

Chloe and Mabel both nodded their heads. *Perfect.*

I had **66** rank 2 core crystals in my stash and chose 20 of them, then hit the confirmation notice. The elemental suddenly started shuddering and growling as its stone body started to grow.

Instead of having single, rocky stumps for limbs, they now consisted of two parts. Both the arms and the legs. One part resembled the lower arm, from wrist to elbow, and the previous one from the elbow to the shoulder. The same was with the legs. The upper part went down to the knee, and after the fist-sized mana hole, went down to the foot. The elemental still floated but looked more dangerous with jagged pieces of molten rock protruding from its shoulders and the previously stumpy part of the limbs.

The outer, rocky skin suddenly exploded, leaving an imp-like elemental with sharp, pointy ears and a fluffy tail with a spear-spike at the end. Its size changed dramatically, growing to near my height, with thick arms and shorter legs. The tip of its tail even started flickering before a wicked flame rose. The head was now more pronounced with a helmet-like shape. Two black beady eyes stared out at me as I smirked.

"You good?" I asked. "Can you fight?"

The elemental nodded and flapped its stony wings, floating nearly three feet off the ground. I hadn't even noticed them as I'd been focused on its body. Shit, it did look huggable now, but I wasn't going to admit that to Chloe.

"What can it do?" Mabel asked.

"I don't know. I have no idea how to check."

"Aren't they autonomous? I could swear I read that about them in a book," Chloe said. "Back in the library."

"Is that right?" I asked, nodding at Chloe, and then turned back to the elemental. "What she said about you being

419

autonomous?" It nodded and let out a mock-growl. "So, I can tell you what to do and you'll do that to the best of your ability?"

It nodded again.

"We need to give it a name!" Chloe hissed, excitedly. "Oh, what about fireball!"

"You can't call him 'fireball', or you might accidentally launch one at someone else!" Mabel protested.

"That is true. Wait, what about—."

"Pyro. I'm going to name him Pyro," I said, interrupting her before she could get going.

"Yeah, I guess it works," she mumbled, obviously annoyed.

A strange sensation flooded over me, almost as if someone or something was watching and studying me. Like I could feel their gaze on me... physically. I looked around into the distance, but no one was there, save for the viper, the beastkin, and us. And no one was really moving. The beastkin were cowering, or dead, I couldn't really tell, and the viper seemed content to wait for someone to come close enough to eat.

"Pyro: Thank you for naming me. That was the last step to making me fully autonomous."

"Shit, it can talk in party chat!" Chloe whispered and quietly clapped her hands. "I like him even more!"

"Pyro: What do you want me to do?"

"I need you to protect the girls and support me when you can. Your main task is to keep the other monsters away from them. If there are any. Once they're safe, you'll support me to the best of your ability."

"Pyro: Yes, master. As you wish."

I grinned, excited to see our little, floating piece of smoldering flame and lava in action. I felt like a father, watching my magical baby head off for the first day of school. Only it was to fight a massive, venomous snake in a magical dungeon, in a magical tower. So, yeah, similar.

"Why are you so excited?" Chloe chuckled. "It's not like this is your first battle."

"No, it isn't, but he," I said, pointing at Pyro, "is awesome and I can't wait to see him in action. And I want to beat the stuffing out of that snake! And if we can, save those beasties so that big, cocky bastard can admit he was wrong for turning us down. They'll help build our name and brand by spreading the story."

"Our brand?" Chloe snorted, "Next thing, you'll be naming our group and printing it on t-shirts. Go, team!"

"What's holding you up?" Mabel asked. "If you're so fired up, then don't let us hold you back. Let's go beat this snake's stuffing as you said!"

"Close enough, Mabel. Close enough," I said and pulled my pen-blade out and readied myself. The battlefield was a mess, but it had come to a lull. If we were to run in just like that, the ADDS would swarm in, surround us, and the snake would finish us off. We couldn't fight battles on all sides. No, we had to manipulate the battlefield and force the confrontation to our design.

"I destroyed the tree; I'm hoping that means the environment can catch fire and damage the monsters?"

"Yes," Chloe replied. "Let's see those ADDS try and hide in burning grass. Bring on the chaos, baby!"

"Take two of trying to be cool while simultaneously burning down the world. Mabel, hold my beer."

I focused a fireball in my left hand and started drawing a whirlwind glyph. The moment the fireball shot out from my hand, I drew the last line and unleashed the gust of wind. The two combined with the fire spell and created a flaming inferno.

The tall, dry grass and reeds immediately burst into flames, the firestorm throwing heat and scorching embers in a wide swath. The wind swirled in, adding to the destruction and helping to push the firestorm directly at the Viper King.

"Up, up, down, down, high kick," Mabel shouted, and excitedly held her hand up. "Slap hands!"

"I've never been so proud," I said and gave her a high five as a lone tear rolled down my cheek. "You've just made my day, girl!"

421

"JD: I'll wait until the flames are close by and stop it with an ice storm. You need to get into the burned area then."

"Pyro: No need. I'll absorb the fire before it can reach them. It will only make me stronger, anyways."

"JD: Alright, Pyro. I'm trusting you with their lives. And why do you sound so human now?"

"Pyro: We take on our summoner's characteristics."

"Chloe: Shit. If one of him wasn't enough," she mocked.

I winked at her and jumped over the flames in the middle of the path, as they had burned down the fastest and charged right down the smoldering, charred path and moved straight at the three-horned viper. Shapes and forms slithered in all directions, around me, some rising clear of the grass, while others shriveled up and died in the flames before me. Several made it free from the fire and came right at me. They were somewhere between ten inches thick and several paces long, all horns and scales and teeth... but they were all burned or on fire. Damaged and weakened.

I slashed through the first, killing it with a single strike. Two more slithered toward me and slammed into my shield, chipping away at its reserve.

Mana shield has sustained 12 damage.
Mana shield has sustained 21 damage.

They flopped to the ground and twisted their bodies around my legs, trying to crush me as their teeth gnashed at my shield. The damage was racking up quickly and a slight panic set in.

"Fireball."

I slammed my hand into the one and it screeched, slithered away, and died as the flames burned it alive. My blade sliced through the third and then a fourth. More of them were trying to get through the flames, but a sudden ring of fire erupted around them, steadily becoming smaller.

The flames were four feet tall and so hot I had to take a step back. Dozens of snakes hissed and screeched. Or, it could have been the noise of the fire—the hiss, squeals, and pops of the grass, rocks, and sticks as they superheated.

I glanced over at the girls. They seemed all good. Chloe was putting her sword to deadly work, cutting down swarming snakes as they appeared from the grass. She twirled and cut two in half with a single cut, stopped her momentum, and slashed back in the other direction, sending a rippling wave of fire into the grass. Another wide swath of grass went up in flames, the dark, slithering forms hiding in its folds screeching and retreating.

Mabel strummed her zither, a spiraling, green buff enveloping Chloe. Then she abruptly changed her tune, only to have a rock twenty feet to my left explode in a shower of jagged chips and dust. I covered my face and retreated.

"Sorry," Mabel called, "I didn't know it would explode like that."

I couldn't argue with the results. A dozen dead snakes laid within the rock's dusty crater.

"Don't apologize. Keep doing exactly what you are doing! But I need you two to move forward. We need to advance together."

"Got it!" Chloe yelled, casting a wave of fire right into a thigh-thick serpent as it moved to strike Mabel.

I cut down a small snake as it lunged at my feet and turned to the beastkin. By now, we'd garnered their attention, so I waved my hands and shouted, "Advance with us! I can't protect you if you stay out there!"

"We're coming!" their leader roared, his voice carrying. But the swarming snakes abruptly changed directions, now moving directly towards the other group.

"Pyro, can you help them?"

"Pyro: I can, master. Give me a moment."

I watched as a massive infernal ring blossomed, first glowing on the ground near the beastkin, and then erupting in tall, mana-infused flames. I closed the distance and launched an air slash at the ring, fanning the flames and creating a safe entry point. Two of the stronger fighters grabbed the wounded and immediately pulled them into the protective circle. Once the wounded were safely inside, Pyro lifted his rocky arms into the air, and the fire crept outward, closing the gap.

Third Dungeon Dive II

THE THREE-HORNED VIPER UNCOILED as we pushed closer, the light from the burning grass reflecting eerily in its large green eyes. Its forked tongue flicked out into the air, tasting our presence as it sized us up. It repelled from the light but then abruptly launched itself forward. I swallowed hard, just as the enormous snake spewed thick poison into the air, the liquid dousing some of the flames. But a magical gust of wind hit and fanned the flames, pushing them into new, dry grass.

"I'm controlling this battlefield," I said, as the snake recoiled and hissed at the new fire blocking its path.

I darted off to the right and it moved to track me, leading the viper away from the girls and the beastkin as I held my pen-blade to the side. *Mana Infusion.*

"JD: Can you get this thing's attention? I want to hit it with something, but don't want to get my face bit off."

"Chloe: No problemo, Amigo!"

"Chloe: Pyro, can you hit that thing with a fireball?"

"Pyro: Of course, I can."

I watched Chloe sprint through the grass behind and to my left, and the fire elemental float behind and to my right.

Four.

Three.

I counted down mentally, timing my movements and my attack for just the right time. The viper king watched me, but tracked Chloe, and Pyro, too, seemingly indecisive as to who was the bigger threat.

Chloe cast her fire wave, right after Mabel's buff lit her up like a Christmas tree, then Pyro surged brightly and cast a streaking fireball. The fireball hit first, heat splashing over the viper's side and pushing it left. It tried to streak out of the way of Chloe's wave, but that forced it to move, right at me.

I charged in as the mana ball gathered in my blade and then formed along the edge, spreading out to form a thin mass of power that would add strength and cutting ability.

"Mana Discharge!"

I jumped through the raging fire, my mana shield taking the damage and I struck hard, my pen-blade hitting the creature's nose. The built-up mana discharged in a flash of light, heat, and ear-popping sound, shredding the skin and scales on contact.

SKILL USED: Mana Discharge
MANA USED: 25
DAMAGE DEALT: 261

The viper reared back, shuddered, and shook its massive head, one of its fangs falling free in the process. A massive fireball struck its neck, burning right through the outer scales. Flames seared the flesh beneath, forcing the boss into a ground-shaking roll.

"JD: Keep it up. Hit hard with everything you have. Don't let it regroup or go on the offensive."

"Sword Aura!"

I cursed under my breath as Chloe got in way too close, sending another blow amplified with mana and the fire element. It exploded against the viper's scales, sending it crashing into the ground.

Several debuffs hit the Viper King one after the other. *Ooze, Debilitate,* and *Malice.* Pyro sent out another *Fireball* that hit its stomach area and immediately burned through the tough skin, exposing charred, oozing flesh.

Chloe used her mana flash and disappeared, only to reappear in an angry, blinding flash of mana right next to the viper's head. I saw her appear, saw the mana-infused attack and gleam of her blade, and the whole snake shook. She immediately ducked a bite and retreated as Mabel's zither music turned sinister. Numerous snares appeared, erupting from the ground and wrapping around the snake's body—her offensive skill, playing as an undercurrent of different notes, slashing into the scales and the skin beneath, digging deep.

All of that happened in a flurry of movements and brought the boss's health down to a hair under **1,000**.

"We're almost there!" I yelled. "Keep at it! Pyro! Pull back! Take care of the small serpents. Keep them off our backs!"

He flew off like a jet, propelling himself by using fire, and landed amidst the smaller vipers. A ring of flame appeared over him and dropped on the snakes, burning them to cinders. Dozens of vipers died in mere seconds. Then we watched as our friendly neighborhood elemental guided the burning ring over to envelop the Three-Horned Viper King's snared body, immediately burning part of the tail.

"Pyro: I have no more mana. All I can do now is melee."

"JD: You did more than enough. Retreat and protect Mabel."

"Pyro: Yes, Master. I will protect Mabel."

Chloe moved in next to me.

"What do you say, love?" she laughed. "Want to finish this thing?"

Movement off to my left caught my attention and just then I noticed three of the beastkin heading straight toward the boss snake. They were only thirty feet out and going straight at the viper, their claws bared.

427

"You all had your chance," I yelled, pointing my blade at them. "Stay back and let us finish our work or you'll have to fight us next."

"You won't kill us! You're a good man!" the big guy yelled back, a feral snarl exposing the tips of his fangs.

I liked to think of myself as a good man, but even good men could be pushed to do bad things. We weren't back on Earth anymore. The stakes were raised, and there was no guarantee Chloe, Mabel, and I would survive the first year at Zenith. Not unless we cultivated enough strength to make it happen. This viper was a big kill, and no one would blame me for fighting to protect our victory.

Plus, we pretty much saved their asses from getting eaten, so... our kill.

"Air Slash!"

I sent two hits his way, making sure one missed wide, while the second caught him right in the chest and blew him off his feet. The others stopped, but I didn't have time to waste on them. Chloe was already standing right next to the viper, hacking at the beast to finish it off. I looked at its health and saw it was down to **398...364...301.**

I whooped and charged in, sending another air slash its way, and noticed I was pretty close to having used most of my own mana pool. If it came down to a fight with the other students, I would need some in reserve.

The Viper finally reared up, having broken free from Mabel's snares and recovered from the burning flames. It surged off the ground and towered above us. Several of its scales started glowing and then blasted toward us, hitting me straight in the face, or rather my mana shield.

Mana shield has sustained 103 damage.

The impact knocked me off my feet, despite the attack not having gone through my mana shield. Either way, I felt it. Chloe hadn't been so fortunate. She lay on the ground a dozen paces away, clutching what I was sure was a broken arm.

A burning chunk of magma flew past me and struck the Viper King's throat, instantly melting through its skin and passing through its neck, only to erupt out the back side. The massive serpent bent in on itself and dropped on its back, its skin going opaque.

I turned to find Pyro floating towards me, with Mabel at its side. One of the elemental's arms was missing a segment.

"Did you launch your hand at it?"

"Pyro: Yes. I did not have enough mana for a fireball. I'm sorry. I thought you were in danger."

"JD: Don't apologize, you did better than expected. I think you helped more than you realize."

I let out a pent-up breath and stumbled over to the boss's corpse, looting it with a raised hand. To my surprise, all of the snakes and their loot suddenly appeared in my rift. Now we wouldn't have to walk around and loot the smaller snakes, or at least those that were still salvageable.

ITEMS RECEIVED:
Horned Viper: 83
Core crystal Rank 1: 141
Core crystal Rank 1: 37
Fres: 9,627
Three-Horned Viper King's Reverse Scale Pendant: 1
Viper Scale Earrings: 1
Viper Wristbands: 1

SPECIAL ITEMS RECEIVED:
Three-Horned Viper King Belt: 1
Three-Horned Viper King Core: 1
Three-Horned Viper King Ink Pouch: 2

I read the ink pouch's description, interested to see if it was the same kind of upgrade material I needed for my pen-blade.

NAME: Three-Horned Viper King Ink Pouch
TYPE: Upgrade Material
DESCRIPTION: Ink Pouch taken from a Three-Horned Viper King.
Used in upgrading certain weapons like the Pen-Blade and the Quill-Blade.
STATS: *+15* Attack from rank 6-10

My heart skipped a beat, both because I knew that I had more upgrade material that would up my attack power, and because I was short 2 ink pouches to get up to the required upgrade so I could use them. I'd have to ask around and see if anyone got some pouches once we were done here.

We got four items aside from the usual, which was surprisingly good in my eyes. Any piece of equipment we looted was a step closer to getting where we needed to be, even if those items weren't as good. If they weren't items someone in the party could use, we'd sell them, baby!

"What about us?" the beastkin leader asked, startling me from my thoughts. I raised my weapon, but the girls and Pyro were already there.

"You? What does that mean? I'm sorry if this comes off a bit dense, but the way I see it, we saved your lives. There is no greater gift a person can receive than that of continued existence."

"How dare you speak to me like that? I am royalty!"

I turned and pointed at the viper king's corpse, "Did it care that you are royalty?"

The beastkin begrudgingly followed my pointing arm and looked at the massive, dead snake. The one that had very nearly killed him and his group. But he refused to answer me.

"I tried to warn you before you came in here. And I didn't do it to steal your spoils, or tag along and gain a little bit of experience.

We weren't sure you all knew what you were walking into and wanted to make sure none of you got hurt. And what did you say to me?"

I knew exactly what he'd said, as his voice and condescension still burned fresh in my mind. But he still didn't answer. Still wouldn't admit his arrogance and pride had gotten his people hurt. Or, worse, killed. How was I to know if one of his party members was laying still and cold somewhere in the scorched grass?

"So, to answer your question, me. I have the right to talk to you like that, you arrogant prick. And I hope your party members do, too. I hope they scream at you and kick your ass." I got right up into his face and jabbed a finger into his chest. Truly a chore, as he was more than a head taller than me. He backed away a step, his ears lowering.

I walked back over to my group, face hot, and hands balled up into fists. I'd wanted to hit him but knew that kind of violence would probably hurt less than the truth, and I already threw that in his face. I pulled the accessories out first, hopeful they would be half-decent. After all, this was a high-ranking boss when it came to the first floor. I wanted good gear so I could compete with the damned royals.

NAME: Three-Horned Viper King's Reverse Scale Pendant
TYPE: Accessory, Necklace
POWER LEVEL: 44, **SLOTS:** 1/1
DESCRIPTION: Necklace made from a King Viper's reverse scale.
STATS: Health + 40, Defense + 40
SPECIAL: Reflect + 30 Poison Damage when receiving damage every second for five seconds. Poison damage is stackable.

The pendant was really something. For someone who would be receiving constant damage, a pendant like that was incredible. You could put someone out front, and see the enemy try to hit them, only to inflict poison damage back on themself. Now if we had an item or weapon that could prolong the duration or cause additional poison damage…shit. It made me want to be a tank.

The earrings were next.

NAME: Viper Scale Earrings
TYPE: Accessory, Earrings
POWER LEVEL: 24, **SLOTS:** 1/2
DESCRIPTION: Earrings made from a viper's scales.
STATS: Health + 40, + 20 Defense
SPECIAL: Reduces Poison duration and damage by 50%.

The earrings were nothing to write home about. They would benefit someone with the extra stats they offered, but even if they were nothing special, whenever an item added a 10% or higher boost in a single stat, it was worth keeping.

Two more items to go, and the first were the wristbands.

NAME: Viper Wristbands
TYPE: Armor
POWER LEVEL: 54
DESCRIPTION: Wristbands made from tough viper skin found beneath the scales.
HEALTH: 50, **MANA:** 20
ATTACK: 20, **DEFENSE:** 20
MANA SHIELD: 50

I was happy with the wristbands. No special traits, but the stats they added were more than sufficient. I put them away and pulled out the main item next: the belt.

NAME: Three-Horned Viper King Belt
TYPE: Armor, Set Item
POWER LEVEL: 80

DESCRIPTION: A belt made from the tough skin beneath the Viper King's Armored scales.
HEALTH: 100, **MANA:** 50
DEFENSE: 50, **MANA SHIELD:** 100
SPECIAL: Set item 1/2. Adds + 20 Poison damage for 5 seconds on hit. Stackable.

"Alright, so, I'm at a loss on what to do with the items. They're...pretty good." I held them out for the girls to see, and they studied them.

"Can we make suggestions?" Chloe asked. "Otherwise, I think we might be sitting here for a while."

I nodded. "Sure. Hit me."

"So, I'd like the earrings, and maybe Mabel should get the wristbands. The belt and pendant probably make sense for you if we don't recruit a tank. What do you think?"

"Well, I'd be more than happy to get either the earrings or the wristbands," Mabel said, scratching her chin. "Boosting stats should be a priority and they all do that one way or another."

"Alright," I replied and handed them the two items. I equipped the pendant and the belt and immediately felt a short surge of power pass through me. I grinned as I thought about all the poison damage I'd do when we came upon enemies who liked to get their hands dirty.

Chloe took the earrings and put them on immediately while Mabel fitted the wristbands. They disappeared, though. I had no idea why, or how, and truth be told, I didn't care. They didn't exactly match her outfit, so it was for the best.

The young feline-beastkin from the first time we met coughed to draw my attention. I turned around and waited to hear what she'd have to say.

"Sir JD, do you have a moment?"

I almost snorted. The sound of "Sir" before my name just sounded ridiculous. But her face was pale and her eyes bloodshot, which tempered my attitude more than a little. She looked to be in a great deal of pain.

"I would like to thank you for helping us, despite our... shortcomings. You saved our lives, so if I can ever be of help in the future, please seek me out. He will never admit it, but we are a proud people that still try to walk an honorable path. A debt now exists between us, one I *will* see repaid."

I put on as genuine a smile as possible, which was hard as her leader sulked and stared at the ground. *Proud? More like arrogant.*

"You should steer clear from guys like that. If I'd been an evil dude or mad about your attack, I could have easily hurt you and blamed it on the viper. Weak leaders just get other people killed."

"I know, please, I mean *we* know. Things happen and yeah... things just happened."

"Take care next time," I said, and turned my back on the group of beastkin, then strolled over to my girls and started making our way out of the zone.

The next smaller boss was in that direction, and I wanted to get to it and do some scouting before anyone else decided on throwing monkeys at our wrenches. Sure, the dungeon instance might have been bugged, but it might also have been purely by coincidence. I'd have to ask Scarlet about it.

"Mabel: What else did you get from the snakes and the boss?"

"JD: A lot of corpses, some crystals, and upgraders for my weapon. Want anything?"

"Mabel: No, I don't. You'll feed and clothe us anyway so it's not like I need anything. You're pretty lucky with the upgrader materials though."

"JD: Pretty much, but fortune favors the bold. We'll keep pushing forward and eventually pick up stuff for your zither and Chloe's sword."

A shout echoed behind us, and I jerked to a halt. We spun only to find beastkin were already busy fighting a bunch of respawned vipers. Damn, that was fast. Was it supposed to happen that fast?

I thought they'd go home the moment we saved them, but they weren't interested in doing so, apparently. I opened my map to check if everything was still in order and only saw four large dots. The Venus Queen hadn't respawned and neither had the Viper King. So, why were the smaller serpents coming back?

"Hey, did you hear that?" Mabel asked, suddenly.

"Where, what? Over there from that trunk?" Chloe asked, following the elf's gaze.

"I thought I heard someone." She immediately moved off the trail, creeping towards a grove of trees.

"No, I... wait," I said, running to catch up.

I trusted the elf's hearing more than my own, so I followed her closely to a broken tree trunk. She searched it for a moment, before putting her weight into it. The trunk suddenly shifted and fell over.

"Shit, is that a hidden entrance?" Chloe said excitedly. "More treasure?"

"Do treasures cry or groan," I replied, now hearing what Mabel had heard from the trail. "Get back, I'll cut through the bush."

I lifted my pen-blade, but Pyro stopped me.

"Pyro: I feel a life source there. It's not a beast."

"JD: Are you sure? Is it human like me?"

"Pyro: No, but it is similar. Very similar."

I immediately stashed my blade away. "Is anyone there? Can you hear me? Can you respond?"

A whimper sounded from beyond the brush, weak and strangled. Then it gained a bit of strength.

"Help!"

I stepped in and started pulling the bush apart, scratchy branches clawing at my robes. I broke a few branches, stepped on others, but finally pulled myself in far enough to see... someone. I froze. It was the red-haired giantess. She was curled up in the dirt, half-covered with debris, and shaking badly. Large dark-blue splotches marred her skin where the vipers had ravaged her. Blood crusted half her face, and one leg was swollen and bent at an odd angle. I didn't know how she'd gotten in that spot, or how she'd gotten in such a terrible state, but shit. She evidently possessed an iron will to survive.

"Mabel! Get in here. We need you!"

Mabel ran in without hesitation, while Chloe pushed up against me to see what was going on. The elf adeptly picked her way through the brush and knelt next to Skadi. She pressed her palms against the larger woman's back and a green healing wave immediately passed between them. I watched Skadi's body start to glow as Mabel's magic ate away at the poison. Mabel suddenly cried out and threw her hands up.

"She's... so heavily poisoned that... some passed to me."

"Damn it!" I cursed. "Give Mabel the earrings, hurry!"

Chloe unequipped them and then let Mabel put them on. The poison dissipated within seconds then she healed herself once to bring her health back up.

"Umm, how do I make her equip the earrings? She's unconscious. And her ears aren't pierced."

"Make holes for them," Chloe said.

"What? Are you serious?"

"If it comes down to her getting her ears pierced or dying, which one do you think she'd pick?"

"Good point," I said, pulled my pen-blade free, and moved in. I brought the tip of the blade to her earlobe, but couldn't push it through, no matter how hard I tried. Skadi suddenly stirred and her eyes fluttered open.

"Hey there, red. You might want to equip these earrings before you pass out again. Ugh, or die," I whispered.

"You sure? I might not give them back," she replied weakly. "They look purdy."

I snorted, as they weren't pretty at all. "Just put them on already, funny girl. You've got a lot of poison flooding your body right now. I kind of like to see you survive."

"Wait, what?" she muttered and pushed herself up in a sitting position. "Then I would be able to thank you for saving me."

She equipped the earrings and immediately started to waver. We watched as greenish poison trickled out through the bite wounds on her arms and legs. It pooled on the ground, mixing with the dirt, and killing the grass.

"Is she going to be alright?" Chloe asked. "Shit, that looks really nasty!"

I almost told her to get back and stay away from the poison, but she was already inching away from the muddy puddle.

"I think she will be okay," Mabel said, "Once her health is recovered. Most of the poison is already gone." The elf pushed another healing spell into Skadi, bringing her health up.

A few minutes later, Skadi pushed herself up and stood on weak legs. But she could stand. Most of the bruising was starting to disappear as well. Mabel healed her yet again, bringing some healthy color back to the giantess.

"Shit! Fuck, that hurt!" Skadi cursed. "Thick-skulled idiots got themselves killed and I barely escaped!"

"Who did? Your party?"

She nodded and spat another wad of blood. "Yeah, I joined a random group so I could do some diving. Those bastards tricked me. I just wanted to tag along, but they actually joined me as a permanent member of their party. Can you believe that shit? I'm debuffed now because of them, and unless I find a new party within **24** hours, I'll permanently lose my party bonuses."

"Shit, that's... not good," I said, looking over at Chloe and Mabel. None of them said anything since they didn't want to be rude. "What's the penalty?"

"It says that I'll have a permanent *-10%* to all stats."

"Chloe: Fuck no! I'm not sharing you with another one. Especially her. Please don't ask this of me!"

"Mabel: I don't care, but she's a tank from what I can see. And she's already said that she wants to join our party. Isn't that a

win/win situation? I mean, I just don't want to room with people that don't want to be there, or that don't like me."

"Chloe: More like a Win / Loss situation! More time with others means less time with me!"

"JD: If that's all you're worried about, I can make it clear I'm not interested in her like that."

"Chloe: Oh? Are you sure? Just look at that thick ass and those big tits. She already told you that her people view sex as a full-contact sport. And let's be honest, our dorm room has already proved to be a high-action zone."

"JD: I'm not looking to shack up with every girl I meet."

"Chloe: Oh?" She smirked between sentences. "Fine, but if you go back on your word I'm leaving. If she proves to be a good chick, sure, we can figure something out, but it's too early to just pass you around like a dildo."

"Are you guys alright? You're staring off into space," Skadi asked.

"Yeah, sorry. We were thinking about it, and we've agreed to offer you sanctuary... if you can promise to behave and pull your weight," I explained.

"My weight?" she asked and then frowned. "Is that supposed to be a jab at my size?"

"Huh? No, it's just a saying...?" Chloe asked, putting herself between the giantess and me. "Yeah, sure, you're thick but like sexy-thick, not bad-thick."

"Hah! I was just kidding!" Skadi laughed.

"See? She's just like a freaking kid," Chloe hissed and turned to stare at me. "Her word might not mean much."

"Hey!" Skadi said, her smile disappearing. "We love to joke, but a word is everything to my people! I would sooner break my own arms and legs than break my word."

"And who are your people?" I asked. "I'm not from around here so I have no idea."

"We are the sons and daughters of Ymir!"

"Ymir? The Jötunn? Norse mythology?" Chloe asked. She watched the giantess with a completely different expression. Admiration? Reverence? Surprise?

"What is Norse mythology?" Mabel asked. "I've never heard about it."

"Never mind," I chimed in. "We'll fill you in later. If we're talking about the same Jötunn, they are an incredibly proud and strong race."

"Mabel: What are the Jötunn?"

"JD: Norse mythology. Frost Giants. The ones that fought the Aesir Gods. You know? Odin and Thor? Legendary gods from my world. Maybe others too?"

"We are a proud race, JD. When I make a promise on my ancestry, I keep it. So, what is it? Just speak it and I will make it so."

"Life in our dorm has been... interesting," I said, pausing as I tried to describe our housing arrangement. Things had been less complicated before the other night when Mabel thanked me. "Chloe is my... woman, and Mabel is, well, she's kind of in the process of becoming one, too. Unless they give their blessing, you are not to make any romantic or sexual advances on me. And you're to be loyal to the whole party, not just me."

"Yeah, what he said," Chloe added. "No fucking JD unless I say so."

Skadi shrugged and then nodded as if she'd expected something more serious. "I can live with that, so here. I, Skadi Medvarna, promise not to make any inappropriate advances on anyone from the party, and that I will do my best to stay loyal to all of you as long as it doesn't lead to my death."

"Satisfied?" I asked as Chloe looked from the giant to me. She nodded.

I did the one thing left and sent her an invitation to our party. The odd, pleasurable, almost orgasmic sensation rippled through me again, and I felt a boost kick into our stats, at least in the **Health** and **Defense** departments.

439

I opened the party menu, just to see what her power level was. Surviving so many snakebites already told me she wasn't a pushover, but I wanted to know exactly what we'd added.

NAME: James (JD) Wright
POWER LEVEL: 819
CULTIVATION: Realm 1, Rank 5

NAME: Chloe Sullivan
POWER LEVEL: 343
CULTIVATION: Realm 1, Rank 4

NAME: Mabel Karash
POWER LEVEL: 313
CULTIVATION: Realm 1, Rank 4

NAME: Skadi Medvarna
POWER LEVEL: 620
CULTIVATION: Realm 1, Rank 4

"Huh, you're rank four as well," I said, not hiding my surprise. "And here I was thinking you were just a big talker."

"A—big talker? I am a giantess. Should I talk small? Just because I look good doesn't mean I can't fight!"

"I can see that. You're still full of viper bites, though," I chuckled and crossed my arms. "You're interesting, and I think we'll get along just fine... as long as you behave, don't eat all the food in the fridge, and work on behalf of the team."

"I eat surprisingly reasonable meals, thank you very much," she said, putting her hands on her hips.

"Good," Chloe said, tracing her index finger along Skadi's jaw. "There are a few things you'll learn very quickly about our little group. JD here is very direct most of the time. Mabel is adorable and painfully naive. And me? Well... I'm me. So far we've worked very well together."

440

Skadi didn't appear to know how to respond, so she looked away and pushed out her chest.

"Skadi, how much health and defense do you have?" I asked, changing the subject. "You're a tank, right?"

She nodded and her confusion turned into a smile. Her eyes sparkled.

"I've got a little under **2000** Health and just over **200** Defense. No gear at all. That is why I joined that group for this dive. They promised me gear in exchange for my help."

"Right. That is impressive if I may say so. You people are well known for your constitution! And what about skills? What can you do?"

"We are, yes. Our bodies are turned into mountains, transformed into the very rock from which our ancestors sprang. We can withstand punishment and barely feel any pain," she said proudly.

Well, it was something to be proud of in my book.

"As for my skills, I've got two. **Provoke** and **Taunt**. Provoke makes everything in a certain radius go bat-shit crazy for me, while Taunt does the same thing but only to a single enemy."

"Interesting. What else?"

She shrugged. "Nothing really. I fight with my fists, elbows, knees, and feet."

"Wait, that's really it?" Chloe asked.

I wanted to remind her that she only had a single skill before I bought the others, but then thought better of it. You didn't give a woman a gift and then remind her about it as leverage. Ever.

"It doesn't matter. We'll get her the buff skills you're using and check in with the peddler in the bazaar and see what's available for her discipline.

"So, what now?" Skadi asked. "Do we go home and celebrate. My people have a tradition of going swimming naked in icy lakes. It is how we bond. Or do we kill some monsters?"

"No skinny dipping for now," I replied, though inside I felt a bit disappointed. Despite Chloe's objections, I was fascinated with the idea of getting her naked.

"I think maybe we'd be better served to let you heal up. Remember, there is always tomorrow."

A Bit of Payback

"So, where are we going next?" Mabel asked. "Where's the next boss?"

"We go over there," I said, pointing toward a narrow trail, encroached on all sides by thick brush. "It leads us to a large empty space, and from there we can get to another smaller boss before we have to fight another bigger one."

"Great!" Skadi laughed. "I'm all good again. My health is almost back up and by the time we're there, my mana will be, too."

"Right, but before we go, here."

I handed everyone beast crystals and wrapped my hand around one as well, drawing on it just to freshen up. The girls whispered and chatted behind me, but as soon as I moved into the narrow passage, I lost track of everything, save what lay before us. The next zone was filled with flies. Flies as far as the eye could see.

"Eww, that's so freaking disgusting!" Chloe groaned, pressing into me from behind. "Just look at them!"

"Yeah, they sure... don't look that appealing. And think, where there are flies, there is usually..."

443

'Don't you dare finish that phrase," Chloe snapped, "Nope-nope-nope."

"There is what?" Mabel asked, innocently.

"Do we have any area of effect skills?" Skadi asked as she stretched her arms.

"We can create one, but they're spread too far out," I replied as I glanced over at Chloe. "You're good to cast Aura?"

She nodded.

"Yeah, I'm full again. You want to create an inferno and burn us a path?"

"Yeah, but they'll just swarm back in and replace the dead ones."

"Let me help," Skadi said. "I'll use skill and gather them all around me, then use your attack. But you'd better not kill me in the process. I don't want to almost die twice in a single day. "

"How do we do that without you getting burned by the fire?"

"Oh, as long as I get clear quickly, I won't. See, after I get hit by any kind of physical or magical attack, I become invulnerable for five seconds."

"Is that an innate ability? Or a skill?"

Skadi scratched her nose and shrugged, her short red hair bobbing around her head.

"I don't know what an innate ability is, but this skill is something I gained when I came of age. We call them racial traits, but they are probably the same thing."

"That is interesting," I whispered. "We can use that to create so many scenarios to lure and kill large groups of monsters... as long as we're careful about getting you out of the way in time."

"Yeah, that's pretty neat. Why don't you just run on out there, I, uh, want to see you in action?" Chloe said, her gaze stuck on Skadi's impressive cleavage.

"Why are you staring at my chest like that?" Skadi asked, taking a step away. "I don't like girls like that."

444

"Who said I was into you?" Chloe protested. "I'm just a fan of anatomy, that's all. And from one woman to another, I can appreciate a rockin' pair of breasts. Man, those are impressive."

Skadi lifted her eyebrows, pulled her top up self-consciously, and ran off. She wove through the throng of flies and stopped when she was right in the thick of them, surrounded on all sides by dark clouds of buzzing creatures. Then, she spread her arms and shouted something in a tongue I didn't recognize. A red glow appeared in a circle around her, at least forty to fifty yards in diameter, and the flies instantly responded. The swarms buzzed angrily and moved, flowing towards her. She ran around a large tree and a rock, shaking them off as her aura faded.

"Skadi: I'll get the second group next. These suckers won't stay still for long, so make sure you are ready."

"JD: Coming."

"Chloe: Oh, look, she knows how to use party chat!"

"JD: Chloe, stop antagonizing."

I ran into the space as Skadi prepared to gather the rest of the flies. The girls followed.

"Ow, they bite!" Chloe gasped, after slapping her arm hard. I turned to find her wiping the messy remains of a dark fly from her hand. A small, red welt had already appeared on her left arm. She looked up to our giantess friend, now being swarmed by unfathoMabel clouds of the beasts. I had a feeling she'd respect Skadi more after we were done.

The glowing red aura appeared again, and the flies started to converge. She jogged back toward the first group, passively swatting the pests away from her face. I looked down at Chloe's welt and cringed, then checked Skadi's health. It hadn't wavered, not even a little.

"I'll target the center the moment she's in range," Chloe said as she pushed me forward. "You need to get in closer. We want our inferno to form as close to the swarm as possible, otherwise, the heat might make them scatter."

"Good call," I said and moved forward.

"Guys! Come on!" Mabel hissed. "She's almost there!"

I ran toward the swarm just as I felt a wave of heat blossom behind me. The aura attack came in hard and fast as I stopped just within striking distance of Skadi's gathered swarm. I pulled my weapon up and traced the familiar ink lines for a tornado glyph. It glowed to life and the wind kicked up, combining with the passing flames to create our telltale inferno.

Struck by sudden inspiration, I drew two more glyphs, one to the left of the inferno and one to the right, but reversed them, so the rotations would spin inwards, towards the fire. They ripped forward, swirling quickly past the firestorm, and as I'd hoped, caught the flies that tried to escape and flung them back into the fiery storm.

"Hah! Now that was a kick!" Skadi laughed as she jogged back to us. Mabel healed her as she knelt to catch her breath. I studied the giantess, only to find that her clothes were singed and burnt in several places. A patch on her left thigh, one on her belly, and a third on her right shoulder. The fabric had been burned clear through, showing skin beneath.

"You need new clothes," Chloe chuckled as she pointed at her stomach, but then frowned. "Shit, just look at those abs. I need to start working out more."

"Oh, I love to exercise. I will help you work out," Skadi said.

"It all depends," Chloe paused, "Are we talking about lifting weights, running, and pushups, or the kind of physical games you told JD about. I think both could be fun."

Skadi's cheeks reddened a bit. "You are a horny girl."

"I would categorize it as a healthy drive for a woman my age."

"Ahh! Stop it, Chloe. You're going out of your way to make her uncomfortable."

"It's not really out of my way..." she grumbled, as I walked off to gather all the loot from the flies dropped. There was nothing left of them, not opaque bodies, or mounds of ash, just a single pile of loot.

ITEMS RECEIVED:
Swapper Fly: 41
Core crystal Rank 1: 14
Core crystal Rank 2: 2
Fres: 3,122

I stared at the loot notification and tried to speak, but I couldn't. Almost 3,122 Fres from a single used skill. Or rather five used skills if you wanted to be precise, but this was insane. Just how much did people earn in the higher dungeons if this was the kind of loot that dropped on the first floor?

"Now that Skadi has joined, we need to look into upgrading our dorm a little more," I said as I walked back to the girls. They didn't respond, and only when I turned did I realize they were fighting... wrestling? Then Chloe laughed. "What—is going on?"

"Get her... off of me! Please!" Chloe gasped, looking to me for help. Her face was flushed red.

"I called her bluff," Skadi said, pinning Chloe to the ground, then proceeded to tickle her in increasingly sensitive spots. "I told her that wrestling was the best form of exercise, and she said she was game anytime. So, I decided to see if she was all talk or not. She has many weak spots."

"Weak spots?" Chloe asked, laughing and trying to push the bigger girl's hands away. "I'm ticklish, you maniac."

"And now I know," Skadi said and pushed off to stand, leaving Chloe curled up into the fetal position on the ground. "What did you just say about upgrading the dorms?"

"We're about **50** rank 1 crystal cores short," I said after taking a look in my rift. "It's pretty doable if we find another boss or a few spawns like the flies."

"I have **70** on me," Skadi said and dusted her rear off with a surprisingly loud smack. Honestly, it almost made my ass sore, too. "I don't mind pitching in, since it will benefit me as well."

"It will indeed," I replied. "We only have one bedroom right now, so we need a room for you and—."

"And what?" she asked with a raised eyebrow.

"We might be having another party member soon. He's a mabiju."

Skadi snorted and laughed once—a loud, almost barking noise. "Are you sure? They're known to be odd. Also, untrustworthy. But strong."

"Yeah, strong," I replied and pushed both hands through my hair. "I don't know, but he seemed alright. He's a loner as well and…well, yeah. He killed a much stronger mabiju without any issues."

"Right. But is this a done deal?" she asked just as Chloe snaked around her and jammed her hand inside Skadi's waistband. The giantess lunged aside and hid behind me.

"Stop it or I'll punch you!"

"I deserve a rematch. You took me off guard," Chloe said.

"Enough! Chloe, you called out a giantess, and she owned your butt. Save that for later, when we're not tromping around a dungeon. Then again, you might want to rethink it. She's more than your match."

Chloe leaned in and whispered into my ear. "She tickled me so hard I almost peed. Is it weird that it turned me on?"

I laughed. "It is a little. Yeah. But just a little."

"Let's kill our next boss and move to the next one. And stop harassing her, Chloe. We're not out on a picnic," Mabel said, snorting impatiently.

Chloe looked stung, turning from the elf to me.

"Don't look at me," I said, defensively. "She's not wrong. We're not on a picnic."

I readied my pen-blade and turned around, only to find Pyro hovering a few feet away. I had almost completely forgotten he was there. I also had no idea if he understood anything that was going on. A large part of me hoped that he couldn't, as we were undoubtedly putting on the wrong kind of show.

"Come on, Pyro. Let's get a move on."

"Pyro: Yes, master."

448

We stopped at the crossroads, where we could simply turn left to leave the dungeon or continue straight to the unexplored zones. I pulled up my map and studied it. A fork in the road sat just a ways ahead. The path to the right led to a bigger boss, while the straight leg of the path would take us to a smaller, weaker opponent. It wasn't even a question at this stage, as I wanted to give Skadi a bit more time to see how we worked as a team before we tackled the stronger zone bosses or the floor boss.

"As long as everyone is up to it, we're going to bypass the floor boss and take on the last zone over there," I said, pointing at the shimmering wall in the distance. "Same tactic, but with the addition of Pyro and Skadi. She'll keep the monster's focus on her, while we stack as much damage as possible. Only use skills without an area of effect, so we don't hit her as well."

"Alright," Chloe replied. "Then I can only use Mana Flash. My aura does deal some splash damage. That's going to limit me on how much I can do."

"I can focus my attack on a single target, though. So, I should be good," Mabel added.

"I will get right up in their face to use my fists and feet!" Skadi laughed and slammed her right fist into her left palm. The impact was impressive, and at that moment, I appreciated her for the brawler she was. *Welcome to the party!*

I opened my map one last time to confirm nothing had changed, only to see our target boss blink out of existence.

"Shit biscuits," I cursed, "Someone just killed the boss."

"How?" Chloe asked, pulling her map up. "There shouldn't be anyone else in this instance. Fuck, you're right. It *is* gone."

"Maybe we should check it out," Mabel suggested. "This floor has already been glitchy, as you said, JD. Maybe it just hid or something."

"It can't hurt to check it out."

We approached the shimmering barrier to the next zone just as a small group exited and walked right at us. They didn't look dramatically stronger, but there was definite discipline in their

449

demeanor and how they moved. And as icing on top of the cake, their group was a mixture of blood and dark elves. *Great.*

"The boss is already dead, human," the lead elf in their group said as he tried to push past me. His blood-red hair and pointy ears immediately irritated me.

"Yeah, thanks," I muttered and turned to leave.

"Hey, wait up. Is that Mabel?" another elf in their party asked, leaning around me and pointing at her.

"It is none of your business," I said, moving to once again block my friend.

"Oh? And I guess that makes you what, JD the Destroyer?" the young blood elf laughed.

"Destroyer?" I asked.

The small group continued to chuckle and laugh, which struck me as odd, considering I'd killed one of them in a duel. Was that really something their kind found funny?

"Have you ever killed someone in a duel?" I asked, coldly, looking right at the leader.

His laughter died away. "No. I have not."

"Then why are you laughing? Because only a fool laughs about something he does not understand."

I looked around their group and my gaze locked on a familiar face. He was the elf Scarlet had blasted against the wall and sent to the infirmary. Now wasn't this a pleasant reunion?

"What are you staring at?" he snapped, as he noticed my attention. His eyes were full of pride and anger, but I could tell he didn't know what to make of me. I could read him like an open book. He'd fight me if the opportunity arose, but only when his group had the upper hand.

"Oh, nothing really. Just looking to see if your head healed after the headmistress bitch-slapped you all the way across the corridor. Are you sure you're alright? You look a little confused."

All four elves took a step back and drew their weapons. The leader, whom I'd just provoked, stepped closer, sneering threateningly. I stood my ground and watched as his hand trembled.

"You don't want to do this, human. Why don't you go back to your room and leave the fighting to the real warriors? The royals."

I sincerely hoped they wouldn't be foolish enough to attack, but it felt like we were a single insult, wrong look, or flinch, away from a brawl. And if it came to a fight, I wasn't going to hold back.

"Mabel: JD, please don't fight them unless they attack first. Do it for me, alright? Please."

"Chloe: Why? We can take them!"

"Skadi: I think she's right. That guy is dangerous. A humiliated elf is an unpredictable elf."

I stared him hard in the eyes for several long seconds and refused to back down. I didn't have to fight him, but I didn't have to lose face, either. I would stand up to him and do it for Mabel. But only if I didn't have any other chance. I still decided to do her the favor and try to avoid a battle.

"I yield the road, your royalness. Please forgive this humble human for blocking your path."

"See? Who said that humans couldn't be tamed or trained?" the dark elf sniggered.

"Please, go ahead. We don't want any trouble," Mabel said as she pulled Chloe aside. Skadi just stood there, tall as a mountain in comparison, and forced the elves to go around her. She immediately became so much cooler in my book.

"JD: Don't worry, I have something much better planned."

"Chloe: Are you looking to fight them in the arena?"

"JD: No, I'll show you. Watch and follow my lead."

Chloe grunted and kicked a clump of grass. She'd wanted to go at it right then and there. I looked toward the center of the zone and saw all the monsters had been cleared. They were thorough just like we had been. The group would have quite a few crystals on their hands. Good, I liked it already.

451

We followed after them, keeping a safe distance. I used my map to track their progress and formulate my plan based on which room they entered and how. Chloe continued to grumble about payback, while Mabel thanked me for not fighting, and Skadi wondered how a blood elf chin would feel against her knuckles. I *really* liked my group!

I stopped and waited for two excruciatingly long minutes before I opened my map, confirmed what they were doing, and then told the others my plan.

"Here's what we're doing," I said, leaning in. "There are two boss-level beasts beyond this barrier. But our elf friends have been very careful to only fight them one at a time."

"Oh, are we going to pee in their Wheaties?" Chloe asked. And considering the looks, I was the only one that got the reference.

"Yes, we are going to spoil their well-laid plans. I think it is time to make these pompous elves some humble pie." I turned to Pyro.

"What can you tell me?"

"Pyro: What do you mean?"

"Have they begun fighting? And which boss is it?"

Pyro pushed his head through the barrier, his body becoming translucent before he pulled back. He looked up at me with his big, flaming eyes.

"Pyro: They're approaching the boss from two sides and... they have only now begun their assault."

"What boss are they fighting? The Leech Queen?"

"Pyro: No. The Gargantua. The Leech Queen is in a separate chamber and has not been alerted to their presence."

"That's terrific!" I laughed. "I don't think she would want to miss out on all the fun. Don't you?"

"If I were a giant, slimy worm creature and found out a bunch of elves was partying next door with a giant cockroach, I would want to join in," Chloe said, beaming.

452

"Let's do this the smart way," I said. "Pyro, you are going to sneak into the next chamber, get the Leech Queen's attention, and lure her out."

"Oh! I love this plan," Skadi said, clapping me hard on the shoulder. "You want to let them die, so we can step in, kill the bosses, and then loot all of their bodies?"

"I'd rather not have their deaths on my conscience. But I think we could help knock them down off their snobby pedestal. Their loss is our gain no matter how I look at it."

"Oh, you sly fox!" Chloe chuckled. "Even if we don't kill either of the bosses, it'll totally be worth it to have to bail those stuffy pricks out of a jam!"

"Wait, are you sure you want to do this?" Mabel asked, her voice weak and wavering. "The mistresses can see everything we do here. They'll know that—."

"Yes, they know that the blood elves have been messing with us for a while now. That they are conceited douchebags that not only think slavery is okay but also abusing the duel system to kill students they believe are beneath them. They also know that sometimes, shit goes down in the dungeons. I doubt they're okay with one group simply murdering another, but if a little justice is dealt out?" I said, letting the question hang before the group.

"JD: Pyro, you follow me inside. The girls will wait for ten seconds."

"Pyro: Yes, master."

The girls nodded and waited as we disappeared into the next zone, passing through the shimmering wall. I dropped to a knee the moment we were inside and looked for cover. Finding a good spot behind a large boulder, I observed the elvish group's movements. They were already busy fighting the Gargantua but appeared to have their hands full with the giant insect.

"JD: Pyro, moving quietly and out of sight. Go find the Queen and lead her to them."

Pyro didn't acknowledge my order in chat but immediately zoomed off to my right, moving tactically towards a second chamber, one that was shielded from view by a dense copse of trees. He disappeared from sight and several seconds later I felt a slight drain on his mana. A low, resonant vibration passed through the ground, followed by a puff of smoke from his direction.

"Chloe: We good to come in?

"JD: Yeah, you're—oh shit! He's literally on fire!"

I chuckled as the elemental flew back through the barrier, an enormous slug-like creature hot on his heels. The Leech Queen spewed a nasty stream of mucus at Pyro, but he cut behind a clump of trees, narrowly missing the attack. The queen flattened the trees, slithering, grasping tendrils stretching out of her mouth and reaching for my elemental. But it was too fast.

They broke into the clear, the other group and the Gargantua coming into view, and the leech immediately noticed.

"JD: Pyro, unsummon or something. Don't attack anyone."

The elemental disappeared, leaving the Leech Queen slithering in large, wet circles, tearing up the grass and dirt as she hunted for him. Then her head came up as the blood elves screamed and hollered, and as I'd hoped, went straight for them. If I didn't know better, I'd say the mucus-covered beastie was smacking her lips in anticipation.

Shit Gone Wrong

"THERE'S A SECOND BOSS!" one of the four elves yelled. I didn't know who the voice belonged to, but it's not like it mattered. I wasn't going to be inviting them over for parties or gaming nights.

"Distract it! Both of you!" their leader called. I recognized his voice easily enough, however.

I watched as the queen slithered in, bypassing the first elf's spell and grabbed the second with her tendrils, picked him up, and then slammed him against the muddy ground. His shield held for the first strike and then the second, but immediately started to flicker. She released a cloud of spores, the foggy attack enveloping her head and the struggling elf. The second blood elf cast a fire spell, but instead of hitting the leech, it ignited the growing spore cloud, detonating and engulfing their party member in heat and flames.

The caster froze, his face turned to a mask of horror when he realized he'd just killed his own party member. It was dumb luck that the fire also damaged the Leech Queen, following her trail of spores right back into her mouth.

"Did he just kill his own..." Chloe started to ask.

"Damn, that escalated fast," I said, taken off guard by how fast the elves devolved into chaos. They had seemed organized and like a good and smart team, but shit...

The Gargantua overpowered the other two with disappointing speed, picking the first up in its pincers and stomping the other with a massive, hook foot.

"My god, I thought they would struggle to fight two at the same time and have to fall back, to admit defeat, but they're getting murdered. Do we stay back?" I muttered.

"No. We save them if we can. Otherwise, we're no better than they are," Mabel said with a hint of urgency.

"What happens if we don't? Someone needs to ask. Will the bosses kill each other?" Chloe added. "They're monsters, after all. Territorial."

The three elves were trying to fall back, to regroup and hold the two monsters off, but they didn't seem to have the strength or the team chemistry. At least not anymore.

"JD, please. They are evil, pretentious, and horrible elves, but I do not want their deaths on my conscience!"

"Pyro, come," I ordered. "Attack the queen from the side, but don't let her catch you. Lure her away from the Gargantua so we can isolate her."

The elemental appeared out of nowhere, draining my mana.

Pyro: Very well, Master.

"What about us?" Chloe asked. "What do you want me to do?"

"Chloe, use your aura to give the elves a chance to retreat. Mabel, hit Chloe with your buffs, then hit the leech with every debuff your mana will support."

Skadi's massive arm snaked around me and pulled me aside.

"You will fight by my side then? Together, we will tear our enemies apart?"

I watched as Chloe threw a scalding wave of fire into the Gargantua's face, driving the beast back and cutting it off from the wounded, retreating elves. A green, glowing ribbon buff, and then

456

a blue one illuminated her silhouette, and before the second one had even faded, she'd launched another wave of fire.

"Yes. Something like that. let's kick some ass." Skadi smiled broadly and let out a loud battle cry. Then she kicked forward into an impressive run, the ground vibrating beneath her feet.

The Leech Queen surged into view suddenly, Pyro trapped in her tendrils while her back burned. Chloe dove out of the way, as the enraged beast made straight for the struggling elves. I reached Mabel just as she screamed.

"What is it?"

"She's going to kill them. They're... they're childhood friends," she whispered, struggling to strum an offensive spell on her zither. "I've known them for decades even though...we haven't always seen eye to eye. They weren't horrible to me. They weren't the really bad ones."

Shit, I thought. Here I was thinking these were elves responsible for not only enslaving Mabel and her people but abusing them over the years. I'd never considered that the younger generations of blood elves and dark elves didn't agree with the treatment. Maybe they were victims of established racial pressure.

"I'll help."

She nodded.

"Please, JD. Especially the one with the fiery red hair. His father helped us out during a... bad mess."

Not wasting time with words, I sprinted for the elves, who slowed the Leech Queen with an impressive barrage of fireballs. The problem was, she had Pyro clutched in her tendrils, and the elemental's body was blocking the worst of the attacks.

"JD: Skadi, keep the Gargantua busy. Chloe and I will finish the Leech Queen and come to you."

"Skadi: Okay, but hurry."

I grabbed another crystal from my rift and held it in my left hand just in case. Sword Aura flashed brightly, hitting the Leech Queen beneath her head. She screeched and thrashed, but refused to release her hold on Pyro. Then she surged forward, once again making for the retreating group of elves.

I worked my pen-blade up, down, and across, cutting as I tried to free my struggling elemental. The first two cuts missed the mark, but the third hit one of her tendrils, dark blood spraying into the air as the snake-like appendage fell free. I dove aside as she lunged for me, her bulk almost crushing me into the ground.

"JD: Holy crap, she really wants those elves."

"Mabel: She's going for the easiest prey. It's what many of the higher-level beasts do."

I cut hard, the slash catching the dark creature and cutting into the blubbery flesh. But it wasn't nearly deep enough. Chloe hit her with a wave of fire, but the fire didn't deter her either. I ran to keep up. She wasn't fast. But unfortunately for the elves, they were slower. I watched the Leech Queen close in, vibrating hungrily. Then an idea struck me.

"JD: Pyro, can you cast fire into her face? You're right there."

"Pyro: I'm sorry, Master. She has me too tightly, and I am facing away. So, I cannot throw my fireballs."

"JD: Do you have any area attacks? Anything you can use to burn yourself free.

The chat was quiet for a moment, then the fire elemental responded.

*"Pyro: Actually yes. I have **Ignite**. But it will burn through a lot of my mana."*

"JD: We have crystals. Do it, now!"

A searing, bright flash suddenly blossomed in a bright halo around the Leech Queen's head, the sizzle, and pop of burning flesh almost as loud as her angry, pained screeches. I cleared her side just in time to see my elemental glowing brightly, his mana-fire raging out from between his magma body parts.

I hurled an air slash forth, and my aim was true. The wave of condensed air hit between Pyro and the queen's face and separated two more of her burning tendrils. The elemental fell free, immediately casting a fireball into her body.

The Leech Queen swung around and lunged for me, her face a mass of burning, smoking flesh but I jumped out of reach. I put my left hand up and summoned a fireball, funneling the crystal's full mana into the spell.

"JD: Pyro, fireball!"

"Chloe! Back!" I yelled. She swung and missed for the queen's body and then retreated behind a mass of boulders as I launched the superpowered fireball at the queen. My elemental surged brightly and launched an attack of his own.

I glanced at my mana, confirmed it was still good at over **80%**, and sprinted out from cover. Pyro's attack hit first as he was closer, but mine exploded against her side with a tremendous boom, blasting clean through her thick flesh and setting her innards on fire. I scanned her quickly to see the current state.

NAME: Leech Queen
TYPE: Zone-Boss
POWER LEVEL: 740
HEALTH: 3,199, **MANA:** 600
ATTACK: 180, **DEFENSE:** 90
WEAKNESS: Fire, Sword

The Gargantua suddenly slammed into her from the other side, pushing her over on her side. I cast an Air Slash, and then another, and another as I stepped in and out of reach. Three attacks found their target, leaving me at just under 50% mana.

The cockroach boss's feet stamped into her as she hissed and writhed, spewing that green acid right into his face, but a cockroach was a cockroach. Those things were resilient as hell. Its head and shell smoked, bits and pieces falling free, then I noticed Skadi hanging from one of his legs, fighting to pull herself within reach of his body.

"JD: Skadi, get out of here!"

She immediately dropped and rolled, a split second before the second ring of fire engulfed both beasts. Chloe's Sword Aura

459

joined in, cutting through two of the roach's legs. It dropped on its side as Pyro's fire ring tightened in on them both.

"Pyro: I'm out of mana, master."

"JD: Go check on the elves. Make sure they are a safe distance!"

The elemental strafed past the two bosses and disappeared as I jumped into range of the burning queen's body. I pulled my blade back. Mana Infusion. I grabbed another crystal and immediately drew on its power, letting it course through me and into the blade. A surge of pain hit me as the mana charge finished.

"Mana Discharge!" I snapped as the blade came crashing down against her neck, right in the smoldering hole created by both fireballs. The queen's insides exploded into a fine green mist, dropping a mass of loot as she died.

Skadi jumped forth and caught the Gargantua's massive pincers, just as it emerged from the darkening smoke. It had been right there next to me, so close it could have reached out and cut me in half, and I didn't even realize it. My giantess friend howled and pushed the giant cockroach back and over, showcasing some breathtaking strength. She punched its head in a strong uppercut and kicked it aside, but the carapace was simply too strong without... hah, the necklace.

"Skadi! Catch!"

I cocked back my hand and hurled the necklace her way. She snapped it out of the air, pulled it over her head, and spun in one, seamless move. Hell, without even checking the stats. She launched a straight jab into the cockroach's face just as it swung a hooked foot into her body. The blow staggered her, but only a half-step, and this time she glowed green.

"Finish it o..." I started to yell, just as a jolting bolt of lightning hit my shield, knocking me to my knees and blurring my vision. Hell, it actually scorched my mana shield.

MANA SHIELD SUSTAINED: 213 DAMAGE

I glanced over to find the blood elf, his palm facing me, and his teeth bared. Half his face was burned, one eye was swollen shut, and his left arm hanging limp at his side, but he was still standing.

"No, Ascal, stop! Please! We helped you," Mabel screamed, running up from behind a tree. She put herself between me and the blood elf, her hands held up protectively. "I asked him to save you!"

"I can't, Mabel. You are mine! That is always how it was supposed to be. Don't you understand that?" the elf cried, a glowing ball of lightning appearing in his palm. "I can't stand the thought of someone else being near you, touching you... being with you. I'll give you this one chance. Leave him and join me! You belong with your own people."

This sounded more serious than I realized—like, he'd developed romantic feelings for her and never been able to voice them. Jealousy could fester, and easily become something far darker. And here we were.

I pushed myself up and put my hand on her shoulder, but she refused to move aside.

"She has the right to choose. Don't we all deserve that right?" I asked.

"I'm not talking to you, human."

"Mabel: Please, let me do this."

I didn't push past her, but I didn't back away either. I understood well enough. This was a battle she had to fight for herself.

"You were always good to me, Ascal. So was your father, although I understood he couldn't let others know. But I won't live like that again. I can't. JD, Chloe, and Skadi, they're my friends. I'm with them because I choose to be, and if that one decision is the closest I get to being a free elf, then by the goddess, I am going to stand by it! And I am going to enjoy it, for as long as it lasts."

461

The crackling ball of lightning in Ascal's hand grew brighter, the arching branches of lightning growing more violent.

"JD: I'm sorry, but I don't think he's listening. Get behind me before you get hurt."

"I wasn't just nice to you, Mabel," Ascal yelled, tears now running down his ruined cheeks. "Didn't you see it? I loved you. My father has been negotiating a deal with Emron's family for some time. He was going to purchase you for me. Then you can be mine. All mine. Not his! Mine!"

"I don't want to be owned, Ascal! Why is it so hard for you to understand that?"

"I can't stand it! The thought of that pale creature touching you!" The blood elf reared back as if preparing to throw the lightning bolt forward, just as Chloe appeared through the smoke.

Her gleaming sword streaked in and slammed into Ascal's mana shield, knocking him sideways. The shield crackled, but it didn't disappear. The blood elf howled, caught his balance, and reared around.

"Don't you hurt them!" Chloe snarled, holding her sword ready.

"Pale, pathetic worm. You dare strike me!"

"Ascal, no!" Mabel screamed as the blood elf's arm came forward.

Chloe was faster. She stepped in, cutting hard right at his midsection, only this time the blade broke right through his mana shield and sunk into his side. Everyone froze.

"My God, why didn't his shield hold?" Chloe gasped. "Why didn't it hold?"

Several scorching lightning bolts struck the ground beside Ascal and Chloe, the headmistress and Zafir appearing in a flash. The short man picked up the elf in his arms, and Scarlet turned to me, her face pulled tight, just as they disappeared again.

Chloe dropped her sword and fell to her knees, screaming and covering her face. Mabel was crying, and Skadi limped towards me and dropped to a knee, panting as she tried to catch her breath.

I looked behind her to the Gargantua. Its legs were still twitching, but the giantess had used the pendant to deadly effect. She'd also caved in half of its skull.

I ran past Mabel and dropped down next to Chloe, throwing my arms around her.

"It was supposed to hold," she mumbled over and over again, tears running down her cheeks and nose. I pulled her into a hug and squeezed her tight. Chloe returned the embrace for only a moment, before pushing away. Her eyes opened wide, and then she turned and vomited.

"Hey, it's not your fault, alright?" I whispered and rubbed her back, working to keep her hair out of the mess. "You did it to protect us. If it is anyone's fault, it is mine."

She shook her head as she hiccupped, and more tears rolled down her cheeks.

"I killed him! I killed a person, JD!"

I hugged her again, understanding all too well how she felt—the lump in the throat, the hot knife in the guts, and worst of all, the smothering cloud of regret and guilt that likely covered her thoughts.

"What have I missed?" Skadi muttered, finally standing up straight. I turned, taking in her expression of shock and disbelief. Perhaps we should have warned her about our elf troubles.

"Mabel, are you okay?" I asked, but she didn't appear to be able to respond.

Skadi walked over to the moon elf, grabbed her by the shoulders, and gave her a shake. Mabel sucked in a startled breath and seemed to come to her senses.

"JD! I'm sorry! I'm so sorry!" she cried and ran at me, almost knocking me over. Skadi caught us just as we were about to fall over and embraced us both.

"No, it's me who's sorry, Mabel," I said. "I really am. I felt threatened and thought this would earn us some respect. I didn't know you had a history with him. I just thought he was like Emron. I thought they were all responsible for your mistreatment.

463

You and I share a connection now. We're not just in a party, but we're family. All of us. And I will fight to protect you."

She nodded and sniffled, pushing away.

"Just give me a minute," she whispered and walked slowly towards the boulders Chloe hid behind earlier.

I silently cursed my decisions as I watched Mabel walk off, then smoothed back Chloe's hair. She looked up at me with glassy eyes and tear-streaked cheeks.

"Thank you," I whispered, after pulling Chloe to her feet. She wiped her mouth and face on her robe. "You saved my life, Chloe. Judging from his anger and the first lightning strike, I probably wouldn't have survived another. Without you, Scarlet would have had to peel my crispy-fried carcass off the ground."

She nodded weakly but tears continued to bubble from her eyes. I had an idea of how I must have looked after my duel, and it was a sobering moment. This shit wasn't a game. It might have felt like it at first, but I suffered no delusions anymore.

"Go get the loot. I'll be fine," she whispered and pushed me toward the two piles.

I frowned but nodded. The loot didn't feel like a priority, but it would give me something to do while the others collected themselves.

I walked over to the two piles and held out my hand.

<u>ITEMS RECEIVED:</u>
Gargantua: 1
Leech Queen: 1
Core crystal Rank 1: 49
Core crystal Rank 2: 14
Fres: 4,332

<u>SPECIAL ITEMS RECEIVED:</u>
Leech Queen Earring: 1
Gargantua Cape: 1
Gargantua Shoulder Pads: 1

464

I checked back on Chloe, but she'd turned away, and Mabel was still crying behind the boulder. Skadi stepped up and looked down at the corpses, but she didn't speak either.

I checked the loot in the meanwhile.

NAME: Leech Queen Earrings
TYPE: Accessory, Earrings
POWER LEVEL: 30, **SLOTS:** 1/2
DESCRIPTION: Earrings made from molten Leech Queen Fangs.
STATS: Mana + 50, Attack + 20
SPECIAL: Add 20 poison damage on attack for 5 seconds. Stacks

NAME: Gargantua Cape
TYPE: Armor, Set Item
POWER LEVEL: 62
DESCRIPTION: Cape made from Gargantua Carapace.
HEALTH: 120, **DEFENSE:** 40
MANA SHIELD: 100
SPECIAL: Set item 1/6. On 2/6 adds Defense + 50, 4/6 adds Health + 200, and 6/6 Tremor Skill.
SPECIAL: Tremor Skill creates a small earthquake around the user, dealing damage to everything in the vicinity.

NAME: Gargantua Shoulder Guards
TYPE: Armor, Set Item
POWER LEVEL: 43
DESCRIPTION: Cape made from Gargantua Carapace.
HEALTH: 80, **DEFENSE:** 30
MANA SHIELD: 50
SPECIAL: Set item 1/6. On 2/6 adds Defense + 50, 4/6 adds Health + 200, and 6/6 Tremor Skill.

SPECIAL: Tremor Skill creates a small earthquake around the user, dealing damage to everything in the vicinity.

The earrings were great for Skadi, and even if she didn't want them, we could always trade or sell them. The cape and the shoulder pads were…awesome. That was the only way I could describe them. Pure student versus student items. Or student versus someone else who wasn't a monster or a beast, that is. I found their stats and perks to be a little ironic, considering what we'd just been through.

"Skadi, take the earrings and give yours to one of the girls."

"Are you sure?" she asked, studying the new piece of jewelry. "I mean it's not like I don't want them, but I already have a good survivability."

"You more than proved that," I said, gesturing to the Gargantua's corpse.

"You were busy with the leech, and then that really angry blood elf. So, I did what I had to. Besides, it didn't want to stand still, so I beat its brains in." She unequipped the old earrings and put the new ones on.

"Mind if I keep both?" she whispered. "There are two earring slots."

I snorted but nodded. "Yeah, you can. And, heh, thanks for earlier, you did well."

I turned back to Mabel now sitting on top of the boulder. Chloe was moving around and met my gaze. She nodded, indicating she was getting better. I walked over and she immediately put her arms around me, pressing her face into my neck and pulling me in tight.

"I don't want to feel that ever again," she whispered.

"I hope you don't have to."

"Can you be honest with me for a moment? Just be straight, okay?" she asked.

"Sure."

"Do you think less of me now?"

I shook my head and smiled. "If anything, I think my feelings for you got stronger."

It was the truth. Seeing how far she was willing to go only confirmed that she cared as much about me as I did for her.

"What now? Do you think the headmistress will punish us? Punish me?"

"No, I don't think so. It was self-defense... and at this point, we don't know if he actually died. In reality, they would have all died if we hadn't come to their aid."

"I guess you're right. So, what now? Do we try to clear the floor? Come back later? Because I can't lie, if I have to go back to our room, I'm just going to go over this stuff again and again," Chloe said.

I glanced over at Mabel.

"Yeah, let's do that," the elf said, dropping off the boulder and walking over to us. "What's done is done, right? And I'm sorry about what happened earlier, my friends. It's just...I don't know. I've known elves like Ascal my entire life. But that is just it. In that life, I was a slave, a piece of property. If I want something more than that, then I have to wash my hands of it all. I do not want to see them hurt or killed, but I refuse to shed any more tears over them."

"Mabel, we've got your back. One day, I will find a way to win you your freedom. I promise. But we're treading a thin line here. If they consider us their enemies, then we'll have to do the same. I don't mean them any ill will, but I won't stand idly by if they try to harm anyone in our group."

"I understand. And trust me, I know *what* they are. They're evil. But you get used to it when you're around them every day of your life," she whispered. "But yes. I will make it up to you all."

I put my free arm out and waited for her to come into my embrace.

"There's nothing to forgive. You did what you thought was right. I'm just happy we all made it out unharmed."

467

"Good but depleted," Skadi said. "I would like several crystals if it's alright."

I nodded and handed her **10**, then did the same with the others. They took them without comment and stashed them away.

"So, over there next?" Chloe asked, pointing at a large stone gate. The air inside the large archway shimmered with faint, blue ribbons of energy. "Or do we go back?"

"Yeah. That's the last zone if you girls are ready, but first, we need to shuffle the items around a bit."

"Yeah, I think finishing this will do us better than just moping around," Mabel said as she met Chloe's eyes. The other girl nodded.

"What did we get?" Chloe asked.

"An earring perfect for Skadi. It adds poison damage on every normal hit. Then there are two tank-ish items I planned to use on myself."

"Yeah, I'm good with anything," Chloe muttered. "As long as Skadi can keep them off me, I can rain down fire."

I studied our items one more time, struggling with the feeling there was a better combination I was missing. After a short study, I came up with the best tradeoff.

"Skadi, you get the reverse scale pendant and the Leech Queen earrings. Mabel takes the vine ring, mana surge ring, and the viper belt. Chloe, thorn ring, aspire boots, and the viper earrings. Those combinations seem to max out your stats and roles perfectly."

We shuffled the items around until everyone had the right gear, and they all looked happy. Which made me happy, as well. The new gear bumped my stats through the roof, and the girls received some extra health and stats bonuses.

"Everyone good?" I asked once everyone was done re-equipping.

"I'm good," Chloe said, managing a toothy smile. "But we get dibs on the next few *juicy* items. We're trailing behind you on the old power level, and that ain't gonna fly forever..."

I nodded. "You're right, and we'll amend that. Including items to upgrade your weapons. What about you Mabel, Skadi?"

"I'm fine," Mabel said, with a satisfied nod. Her smile looked genuine enough, so I moved onto Skadi, who gave me two thumbs up and a grin.

I checked my stats one last time before we went head-to-head with the floor boss, wanting to bask in their greatness one more time before I was ripped to pieces and eaten.

NAME: JD, **AGE:** 24
WEAPON: Pen-Blade
CULTIVATION: Realm 1, Rank 5
POWER LEVEL: 988 (442 + 147)
HEALTH: 1295 (+315**), MANA:** 669 (+97)
ATTACK: 317 (+27**), DEFENSE:** 287 (+52)
MANA SHIELD: 1200 (+180)

I gave our party one last glance as well, to see how their power levels had changed from last time and smiled.

NAME: James (JD) Wright
POWER LEVEL: 988
CULTIVATION: Realm 1, Rank 5

NAME: Chloe Sullivan
POWER LEVEL: 608
CULTIVATION: Realm 1, Rank 4

NAME: Mabel Karash
POWER LEVEL: 591
CULTIVATION: Realm 1, Rank 4

NAME: Skadi Medvarna
POWER LEVEL: 871
CULTIVATION: Realm 1, Rank 4

The party buff was something that we would need to invest in when we got our hands on more crystal cores. The bonus we'd already gained was astonishing and the girls were easily receiving almost **200** power from the party, while my gains were smaller. But that would change as we equipped them with better gear, and they gained strength. Still, any bonus was welcome even if it was just 10 health. It could mean the difference between life and death.

"Okay. If you ladies are ready, let's do this."

CREATION MAGIC

SEVERAL GROUPS of smaller leeches and cockroach-like beasts attacked us immediately as we entered the next zone. We made quick work out of them. Skadi used Provoke to gather them in a group, and Pyro made short work of them with his fire rings.

We pushed through to the gate, arriving at the boss area efficiently. We weren't really in the mood for games after the ordeal with the elves, after all. I sat down and collected my thoughts until Pyro had regained all his mana. Once he was done, we quietly stacked up before the barrier, and the air around us shifted. It was colder, practically crackling with mana. The floor boss waited in the next room, and something told me it knew we were there.

"Pyro, please scout the other side and tell me what is waiting."

"Pyro: Yes, Master."

The elemental passed halfway through the barrier but then returned almost immediately.

"What's wrong? What did you see?"

"Pyro: The boss stands dead center of the space, waiting. It is also surrounded by approximately two dozen smaller beasts. They aren't terribly strong, but together they could be dangerous."

"Alright. Can we enter without getting attacked?"

"Pyro: Yes, you can, Master."

"Girls? Are you sure about this? It has been a... day. We could always rest and recoup and come back later."

Mabel and Chloe nodded. Skadi, who stood just to my right, saw them and Skadi scowled.

"Come on girls? Get fired up! We are about to charge into battle, where fist and blade meet flesh and blood. If your heart isn't in this, then someone will get hurt?"

"It's okay, Skadi, I know the girls. They aren't as rah-rah-rah as you are. But they'll kick some ass. The question is, are you ready? This is the big bad of the first floor?"

"Pfft!" She blew a raspberry and waved me off. "I was born for this, literally. Giants were made to fight beasts and get thrown around. Don't worry about me."

"I love the attitude, though I hope we can avoid the 'get thrown around' part."

"I live for it. Like I said before, everything we do is a high impact sport. Once the girls are okay with it, I plan on showing you." She winked and abruptly stepped through the shimmering wall. The barrier suddenly turned red, indicating danger.

"Is this what it did with the barrier outside the viper's zone?"

"Yeah," Chloe replied, tightening her grip on her sword. "It had turned red from the inside out if I remember correctly."

"Skadi: You can come in, but don't move once you're inside. There's a lot of these bastards and they seem very aware of everything going on."

"Alright, here we go. If you've got any doubts, now's the time to voice them. If not, let's go kick some ass and clear our first floor."

Mabel and Chloe both shook their heads, then they looked to one another.

"Let's do this!" Chloe said.

"Should we get their asses and collect their names?" Mabel replied, with a grin.

I snorted appreciatively. This was my party, and I loved the shit out of them.

I took a deep breath, turned, and walked through the archway. The zone on the other side was dense jungle, with thick tree line filling the outer edge. Massive fronds and ferns covered the ground, dripping moisture from their leaves. *Shit.* I held my hand out just as a large raindrop hit me on the top of the head. Yes, of course it would be raining.

A peel of distant thunder shook the ground while I turned my attention towards the center of the zone. The ground cover gave way to grassland, where large rocks, person-sized boulders, tree stumps, and a mass of monkey-like creatures congregated. The largest sat on a rock at the very center. It rose and stretched its muscular arms. Okay, not a monkey. It was a gorilla.

My eyebrows rose when I saw the beast tower over the already sizable, smaller counterparts. It stood at least twelve-feet-tall with massive arms and legs, each as thick as tree trunks. Its torso was all muscle and armored skin. Not what looked like scales, from what I could see, but definitely not normal animal flesh. Reinforced leather?

It yawned, showcasing some impressive canine teeth, then settled back onto its rock, and snorted. The smaller beasts jumped at the noise and turned, considering their leader. Then they turned back and resumed their pacing. Vigilantly. Then I realized they weren't just pacing aimlessly. They were walking set routes, back and forth. They were patrolling.

Chloe and Mabel stood next to me, while Skadi stood just beyond them.

"Skadi: What's the plan?"

"JD: I was going to say, 'simple'. That we should take out the ADDS first, and then take on the boss. But I don't think anything that simple and straightforward will work. The smaller ones are patrolling. That means they're smart. And I'm guessing they'll alert the boss once anything happens. Which probably means they'll swarm, surround, and kill."

473

"Mabel: Smart is scary. Should we have Skadi lure the ADDS away and try to fight them separately?"

"JD: That might work. The only question is, will the boss join in? If Skadi runs in and Provokes them, they'll just swarm her. Now, here is how we could make it interesting for our beastie friends. What if we use her five seconds of invulnerability to our advantage? While the ADDS move towards her, we do the same thing, but physically target the boss. Meaning, once the smaller ones move off, we surrounded the boss with a fire ring to isolate him. Then we hit him with a fireball to make sure we've got his attention."

"Chloe: I like how that sounds. Except, we're not going to want to leave Skadi on her own for too long. What if we had Pyro move in to support her?"

"JD: That could work. And maybe we position you and Mabel between the two, so you can provide offensive and defensive support for both groups. Mabel, there are lots of decent-sized rocks in the field. Those could make really nice bombs, if you get my drift."

"Mabel: Yes. I just want to make sure I don't target any too close to you all. I've seen one mana shield fail today. I don't want to see two."

"Chloe: This sounds like an awesome plan. Let me buff up first. I'll need half a minute."

"JD: Alright. Skadi, are you good with this plan?"

"Skadi: This feels like a good day to die! I will sing the songs of my ancestors and rain the wrath of the giants down on our enemies!"

"JD: Okay, I like the second part. Bring the wrath and the pain. The dying part? Let's avoid that at all costs.

"Skadi: Ahahahaha. We will see. We giants welcome death, and the promises of our next life!"

I sighed inwardly and readied myself as Chloe activated her buffs. Mabel did, too, the colorful ribbons of positive magic appearing over herself, me, and Skadi.

"JD: Ready?"

All three girls nodded, but Skadi appeared practically out of her mind with excitement. She was one of those who lived for the thrill, and I had to admit that I wasn't far off, either. Casting magic and killing great beasts provided a boost unlike anything I'd ever felt before.

Skadi moved off to the left, sneaking into position before activating her skill. I turned back to find that the floor boss had fallen asleep. Even better for our plan, as that almost ensured she could get the ADDS away without pulling him in, too. Chloe and Mabel snuck right up the middle, Pyro drifted right to support Skadi, and I went right. This was a tactic of timing, so if we did everything right, these beasts wouldn't know what hit them.

"JD: (Skadi and Chloe) Once we get the ADDS' attention and moving, let's hit them with an inferno. Pyro. Be sure to surround the boss with that fire ring so he can't join in. It is important to isolate him and take out those smaller beasts quickly. If we do, then we immediately turn our combined attention to him. Their game is to surround, overpower, and kill. Let's turn that same scenario right back on them."

"For the glory of Jotunheim!" Skadi hollered as she jumped out of the fronds and activated Provoke. She immediately glowed wicked red. The entire group of the ADDS looked her way, their eyes flaring up. They swarmed towards her, moving with terrifying quickness. Once they were past Chloe and Mabel's hiding spot, I closed our trap.

"JD: (Chloe and Mabel) Now!"

The girls and I popped up, Mabel's zither strumming a quiet chord as Chloe's sword heated up. I ran right in behind them as Sword Aura shot past me. I pulled forth a spare crystal in my left hand and imagined the glyph for Wind Gust. Three brush strokes connected, and I slashed along the lines, activating the skills. The two separate wind gusts caught up with the Aura, erupting into an eyelash-singing explosion of fire that scorched the beasts' fur.

475

A ground-shaking roar split the rain's gentle white noise and I turned to find the zone boss pounding his chest atop the rock. He paced back and forth, unwilling to pass the perimeter of Pyro's impressive fire ring.

"JD: Pyro, good job. Keep that ring blazing! Create another ring around the ADDS if you can."

"Pyro: Yes, Master."

A giant ring of flames appeared around Skadi and the ADDS and immediately started to shrink, to cluster them together. Sword Aura flashed in, adding to the blaze just as Skadi leapt through the fire and rolled. She stood, her hair literally on fire. Mabel ran up, tore a wet frond from a plant, and used it to pat out the flames.

"Shit! They hit me faster than I thought they would!" Skadi gasped, catching her breath. "My invulnerability window ran out really quick!"

I checked her out, and confirmed that she wasn't hurt, but she'd have to consider a haircut when we were all done. Mabel used Heal, recovering the little health she'd lost. Several of the ADDS jumped through the flames, while most perished in our inferno. Chloe cut down the first two, while Skadi finished the third, hitting it with an impressive punch and sending it flying back into the undergrowth. I caught the fourth with a well-placed slash and cut it in half.

A turned to congratulate the others just as something crashed into me, and I went airborne. I felt the air and rain wash over me, then I was tumbling, crashing through the ferns.

MANA SHIELD SUSTAINED: 174 DAMAGE

I shook off the disorientation and sat up. Luckily, my blade was still in hand. I managed to my feet and turned, only to find the floor boss standing over the others, smoke wafting off his hide. It shot me a deathly glare, then pounded its fists against its chest. The sound and violence pushed even Skadi back, and immediately formed a cold sweat on my brown. I scanned him and tightened the grip on my pen-blade.

NAME: Gorilla King
TYPE: Floor-Boss
POWER LEVEL: 1,030
HEALTH: 4,500, **MANA:** 900
ATTACK: 250, **DEFENSE:** 150
WEAKNESS: Fire, Poison

"Okay, team, let's show this Gorilla King our mean faces!" I hollered and moved in.

Skadi roared and crashed into him from the side. She glowed purple for a second and he turned his attention to her.

"Taunt!" she yelled, using her aggro skill to keep his anger on her.

"Pyro! Attack!" I snapped.

Mabel's fingers ran across the zither's strings, forming glowing snares that snaked around the boss's arms and chest. The debuffs hit him next. I watched in horror as he ripped easily through the snares, while Skadi pummeled with a vicious left and right.

"Mana Flash!" Chloe appeared next to him in a brilliant flash of mana, delivering a savage sword strike, then phased out again before the Gorilla King could grab her.

"Skadi! Keep hitting him! He's weak against poison!"

"Sure thiiiiiiing," she yelled back just as the boss kicked out, catching her in the chest. She flew back into a tree, the force breaking the trunk and toppling it over. I watched as a decent chunk of her health dropped from the strike and hitting the tree.

"Mabel! Keep it fully debuffed and use what mana you can spare to heal Skadi! Don't waste it on attacks!"

"On it!"

I slid in from behind, slashing the pen-blade across the back of its legs, targeting its hamstrings. I had to cripple it, if possible. That way we could try and keep it at a distance.

DAMAGE DEALT: 137

I loved my attack power. Even normal attacks did decent damage in comparison to their health pool.

I pulled back as it turned to face me, swinging its massive fists my way. At the last moment the boss stopped and turned toward Skadi again as she Provoked him. Damn. I loved her aggro skills!

Skadi jumped in and connected with a solid kick to its midsection but jumped back just as Chloe's Sword Aura crashed in, covering its left arm with raging fire. The gorilla brushed it off as if the attack was a mere bug, literally sweeping the fire off its skin. Although, some of its fur was burned away now.

"Air Slash!" I launched two mana slashes in quick succession, jumping out of the way just as Pyro launched another Fire Ring.

"Pyro: Down to 30% mana."

"JD: Do you have any ordinary attacks?"

"Pyro: I have ranged attacks that count as elemental but don't cost any mana. They won't do much damage. And I am also running out of time on this summon."

Three debuffs struck the Gorilla King right after my slashes hit. It roared and thrashed its arms as if trying to pummel the fire, but we were all too far away to harm. Then it jumped into the air and came crashing down, slamming its fists into the ground. The resulting shockwave knocked everyone but Skadi and Pyro off their feet.

"It's shaking the debuffs off. I can't get them to stick for longer than several seconds! I'm doing my best!" Mabel yelled, crawling back to her feet. The Gorilla King tried to push through the fire ring but pulled back, shrieking angrily.

"Chloe! Use aura whenever it's available! Target a single spot!"

Skadi tried to jump in, but the fire held her back as well. The Gorilla King watched her carefully, then extended both arms and spun in a circle, lashing out through the fire and somehow hitting her. She grunted and fell away.

"Damn thing knows I won't cross the fire. He's using it against me now," Skadi yelled.

I grabbed another crystal and focused the energy into my body, molded the mana into my free hand, and sent a spell his way.

"Fireball!"

Unfortunately, my magic wasn't even close to Pyro's strength, and my fireball hit with far less impact and flame damage. The rings had already drained most of my elemental's reserves. He not only wouldn't recover mana fast enough to be a benefit but was also running out of time on this summons.

"JD: Pyro, we're going to have to play the risk game. Don't summon anymore fire rings. Save what mana you have left for offensive attacks. Skadi, be prepared to go head on when that ring goes cold."

"Pyro: Yes, Master."

The elemental floated just outside the fire ring, trying to draw in some of its aggro as he shot fist-sized fireballs at his body. They didn't do much damage, but I did notice something. When the boss wasn't able to slap the fire away, his fur was starting to catch fire.

"Pyro! Focus on the same spot! Chloe! Aura on the burning fur! Wait and attack together. Hit his back, where he can't reach!" Then I turned to our tank. "Skadi, get him to turn to you."

"Hey, monkey boy! I have some bananas," Skadi yelled and activated Taunt.

He stopped spinning, his eyes flashing red just like the monkey's eyes had done before. I rushed in and slashed three times, just as Chloe and Pyro launched fire attacks at his back. His fur started to burn, dark smoke wafting off his body.

The massive gorilla slapped at his back, growled, and let out a deafening bellow. I staggered back, my limbs suddenly heavy and numb. I watched the debuffs drop away and the fire ring went dark. *Shit! He just wiped everything clean.*

YOU HAVE BEEN HIT WITH: THE KING'S ROAR MOVEMENT SPEED – 30% FOR 15 SECONDS.

Before we could move, the Gorilla King jumped at Skadi, pummeling her three times in quick succession. Then he grabbed her by the legs and hurled her bodily into the tree line. Chloe sent an aura attack his way, but it didn't do much more than piss him off.

I checked him again quickly, but he was only down to 1,721 Health. Pyro didn't seem inflicted by the slow debuff, either because he was a summon or that he had an innate immunity. He continued to harass the king, peppering his back with fireballs and slamming his body into the massive gorilla's left leg. The Gorilla King spun and hit him with a fist, sending the elemental twirling through a few trees, but Pyro launched three quick fireballs, somehow hitting all in the exact same spot. I watched as the fur burned, and in a moment of triumph, his skin split and burst wide open. The monster dropped to its knees and stumbled, face planting on the muddy ground.

"He's not shaking the debuffs anymore! He's stunned, this is our chance," Mabel yelled as the Gorilla King glowed three times in quick succession.

I charged in and hacked at the damaged shoulder, sending in a fireball of my own.

SKILL USED: Fireball
MANA USED: 20
DAMAGE DEALT: 372

My mana was down to 40% but his health was down to 1,478. I kept hacking at the skin, and felt Chloe initiate a skill, a split second before her mana flash blinded me.

"Boom!" she cried, appearing next to the stunned boss, her sword crashing in and hitting hard.

The left arm now hung by a strip of tattered muscle and skin, but the monster didn't seem to register the pain as it raged thrashed. It flashed again, snarled, and started to push off the ground.

Skadi appeared from behind a tree, staggering drunkenly and activating Taunt, just as our damaged gorilla friend staggered off the ground. He pounded his one good arm against his chest and roared, releasing a massive blast wave that scattered us like dry leaves.

MANA SHIELD SUSTAINED: 297 DAMAGE

I hit hard and rolled, the plants relatively soft and spongy beneath me. At least we had that. I pushed up, wiping blood from my face. I'd split my lip again and my nose felt broken. Damn, I really hoped it wasn't crooked.

I limped back into the fray as the Gorilla King cracked Pyro with a hard punch and almost scattered the elemental's magma body parts. The boss's fur was dissolving, still burning like a growing roadmap across his back, but the flesh was regrowing over the gaping shoulder wound, too. And if that wasn't weird enough to behold, new fur was growing in, but it wasn't black like before, but silver.

Mabel was with Skadi, using Heal as the other woman staggered to her feet.

"Down to 40% mana! And I don't know how many of those hits I can bring Skadi back from!" Mabel yelled. If this lasted much longer, we'd be without support, and I was down to just under 30% myself.

"Role call!"

"I'm out!" Chloe yelled from my left. "One skill left!"

"I don't need any! Hell, I don't really have any!" Skadi laughed.

I almost laughed with her, if the stakes weren't so high. But I did silently vow to rectify that issue with our party's skillset, if we survived the Gorilla King, that is.

"Can you occupy the beast for a few seconds?"

"Sure thing now that I'm healed! But if Mabel doesn't have enough mana for more healing magic, let's make sure we finish this monkey off before I get sent to my ancestors. Okay?"

I searched for Pyro, but he wasn't attacking. The freaking elemental was actually hiding behind a boulder, trying to blend in.

"JD: Pyro! What are you doing?"

"Pyro: I'm hiding. Master. That beast is too strong. Another few hits like that last one and I would be a pile of glowing rubble."

"JD: So, you are just going to wait until your summon expires?"

"Pyro: I might be a magical being, but it still hurts if I die. Even if I can revive again. I will fight with you all together, but please do not ask me to sacrifice myself."

"Chloe: Are you guys hearing this? Pyro has some backbone. I'm starting to like this guy, ugh, pile of magma, ugh, fire elemental."

"JD: What a great time to find his spine. (Pyro) Yes, fight with us."

I thought hard about how to proceed next as the Gorilla took its pain and frustration out on one of the remaining trees. It roared and toppled it with a single, powerful strike. Then Skadi stepped into the clear and activated her Provoke. She cracked her knuckles and made for him, just as he slammed his hands into the ground, dug out a chunk of hard soil, and then threw it right at her.

"Shit!" she cursed and jumped out of the way. The chunk of rocky ground hit a boulder behind her shattered, peppering her back. But it stirred something in my mind. The Ink. Creation magic through the use of a pen.

"Anyone know how to use creation magic?"

"You need ink!" Chloe yelled as she slashed across the Gorilla's hind leg and retreated as it turned.

"And a pen?"

"Yeah! Then use the ink as if it was an item!"

Skadi stormed toward the Gorilla, using Taunt to pull his attention away from Chloe. A second chunk of rocky earth shattered between her and Mabel, hitting the latter with debris.

"Scatter! Get clear and hide if you can," I yelled as I pulled the ink from my rift.

DO YOU WISH TO USE THE THREE-HORNED VIPER KING INK POUCH?
YES / NO?

"Yes!" I laughed. It had been so easy that I felt embarrassed. Ink. Damned ink! All I had to do was take it out of my rift, but how was I supposed to know? I'd have to think about this more in game-like terms and not as something abstract. Keeping that in mind, I considered how best to use it.

A black canvas appeared in front of me as time froze and a timer appeared, counting down from **30**.

Gorilla. Tough skin. Agile. Strong. What would be the best thing to hurt it while using poison? If the new fur was stronger than the old stuff, nothing would do—no, there was something. I grinned as I remembered a strategy game I used to play as a kid, where you could use ballistae to hurl oversized projectiles at the enemy.

Thanking whatever deity or higher power was watching over me, I plunged the tip of my pen-blade into the ink pouch and started drawing on the black canvas.

25.

24.

23.

I tried not to think about the timer and instead thought of how to structure my drawing, but my hand moved on its own, drawing intricate details on the canvas. A shimmering and stationary ballista appeared on a rotating pedestal. The weapon sat atop a sturdy frame. But that was it. I was out of ink. Shit! Gritting my teeth, I used the second pouch and started drawing the tight rope, a projectile, and a lever. It wasn't quite as large as I hoped it would be, but the bolt was covered in dripping green poison. Poison so corrosive it seemed to eat away at the metal itself of the bladed tip.

"Taunt him again! Skadi!"

My giantess friend seemed to snap out of her stupor. She nodded and glowed red, but the Gorilla King didn't respond.

"Pyro: I am here!" The element practically yelled into the chat, just as I was moving to pull the lever. Then the elemental appeared in the air above the Gorilla King's head and dropped like a boulder. He hit like a literal ton of flaming rocks and erupted on impact staggering the beast back.

I put my hand on the lever and stared through the targeting mechanism, while using my left to move and aim the weapon.

"Do it!" Mabel said from my right as she cast Debilitate and Slow. I took in a deep breath and slowly squeezed the trigger, waiting as the gorilla boss slowly turned to face me. The thick bow and rope snapped violently, launching the bolt forward with tremendous velocity.

"Fuck! That was close!" Skadi cursed as the bolt struck in the gorilla's gut and punched all the way through, exiting its back with a messy squelch. I didn't know it right away, but kept flying, and very nearly hit her, too.

The boss let out a deafening bellow, debuffing us, but the noise died away quickly. It staggered as the poison spread, coloring the fur with green and red blood.

The ballista disappeared from before me, so I ran forward. I ran as if my life depended on it. Every step launched me several yards, as I poured mana into my legs and feet. But before I could make it into striking distance, the boss dropped, his body going opaque and loot tumbling forth.

I struggled to halt my momentum, and it took Skadi catching me so I wouldn't overshoot.

"I don't get it?" I gasped, trying to catch my breath. "Why did it die? It still had life."

"My poison dot damage suddenly spiked after you hit him with the bolt," Skadi said, pulling the bolt from the ground and inspecting it. It went up from **21** points of damage per second to over **100**. That is it. We stacked the right multipliers and you hit it home with the big stick."

"Heh! Well, I'll take it," I muttered. "Poison really stacks when you ram it home with a really big arrow. We'll have to get more of that kind of gear for you."

"For all of us," Chloe murmured. "I'm more or less useless when on cooldown. Fire doesn't fix all problems, I have found."

"Are you guys forgetting something?" Mabel asked, joining. "JD created a freaking glorious siege weapon, from thin air!"

"Yeah. About that," Chloe whispered. "How did you do that?"

Skadi watched us quickly.

"Creation Magic. I used the ink pouch, or rather two. They should have given me *+30* to my attack instead, but I figured out continued survival was more important, right?"

"You drew it? During battle?" Chloe laughed. "Wait, you're not joking, are you?"

I shook my head.

"No, I'm not. Time froze for about thirty seconds, giving me just enough time to draw the ballista's rough shape. The ink and my mana did the rest. Which begs the question, is this why they consider the pen-blade to be so overpowered? Creation magic? Now that I've done it, I can't say that I agree. I need ink, so I won't be able to use it to its fullest potential if there isn't any available. Considering we've cleared this entire floor and I've only found it twice."

"Maybe, but we can always buy it. It also might be an item that drops more readily from stronger enemies on the higher floors," Mabel said. "It is weird, though. I didn't feel a break in the action, and you said things paused, for what? **30** seconds? Maybe that only happened in your mind."

Chloe hit my shoulder. Then she leaned in and kissed me. Mabel threw her arms around me, and unfortunately, so did Skadi. I think all of my ribs popped from her embrace.

"You realize this means we celebrate, right?" the giantess asked.

"Of course, it does," I said, but first, how about we check out this loot?"

ITEMS RECEIVED:
Silverback: 41
Gorilla King: 1
Core crystal Rank 1: 49
Core crystal Rank 2: 13
Core Crystal Rank 3: 3
Fres: 5,834

SPECIAL ITEMS RECEIVED:
Gorilla King Core: 1

A prompt appeared, startling me as I was reading the loot. I stared at it and frowned.

DO YOU WISH TO ENTER THE 1ˢᵗ DUNGEON'S HIDDEN AREA?

YES / NO?

CONVERGENCE

THIS WASN'T SOMETHING I'D EXPECTED. It was an offer to go to a hidden area, but considering the boss had been cleared so many times until now, just how hidden could it be?

"Did you girls get the same prompt?"

"What prompt?" Chloe asked. "We got nothing."

"I got a prompt asking me if I want to enter the **1st** dungeon's hidden area."

A flash of thunder struck the ground next to us, and then another, and another until all mistresses stood before us, practically glowing with energy.

"What's going on?" I asked, with more than a little trepidation. "We can explain what happened with the elves."

"We're not here about that. We're here to bid for the hidden area," Salina, the Mistress of Finances, said. She held herself with an air of importance—her back straight, chest out, and hand resting on the pommel of her sword. *Damn, they look impressive.*

"Mistress Salina? Scarlet, Leona, Freya, and Eliana. Right? I don't understand."

"Oh, you have a good memory," Scarlet replied with a nod. "First off, I want to tell you that Ascal isn't dead. He survived and is recovering. Although, blood elves have long memories, and hold onto grievances better than any race I have ever encountered."

"I've come to realize that. Yes," I said.

"What about the elf in their group. The one that didn't make it?" Chloe asked, quietly.

"No one killed him," Scarlet said, interrupting her. "If that is what you are asking. Students die in the dungeons all the time. It is part of the tower's natural order, the only way to adequately prepare you for life beyond our walls."

I frowned.

"But he was royal," I said. "Won't they demand something... anything. I don't know, some kind of..."

"Revenge?" Scarlet said, interrupting. "Whoever kills a royal is hunted down, tortured, and killed. But if one dies here, they will do nothing. They understand the way of this world."

"So, you're here to make offers?" I asked.

"As Salina said, yes. I will give my offer first, though, as is fitting for my station as headmistress. You can accept mine or choose to hear the others."

"Hey, that's not fair! You're going to use Ascal's life as part of the trade!" Leona protested.

"No, I won't, but I thought they deserved to know before the haggling began," Scarlet argued.

"What does that mean?" Chloe asked.

"I think it means they are offering to kill the elves that survived from the dungeon," I said, leaning into her. Scarlet winked, that haunting red glow burning to life in her eyes.

"Loyalty and gratitude means everything here. Besides, I believe young JD here knows very well who has been keeping him safe up till now. And who will likely continue to do so moving forward. That has to be worth something, as well. Don't you think so?"

Shit. She just admitted she's been the one helping me!

The other mistresses snapped their fingers and disappeared, leaving Scarlet standing alone before us. She chuckled quietly. But it was an eerie noise, one that made the hairs on my neck stand on end. There was a strange power dynamic between the mistresses. One I wasn't entirely sure I wanted to unearth. She extended her hand and gestured me forward. Only me.

"So, headmistress, what is it that we have to do in order to repay our... debt?" I asked, when I was standing before her. She straightened her dress, cracked her neck, and made a grand show of considering her response. Funny, considering she already knew exactly what she wanted to ask.

"I want you to give me access to the hidden zone. If you do, I'll gear your group in low—," she saw my frown deepen and scowled before continuing. "I'll gear your group in mid-grade armors, accessories, and weapons. You will get a yearly stipend in advance, and I'll make the problem with Ascal's family go away."

"Chloe: Do you really want to barter with her? I think she might give us more the way she mentioned the hidden zone."

"JD: No. But yes? I don't want to overdo it. If she's offering to help with the Ascal problem, then that just might mean we gain a little safety moving forward. Your lives are worth more to me than any hidden zone."

"Skadi: I'm glad to hear you say that. It tells me I made the right choice to join you. I can respect honesty as well as loyalty. You have my renewed word that I'll never do anything to harm this party, JD."

"JD: What about you, Mabel?"

"Mabel: Do what you think is right. But if Ascal doesn't have to die, please see to that. I don't want to see anyone else hurt."

Scarlet frowned as a knowing glance passed between Mabel and me.

"Are you having a good, little party chat?" she asked.

"Yes, we are. I was just telling them how happy I was that the problem went away. But..." I paused, considering how to

489

continue. "If it is at all possible, I would like it if Ascal survived. His party members, too."

"Oh. Mercy? A trickier path, to be honest. But not impossible. It depends on whether you accept my terms."

I nodded and put on what I hoped looked like my most honest smile.

"I accept under the condition that we can come to you whenever we need information. And that Ascal and his party members survive."

"And that you give him a skill or two for the Pen-Blade!" Chloe added, stepping up next to me and putting her arm around my back.

"One skill of *his* choice, and you get to call on me for information three times."

Scarlet's voice didn't betray any hint of nervousness or anticipation, but I wasn't going to push her. She could just as easily make our lives miserable as she could make it easier.

"I agree, Headmistress. Now, how do I send you there?"

"Simple. Take my hand and accept the offer. I'll do the rest."

"What about the girls? Will they be safe here?" I asked, looking over the three.

"Yeah, they will. The boss won't respawn for some time. I have seen to it."

"I'm ready in that case."

For some reason I had a feeling I'd come to regret this, but in the end, my party and my girls were more important. Sure, we'd get good gear, as well as cultivation, but in time. Scarlet appeared to be a path to accelerate our progress significantly.

Scarlet pushed herself into me at the last moment as I accepted the summons and a bright light enveloped us. It dulled all of my senses and I couldn't see, hear, or even feel her body pressed against me. But before my panic could fully blossom, we appeared in a small grove. On the far end sat a pedestal, a single, gleaming chalice sitting on top. Some kind of glowing, golden liquid sat inside, a peculiar mist drifting upwards and into the air. Whatever it was, it smelled heavenly.

"Yes! It's there! It really is!" Scarlet gasped.

"What is?" I asked, following a few steps behind her.

"The highest grade of mana imaginable. A single drop is worth as much as a rank **6** core crystal."

My eyebrows rose.

"Huh? I think I feel cheated right about now," I muttered. "Shouldn't that be enough to get me halfway through the first realm?"

"Halfway? All the way to the second realm!" she exclaimed. "But that's your loss as we already agreed on the deal."

"Not even a little bit? A gulp? A sip?"

"If I manage to break through, you can keep the rest," she said, the glowing liquid gleaming in her reddish eyes.

She stepped up and picked up the chalice, then without hesitation, pressed her lips to the edge of the chalice and drank, sip by sip. Seven sips in, something started to happen. A bright, golden glow enveloped Scarlet's body. It shifted from red, to orange, and finally yellow.

"Headmistress? Is that supposed to happen?"

Her head snapped around as she grinned, a horrible gleam burning in her eyes. But before she could speak, a massive explosion erupted before her and threw me back. I felt the heat, the air moving against me, and then the grass as I hit, tumbled, and rolled. My vision swam and I might have blacked out. I don't remember coming to, only that my vision was black one moment and then my hands were before my face the next.

I groaned and pulled myself to my feet and spotted Scarlet. She tore at her robe, ripping it to shreds. Then she tipped back and screamed. "I'm... finally! I'm... breaking through!"

A notification popped up, startling me as I watched the beautiful, now naked, and kind of terrifying woman swell and pulse with obvious energy. She howled, that odd red light burning brightly in her eyes, and she turned to face me. She faced me, but I don't think she actually saw me. At least, I hoped she didn't.

I quickly read the message.

CONGRATULATIONS TO HEADMISTRESS SCARLET OF THE "ZENITH ACADEMY" FOR BREAKING THROUGH TO THE FOURTH REALM. SHE IS NOW THE 11TH RANKED CULTIVATOR WITHIN THE TOWER.

"I did it. And thanks to you, JD," Scarlet whispered, closing the distance between us. She didn't take a step, or jump, or run. She just kind of slid along the ground. *Creepy.*

The chalice was still in her hand, but I wasn't sure if anything was left inside. The mana radiating from her body made me tremble, made my skin ache, and my eyes buzz. Just being near her sent shivers down my spine and made my bones feel old and brittle.

"Drink."

She moved in close, her large breasts heaving. I tried to look anywhere else as she pressed the chalice to my lips, put her hand against my back, and forced my head back. I felt the drops enter my mouth and slide down my throat. Twenty-one drops the fiery, enervating liquid.

I felt heat blossom in my chest, and then it felt like a nuclear bomb of the purest pleasure detonated inside me. All of my muscles ruptured, my blood vessels exploded, and my skin tore as everything that made up me pushed outward. I ceased to be in the next moment but felt myself pulled back together and came to sometime later. I had no idea how much time passed, only that I was lying on the ground, my head propped up on her lap. I became very aware that she was still very naked.

"How are you feeling?" she asked, her mouth pulled up in a mischievous smile.

I sucked in a breath to speak but couldn't push out the words. It was pain... everywhere. Horrible, aching, singing, burning-you-to-the-core pain.

"Hurts. Everything," I finally managed.

"Give it a few minutes, but you'll have to process all the mana gathered inside your meridians and core. Give it a week before you do any more fighting, then come see me for your rewards, alright?"

I nodded without even understanding what she meant by 'rewards' or by 'not fighting'. My mind was simply too jumbled.

"Can I... have you... in your room?" I struggled to put a sentence together. But I think she knew where my thoughts were headed.

Her mischievous smile deepened as she leaned in and kissed me. I felt her hand slide down my chest and over my stomach, the strength and energy pouring off her skin almost making my testicles ring like Christmas bells.

"You rest," my young champion, "And when you've gathered and honed this new strength, come and see me. I have a lifetime of tricks you might find... enticing."

The next thing I knew I was standing in the clearing, just beyond the Gorilla King's carcass. The pain had faded somewhat, and my throat wasn't so dry anymore. Her last words bounced around in my brain, and I couldn't help but think about her electric touch. Would I survive a sexual encounter with a woman like that? Did I want to?

"Shit, maybe," I whispered as Scarlet appeared next, but only for the briefest of moments. One moment she stood there, in all her naked glory, and then she was gone.

"Wait, what happened? Why was she naked? And why do you look like someone gave you a drink filled with roofies?" Chloe demanded. "Did you two? Did she...? You know?"

"Realms. Breakthrough. Didn't you receive the notification? It was... weird," I said, my brain still more than a little scattered.

"We did," Skadi replied, coming up next to me and patting my shoulder. "And I see you've gone all the way to the **9th** rank. Shit, there must have been something truly special hidden in there!"

I scowled, knowing exactly what had happened, but wasn't as willing to tell them as I'd liked.

"We didn't do anything," I said, rubbing my eyes. "But she broke through, and there was screaming, and clothes tearing, and eyes glowing. It was all very strange and kind of scary. I also get the feeling that she could kill me with a snap of her fingers, so I'm just going to stop talking now before she reappears and does something. Besides, what could I do if a woman like that got an idea in her head?"

Chloe blew out a pent-up breath. But she didn't speak.

"It has been a very intense time. Can we, say, finish with this floor so I can go get a bath and eat? Maybe fall over dead, or... go find a TV to steal so we can stay in bed for the next week? I don't want to deal with dungeons and stuff for a while."

Skadi moved in and hooked her arm around my back, helping me to stand upright.

"Got you, boss."

Mabel nodded, moving in my other side.

"I don't know what a TV is, but if you like it, then I will like it, too." She smiled and gave me a peck on the cheek.

We walked in silence, all the way out to the crossroads. But a new path had appeared. One leading to another portal.

DO YOU WISH TO MOVE TO THE SECOND FLOOR?

YES / NO?

"Yes," I said, before realizing what I was doing. Shit, part of me thought it was the prompt to leave the dungeon.

The weird, pseudo-peeing, tingling sensation washed over us as we teleported. And in a flash, we weren't standing on the next floor, but in the tavern. A new prompt floated right in front of our faces. And we weren't alone. Everyone was staring at the glowing window, their faces twisted in horror and shock.

I focused on the message and read out loud.

WARNING! IMMINENT BEAST WAVE DETECTED!
THE KING STAGE EARTH TORTOISE
HAS STARTED MOVING.
TIME UNTIL CONVERGENCE: 720 HOURS.
TARGET: WALLED CITY OF SKLAVA

Shit, and there I thought things couldn't get any worse.

ABOUT THE COMMUNITY If you want to become invested in this amazing genre, then please visit the various community pages listed below. The other authors will usually take some time and chat with you, reply to any questions, or goof around. Don't be shy. Give them a visit and say hello!

Harem Lit FB Page
Harem GameLit FB Page
Western Wuxia FB Page
Cultivation Novels FB Page
LitRPG Books FB Page
Amazon LitRPG Page

ALSO BY CASSIUS LANGE

MANABORN

Book 1 (Out Now)
Book 2 (Coming Soon)

ZENITH ACADEMY

Book 1 (Out Now)
Book 2 (Coming Soon)

ASH AND FIRE

Book 1 (Coming Soon)

STATS:

NAME: JD, AGE: 24

WEAPON: Pen–Blade

CULTIVATION: Realm 1, Rank 9

POWER LEVEL: 1666 (897 + 147)

HEALTH: 2065 (+315), MANA: 1264 (+97)

ATTACK: 527 (+27), DEFENSE: 462 (+52)

MANA SHIELD: 2250 (+180)

<u>INVENTORY:</u>

Fres (cash):	87811
Fres (card):	89400
Core Crystal Rank 1:	316
Core Crystal Rank 2:	132
Core Crystal Rank 3:	5
Horned Viper: 83	83
Swapper Fly: 41	41
Silverback: 41	41
Gargantua: 1	1
Leech Queen: 1	1
Gorilla King: 1	1

SPECIAL ITEM RECEIVED:

Gorilla King Core: 1   1

GEAR:

NAME: Pen Blade (R4)

TYPE: Weapon, Upgradeable

POWER LEVEL: 42, RANGE: 6

ATTACK: 30

DESCRIPTION: Blade crafted from the feather of a ??? and steel mined deep within ???.

Can be used to cast magic and as an ordinary sword.

NAME: Heaven-Defying Palmire Robes (R9)

TYPE: Full-body armor, Scaling

POWER LEVEL: 420

DESCRIPTION: Symbiote armor crafted by the finest Elven Palmire silk only found in the Elven kingdoms.

Infused by a rank 9 Heavenly Tiger named Core.

HEALTH: 600, MANA: 300

ATTACK: 120, DEFENSE: 120

MANA SHIELD: 600

NAME: Heritage Bracelet (R9)

TYPE: Accessory, Scaling

POWER LEVEL: 372

DESCRIPTION: Bracelet that feeds on the owner's health during battle. When active, improves attack power of mana-based attacks by 3% for every rank.

CURRENT BONUS: 15%

HEALTH: 240, MANA: 480

ATTACK: 120, DEFENSE: 60

MANA SHIELD: 720

NAME: Gargantua Cape

TYPE: Armor, Set Item

POWER LEVEL: 62

DESCRIPTION: Cape made from Gargantua Carapace.

HEALTH: 120, **DEFENSE:** 40

MANA SHIELD: 100

SPECIAL: Set item 1/6. On 2/6 adds Defense + 50, 4/6 adds Health + 200, and 6/6 Tremor Skill.

SPECIAL: Tremor Skill creates small earthquake around user, dealing damage to everything in the vicinity.

NAME: Gargantua Shoulder Guards

TYPE: Armor, Set Item

POWER LEVEL: 43

DESCRIPTION: Cape made from Gargantua Carapace.

HEALTH: 80, **DEFENSE:** 30

MANA SHIELD: 50

SPECIAL: Set item 1/6. On 2/6 adds Defense + 50, 4/6 adds Health + 200, and 6/6 Tremor Skill.

SPECIAL: Tremor Skill creates small earthquake around user, dealing damage to everything in the vicinity.

BASIC SKILLS:

SKILL NAME: Creation Magic (???)

SKILL NAME: Mana Charge (B)

TYPE: Basic, Mana, **RANGE:** 1 pace

DESCRIPTION: One of the Foundation type skills used in all of the branches. Mana Infusion is used to gather mana into a weapon or the body and then use it to either attack or defend against attacks.

BASIC: +20 Attack, +50 Health on mastery, Charge Time: 5 sec

ADVANCED: +50 Attack, 100 Health on mastery, Charge Time: 4 sec

MASTER: +100 Attack, 200 Health on mastery, Charge Time: 3 sec

SKILL NAME: Mana Discharge (B)

TYPE: Basic, Mana, **RANGE:** 10 paces

DESCRIPTION: One of the Foundation-type skills used in all branches. The skill is used to attack an enemy with a burst of mana that can add to physical damage.

BASIC: +40 Attack on mastery, Damage: Attack x 1.25, Mana: 25

ADVANCED: +80 Attack on mastery, Damage: Attack x 1.45, Mana: 40

MASTER: +160 Attack on mastery, Damage: Attack x 1.8, Mana: 60

NOTE: Mana Discharge can be used with or without a weapon.

PASSIVE SKILLS:

SKILL NAME: Body Tempering (B)

SKILL NAME: Mana Tempering (B)

SKILL NAME: Forge

SKILL NAME: Weapon Soul (B)

TYPE: Basic, Mana, **RANGE:** 1 pace

DESCRIPTION: The most basic Weapon Cultivation skill. It allows you to connect your weapon to your soul and allow it to start absorbing mana. Once learned, you can never lose your weapon as it becomes a part of the user.

BASIC: +50 Attack on mastery

ADVANCED: +100 Attack on mastery

MASTER: +200 Attack on mastery

ELEMENTAL SKILLS:

SKILL NAME: Air Slash (A)

TYPE: Elemental, Mana, **RANGE:** 20 paces

DESCRIPTION: Air Slash is the most basic wind-elemental mana attack, but also the most versatile. Can be molded into many types of attacks. Mana usage goes up with every added layer of Air Slash.

BASIC: +20 Mana on mastery, Damage: Attack x 1.1, Mana: 7

ADVANCED: +50 Mana on mastery, Damage: Attack x 1.25, Mana: 10

MASTER: +100 Mana on mastery, Damage: Attack x 1.4, Mana: 12

NOTE: DAMAGE DROPS 20% FOR EVERY 5 PACES

SKILL NAME: Ice Shard (B)

TYPE: Basic, Mana, **RANGE:** 30 paces

DESCRIPTION: One of the basic elemental spells.

Highly versatile yet destructive in the right hands.

BASIC: +30 Attack, +20 Mana on mastery, Damage: Attack x 1.4, Mana: 20

ADVANCED: +60 Attack, +40 Mana on mastery, Damage: Attack x 1.6, Mana: 25

MASTER: +120 Attack, +80 Mana on mastery, Damage: Attack x 1.8, Mana: 30

NOTE: Attack goes up/down by 50% depending on elemental affinity

NOTE: Ice Shard can cause debuffs that slow or freeze the target.

SKILL NAME: Fireball (B)

TYPE: Basic, Mana, **RANGE:** 20 paces

DESCRIPTION: One of the basic elemental spells.

Highly versatile yet destructive in the right hands.

BASIC: +30 Attack, +20 Mana on mastery, Damage: Attack x 1.55, Mana: 20

ADVANCED: +60 Attack, +40 Mana on mastery, Damage: Attack x 1.75, Mana: 25

MASTER: +120 Attack, +80 Mana on mastery, Damage: Attack x 2.0, Mana: 30

NOTE 1: Attack goes up/down by 50% depending on elemental affinity

NOTE 2: Fire Ball can cause debuffs that cause fire damage to target

SKILL NAME: Summon Fire Elemental (B)

TYPE: Summon, Mana, **DURATION**: 60 Minutes

DESCRIPTION: Basic Summoning spell to create a fire Elemental.

BASIC: +50 Health, +30 Mana on mastery, **STATS:** User x 1.1, Mana: 50

ADVANCED: +100 Health, +60 Mana on mastery, **STATS:** User x 1.4, Mana: 70

MASTER: +200 Health, +120 Mana on mastery, **STATS:** User x 1.7, Mana: 85

NOTE 1: The summoned Fire Elemental lasts for 60 minutes or until killed.

NOTE 2: The user's stats are multiplied with a modifier depending on mastery.

NOTE 3: Summon stays active for 60, 120, and 240 minutes depending on mastery.

CPSIA information can be obtained
at www.ICGtesting.com
Printed in the USA
BVHW090616111121
621212BV00008B/562

9 781733 809566